Uncontrollable

Also by Shannon Richard

Undone
Undeniable
Unstoppable
Unforgettable
Undressed
Unsung

Uncontrollable

SHANNON RICHARD

New York   Boston

Copyright © 2016 by Shannon Richard
Cover design by Elizabeth Turner
Cover copyright © 2016 by Hachette Book Group, Inc.

Forever Yours
Hachette Book Group
1290 Avenue of the Americas
New York, NY 10104
forever-romance.com
twitter.com/foreverromance

First published as an ebook and as a print on demand: November 2016

Forever Yours is an imprint of Grand Central Publishing. The Forever Yours name and logo are trademarks of Hachette Book Group, Inc.

The publisher is not responsible for websites (or their content) that are not owned by the publisher.

The Hachette Speakers Bureau provides a wide range of authors for speaking events. To find out more, go to www.hachettespeakersbureau.com or call (866) 376-6591.

ISBN 978-1-4555-6507-8 (ebook)
ISBN 978-1-4555-6511-5 (print on demand)

To Sarah Elizabeth Younger
Because of you I was able to achieve this dream of mine.
You read my writing and found something promising in my words.
Since the very start you've been much more than an agent.
You've been a mentor, a confidant, my biggest advocate,
and, most important, a friend.
Thank you.

Acknowledgments

I first off want to say thank you to all of my readers. There was a bit of an extended gap between *Unsung* and *Uncontrollable*, but I appreciate your patience and sticking with me through it. This book was a little harder for me to write, but in the end I'm very proud of what it turned into. I hope that you enjoy Beth and Tripp's story as much as the other books in the Country Roads Series.

Mom and Dad, there is no doubt in my mind that I need to say a big ol' thank you to the two of you. This past year has held many new adventures, adventures that wouldn't have been possible without your support, guidance, and love. To my father for spending a weekend with me painting the rooms of my very first house. It's a memory that I will never forget. And my mother, who came and did a marathon decorating weekend and helped me figure out the perfect place for all of my belongings.

I had a number of sounding boards for this book, sounding

boards that would always write back to my text of *question* with the simple response of *answer*. Jessica Lemmon, you've constantly been there for me and I value every single piece of wisdom you give me. Amy Lipford, you're always there when I need you for a little legal advice (book related, of course). And then there are my two awesome Beta Readers, Nikki Rushbrook and Katie Crandall. Thank you so, so, so much for all of your invaluable feedback. Both of you had a special love for Tripp. All of you helped me figure out the path with this book.

I was blessed enough to have become friends with Tara Wyatt this year, yet another one of my oh-so-amazing sounding boards. It blows my mind how close you can get to a person who lives almost 1,800 miles away (and yes, I Googled that). You helped me out in ways that went above and beyond. Also, our music-loving souls sing to each other.

Thank you to everyone at Grand Central Publishing. I appreciate the hard work that every single one of you puts into my books. Jessica Pierce, I'm grateful for all of your wisdom and insight that helped me in writing this story...and all of your patience in waiting for me to *finally* get this book to you. Also, your love for Penny made me so freaking happy. Like, *unbelievably* happy. And Megha Parekh, you helped me from the very start of plotting out this book. Your fingerprints are still all over this story and I wouldn't have it any other way.

This is where I have to say a little bit more about the woman who this book is dedicated to, Sarah E. Younger. There has never been a moment that I doubted your dedication to what you do, day in and day out for your authors. I know how much you care, and it's a whole hell of a lot. But it goes beyond that, so far beyond that.

You stand up for all of us, and are just so freaking good at what you do.

And finally, I must say thank you to Sarah's father, firefighter Chuck Younger, who helped me figure out a few of the ins and outs of my hero's job. Any deviations from what things actually go on at a firehouse were entirely of my own doing. Also, I must say, your daughter is one awesome lady. You and Mrs. Younger did an excellent job. There are certain kindnesses in this world that are part of how you are raised, and that kindness shines from Sarah.

Uncontrollable

Chapter One

It's Not Just Another Friendly Day in the Neighborhood

The steady knocking was only getting louder, ricocheting against the inside of Tripp Black's skull. He hadn't gotten a full night's sleep in four days and it was beginning to catch up to him. Who the hell was he kidding? It had already caught up to him.

Normally he was up and at 'em at the crack of dawn, out of bed and working through his first cup of coffee before the sun was even up. But not today. He'd been hoping when he'd finally crawled into bed after five that morning that he'd get to sleep in.

Apparently that had been too much to ask for.

It was unseasonably warm for early spring, and a string of thunderstorms had rolled through over the last week. Not a single night had gone by without some crisis pulling Tripp from bed. But that was what came with the job when you were the town's resident Fire Chief.

Mirabelle was a relatively small beachside town right on the Gulf of Mexico. Tripp had moved here three years ago in hopes of a quieter life…though it wasn't all that quiet at the moment.

The knocking turned into banging.

What the hell?

He pulled his head from where it was buried in the pillow, cracking one eye and blearily looking over at the alarm clock. It was almost eight in the morning. Three hours...he hadn't even gotten three hours of sleep. He'd been at the Wilkins's for most of the night trying to get the family out of their house, which had been almost split in two by a tree.

It took more effort than he was prepared for to pull himself from bed, probably because almost every inch of his body felt like it had been worked over with a two-by-four. The tightness in his arms was courtesy of fighting with the hose during the warehouse fire on Sunday, the twinge in his lower back from carrying Mr. Phillips down four flights of stairs on Monday, the soreness in his legs from the three car pileup that had happened on Tuesday, and so on and so on.

He could keep going, but just thinking about the last week made him hurt even more. So instead he focused on navigating through his dim bedroom. The thick navy blue curtains on the windows did a decent job of blocking out the light, but a few rays of sunshine managed to peek in through the sides, outlining the furniture in his room.

He just made out the pair of athletic shorts hanging from a chair in the corner, pausing only long enough to pull them on. After a quick shower when he'd gotten home, he'd collapsed onto his bed bare ass naked, his preferred way to sleep. He had no idea who was currently trying to knock down his door with their fist, but giving them a little show wasn't exactly on his morning agenda.

Another round of thunderous blows echoed in the air and he

wrenched the door wide before the noise split his head in two. But there was no helping the pain behind his eyes, because the second the door was open he was blinded by the light.

He squinted out into the sunshine, the only thing he could see a splash of hot pink directly in front of him. "For the love of everything good and holy, what do you want?!" Yup, yelling had been a mistake; it just made his head hurt even more.

"What. Do. I. Want?" The words came out clipped, a barely controlled rage behind each and every syllable.

Tripp closed his eyes and groaned at the voice that filled his ears, then rubbed at his temples. Whatever was about to happen wasn't going to be pleasant. It never was when it involved his neighbor. He'd bought the house he was now residing in almost four months ago, and it had taken him about a week to figure out he'd made a *very* bad choice of location.

Appearances could be deceiving, and the prime example of that was standing before him.

Beth Boone was a tiny little blond thing, five-foot-three? Five-foot-four? Tripp had met her on a number of occasions before he'd moved in next door. They had quite a few friends in common and had become acquainted with each other over the years, but he'd had no idea what he was getting into when he'd become her neighbor.

None at all.

The woman was a pain in the ass, but she wasn't the only problem. Nope. Her three wards were just as big of an aggravation.

Beth's sister and brother-in-law, Colleen and Kevin Ross, had died in a car accident last year. And okay, he had to give the woman a certain amount of credit and respect, as she'd moved back to

Mirabelle to take care of her two nieces and nephew. And he'd be a cold-hearted bastard if he didn't have any sympathy for the family that had been left behind, because he totally did. He'd dealt with too much death in his life to not be fully aware of the pain that came with a loss like that.

Didn't change the fact that Beth Boone was a pill.

Tripp opened his eyes again and the woman before him came into focus, along with the creature at her side...a creature that belonged to him.

His dog, covered in mud.

Shit.

"Your *damn* dog got into my yard *again*," Beth ground out through clenched teeth.

Duke—as in *The* Duke, named after the one and only John Wayne—was a rescue puppy who'd been abandoned at the firehouse last summer. Though *puppy* should be used loosely; Duke was over a hundred pounds and still growing. Normally his fluffy coat was a fifty-fifty mix of white and light brown, but at the moment he was entirely the dark brownish black of whatever muck he'd rolled around in.

Tripp's sleep-hazed brain was having a hard time processing the scene in front of him, especially when his eyes landed on Beth. For the first time since he'd opened the door, he really looked at her.

Her blond hair had been thrown up in a messy bun, but a good portion of it had fallen out. A glob of brown mud plastered her bangs to her forehead, and there were streaks on her cheeks, like war paint.

His eyes moved down, landing on the multiple paw prints

stamped on her T-shirt. The hot pink cotton material was soaked and plastered to her body like a second skin.

Dear Lord, she wasn't wearing a bra. Absolutely nothing was left to the imagination. *Nothing.* He'd seen the woman in a bathing suit before, so he knew full well what she was hiding under those baggy nurse scrubs that she wore every day. Soft curves and perfect breasts. Perfect breasts that would be a pretty good handful and were in no need of a bra to be perky.

And that was *just* what he needed first thing in the morning, for her clearly displayed nipples to make him tongue-tied. Not that speaking was going to help him, because it was at that moment when Duke decided it was time to shake, splattering mud on everything within ten feet.

Beth let go of the dog, probably instinctively fearing being thrown around like a rag doll with the movement. Because really, Duke outweighed Beth by a few pounds. He was surprised she'd been able to drag the dog back over to his house in the first place.

But Duke had absolutely no bite in him. When it came right down to it, he had pretty much two modes: scared of everything or spaz. Option one had him cowering in the corner at the sound of the vacuum, or sprinting into the house when Tripp mowed the lawn, or eating through a door when he was home alone during a thunderstorm. Option two had him tripping over his too long feet as he tried to chase a ball, or knocking things over with his rapidly moving tail, or attempting to lick someone to death.

No more evidence was needed as to what mode Duke was in at the moment. He was currently rubbing his head against Beth's thigh, painting her skin with even more mud. Tripp had to give it to the dog, though, because he'd bet good money there wasn't a person in a hundred-mile radius who wanted to play less in that moment than Beth did. But Duke was oblivious to the fury radiating off the woman.

Tripp, on the other hand, was not.

It couldn't have been more than twenty seconds since he'd opened the front door, twenty seconds of Beth glaring at him with daggers in her blue eyes. The visible portions of her face and neck were turning red hot with rage.

"I'm sorry, Beth. I don't know how he's getting out of the yard." Which was the truth. Tripp had gone over his backyard more times than he could count trying to figure out an escape route from the fence. He'd come up with absolutely nothing.

Duke wasn't exactly used to the freedom that this backyard provided. For the first six months of the dog's domesticated life, he'd been confined to a postage stamp–size piece of grass attached to the townhouse Tripp had rented. Now he was getting access to about half of a football field, complete with a pool that he loved to take daily dips in.

There was a doggy door to the backyard to give the pup the ability to come and go. But because of that easy access, there'd been more than a few mornings where the trail of water on the kitchen tile from an early morning swim had left Tripp flat on his back and staring up at the ceiling. It had taken a month, but Tripp had gotten Duke to break that habit, and he now only dove in when he was given permission. The dog was capable of listening…sometimes.

"Duke," Tripp snapped his fingers.

The dog pulled his attention from Beth—and stopped rubbing all over her—as he looked over to his owner. But that was about all of the focus Tripp was going to get. A squirrel jumped from the roof to a tree in front of the house and the dog tore off like his ass was on fire, barking madly.

"You need to figure out how to keep that dumb beast under control." She pointed to Duke, who was unsuccessfully trying to climb the tree as he attempted to get to the squirrel. "He destroyed my flower beds, ripped up *everything*. So close up that doggy door, put him on a leash, maybe actually train him, or give him to someone else. I don't care, but I'm sick and tired of dealing with this. He's an obnoxious menace and has absolutely no concept of boundaries."

Okay, so yes it was true that Duke had in fact gotten into her backyard...again, and that he'd done something with a whole hell of a lot of mud included. It was also true that the dog wasn't *always* the brightest crayon in the box. But no one called Tripp's dog dumb.

This was the portion of the morning where little Miss Perky Tits crossed the line.

"Ha! Boundaries! You want to talk boundaries, Beth? How about the fact that I've caught your teenage niece and her friends in *my* hot tub. Or what about the fact that I've had two flat tires on my truck because of various toys that I've run over on *my* driveway. Or what about the fact that there is peanut butter *everywhere*. On the door handles. On the mailbox. In my garage. And I *hate* peanut butter, so it sure as hell isn't coming from me."

Her eyes narrowed as he'd gone through the list, her mouth getting tighter and tighter.

"You think you're the perfect neighbor?" he asked. "Think again. I've had to deal with plenty myself. Maybe you should figure out how to use a leash, too."

As soon as the words were out of his mouth he knew he'd gone too far. But he didn't have a chance to take them back.

Beth took a step away, her nostrils flaring as she breathed deep through her nose. "God you're an asshole."

All right, maybe he didn't want to take it back. So he said nothing as she turned on her heel and headed down the pathway.

It was then that he got a good long look at the back of her. Her cotton shorts weren't even discernible at this angle they were so covered in mud, and the backs of her legs were just as bad. Duke must've knocked her down into all of that mud. And really, he should feel bad about what had just happened but he was hard pressed to, considering everything. His dog wasn't the only one who was a "menace."

A loud bark rent the air, pulling Tripp's gaze from the retreating woman. Duke was now rolling around in the yard, scratching his back on the grass like it was the greatest thing in the world.

Spaz. But he was Tripp's spaz, and he wasn't going anywhere. Well, he wasn't going anywhere besides to get a bath. Stat.

* * *

"Arrogant."

Slam!

"Asshole."

Slam!

"Egotistical."

Slam!

"Dickhead."

Slam!

Six hours. It had been six hours since Beth had walked away from the neighbor from hell—and the demon dog that was determined to make her life miserable—and she was still fuming. So much so that she was taking it out on the filing cabinet in front of her. If she had a baseball bat she'd crack the sucker open like it was a piñata.

Maybe you should figure out how to use a leash, too.

God, he was such a jerk. She needed to keep reminding herself of that fact...and not think about the way his thick dark brown hair had been tousled all around his head, and how it had been so damn sexy it should be illegal. Nor should she be thinking about how the lovely scruff on his face was in that land just beyond five o'clock shadow and going into beard. She loved a good beard.

Loved. It.

And she *really* shouldn't be thinking about how his shorts had hung perilously low on his hips. Or the dusting of hair across his abs—abs that had abs—and how it reached down beyond the waist band of those perilously low-hanging shorts.

Then there was the tattoo inked on his left side and down his ribs. She really shouldn't be thinking about that either, but she was a sucker for tattoos if there ever was one. His was a shield with crossed axes, a side profile of the patron saint of firefighters at the center, and the words "St. Florian Protect Us," written around it.

From his chocolate brown eyes to the chestnut of his hair, all the way to his tanned toned skin, he was all shades of warmth. Too bad he was a cold bastard. Not even his sexy sexiness could make up for that fact that he was a...

"Prick," she mumbled to herself as she slammed another drawer shut.

"What did the filing cabinet ever do to you?"

Beth turned and looked over her shoulder to find Denise Morrison standing in the doorway, eyebrows raised high above her hazel eyes and hands on her slender hips. It would've been an intimidating pose if it was anyone else making it.

Beth knew better. Denise could be sassy with the best of them, but she was the queen of politeness and about as nice as they came. Besides, how could the woman be intimidating when she was currently sporting light pink scrubs?

Denise and her husband Trevor had retired before they'd moved down from Philadelphia six years ago. They'd lived in Mirabelle for two years before Trevor's death. The pancreatic cancer had been swift and unforgiving.

These days, Denise found that being busy was the best policy. She'd gone from volunteering to getting a full-time nursing job at the hospital. Then there was the fact that she had her hands full with her three grandchildren. Her daughter Paige and son-in-law Brendan King had a three-year-old, Trevor, named after the late Trevor Morrison, and twin girls. Sarah and Molly had entered the world last September. Denise babysat as much as possible and absolutely loved having her family so close.

Over the last year, Denise had become one of Beth's very good friends and a pretty excellent confidant. They got each other, part of it being that they both understood how hard it was to lose someone they loved.

"It's not the filing cabinet." Beth sighed, tired of it all. She was so beyond sick of the line of jerks who'd paraded through her life, each one worst than the last.

Though no one could top her ex Mick. It wasn't a coincidence that "Mick" rhymed with "prick," because that man was King of the Pricks—wore a fucking clown and held the damn scepter, a scepter he could stick straight up his…

"Uh oh." Denise's eyebrows rose higher. "Who is he and what did he do?"

"My jackass neighbor and so many things."

"What happened with Tripp now?" Denise asked as she leaned against the doorjamb, folding her arms across her chest and settling in for the conversation. She knew full well everything that had happened since Tripp had moved in. And just like everyone else she thought that he was a nice guy.

"Living next to him—and his dog—is *not* just another friendly day in the neighborhood. Everyone is under that man's spell except for me." Beth didn't fall under spells…well, not anymore. She'd been disillusioned good and proper over the last year. And really, what with the fact that she was now responsible for three other people, she couldn't afford to be disillusioned by anyone or anything. It wasn't just her she had to worry about these days.

"Okay…so let's hear it. What happened?"

"I'm only going to tell you if you promise you will be on my side no matter what."

"Cross my heart." Denise moved one of her hands and made the motion over her chest.

And with that Beth launched into her morning…which had been on the heels of a ridiculously long night…which had occurred during an even longer week.

Oh, who the hell was she kidding? Days? Weeks? Months? It had been the longest most difficult year of her life.

Thunderstorms didn't go over very well in the Ross house,

hadn't since Colleen and Kevin had died in a car accident during a particularly horrible one ten months ago. And whenever a bad one rolled in, the kids slept with Beth. Much like they had the night before…and the night before that…and the night before that.

Nora always commandeered the left side of the king-size mattress, needing a little bit more space than the other two as she was a fully grown seventeen year old…though, her "fully grown" was exactly five feet tall. And by morning all sixty of those inches would be sprawled out like a starfish.

Grant occupied the lower right side of the bed. As he was eight years old, he didn't require as much space. But he slept on Beth more than he did the actual mattress. His arms wrapped around her waist while he used her stomach as a pillow. Who needed blankets—which were always stolen anyway—when she had her own personal heaters?

And last, but certainly not least, was Penny. The three-year-old claimed the top of the bed, her tiny toddler body buried in the pillows. The second she got settled, she'd stick her foot out and whisper, "hold please." It was the only way she'd be able to fall asleep.

None of the three children were stationary sleepers, and without fail Beth always woke up with knees in her back, an elbow in her stomach, a foot in her face, or all of the above. That morning had been no different. If she'd gotten two solid hours of sleep she'd be shocked.

She'd just gotten all the kids out the door and on their way to school when she'd gone into the kitchen for a very much needed second cup of coffee. And that was when she'd spotted the damn dog.

Freaking Fido from Hell was in her backyard, again. He was rolling around in her flower beds, flower beds that she'd dropped two hundred dollars to fix up the previous summer. Flower beds that were now good and thoroughly destroyed.

"So what happened?" Denise asked when Beth got to the part where the demon dog had made a meal of her rose bushes.

"Well, when I tried to get him, he thought I was playing and started running around the yard." A yard spotted with mud puddles from all of the rain over the last few days. "I think I fell about half a dozen times before I finally caught him."

"So you marched over to Tripp's house covered in mud?" Denise bit the corner of her lip to suppress a laugh.

"Oh no." Beth pointed to the treachery on her friend's mouth. "Don't even. *My* side, remember? You aren't allowed to be amused by this. I'm fully aware of how ridiculous I looked."

Denise held her palms out in surrender. "I'm sorry." She waved a hand through the air in a *please continue* motion as she settled into the chair across from Beth.

"I banged on his front door for a couple of minutes until he could be roused from his sound sleep. And, get this, he had the nerve to yell at me. He's sleeping in, oblivious to all of it, while I'm chasing that bear of his around the yard and he gets angry with me. And then he tells *me* to put my kids on a leash. Can you believe that?"

Denise was silent for a moment, chewing the corner of her lip, but this time it wasn't in amusement.

"What?" Beth narrowed her eyes.

"I didn't say anything."

"You didn't have to; that expression says it all. You're about to make excuses for him, aren't you?"

"Look, I'm not on his side about the dog. Not by any means. He should keep his animal on his side of the fence. And that comment about the leash…that was…uncalled for and *way too* far."

"But…?" Beth folded her arms across her chest as she leaned back in the chair.

"Is this real-time talk? Or am I still supposed to just agree with you?"

Beth thought for a second before she sighed. "Real-time talk." She knew that Denise had her best interest at heart…even if it was going to be something she didn't want to hear.

"Your kids have been known to go over onto his property."

Okay…so this was the one part of the argument from that morning that Beth had flat out lost. Her nieces and nephew had been playing with the borders of the boundaries as well…Nora being the worst.

That had been a fun encounter in December. Tripp had been standing on the front porch at three in the morning with Nora and two other girls Beth had never met before. They'd all been wrapped in towels and shivering in the cold night air.

"I believe one of these belongs to you," he'd frowned at her. And that was the day she'd discovered just how attractive surly could be.

Not that she thought about that a lot…no, not at all. She shook her head, pulling herself back to the conversation with Denise.

"They've had their moments," Beth admitted more than a little grudgingly.

"Now you know I'm not saying you weren't more than justified to be upset about what happened this morning. I would've been fuming mad if someone or something was responsible for messing up my garden."

Of that Beth had no doubt. Denise's garden was an oasis if Beth had ever seen one. It was a passion that both Denise and her late husband Trevor had shared. Denise had told Beth many times that being out there was the best sort of therapy for her, even if it was bittersweet. This was yet another thing the two women had in common, as Beth felt the same way about gardening because of her late mother.

"What are you two chatting about?" The voice of Vanessa Cartwright wafted through the room about a second before her Chanel perfume.

Beth pulled her eyes from her friend and turned to the doorway, where the receptionist for the women's health wing of the hospital stood. Her long auburn hair stretched down her back in a curtain and her super model long legs were only half covered by her silvery gray Dior wrap dress that went perfectly with the black Louis Vuitton pumps on her feet.

Beth didn't get to wear shoes like that very often. Her footwear was all about the practical and what didn't have her feet screaming for release at the end of the day. Case in point: the hot pink and lime green tennis shoes she was currently sporting.

But Vanessa and Beth lived very different lifestyles. Where Beth was the one going home at the end of the work day to take care of three children, Vanessa was the one getting taken care of. Her current boyfriend was a former investment banker who'd retired at the age of forty-five and moved to the Gulf Coast to spend his days on his boat. These days he also thoroughly enjoyed lavishing his twenty-seven-year-old bombshell girlfriend with gifts.

There were three things that Vanessa loved the most: expensive things, rich men, and good gossip. Beth liked Vanessa just fine, the girl was as sweet as pie...but a vault for secrets she was not.

"Beth is having gardening problems." Denise immediately diverted from their main topic of conversation.

"Oh." Vanessa wrinkled her nose at the distasteful thought of dirt getting underneath her pretty pale pink manicure. "I can't help you there."

No shit, Beth thought...and was proud she hadn't voiced those words out loud. Besides, it wasn't Vanessa's vault that Beth was having a supremely shitty day. So she kept her mouth shut and finished filing the last of the folders while Vanessa and Denise started talking about the latest episode of a reality TV show they both watched.

"I mean I would've picked the cop over the lawyer," Denise said. "He was adorable and super sweet."

"No, it was the lawyer all the way for me. He had the looks and the money. I mean don't get me wrong; the cop was cute, but cute doesn't always cut it. Maybe if he had a few more muscles like some of *our* public servants...well, that would've changed my vote. Speaking of public servants...Beth, I heard what happened with your neighbor this morning."

"What?" Her head came up as she looked over at Vanessa. What the hell had she heard? What was Tripp telling everyone? That she'd barged over to his house raving like a lunatic?

"A massive tree crashed down through the Wilkins house around three last night. Landed right across the hallway separating the master bedroom from the rest of the house. They're on the second floor so they couldn't exactly climb out the window to get to their kids. Jefferson is, what? Two? And Mary is only a few months. They were both crying up a storm in their cribs for twenty minutes or so before anyone could get there."

Oh dear…a sinking feeling started to settle low in Beth's stomach. Why did she get the feeling she was going to come out of this conversation feeling like a jerk?

"Dorothy was beside herself and Bobbie was about to jump out the window to get to the kids. Tripp was the one who got to the house first. He made sure the kids were safely out and then got Dorothy and Bobbie out, too."

So Tripp had been out in the middle of the night saving babies…and here she was complaining about a messed up garden.

No, she didn't feel like a jerk…she felt like an asshole.

Chapter Two

The Never-Ending Storm

Beth pulled into her driveway at 6:03. She shut off the engine of her white Trailblazer and leaned back in the seat, taking a deep breath and rubbing at her throbbing temples.

From start to finish the day had sucked and her exhaustion was emotional, physical, and mental. The thought of cooking had been pure misery so she'd ordered two pies from Papa Pan's Pizza and picked them up on the way home. One a thin crust with extra cheese and mushrooms for her and Grant, the other a deep dish with pineapple and ham for Nora and Penny. The Hawaiian had been Colleen's favorite, too.

God, Beth missed her sister.

Her eyes popped open and she focused on the house in front of her. It had been Colleen's dream home from the very start. Even though half the inside had needed to be remodeled when they bought it, she'd seen every part of its potential at first sight. There was a massive front porch and a beautiful brick staircase that led up to the bright red front door. It had a bit of a plantation feel to it with its white columns, but as it was only one story it wasn't os-tentatious.

Beth's favorite part was the backyard that looked out to the lake. Nothing sounded better than curling up in the hammock on the screened in back porch and enjoying a beer while watching the sunset.

But as another storm was rolling in off the horizon, making everything as gloomy as possible, that wasn't going to be a reality. The sun was nowhere in sight, covered up by the big black clouds that hovered low.

Odds were it was going to be another long evening of Beth sharing her bed with three scared kids. It wasn't all that shocking that ten months since their parents' death, they were still having difficulties with storms…especially at night. Nope, not surprising at all, as they'd been asleep when the sheriff's department had shown up on the doorstep to tell them that their parents were gone.

Kevin and Colleen had been driving back from dinner to celebrate their nineteenth wedding anniversary. Lightning had struck a tree and snapped it in half, leaving part of it lying in the middle of the road. Kevin had slowed the car as he'd rounded a bend in the road, but the driver of the SUV behind him had not. Four people had been involved in the accident. None of them made it out alive.

Nora had been babysitting and had fallen asleep on the sofa waiting for her parents to get home. The Atticus County Sheriffs department contacted Wallace Boone, Colleen's and Beth's father, before they'd gone over to the Ross house with Wallace. It was only after telling the kids that her father had told Beth. Beth would forever remember the phone call she'd gotten just before midnight.

"It's…it's your sister…" That was as far as Wallace had gotten

before he'd started sobbing into the phone. But he didn't have to go any further, because Beth knew. She knew her sister was gone.

The whole thing was so fucking unfair. And yes, Beth had heard it so many times before: *life's not fair*. But she knew full well what it was like to lose a parent at a young age. Knew what it was like to grow up without her mother. Knew what it was like to feel like a part of herself was missing after her own mother's death.

And Nora, Grant, and Penny? Well, they'd lost both of their parents in an instant.

Beth forced herself to come back to the present moment before she lost it…because once lost, there was no guarantee she'd get it back.

As she got out of the SUV, her eyes immediately darted over to Tripp's house. His big black truck was parked in the driveway. Her mood took another dip as she thought about how she'd dealt with things that morning. It hadn't been the best and she knew it. She was going to need to figure out how to coexist with the man.

Maybe she'd get a brainwave with a stomach full of cheese and dough…and that beer.

She grabbed the pizzas from the back seat just as a car pulled into the driveway of her other neighbors' house, the O'Bryans. Miles and Corinne had lived there as far back as Beth could remember. They had two kids, Melanie and Hamilton.

Even though there was a two-year age difference between Mel and Beth—Beth being older—they'd always been incredibly close growing up. As college had brought both of them up to Tallahassee, they'd actually been roommates for a couple of years when their time at Florida State had overlapped. Keeping up with each other after school had never been a problem. They'd always made the effort with each other and Beth had been one of Mel's brides-maids when she'd married her husband almost two years ago.

Another thing Beth and Mel had in common was the similar age gap between them and their siblings. Mel was ten years older than her brother, while Beth had been twelve years younger than her sister. Apparently it was a common theme in both of their families; Colleen and Kevin had waited nine years between having Nora and Grant.

Hamilton just so happened to be a year older than Nora. For over a decade—which was how long they'd been neighbors—the two had been best friends... *had* being the operative word.

Nora was good and truly immersed in the anger portion of grieving. She listened to pretty much no one, and was under the impression she knew absolutely everything. And yes, Beth shouldn't be surprised that Nora was being a rebellious teenager. But the transformation had taken place right before the holidays. And that first Thanksgiving without Colleen and Kevin had been pretty freaking awful... and it hadn't just been Beth who'd dealt with the fallout.

Gone was Beth's sweet niece—who'd always been a little bit on the sassy side, but it was a sass filled with sugar. Gone was the girl who'd come up and wrap her arms around Beth in a good, long hug. Gone was the girl who'd curl up next to Beth on the sofa. Gone was the girl who usually had a smile turning up her lips.

Pretty much the only affection Beth got from her niece these days was during those stormy nights when Nora was scared. Since Beth hated it when the kids were scared, it wasn't exactly her favorite form of affection.

Nora's new anger-filled attitude had come with a new set of

friends. Friends that Beth wasn't a fan of in the slightest. Friends who liked to wear short skirts, and low-cut shirts that would be more accurately described as bras. And the thing was, even though Nora was on the shorter size, her chest hadn't gotten the memo about her tiny frame. She was in the "D" range where a lot of her friends weren't nearly as ample. What looked inappropriate on the other teenagers looked downright indecent on Nora.

There was also the fact that Nora was getting to that age where sex was becoming a much more prevalent thing. One afternoon when Beth had gotten home early, Nora had had a friend over, and Beth had overheard a rather descriptive conversation about oral sex. When Beth had tried to talk to Nora about it later, there'd been an explosive fight that ended with Nora getting grounded for a week—not because of the topic but because of Nora screaming *It's none of your freaking business*—and the slamming of a bedroom door that caused the entire house to shake.

God help Beth when her niece started dating. She'd thought more than once about building an add-on tower to the house and locking the girl up until she was twenty-two...or thirty. Thirty was a much better age.

If only.

Beth slid the pizza boxes back into the SUV and dropped her purse on the seat next to them. Then she closed the door and headed across the yard and over to the O'Bryans' driveway. Corinne got out of the car, an exhausted smile on her face, and waved as Beth approached.

"You have a long day, too?" she asked.

"The longest." Corinne nodded as she walked around the car to the backseat on the passenger side. "There were three birthdays today…so we had all three of the dreaded C's: cookies, cupcakes, *and* candy."

Corinne was a preschool teacher, had been one for almost thirty years now.

"I can barely keep up with my three; you are Wonder Woman handling seventy of them with sugar rushes."

"Yes, but there are ten of us and I get to give them back at the end of the day," Corinne said as she opened the back door to reveal Penny bouncing in the car seat.

"Aunt B!" she exclaimed excitedly.

Penny had just started going to preschool that year, and Corinne was kind enough to take the little one in the morning and bring her back every evening.

The woman was a freaking godsend.

Corinne had the little girl unbuckled in a snap, and before Beth knew it, her niece was shooting across the space, her blond ponytail bouncing as she ran. Beth kneeled down low as Penny wrapped her little arms around Beth's neck and kissed Beth's cheek.

And just like that, some of the crap she'd dealt with that day melted away.

The child had always been exceptionally affectionate, more content to crawl up into someone's lap for a good cuddle than do anything else. The months right after Colleen and Kevin died, Beth very rarely didn't have Penny in her arms.

Because really, how could a person not give in to the little girl when she would look up with those pleading mossy green eyes—eyes the exact same shade as her brother's and sister's…the exact same shade as their mother's had been—and hold her arms wide, saying, "hold you, hold you"?

How did a person say *no* to that?

"How's my Lucky Penny?" Beth asked as she wrapped her own arms around her niece and stood.

"Good!" Penny leaned back just slightly so she could look into Beth's face. "I had a cupcake with a cookie in it."

"What kind of cookie?"

Her little brow furrowed as she tried to remember. "A roreo."

"An Oreo?"

"Yes, that's what I said."

"You save room for dinner? We're having pizza."

"With pineapples?" she asked as her eyes lit up.

"Just for you."

The rumble of an engine could be heard from the end of the street and they all turned to look in that direction. "Hammy's home," Penny said as a big old blue truck rounded the corner and rolled to a stop in front of the house.

A couple of years ago it would've amused Beth to see Hamilton driving such a big vehicle, only because he'd been a fairly scrawny kid. Tall, yes, but a beanpole nonetheless. So him sitting behind the wheel of something that large would've been disproportionate somehow.

This was no longer the case. The boy who got out of the driver's side of the truck wasn't a boy anymore. He was a man.

At eighteen years old Hamilton O'Bryan was a couple of inches over six feet tall, had muscular arms that were bigger than Beth's thighs, shaggy dark brown hair, and was always sporting a decent showing of five o'clock shadow on his jaw. He topped off the whole look with his thick, black-framed glasses, making him look like a young Clark Kent.

Hamilton's transformation over the last couple of years had been twofold. One, he'd hit puberty. And two, he'd been whipped into shape by his brother-in-law, Bennett Hart. Though as close as they were, that *in-law* part could really be erased.

And Hamilton wasn't the only one who'd benefitted from Mel and Bennett's union. The slightly shorter, equally as dark-haired, and a tad bit more muscular eighteen-year-old who was climbing out of the passenger side of the truck was Dale Riggels. He'd transformed almost just as much.

Actually, considering that Dale had been battling cancer the previous year and had lost about thirty pounds when he'd been on chemo, his transformation was just a little more impressive.

"Hammy! Dale!" Penny squealed.

Beth set her niece down and the little girl immediately shot off across the yard.

"PenPen!" Hamilton said as he ran toward her, scooping her up in one fluid motion and spinning her in the air.

The little girl's delighted giggles filled the air as she wrapped her arms around his neck and held on tight. A moment later she was transported to Dale's back, who started running around the yard, making her laugh all the more.

While Penny was carted around the yard by Dale, Hamilton made his way over to Beth and Corinne. As was the usual when he saw her—and she expected nothing less—Hamilton pulled Beth into a hug.

Despite everything that was going on with Nora, Hamilton didn't treat anyone else differently. He was a bigger man in many ways.

"I heard congratulations are in order." Beth looked up at him when he let go of her and took a step back. "Your mom told me you got into five colleges. And that every single one of them has a music scholarship attached."

Hamilton had been playing instruments as far back as Beth could remember. She was pretty sure he was proficient in about ten at this point.

"Yes ma'am." He nodded.

"You know which one you want to go to yet?"

"Still deciding."

"Dale got into a number of schools, too," Corinne called out, sounding just as proud as she did when she talked about Hamilton. "How many was it?"

"Four," Dale said as he came up to them. As he'd been running full tilt around with Penny it was pretty impressive that he was only slightly winded.

"Congratulations to you, too. Any of the same?" Beth asked.

"Three of the same," Hamilton answered.

"That's very exciting." She couldn't help but grin at both of them. "Well, we should get going." She nodded to her niece, who was currently sliding down Dale's back. "I have pizza in the car that's getting cold."

"Oh, pizza!" Hamilton said, looking at his mom. "Can we do that for dinner? I'm starving."

"You're always starving. And I'm making fried chicken and mashed potatoes."

"Ohhhhh, even better." Hamilton groaned.

"You staying for dinner?" Corinne asked Dale.

"Well, I can't miss your fried chicken and mashed potatoes, now can I?"

"No, you can't. Enjoy your pizza," she said, rubbing Penny's head affectionately before grabbing Penny's sparkly purple backpack and handing it to Beth. "I'll see you tomorrow."

"Bright and early. Have a good evening, you guys," Beth said as she reached for Penny's outstretched hand.

"You too, sugar."

Beth headed back to the house, Penny now chattering about the "bwock" castle she'd built.

When they got to the SUV she let go of her still chattering niece's hand. "Can you carry this?" she asked, holding out the backpack.

"Yes," Penny nodded simply, grabbing the bag and pulling it onto her tiny shoulders as she switched topics. Now she was telling Beth the story she'd heard before nap time about an alligator in high heels.

Beth grabbed the pizza boxes and her purse, hitting the automatic locks before they headed for the house.

The auditory assault happened as they stepped onto the porch, the windows barely containing the loud bass. When she opened the front door hip-hop thumped through the speakers, a female voice rapping about a sexual act that even at thirty Beth had never heard of.

"You've got to be kidding me." She stopped by the kitchen first, setting the pizza on the counter before making a beeline for the entertainment center in the living room. Nora's iPhone was plugged into the speakers, and Beth pulled it off the chord, plunging the house into silence... for about a second.

"Hey, I was listening to that!"

Beth spun around to find Nora laid out on the sofa, her computer in her lap and a massive frown on her face. The overjoyed enthusiasm that Penny had shown upon seeing her aunt was not matched by Nora.

Not in the slightest.

Beth missed the days when she and her older niece didn't have the most caustic relationship known to man. Missed them dearly.

"The entire neighborhood was listening to that, Nora. You are not allowed to play music like that."

"Why not?"

"Because they've said about nineteen inappropriate things in the thirty seconds that I've been in the house and certain ears"—she pointed to Penny, who'd followed her into the room—"should not be listening to it."

"You guys weren't even here."

"Yeah, but your eight-year-old brother is."

"He's outside," Nora waved carelessly behind her. "He's fine."

"Have you even looked outside? There's a massive storm coming this way, Nora!" Beth's gaze followed the motion of Nora's hand. As she looked out the windows, a bolt of lightning struck in the distance. Seconds later a rumble of thunder rolled through the air.

It was then that Nora's head popped up to look over the back of the sofa and her mossy green eyes went wide. "It's still...it's still far enough away. And he's probably on the porch."

"He shouldn't be outside at all," Beth said as she headed for the back door and pulled it open. "Goose!" She called out Grant's nickname as she looked at the very much empty porch. "Goose!" she called, louder, her eyes scanning the backyard. "It's time for dinner."

No answer.

"Grant!" She pushed the wooden frame of the screen door, stepping out onto the patio. The massive hundred-year-old oak tree that stood tall in the center of the yard moved with the wind, the leaves rustling on the branches that held them.

"Aunt B?" Beth turned around to see Penny standing in the doorway, her eyes wide and her bottom lip trembling.

"Sweetie, get back inside."

"Come here, Pen." Nora came up behind her little sister and picked her up just as another flash of lightning split the sky. Penny cried out as she wrapped her arms around her sister's neck. "Maybe he snuck in when I went to get a drink or something. Let me check his room."

Nora and Penny disappeared inside the house, the door closing with a snap as Beth turned around and made her way farther into the yard to do a loop around.

"Come on, Goose. You need to get inside, buddy." Something unpleasant settled low in Beth's belly. Out of the three kids, he was the most affected by storms. There was no way he would've missed what was rolling in, and he wouldn't linger outside. Not for a second.

As she got closer to the house the back door opened again and Nora stood on the threshold, chewing on her bottom lip. She dropped her lip from between her teeth and shook her head. "He isn't in the house."

Beth spun back around and called out again. "Grant!"

Then her eyes moved beyond the backyard and to the lake that spread out for about two miles. She spotted her brother-in-law's little green rowboat a hundred yards away, bobbing along while its two paddles floated out across the water in different directions.

Her shaking hand came up to cover her mouth. "Oh, God," she whispered through her fingers.

Chapter Three

How to Save a Life

The continuous high-pitched whining coming from Duke was like nails on a chalkboard. Tripp had been home for about two hours and for the last hour the dog would not stop. He sat by the French doors that led to the backyard, looking through the glass, his long fluffy tail thumping out a steady beat against the hardwood floors.

Until Tripp figured out the escape route Duke was using, the doggy door was going to have to be closed up. He knew the dog didn't need to use the bathroom as they'd spent about thirty minutes out there, Duke doing his business before a round of fetch had been played.

Damn, did that dog love balls. Tennis, baseball, rubber, blue, red, squeaky, anything. Maybe it was because Duke no longer had any that he was so obsessed with them.

Another long whine came from the dog, and this time he stretched his paw up and scratched at the door.

"Duke," Tripp snapped his fingers, immediately drawing the attention of the dog. "No."

Tripp really didn't understand why the dog was so damn anxious to get outside at the moment, because he hated storms. Maybe he was too upset with the freedom that had been taken away from him to be concerned with the storm brewing on the horizon.

Duke turned away from Tripp then stood up and started pacing, and the whining turned to keening.

"What's going on with you, buddy?" Tripp asked, crossing the room and crouching down to rub the dog's neck. Duke gently butted his head against Tripp's chest, the next whine coming out low and painful-sounding.

Tripp moved his hand to Duke's head as he stood and looked out the back doors, his gaze immediately landing on the lake. Normally at this time of the day the sun was setting and the water was a riot of colors. Today it was black and churning.

The doorbell rang, vibrating through the air, before a hurried knock followed. Duke bolted for the front door, letting off a series of booming barks.

"Shit," Tripp groaned.

He crossed the room and grabbed Duke by the collar before he opened the door, not even bothering with the peephole. What was the point? He knew exactly who it was based on that damn knock.

What the hell did she want now?

But as the woman on the other side of his door came into view, he knew this wasn't about her complaining. Her face was white, her blue eyes filled with terror, and her hands were shaking.

"I-I need to borrow your boat. It's Grant; I think he's out on the lake. The rowboat is out there and he isn't answering. I can't…I can't get to him. I don't know if he…"

She couldn't finish the sentence, but he knew the end anyway. Beth wasn't sure if Grant had fallen in.

"Come on." Tripp went into action mode, grabbing Beth's hand and pulling her into the house. He shut the door behind them, letting go of Duke's collar and Beth's hand simultaneously. The dog immediately bolted for the back door while Beth followed Tripp into the kitchen.

"I got home five minutes ago and couldn't find him, and then I saw the boat out there, and…and I kept calling his name but he didn't answer…and…oh, God."

The keys to his bass boat were on a hook inside the pantry. He wrenched them from where they hung and was pretty sure he'd ripped the hook out of the wall in the process. Beth held her shaking palm out in front of Tripp.

"You aren't going out there," he said as he stepped around her and paused for a second, slipping on his deck shoes in two quick movements.

The second the back door was opened, Duke sprinted off to the lake and Tripp followed. Beth was at his heels, which was more than a little impressive as he had about a foot on her in height.

As he opened the latch on the gate Beth made a move to follow him through but he held his hand up to stop her.

"Stay here."

"No, I'm going with you." She shook her head stubbornly.

"Beth, if lightning strikes the lake, there are going to be much bigger problems. *Stay. Here.*" If lightning did strike the lake it would travel across the top of it, a big problem for the metal-bottomed rowboat.

The gate snapped shut behind Tripp and he quickly moved to the end of the small wooden dock where the motorized bass boat was moored. He untied the rope from the post within seconds, and once he was standing securely in the boat pushed off from the dock before moving to the wheel. The motor came to life with a turn of the key and then he was steering the boat through the water.

There were fifty or so yards left to get to the rowboat when another bolt of lightning cracked the sky in half; the thunder that followed ripped through the air. Duke was barking like mad—a whole new level of *freaking the fuck out* that Tripp had never before seen from the dog.

He slowed the motorboat as he got close to the rowboat, but the rumbling engine was drowned out by another explosive clap of thunder.

"Be in there. Be in there. Be in there." The chant was a prayer more than anything else.

The second he was close enough to see over the bow of the boat he spotted the sandy blond head of the little boy. The relief at seeing Grant in there was short-lived. The kid was petrified, curled up in a ball and shaking uncontrollably, his hands covering his ears.

"Grant!" Tripp shouted, making the kid jump as he rolled over and opened his eyes wide. "Come on buddy." He leaned over, holding on to the side of the rowboat with one hand as he reached for the boy with the other. But Grant was just out of reach.

"I can't," Grant shook his head.

"Yes you can. You just need to move a little closer."

Grant still wouldn't move.

Tripp *really* didn't want to have to get into the rowboat. That was going to make this whole thing way more complicated. All he needed was for one or both of them to fall into the lake.

"Grant, you can do this. Just shift over a little bit and give me your hand. I'm going to get you out of here. Come on. Get on your knees and crawl over to me. Can you do that?"

Grant nodded, his little chin trembling as he did what Tripp told him, and slowly sat up. Then he got onto his hands and knees and started to move closer. There were shouts from Beth coming from the shore, but Tripp couldn't make out what she was saying.

Grant froze again as another boom of thunder shook the air, but by that point he was close enough for Tripp to grab. It took very little effort to lift the kid into the boat and seat him safely on the floor. Then they were off again, moving over the black, churning waters and back to shore.

Beth was on the edge of the dock, a clear beacon in the gloom with her lime green scrubs. Tripp slowed the engine again as he pulled in. When he was close enough, he reached down and grabbed Grant, lifting him out and handing him to his aunt.

Tripp followed, climbing out of the boat before quickly tying it back to the dock. When it was good and secure he turned and started running to catch up with Beth and Grant.

She was just stepping off the dock, her nephew still wrapped around her. His legs were at her waist, his arms at her shoulders while he cried into her neck. They all headed for the gate, Tripp moving in front of them so he could push the lever down. The second they were through it, he had his hand at the small of Beth's back and was leading them up the slope of the lawn and to his house. He would've offered to carry the kid, but Grant was wrapped around her like a vise. There was no way the little guy was letting go.

Duke was at Beth's other side, gently whining now as opposed to the full-on freak out he'd been having moments earlier.

"You're okay," Beth whispered over and over again, most likely reassuring herself just as much as she was reassuring Grant.

* * *

For about the fortieth time that night, Beth stuck her head in the door of the master bedroom and counted all three kids fast asleep in the king-size bed. The dim light shinning in from the living room was enough to illuminate the shapes of their bodies under the covers.

It was almost eleven o'clock, over four hours since Tripp had gotten Grant off the lake, and Beth still hadn't stopped shaking.

She'd dealt with high stress situations a number of times in her life. How could she not when she worked with mothers who were giving birth? But this was different. This had been *her* kid.

She didn't feel that way just because they were hers legally now. For all intents and purposes Nora, Grant, and Penny had been hers since they'd been born. They were part of her sister…and they were part of Beth. She'd felt them as they'd moved around in Colleen's belly, been there for all three of their births, had never missed a single birthday for any of them. Had watched Nora take her first steps, witnessed Grant's first giggle, heard Penny say her first word.

They were hers, and today she could've lost Grant. Her stomach churned painfully and she was pretty sure she was going to throw up…again.

It had taken a little while, but once Grant had calmed down he'd explained what had happened. It had all been a series of unfortunate events, starting off with him having a rough day at school.

Every Wednesday a folder was turned in with any forms or papers that had to be sent home for parents to look at. The kids got a sticker if they turned in a completed folder.

Well, Grant's teacher Mrs. Fielding had been out sick with the flu, so when the substitute had been instructed to collect the folders, there'd been one thing missing from Grant's: the sign-up form for "Bring Your Daddy to School Day." When the teacher hadn't given him a sticker because of his missing form he'd shut down.

Beth had given Grant the nickname Goose years ago, mainly because he was so silly, but also because of his laugh. A laugh she rarely ever heard anymore. Where Nora was acting out with her grief, Grant was on the opposite end. His parents' death had made him retreat into himself.

When Grant got home after school, Nora had noticed that her brother was upset. He'd responded to her questions with as few words as possible and a couple of shrugs of the shoulder. As Nora preferred space to deal with her grief, she'd given her brother the same courtesy.

But Grant had done something different that afternoon. He'd gone out into the rowboat, the boat he'd helped his father refurbish when he was five. The boat he and his dad would go out onto the lake and fish or row around in. That afternoon he'd wanted to be close to his dad, *needed* to be close. So he'd lain down at the bottom of that boat and curled up with a blanket and pillow he'd dragged out. Once he'd gotten comfortable he'd started reading from the pile of books he'd brought. He escaped into stories when he wanted to get away from it all.

He'd tied the rope to the boat before he'd pushed himself out onto the lake. Even though he wasn't good at rowing, he knew he could still pull himself back in with that rope. But Grant's "secure" rope tying hadn't been nearly secure enough. He'd fallen asleep in the middle of reading one of those books and hadn't been aware of the boat drifting off... or the storm drifting in.

The first crack of thunder that shook the sky woke him up, and it was then that he'd discovered he was out in the middle of the lake. At that point he'd been too terrified to do anything besides curl up in a ball. He hadn't heard Beth's shouts from the shore, either, and she doubted he would've been able to move even if he had heard her.

It really wasn't Nora's fault. Grant always went out into the backyard unsupervised. But more often than not, he was curled up in the hammock on the porch or at the base of the oak tree with one of his books.

One word from Beth's argument with Tripp that morning came back louder than ever: *boundaries.*

Grant knew he wasn't supposed to go anywhere near the lake when an adult wasn't home. Yeah, her nephew was more than a little lacking in the boundaries department. Who was she kidding? All of her kids were.

The relief of getting Grant back safe and sound had sidetracked any conversation she needed to have with Tripp. It wasn't that Beth wanted to put it off; it was that it was hard for her to open her mouth long enough to formulate words without losing it.

She'd barely been able to say anything to Tripp besides "thank you." Though that might've also had to do with him getting an emergency call pretty much the moment he'd walked her and Grant back to their house. He'd made sure they were in the door before he'd sprinted off.

The storm had blown in and out within two hours, but the winds had picked up steadily in the middle, wreaking havoc somewhere in Mirabelle.

Beth kept recalling the sight of Tripp out on that lake, and something unexpected made her heart clutch. Something she didn't quite understand…not even a little bit.

Hell, Tripp was the man she'd screamed at like a lunatic that morning. The man who every single one of her closest friends liked. The man who hadn't even thought twice before he'd gone out there to get Grant. And he'd done it so fast. He'd been out and back within two minutes. If she'd been the one to go out there? God, she probably would've fallen in trying to get Grant out.

She took one more long look at the kids before she grabbed the handle and pulled the door nearly closed, keeping only a gap big enough to stick her head through. The exhaustion coursing through her body was extreme, but there was no way in hell she was going to be able to fall asleep any time soon.

Instead she headed for the kitchen. An empty pizza box sat on the counter. She hadn't been able to eat anything for dinner, probably the only reason she hadn't thrown up again. At least the kids had been able to calm down enough to eat.

She grabbed the box from the counter and headed for the garage. The fluorescent lights flickered when she hit the switch, illuminating the space and the six brick steps that led to the ground. She slipped her flip-flops on before she headed to the door at the back of the garage. The backs of her shoes slapped against the concrete floor and the sound echoed around in her head.

Just more noise to add to the jumble that was already in her brain.

When she stepped outside she took a deep breath, hoping the fresh air would clear something. It cleared absolutely nothing. In fact, she just felt like she was suffocating.

Everything in her hurt and she couldn't take another step. The box fell from her hand as she sat on the stone path that wrapped around the side of the house. She pressed her back against the brick wall, pulled her legs up to her chest, and buried her face in her knees. The sob that cracked out of her lungs broke her in two...or at least it sure as hell felt like it did.

God. Grant could've drowned today...or been struck by lightning...or any number of other possible scenarios that all ended the same way: Beth losing him.

"Beth?"

Her head snapped up to find Tripp standing in front of her. Of course he'd be the one to witness her having a breakdown. The universe was just that kind.

He was illuminated by the sensor light that had turned on when she'd stepped outside. She'd never felt quite as small as she did in that moment, with him standing over her. He had a foot or so on her when she was actually standing, and weighed a good hundred pounds more...so yeah, he was slightly imposing.

"I'm fine." She pulled her gaze away from him, running her fingers under her streaming eyes.

"I know enough about women to know that word never means what it should mean."

A somewhat bitter laugh escaped Beth's mouth and she looked up at the black sky, resting her head on the wall behind her. "You're right. It never does."

Tripp's boots moved through the grass until they made a low thud against the stone. And then he had his back against the wall as he lowered his body down next to hers. They sat in silence for a moment before he asked, "Did that really happen?"

Beth brought her head down and looked over at him. "Did what happen?"

"Did you just admit I was right?" His chocolate brown eyes were lit up with a bit of humor, and his mouth quirked to the side.

"Only a little."

"You don't have to be 'fine', you know. Or anything else you don't want to be, for that matter."

"I'm failing," she whispered, pushing past the constriction in her throat. "That's what I am, failing at being a parent to those three kids." The confession burned its way out, the words like acid on her tongue.

The bitter, bitter truth.

"You aren't failing. Good God, Beth, you have three of them and you're raising them by yourself. My parents just had me and my mom will be the first to tell you she's surprised I'm here today after all the shit I got into growing up."

"Really?"

"Yeah. I won't get into the details because it would probably just stress you out more to know what boys get into. But considering everything you've got on your plate? I think you're doing a pretty damn good job." He gave her another sidewise smile as he reached up and scratched his jaw, the sound of his beard under his nails filling her ears. "I mean, obviously I say all of these things more than a little grudgingly, as we can't really have a conversation and not get into an argument."

Another laugh bubbled out of Beth's chest, but this one actually held a bit of real amusement. "I'm sorry about this morning. I was out of line."

"So was I. That, uh, leash comment was way too far. And I'm sorry about your garden, too. I'll pay you for the damage and fix it to the state it was in before Duke destroyed it."

"Not necessary." Beth shook her head. "It appears I owe you money for flat tires. And it's going to be a few weeks before I can plant anything. Besides, I love being out there with my hands in the dirt. It makes me…" She trailed off, unsure of how she'd started down this path.

How in the world was it that she was confiding in Tripp Black? The man who until very recently she'd thought was a jerk.

Well, he'd proved her good and wrong, hadn't he? He was something else entirely…something else that she hadn't been prepared to discover. The type of man who risked his life for others. And yes, that was something she'd known before that afternoon, but seeing him in action? Witnessing him do it? That had been beyond eye-opening.

She'd been really, *really* wrong about him.

"It makes you what?" Within an instant those melty brown eyes of his pulled her in, making her feel…what, exactly?

Warm?

Safe?

Comforted?

She had no clue.

Not only that, but her fingers had the strangest urge to reach up and touch the scruff that dusted his strong jaw.

Bad urge. She mentally slapped her hand down. Where in the hell had that come from?

She forced herself to pull her gaze away and look forward at the less than thrilling view of the side of Tripp's house. Yeah, looking into his face had been much better...if not slightly more dangerous. But this was a conversation she wasn't going to have while looking into his eyes.

Nope.

"It makes me feel closer to my mother."

Tripp was silent for a moment before he cleared his throat and spoke. "Her name was Dory, right?"

And just that fast she was looking at him again. She couldn't stop herself. "How?" Her eyebrows raised in question.

"Your dad stops by the firehouse every once in a while for lunch. We've had a couple of conversations."

It just figured that Tripp had won over her father as well. Wallace was a mechanic at King's Auto, which was just a few doors down from the fire station.

"Yes, her name was Dory." Beth nodded as she looked down at her hands, hands that had been taught to do things like create and cultivate by her mother. "Her two favorite things were baking and gardening. So whenever I do either of those things...well, it's like she's here again. Even if it's just for a moment."

"How old were you when she passed?"

"Thirteen. I was sitting at the dining room table doing homework while she ironed. One minute she was singing Billy Joel and…and the next she was gone." She blinked, tears falling from her eyes and hitting the backs of her hands. When had she started crying again? "I can't do it again. My mom, Colleen, Kevin…I can't lose someone I love like that…so…so unexpectedly. I just can't."

Again, again the words were just spilling out of her mouth as if she had absolutely no control. What was even happening?

But her brain didn't have a chance to formulate an answer. A moment later his hand covered hers, his thumb brushing across her knuckles and wiping away the tears that had fallen. "I can't imagine how hard it's been."

"It's fucking awful. Grant could've died today." Saying those words out loud caused more pain to course through her and the second they were out of her mouth she promptly proceeded to break down…again.

"Hey, now." Tripp pulled her into his arms, and she couldn't stop herself from pressing her face to his neck. "I've got you, Beth," he whispered as his hand moved up and down her spine. His other hand palmed the back of her head, holding her steady.

Before she even knew what she was doing, her hands were fisted in his shirt and she was holding on to him with something similar to a death grip. It had been ages since she'd been comforted by anyone like this and it felt so damn good to be in someone's arms.

She hadn't realized how much she'd missed it until just that moment. There was no telling how long they sat there, her tears soaking into his shirt while he held her close.

But the second she found an ounce of composure she felt a whole new emotion: *Mortification.*

Not only had she just lost it in front of Tripp, she'd lost it *on* him.

Yup, just when she thought her day couldn't get any worse. But when she pulled back and looked up into his face, she found something rather unexpected in his expression. There wasn't an ounce of pity in his gaze—something she'd long ago gotten sick and tired of seeing. No, he was looking at her with compassion and sympathy.

"It's okay, Beth. *Grant* is okay. We got him out of there and he's fine."

"You got him out of there."

"Yes, but you got me to help. It was a team effort." He reached up, running his fingers underneath her eyes.

"I think your definition of 'team effort' is a little skewed. What you did, Tripp…I can't, I can't thank you enough."

"What other option was there? Anyone would have gone out there to get him."

"No." She shook her head. "They wouldn't have. There are plenty of people who would've walked away. Plenty of people who wouldn't have taken the risk to save another person."

"Yeah, well, that would make me a pretty shitty firefighter, now wouldn't it? 'You guys get yourself out of the burning building, I'm just going to stand back here and roast a marshmallow.'"

"This is very true," she said as another genuine laugh escaped her mouth. Five minutes with this guy and she already felt a hundred times better. No wonder everyone fell under his spell.

And another one bites the dust.

Oh no…no, no, no. Something funny fluttered low in her belly…something she was in no way prepared for. Not with any man, but especially not with *this* man.

"I should go in now. I don't want one of the kids to wake up and not find me in the house." Nor did she want to do something incredibly stupid...well, something *else* incredibly stupid.

"Okay." Tripp moved first, getting to his feet before turning to her and holding out his hand.

She grabbed it, in no way oblivious to the tingles that shot up her arm as their palms slid against each other. He helped her up to her feet, and she wasn't the least bit surprised that she was just a tad unsteady. What she was surprised by was when his hand let go of hers and landed on her hip.

"You going to be all right?" He took a step closer and reached up to her forehead with his free hand. His fingertips traced her hairline and caught a few strands that had fallen across her face. He brushed her hair back and behind her ear as he looked into her eyes.

"Yeah." She nodded, taking a deep breath. But that deep breath had been a bit of a mistake, because all she smelled was Tripp.

There was the lingering scent of soap—either laundry detergent or body wash, she wasn't quite sure which—making him smell fresh and clean. There was also a hint of something else filling her already foggy brain.

Good Lord, no wonder she'd plastered herself to him when she'd had her little meltdown. Even subconsciously she'd been trying to inhale him. It was then that her eyes dropped to the tear-soaked shoulder of his shirt.

"I didn't mean to..." she gestured at the spot, "cry all over you."

"It's not a problem." He shook his head. "Though I will say, I'd like to have a conversation with you that doesn't involve screaming or crying."

"Deal."

"So we have a truce, neighbor."

"No." Beth shook her head. "Friends before neighbors." She grabbed his forearm for balance as she stretched up onto her tiptoes. The scruff on his jaw rasped against her lips as she placed a kiss on his cheek.

She pulled back to look at him, and for just a second she thought she saw something flicker in his eyes...something that bordered on desire. Nope, that couldn't be right. It was just a reflection from the light. Fluorescents could be tricky little bastards.

Her hands fell away from his body first and he followed her lead, letting go as he took a step back.

"Thank you for everything, Tripp. Earlier with Grant...and for talking to me now."

"Anytime." He nodded as he took another step back, swooping down and snatching the forgotten pizza box from the ground before he straightened. "Get some sleep. Everything will be better in the morning."

"Oh, don't say that. You might jinx me."

"Nah." He shook his head as he grinned at her. "It will be. Good night, Beth."

"'Night, Tripp."

And with that he turned around, stopping at the trashcan to toss the pizza box before he headed off to his house.

Beth wasn't sure how long she stood there, staring after the man who'd disappeared into the darkness.

Chapter Four

The Caveman Phenomenon

Without fail, whenever anything happened that required the need for Beth to *talk it out*, her first thought was always that she wanted to talk to her sister.

Almost a year without Colleen and Beth's immediate reaction hadn't changed one little bit. How could it? Her sister had always been the first person she'd turned to for advice, even when their mom was alive.

It was Colleen who Beth went to when she had her first kiss. Colleen who learned about Beth's first boyfriend while they shared a pint of ice cream. Colleen who took Beth shopping for her prom dress. Colleen who consoled Beth during her first bad breakup...and her second...and her third...and her fourth. Colleen who Beth talked to leading up to losing her virginity... and afterward. It was Colleen who took Beth out for her first legal drink at a bar.

She'd been Beth's constant sounding board. Only a phone call away, or an hour drive when a little extra counseling was needed…counseling that had usually included a glass of wine…or three.

After the backyard, the kitchen was Beth's second favorite room in the house. It had been remodeled to perfection. Colleen's dream laid out in every detail. The appliances were all stainless steel, set into cabinets that were stained a natural vintage oak, and topped with tan and white granite counters. Chair railing ran across the back wall, painted light gray above and dark gray below.

A table for six—the planks stained a similar light brown that matched the kitchen cabinets—sat in front of a wall of windows that looked out to the backyard.

That was where they'd always sat and talked when Beth came over—Colleen's sanctuary. And though it would never, *ever,* be the same without Colleen, those counseling and wine sessions still very much happened these days.

Case in point: Melanie Hart was currently sitting at the dining room table with Beth, sipping a glass of Pinot Grigio.

Beth was more than blessed by the friends she had in Mirabelle. Some she'd known for decades, while others were newer to the fold. But every single one of them had her back. She wouldn't have gotten through the last year without them.

Not a chance.

"So Tripp just went out there in the middle of a lightning storm?" Mel asked, indicating the lake behind the house with her wineglass.

"Yup." Beth nodded, not needing to look out at the lake that had been her biggest nightmare the day before. It had been just over twenty-four hours since everything had happened, and the fear of it was still tying her stomach in knots.

"No second guessing? No questions asked?" Mel shook her head, her blond corkscrew curls bouncing slightly at the movement. "No stopping? Just *bam*: 'I am man. Watch me save.'"

"*I am man. Watch me save?*" Beth repeated, unable to fight the smile that worked at her mouth.

"You know, when they get all caveman." Mel waved her free hand in the air as she brought her glass to her mouth and took a sip.

"Bennett do that very often? Go all caveman?"

Mel glanced over at the living room and Beth's gazed followed. The kids were in there watching *Mulan*. Nora and Penny were on the sofa, snuggled up under a fuzzy pink blanket, while Grant sat in front of the coffee table putting together a puzzle of the Grand Canyon.

They were all thoroughly occupied and not paying attention to the conversation going on in the kitchen.

"Sometimes." Mel grinned hugely as she waggled her eyebrows. "Depends on the situation. But he has been known to throw me over his shoulder and carry me off to the closest flat surface."

A year ago Beth wouldn't have begrudged anyone on having an active sex life. But that was because a year ago Beth had *had* an active sex life. Good Lord, she missed it. Missed losing herself in the intense passion. Missed those real and intimate moments. The anticipation beforehand, the pleasure of it all during, catching her breath afterward. She missed a man's hands on her body...missed the connection...missed all of it.

The last year had been lonely for many reasons; there was no doubt about that. And try as she might, there'd been times when she hadn't been able to stop herself from thinking about the really good sex she'd had with her stupid dickhead ex.

Though the image she was having right now of a man carrying *her* off to a flat surface wasn't Mick. Nope. It was a different man entirely…

Now Beth normally wasn't a betting woman, but she'd put a lot of money on the line that Tripp Black probably knew exactly what he was doing in a lot of *hands on* scenarios in life.

Talented hands or not, she needed to stop with all of her betting and fantasizing and anything else that involved that particular man. Because really, imagining sex with him was dangerous. Unlike her friend, regular orgasms just weren't going to be a reality for her.

Honestly though, Beth didn't begrudge Mel's sex life at all. Those regular orgasms—and what was no doubt still *really* hot sex—were part of the fact that she and Bennett were trying to get pregnant…had been trying to get pregnant for well over a year now.

Mel had always been a positive person, probably *the most* positive person Beth knew. But what with all of their friends popping out kids like no one's business, it was starting to wear on Mel.

About a month ago, on one of the weekends that Papa Wallace had taken the kids, there'd been a Friday night when Beth and Mel had cracked into a bottle—or two—of wine. They'd talked about a lot of things, Mel's current struggle being one of them. It had been pretty damn difficult sitting across from her friend and watching her cry.

Beth could only imagine the frustration that the couple was going through, especially because the fertility specialist hadn't found anything wrong with either of them. For all intents and purposes, they *should* be pregnant.

That had sure been fun for Mel to hear.

"So anyway," Mel said, bringing Beth back to the moment. "What was it like to see him in action?"

"Well, he's very…take charge. Which was good as I wasn't exactly thinking straight, and you know, was more than slightly terrified."

"Understandably so," Mel nodded.

"But when Tripp found Grant in the boat…I knew Grant was in capable hands, knew Tripp was going to get both of them off that lake." She paused for a second, pulling herself away from that very vivid image. "You know, he brought the boat back."

"What?"

"I woke up this morning to find it tied up on the bank, paddles and everything. He must've gone out this morning to get it all."

"Hmmm." Mel grinned as she set her glass on the table. "You're talking about Tripp a lot differently today than I'm used to."

"And how do I normally talk about him?"

"With annoyance…mild displeasure…extreme hostility."

It was true; Mel had listened to Beth vent about the man on more than one occasion. And even though she'd listened, she'd always stood firm on the fact that Tripp was a good guy and Beth just needed to give him a chance. But really that was to be expected of Mel. Besides very few exceptions, she pretty much saw the good in everyone.

"Yeah, well, that was before." Beth reached for the wine bottle and topped off both of their glasses.

"Uh-hunh."

"What?"

"I don't know." Mel shrugged. "Something's just different."

"Well, of course it is…we're friends now."

"*Ohhhh*, your *friends* now?" Mel's eyebrows rose high. "That's a new descriptor."

"We came to a truce." Beth shrugged in an attempt to show it wasn't a big deal at all.

Mel wasn't falling for it. "A truce? When was that?"

"Last night…we…uh…we had a conversation." Beth looked at her wineglass, running her forefinger around the rim and not exactly looking at Mel as she started that part of the story. "I was upset…"

"Obviously," Mel agreed.

Beth finally glanced up. "I might've cried all over him."

"Well, this is getting more and more interesting."

"Interesting? It was humiliating!"

"I'd assume so. But you know what, embarrassing yourself in front of a guy isn't always a bad thing. When Bennett and I started dating, I got a migraine and threw up in front of him. He handled the whole situation like a champ."

"Well, see, you had a couple of things going for you there. First, Bennett is Bennett. And second, the two of you were dating at the time."

"I would hope that Bennett is Bennett."

"You know what I mean." Beth shook her head. "He's a good guy."

"And so is Tripp. Something you've now witnessed."

"Yes, I know, but please reference point number two." Beth held up two fingers. "Tripp and I aren't dating."

"You could be."

"Come on."

"No, you come on, Beth." Mel shook her head. "Don't tell me you don't think that man is attractive as sin."

"You checking out Tripp Black? Do I need to tell your husband?"

"Oh, please." Mel waved her friend off. "My husband has absolutely nothing to worry about when it comes to my eyes. They don't wander. What they do is pick up on something that I see to be a potential relationship between two of my friends."

"Speaking of your husband, where is he this evening?"

"Nice subject change. I'll let you get away with it tonight, but only because I'm feeling generous at the moment." Mel grabbed her wineglass from the table and took a sip before she continued. "Some new video game came out this week and he's currently trying to master it with Hamilton."

"How is Hamilton?" Beth asked, unable to stop her eyes from traveling to the living room and landing on her niece.

Yes, Beth saw Hamilton regularly, the day before being the most recent, but it wasn't like she asked him about Nora. He wasn't going to confide in her regarding that topic. And it wasn't like she could do anything to fix it. Didn't change how damn frustrating it was that after thirteen years of friendship, Nora was ignoring Hamilton when she needed him the most.

"He misses her. He doesn't really bring it up very often with me and he probably talks to Bennett about it fractionally more. I think it's weird for him, you know? They've always been in and out of each others' lives and now … nothing."

"I know. This whole thing is so damn frustrating. I don't know how to help her."

"The therapy working at all?"

"Marginally." Beth nodded. She and her dad had come to the conclusion that the kids needed to start seeing someone last fall. "It isn't like I expected this to be fixed overnight or anything, but I really hoped there would be a little bit more improvement."

"I bet. At least her grades aren't suffering. She isn't sabotaging herself, which is something I've seen before in similar situations."

Mel was a math teacher at the high school, and she just so happened to be Nora's. Yup, she had two close friends that were teachers to her kids, which made it *that* much easier to always know what was going on with them in school.

"I know you worry about her," Mel continued. "*I* worry about her, but she's a good kid. She'll figure it out sooner or later. And even if she is pushing pretty much everyone away, at least she isn't pushing the two most important people away."

Beth turned to the living room just as Nora reached out and ran her fingers through Grant's hair.

It was true. Nora loved her little brother and sister more than anything. She'd blamed herself for what had happened with Grant out there on that lake. Didn't matter how many times Beth told her it wasn't her fault. Grant had known better; there was no doubt about that. He knew he wasn't supposed to go out on that lake. But he'd done it anyway.

And really, it had been Beth's fault. She was their parent now. She was the one who needed to be watching out for these kids. She was the one taking care of them.

So in the end, whether Mel tried to play matchmaker or not, Beth didn't have time for other things...like relationships. She'd been burned before...she didn't need to deal with that again. Besides, if she were to get into a relationship, it wouldn't be just her heart on the line. There were the kids to factor in now. And they were a pretty big factor.

It was safer this way, not getting involved.

Safer and lonely.

* * *

There were few things Duke loved more than a car ride. He sat in the back seat of Tripp's truck, eyes closed and big tongue lolling as the open window blew air into his face. His lips were pulled back by the force of the air in such a way that it appeared he was grinning.

It really was the simple things in life.

Tripp was just hoping that this current calm state didn't go anywhere, especially as they were heading to the veterinarian. If there was any situation for Duke to be in his scared-of-everything mode, it was at the vet.

The last time they were here Duke had lost his balls...or more accurately, had had them taken away. But when Tripp parked the car, the dog looked more disappointed at the loss of the steady breeze coming through the open window than at the location.

The St. Francis Veterinary Clinic was pretty much right at the center of downtown Mirabelle, and about a ten-minute walk from the fire station. It was set up in a three-story, Victorian house painted a dark blue with an identical sage-green house sitting right next to it.

The green one was the home of Dr. Paul Laurence and his wife Delilah. They'd been the owners of both buildings for the last sixteen years. For the first fourteen, Dr. Laurence had been the only vet in Mirabelle. Sure, there were more scattered around Atticus County—and some of the town's five thousand residents did take their animals elsewhere—but Paul had been a pretty busy man running the place on his own.

Now he had help at the practice. He'd hired on Dr. Finn Shepherd about two years ago. Finn was a Mirabelle native, only leaving town for the time it took him to get his degree. He moved back pretty much the moment he'd graduated. Tripp had a close group of friends in Mirabelle, but these days he hung out with Finn the most. Probably because they were the only two bachelors left in their circle.

Well, that and their dogs were siblings.

Finn's dog Frankie had been abandoned at the firehouse last year with Duke. She was just as big as her brother, but where Duke was evenly colored with white and brown, Frankie was mostly white. She also wasn't a spaz.

Tripp got out of his truck and rounded the other side. When he opened the door Duke leaned forward and licked his neck before nuzzling him.

Whatever. Duke could be a spaz all he fucking wanted.

"Come on, buddy," Tripp said as he scratched the dog under his collar. "Let's go get you checked out." He grabbed the leash that sat on the floor of the back seat, clipping it into place before he moved enough for the dog to jump out.

Duke led the way to the building, tail wagging and head held high as they mounted the steps. The second they walked into the office a loud squawk filled the room. There were two receptionists for the clinic: Janet Peterson and Gabby. Janet was an older lady who had been working there for thirty-plus years. Gabby was a white and yellow cockatoo that had been adopted by the practice when her owner died over ten years ago.

The bird sat on her perch by the desk, alerting everyone who worked in the building when anyone or anything walked in the door.

But there really wasn't a need to alert anyone of Tripp and Duke's presence that morning. Seven people—including all three who worked in the building—were standing in the reception area. Well, six of them were standing. The seventh person was of the teeny tiny variety. She was currently being held by her grandfather, a grandfather who was already wrapped around her teeny tiny little finger.

Sofia Lilian James wasn't even a month old. She had violet eyes just like her mother's and a full head of dark brown hair that matched her father's. Her parents, Harper and Liam James, were among the group of people in the room.

Liam hadn't become a fixture in Mirabelle until the summer before. He was a country musician whose career had skyrocketed, something that he attributed to the song he'd written about the woman standing next to him. A woman who'd become his wife last November.

Harper was beautiful, there was no doubt about it. She had long black hair that stretched down her back, killer curves that only a blind man would miss, and a sassy attitude. Tripp had met her shortly after he'd moved to Mirabelle three years ago, but they'd only ever been friends.

There were certain pools he didn't play in when it came to dating or sex. Number one, he didn't mess with married women. That was a hard and fast rule that he never bent in any way, shape, or form. Number two, he steered clear of anything professional. This hadn't been much of a problem since he'd moved to Mirabelle as everyone who worked for the fire department—outside of dispatch—was a man. Number three, he didn't date within his personal circle. So no friends, or friends of friends, or feisty blond neighbors, for that matter.

Not only was Beth in his personal circle, but her front door was about seventy feet away from his.

Though neither of those facts were helping deter Tripp at the moment. Beth hadn't been too far from his thoughts since their conversation the other night…when she'd confided in him… when he'd had his hands on her body for just a moment…or when she'd placed that kiss on his cheek.

Somewhere in the chaos of everything that had happened that day, he'd gone from thinking she was a royal pain in his ass to…well…liking her. There was something about her. Something that had him rethinking a lot of things he'd thought about her in the last few months. She'd been so soft and sweet in his arms…and so thoroughly heartbroken.

He'd always hated seeing women cry; it made him want to fix whatever it was that had upset them. But with Beth? That desire to fix had been *so* much stronger.

And that wasn't the only strong desire he'd had. It had taken everything in him not to turn into that kiss and claim her mouth. Something he'd been more than a little shocked by.

Tripp had never been a man who wanted what he couldn't have, so it had nothing to do with her being off limits. And it wasn't just because she was beautiful, either. Because she was. Oh, who the hell was he kidding? Beth Boone was fucking gorgeous. She was a tiny thing, but she made a case for not underestimating what could come in small packages.

He'd done a double take when he'd seen her in the front yard the day before. She'd been wearing a red T-shirt that had done a fantastic job of showing off just a hint of cleavage, along with the dip of her waist…a dip he'd had his hands on…had felt under his palms. Not that he'd thought about that multiple times in the last two days…nope.

Nor had he thought about the pair of jeans that looked like they'd been made for her. A pair of jeans that were beyond distract-ing as they showcased the curve of her hips…and her spectacular ass.

Yeah, he was full of shit. He'd thought about all of those damn things. *A lot*. He needed to get it together. Stat.

"Tripp!" Delilah Laurence clapped her hands together excit-edly, the sharp slap echoing in the space and pulling him back to the present. "Have you met my granddaughter yet?"

"I have." Tripp nodded, moving closer to Paul in an attempt to get a better look at Sofia.

The little girl was wrapped up in a purple blanket, her pretty eyes open as her grandfather held a bottle to her mouth.

"She gets more beautiful every time I see her," Tripp said, glanc-ing over at her parents.

Harper was leaning against Liam's side, his arm wrapped around her waist and holding her close.

"That would be because she looks more and more like her mother every day." Liam grinned as he pressed a kiss to his wife's temple.

It was at that moment that the *tap, tap, tap* of claws could be heard coming down the hallway from the kitchen. Frankie's massive white head emerged from the doorway before the rest of her body followed. She immediately headed over to her brother and gave him a big old lick across the face.

"I still can't believe how massive they are," Harper said as she pulled away from Liam and moved toward the dogs. "I remember when they were this big." She held her hands about a foot apart in the air before she crouched down next to both dogs and started petting them.

"Yeah, they are considerably larger now," Finn nodded before he took a sip from his mug of coffee.

"I hadn't noticed." Tripp looked at his friend, exaggerating a frown.

"Oh, don't even get started with that." Finn waved his hand in the air before he pushed his black plastic-framed glasses up the bridge of his nose.

"Get started with what?"

"The whole 'it's *my* fault that *you* adopted the dog' thing that you like to do."

"It *is* your fault that I adopted the dog."

"And you don't regret it at all, do you?" Harper grinned up at Tripp as she scratched Duke's chest while simultaneously rubbing the spot between Frankie's ears.

"Nope, I don't."

"Well, we should go get him checked out," Finn nodded to Duke. "That way you can get back to, well, whatever it is that you do."

"Why, Finn Shepherd, are you mocking one of our good public servants?" Janet asked, her steely gray eyebrows furrowing in disapproval.

Janet hadn't seen anything. Finn and Tripp busted each other's balls on a regular basis. If they weren't in a room with this particular audience there wouldn't be holding back of any kind.

"I sure am." Finn grinned. "What are you guys marathon watching on Netflix now? *Pretty Little Liars?*"

"Nah, all caught up on that. We've moved onto *Gilmore Girls* now."

"See, Mrs. Peterson, those are your taxpayer dollars hard at work." Finn shook his head in mock disapproval.

"You mean when he isn't rescuing children from getting struck by lightning on a lake?" Harper asked as she stood, folding her arms across her chest and giving Tripp what could only be described as a penetrating gaze.

The room fell silent and as Tripp held Harper's gaze he felt all the eyes in the room go from her to him in an instant.

"You did what?" Paul asked.

"Yeah," Finn echoed. "You did *what?*"

Tripp cleared his throat, still trying to hold his ground with Harper, as he scratched the back of his neck with his free hand. "It was nothing."

"That's not the way Beth told it." She pursed her lips together as one of her eyebrows climbed high.

And Harper had every reason to be skeptical.

Okay, so he'd be lying if he said he wasn't just a little bit curious about Harper's statement. But the curiosity had nothing to do with wanting to hear what *he'd* done. He'd been there. He knew what had happened. No, it had everything to do with wanting to hear the way *Beth* had told it.

And that desire? Well, he wasn't exactly sure how he felt about it. Another thing that he could just add to the list.

Before Tripp could stop himself he opened his mouth and the question fell out. "And how was that?"

He hadn't thought it was possible for Harper's gaze to narrow further…but it most definitely did. And not only that, but the move was accompanied by her mouth forming a bit of a smirk.

Chapter Five

Thank You Cookies

The sun was sitting low in the sky, sunset about twenty minutes away, as Beth walked across the lawn and over to Tripp's house. She wasn't exactly sure *why* she was so nervous as she headed up the walkway and to his front door…but she was.

It was Saturday, three days since the lake incident, and though she'd seen him a couple of times in passing, she hadn't talked to him since he'd comforted her…and she'd cried all over him.

But she wanted to get past that; she *had* to get past that. They were neighbors and apparently friends now, too. She'd told him so right before she'd kissed his cheek…right before she'd felt his beard rasp against her lips. Not that she'd thought about that multiple times a day or anything.

Good Lord, what the hell had happened? She'd gone from despising him to…well, what exactly was this, anyway? A crush? No…no, she didn't get crushes. That was…ridiculous. Wasn't it? She couldn't be too sure…but the still warm plate of cookies she was currently carrying over to him didn't bode well for her.

Not at all.

Maybe she could just leave them on the mat. Just ring the doorbell and run.

Really? You're going to play ding-dong-ditch?

No. No, she wasn't. Because Beth didn't run from anything…or anyone, for that matter. She dealt with it, and she'd damn well deal with this. And besides, this feeling was probably just lingering appreciation for what Tripp had done for Grant. Yeah, that's what it was.

Had to be, and once she addressed it head on she'd be able to move *on*. Her resolve was firm, which was probably the only reason she was able to lift her hand and press her finger to the doorbell.

A few seconds went by before a shadow moved behind the frosted glass that surrounded the frame. The deadbolt was flipped a moment later and the door pulled open, revealing Tripp Black. He stood there in day-old scruff, khaki shorts, and a hunter green T-shirt. The shirt in question was fit at the top, showcasing his arms and muscled chest but hanging loose around his waist.

"Hey." His mouth split into a grin as his chocolate eyes focused on her.

A small swoop kicked up low in her belly and her mouth went dry.

Shit.

"Hi." That one word was more difficult to get out of her mouth than it should've been. She swallowed hard before she attempted to speak again. "I hadn't talked to you since the other night, or thanked you properly. So I made you *thank you* cookies." She finished more than somewhat lamely as she stuck out her hands, holding the plate for him to grab.

"*Thank you* cookies?" His eyes went to the cookies and then back up to her face, and that smile of his seemed to grow.

How the hell had she never noticed what a great smile he had? Maybe because until recently he'd always been scowling at her. Which made sense, as she'd usually been yelling at him.

"It isn't much. I know nothing will be enough for what you did...but I wanted to do something."

"I don't think you're aware of my love of sweets. This is a pretty good *thank you* if I do say so myself." He grabbed the plate from her hands, his eyes not leaving hers. "You need to be anywhere? Sun's about to set; you want to have a beer with me?"

Beth wasn't exactly sure why she was so surprised by Tripp's invitation, but she was.

"Yes." The answer came out of her mouth before she could really think about it.

And why shouldn't she enjoy a beer with him? It wasn't like the kids would be alone. Her father had come over for dinner that night and was currently watching *Frozen*. Penny had conned him into it.

Maybe it was the prospect of not having to listen to Elsa sing "Let It Go" for the five thousandth time that had prompted her to say yes so quickly. Because really, the next rendition was going to end with her shoving a fork into her ears.

Yeah, that had to be it...and not because he was smiling at her. Nope, it had absolutely nothing to do with that smile.

Liar.

Tripp stepped back from the doorway, making space for her to walk by. Beth moved slightly down the hallway and turned as he shut the front door.

"After you." He looked behind her and she spun back around. She headed down the rest of the hallway that opened up into a big, grand space comprising the living room, kitchen, and dining room.

Beth hadn't had a chance to take in the house when she'd been there the other day...She'd been just *slightly* distracted. It had probably been about ten years since she'd been inside the house that now belonged to Tripp, and absolutely nothing was the same as she remembered.

She knew it from the days that the Schaffers had lived there, and it had been a dark cave with thick velvet curtains hanging from the windows. There'd been floral sofas covered in plastic and they squeaked when anyone sat down. The closed-in kitchen had been filled with dilapidated cabinets and appliances. Every room sported a different wallpaper in some pattern of birds. And Beth's favorite? The mustard yellow carpet that had plastic runners indicating exactly where guests could walk.

The neighborhood had been built in the seventies. When her sister and brother-in-law had bought the house next door it had been in much the same shape, but they'd remodeled each room, one at a time. And now Tripp's house had been remodeled as well.

A chocolate brown leather sectional sat in the middle of the living room. It was strategically positioned so that the big screen TV mounted on the wall could be seen from any and all angles. A plush red and tan rug was stretched out across the cherrywood floors and a coffee table with a stone top and ironwork base sat in the middle. The back wall of the living room had more windows than there used to be, and the sliding glass doors had been replaced with French doors that opened up to the backyard. Light streamed in, making the cream-colored walls appear to glow.

Beth's gaze moved beyond the living room and to the entirely remodeled kitchen. The divider wall had been knocked down and replaced with a breakfast bar. Brand-new wooden cabinets stained a light blond went all the way up to the ceiling and the countertops were made of black granite. A mosaic of white, gray, and black tiles made up the backsplash and shiny black appliances gleamed.

A table for six—which was interesting as he lived alone—sat in the far left corner, where massive windows made up the majority of the ninety-degree angle and stretched up to just a few inches below the ceiling. All of the venetian blinds in the space were open, the exposed windows giving a clear view of the backyard.

A deep, masculine moan filled the room behind Beth and it had her spinning around in an instant. The sight before her had her breath catching in her throat, while a riot of flutters overtook her stomach.

Tripp was taking another bite of the half-devoured cookie in his hand, his eyes closed as he made a second moan of bliss.

This time the flutters flowing through Beth's body were much, much lower than before. It had been a long time since a man had inspired her to feel anything south of the border. Well, any man besides Henry Cavill, but she had old episodes of *The Tudors* to help out with that.

But good Lord, there was something about hearing the sound of pure male satisfaction that had her brain short-circuiting. And this particular man? Well, he was her sexy-as-all-hell neighbor. Her sexy-as-all-hell neighbor who'd been at the forefront of her thoughts the last couple of days. Not that that was a problem or anything, except she shouldn't be thinking romantically about any man at the moment.

No relationships...she needed to remember that...even if he was sexy as all hell.

And okay, Beth would be the biggest liar on the face of the planet if she said she hadn't been fully aware of Tripp and his sexiness long before. Because: scruff...and chocolate brown eyes...and strong sturdy hands...and well, everything else.

Yeah, her saying yes to a beer had absolutely nothing to do with her Elsa aversion and everything to do with wanting to spend a few moments alone with a man...a man she hadn't been able to stand until about a week ago.

Oh, how the tides had turned.

Though, they hadn't always been at odds. He'd been an acquaintance of hers for years now. Hell, they'd both been in Mel and Bennett's wedding two years ago. But Beth had been with Mick then, so there'd been nothing more than appreciation at how Tripp filled out a tux...a sight she remembered vividly.

There were also the countless group beach excursions with their friends last summer where she'd seen him wearing nothing more than a pair of swim trunks. But that had been right after Beth had moved back. She'd been grieving and focusing on settling into her new job description of caregiver to three children. There'd also been the part about getting over her horrendous breakup with her ex.

But circumstances being what they were, she would've been blind not to notice him before...and Beth had twenty-twenty vision. Her excellent eyesight meant she didn't miss a moment of Tripp opening his somewhat dazed eyes as he licked his lips.

Her knees were about two-point-five seconds from buckling.

"Damn. These are incredible, Beth." He pointed to the plate, not taking his gaze from hers. "Best *thank you* you could've given me."

"That's your assessment after just one? Well, aren't you easy?" The words had slipped out before she even realized it.

Tripp's eyebrows shot up in surprise and a sideways grin played across his lips.

Oh, good God. Had she really just said that? What the hell was wrong with her? Apparently she was incapable of having a normal conversation with the guy. "That...that wasn't what I meant."

"I knew what you meant," he said as his half-smile transformed into a full-on grin. "Do you prefer your beer in a glass or the bottle?"

"The bottle is good."

Tripp nodded as he opened a drawer and pulled out two koozies, one teal, the other black. Beth recognized them immediately, as she had one in hot pink at home. They were from the Sleepy Sheep, Mirabelle's most popular watering hole. It was owned by the Shepherds, who just so happened to be more mutual friends of theirs.

Tripp moved to the refrigerator, opened the door, and pulled out two bottles. "How do you feel about Huckleberry Blond Ale?" Tripp asked as he held the bottles up in the air for her to see better.

"Uh, it's legendary."

The beer in question had actually been brewed at the Sleepy Sheep's brewery. Not only was it one of her favorites, but it was seasonal and hadn't been available for a couple of months now. She fully appreciated Tripp's sacrifice of tapping into his reserve supply.

"Good answer." He nodded as he slid the bottles into the koozies.

He grabbed an opener that was magnetized to the refrigerator and the caps were popped off in two quick and easy movements. The crisp sound of the beer's release filled the room and he looped his fingers around the necks with one hand. In his other hand, he snatched up the plate of cookies from the counter.

With a few easy strides he was standing next to her, holding up the two beer bottles. She grabbed the one with the teal koozie.

"Thank you."

"No problem." He stepped past her and headed for the French doors, pushing down the lever handle with the side of the hand holding the beer. The door opened when he bumped his shoulder into it, and he stretched his arm out wide, holding the door for her. The hunter green fabric of his shirt pulled even tighter across his shoulders and chest. "After you."

When she walked by him she couldn't help but glance up at his face. His gaze was focused on her, and those damn flutters in her belly intensified.

Get a grip, woman. All he did was open a door…and look at you with melty brown eyes…and smell incredible. In-cred-ible.

Oh, no no no. She needed to stop it. This was just a friendly drink with her neighbor. Nothing more.

She pulled her gaze from him and kept walking, stepping out onto the deck. The backs of her leather flip-flops slapped against the wood as she looked around his backyard, taking a deep breath of Tripp-free scented air.

The deck stretched out across the back of the house and had a built-in hot tub sitting off to the left. Stairs led down to a stone path that ran around the entirety of a pool that boasted crystal clear water. Beyond that was lush green grass that went all the way to the low wooden gate that butted against the lake. The water was currently a rainbow of colors from the setting sun.

It was the same stunning view she got from her backyard. Well, minus the hot tub and pool...and the massive dog that was doing laps around the space. Duke's long, fluffy tail whipped back and forth as he snapped playfully at the air. He was chasing a butterfly.

Tripp moved across the deck behind Beth, the thuds of his bare feet echoing in the air and vibrating the planks beneath her shoes. She turned to look over her shoulder as he walked toward the hot tub. The cover had been pulled back and steam rose into the air as the jets bubbled up in the water.

"I turned it on before you got here."

"Oh, if you were going to get in, I..." And just like that she lost her train of thought as she imagined Tripp in the hot tub...bare chested...and wet.

Shit. Focus, woman.

"I didn't mean to change up your plans or anything," she somehow managed to say.

His eyes narrowed on her and he shook his head, that smile still playing on his lips. "Beth, I invited you in for a beer. *I* changed up my plans. Come on, you can dip your feet in, watch the sunset, and drink a beer. It will *relax* you."

His emphasis on the word "relax" implied she didn't know what it meant. At this point he probably thought she was uptight or crazy...or both.

The plate of cookies and bottle of beer—which was a beyond-odd flavor combination, but to each their own—were deposited on a low table before Tripp dropped down and took a seat on the edge of the tub. He swiveled his body before sticking his feet into the water. It came all the way up his strong muscular calves, dusted with brown hair, and to his knees.

Really, the thought of soaking her aching feet sounded like pure heaven.

Beth crossed over to Tripp, setting her bottle next to his as she slipped off her flip-flops and lowered herself on the other side of the table. As the weather was beyond pleasant—it was currently in the low seventies—she'd opted for shorts as well, so it was a simple enough move to slide her feet into the rolling water.

The sigh of contentment that escaped her mouth could not be stopped. She closed her eyes and took a moment to appreciate the way the water flowed between her toes and across her arches. She wiggled and moved her feet, the heat working its magic in no time at all.

"I think I need to get one of these." She opened her eyes as she lifted her legs up, her hot pink toes peeking just above the surface before she submerged them again.

"Nice, huh?"

"It's wonderful."

"Bring your suit next time and you can get all the way in."

Beth's head immediately snapped over to look at Tripp. And just like that, her mouth was dry again. She wasn't sure if the offer was one of being friends or…something else.

"To burying the hatchet," Tripp said as he grabbed his beer and extended the neck out to her.

Okay…so it was a friends thing…or a good neighbors thing. That worked…yeah…totally worked.

Beth grabbed her own bottle, staring into his eyes as she clinked the exposed glass against his. "To burying the hatchet," she repeated.

The need to pull her gaze from this man was *real.* So she looked out at the yard, bringing the bottle to her mouth and tipping her head back. The cold beer washed over her tongue, loosening it just a little bit.

Duke was now making his way to the deck, clearing the stairs with ease before he ambled over to them. He nudged Tripp's shoulder, who immediately turned and scratched the dog's chest.

"You thoroughly exhaust yourself?" he asked Duke.

Duke's answer was to unceremoniously plop down on the deck between Beth and Tripp.

"Best part of the day," Tripp said as he looked back out to the lake, now scratching Duke's back. The dog's tongue lolled out and he closed his eyes in ecstasy. "This view is my favorite part of the house, actually."

"Mine too. I love it out here. It was always my favorite part of Colleen and Kevin's house…" She trailed off for just a moment, shaking her head at the words. "Though, I guess it's my house now." A fact she still hadn't quite accepted.

That oh-so-familiar ache blossomed in her chest…an ache that was unavoidable whenever she thought about Colleen…an ache that she knew would never fully go away.

"Do you like being back here? Back in Mirabelle?"

"Yes and no," she shrugged. "It's home, always will be. But there's no anonymity here. Everyone knows everything about you pretty much all the time."

"There wasn't any anonymity where I grew up, either."

"Where was that?" she asked as she took another sip of her beer.

"Kingsland, Georgia. Residents are more than three times Mirabelle's five thousand, and I'd say over half all knew who I was. A lot of that had to do with my father, though: Judge Dominic Brandon Black II."

"Are you the third? Is that where Tripp comes from?"

"Yes, and I couldn't ask for a better man to get my name from," Tripp said with no small amount of pride.

"So your leaving didn't have to do with being in his shadow?"

"Not at all. Hell, I even went to his Alma Mater. Spent four years playing baseball for the University of Georgia just like he did."

"And after that?"

"This is where I deviated from my dad. His passion was in law, but mine wasn't. I enlisted and spent six years in the Air Force."

Beth did the math in her head. Tripp was thirty-five now, which meant…"You joined after September Eleventh."

He nodded slowly, his eyes not leaving hers. "I did. I'd always wanted to be a firefighter, so I figured I might as well do it serving my country for a few years."

Holy crap. She knew this man didn't run away from danger, and instead went straight into it. He was a firefighter, after all. But this…this was different. This was something else entirely.

"Did you have to go over there?"

"I was part of Operation Iraqi Freedom. I was on the bases with the planes mostly, so I wasn't in the actual fight. But I spent about two years over there before they brought me back."

Two years?

"And what did you do then?" she asked before she could stop

herself. She was absolutely more than interested to learn all about him.

They *were* friends now, after all.

"They sent me to Shaw in Sumter, South Carolina. After that I got transferred to Tyndall in Panama City where I finished out my service. When I got out, I spent a couple of years as a civilian firefighter over there. Turned out I missed small town life. I didn't really want to move back home, though." He shook his head. "I liked making a name for myself on my own."

"So you got the Fire Chief position here."

"Yup. And it was pretty perfect, actually. Home has always been near the water for me, which was never made clearer than when I was in the desert."

"A fireman who loves water." She couldn't help but smile. "Makes sense."

"It does, doesn't it?" He grinned back at her. "What about you? Has it only been Mirabelle and Tallahassee?"

"I stayed there after school, found a job that I loved, and started to build my life there."

"Do you miss it?"

"I think I'd miss it more had the circumstances of me leaving been different. My ex had a lot to do with that." She grimaced, an unavoidable reaction whenever she thought about Mick.

"I remember meeting him at Bennett and Mel's wedding. I take it the two of you didn't really end on good terms."

"Couldn't get away fast enough," Beth said right before she tipped back her beer and took a good mouthful. Unavoidable reaction number two: drinking more.

She turned back to look out at the view of the lake, the bright bursts of color reflecting off the water. Even the stunning beauty of it couldn't erase the memories that played out clear as day in her mind.

Two years. That's how long Beth had been with Mick Waters...*Dr.* Mick Waters...general surgeon and genuine asshole.

Though the "asshole" part hadn't been discovered until the very end of their relationship.

A nurse falling for a doctor...it wasn't a new or original story in the slightest. They'd met at the hospital. He was eight years older than her, well respected and liked by everyone, and charming as all get out.

She'd said no the first half a dozen times he'd asked her out. She wasn't interested in being another cliché. It didn't matter how attractive he was with his blond hair and baby blue eyes. Or that he looked like Brad Pitt circa *Meet Joe Black*.

But after the longest graveyard shift of her life—where about a dozen babies had been born—he'd asked her to breakfast. The draw of caffeine and a warm meal had been too much to turn down, so she'd said yes.

Four months later she moved in with him. They'd both jumped into the relationship and never looked back...or so Beth had thought.

It still baffled her mind that she could love someone so fully and not know him, because in the end she hadn't known him at all—a fact that had shocked the hell out of her because they'd never seemed to have a problem communicating. They'd talked about everything; absolutely nothing had been off the table. They discussed the future, staying in Tallahassee, getting married, buying a bigger house to raise a family...*their* family...*their* kids.

But there'd been some things he hadn't been up for.

He didn't want them.

"He didn't want who?"

"What?" Beth repeated as she turned to look at Tripp. He was frowning, his dark brown eyebrows coming down low over his eyes.

"You said *he didn't want them.*"

Shit. She'd spoken out loud and hadn't even realized it. And it wasn't the only thing she hadn't realized. Somewhere between her thinking and accidental talking, she'd started petting Duke.

The dog had moved closer to her, putting his head in her lap. She was now scratching him between his fluffy ears.

Well, this was interesting. She'd screamed and ranted and raved at this dog more times than she could count. But he wasn't even remotely intimidated by her. Yeah, she knew it; her bark was much bigger than her bite. Duke had read her like a freaking book; she was a total softie.

"Beth?" Tripp pressed. "He didn't want who?" he asked again.

She pulled her eyes from the dog who was scooting closer to her and looked up at Tripp again. "I didn't mean to say that out loud."

Besides Mel, Beth hadn't told anyone what had *really* ended her and Mick's relationship. People had probably guessed it, but no one had asked her outright. Yet here she was, telling Tripp.

"Apparently I can't control my mouth when I'm around you. Whether it's yelling, or crying, or telling you personal things that I don't usually talk about." Before she could stop herself she just went for it. "Mick didn't want Nora, Grant, and Penny. Didn't want to raise kids that weren't *his.*"

An admission that had almost destroyed her. Because really,

how was a person supposed to react when the man they loved…the man they planned on marrying…the man they planned on spending the rest of their life with…how were they supposed to react when that man walked away without a second thought?

"Wow," Tripp's frown deepened. "He sounds like a real class act."

"He was an asshole." A bitter laugh escaped Beth's mouth. "He waited a whole week after Colleen and Kevin died—two days after the funeral—to tell me how he felt. It was either him or them. I didn't need to even think about it. There wasn't a choice."

Tripp looked at her for a moment…*really* looked at her, his eyes holding hers so intensely that she was maybe just a little bit breathless from them.

"You know"—he slowly shook his head—"if there's one thing I've learned in life, there's always a choice. A choice to be selfish or to be generous. A choice to take the easy road or the hard road. A choice to quit or to keeping going. A choice to turn away or to walk into the fire."

"Well, your whole adult life has been about walking straight into the fire. God, Tripp, you enlisted after 9/11. You're a firefighter. You save people's lives."

"Last I checked, so do you. Aren't you saving babies these days?"

"I'm an obstetrics nurse. I work with moms and their unborn babies. But I don't put my life at risk every day that I do my job."

"Maybe not. But it doesn't change what you do, does it?" he asked. "I've seen it more times than I can count. When I was growing up, when I was in college, when I was in the military, even now. There are people in this world who don't choose to do good. People who turn their backs on someone in need. People who walk away, sometimes from their own flesh and blood, and don't even think twice about it." He turned his body more fully to face her.

"Beth, there's *always* a choice. And you know what? I think you're pretty damn remarkable for what you're doing for those kids. The other day you said you felt like you were failing. But you aren't. Because when you were given a choice to turn away or walk into the fire, you chose the fire. It's never easy."

"Thank you," she said on a whisper, surprised she'd been able to get those two words past the constriction in her throat. Words...words failed her. How did someone respond to something like that? He'd just called her remarkable.

Duke shifted closer to her, moving so he could push his side up against her thigh. She ran her fingers through the thick, soft fur on his back. She found it comforting, just like she was beginning to find his owner.

"Any time." Another smile turned up Tripp's mouth as he clinked the neck of his beer against hers. He tipped the bottle back and she followed suit, the cold liquid washing down her throat and helping with the tightness.

"Besides, you've got a couple things going for you," he said as he lowered the bottle, pointing to the plate on the stand. "Your chocolate chip cookies are pretty much the best I've ever had."

She raised her eyebrows high. "Pretty much?" she asked, no problem finding her voice now.

That recipe had been honed to perfection by her grandmother and mother. They were without a doubt *the best* chocolate chip cookies ever.

"Hmmm, maybe I need another taste." He set his beer down before he pulled the Saran-wrap back and grabbed a cookie. When he took a bite—that comprised half of the cookie—his eyes didn't leave hers as he chewed thoughtfully. He swallowed before he popped the other half in his mouth, repeating the process.

Yup, watching this man eat a cookie should be illegal. How in the hell could something like that be so damn sexy?

"Okay." He nodded as he grabbed the plate and held it out for her. "I take back the *pretty sure*."

"Damn straight you do," Beth said as she set her bottle down and snatched up a cookie with the hand that wasn't buried in Duke's fur.

"Pretty interesting flavor combination, cookies and beer." She raised her eyebrows before she took a bite of the cookie.

"Well, when it comes to me, I'll pretty much pair sweets with anything."

She laughed as she turned back to look out at the sunset, unable to stop herself from marveling at the moment. She was enjoying a drink and conversation—*good* conversation nonetheless—with her horrible neighbor Tripp Black.

The thing was, he wasn't remotely horrible. Not even in the slightest.

Chapter Six

Pick-Me-Up Pie

Mirabelle, Florida, was about six hundred square miles. About three hundred miles of that was water, two hundred and forty was the Bartlett Forest, and the remaining sixty(ish) made up everything else…seventy-five percent of which was farms and pastures.

For the most part everyone lived just a few miles away from the main part of town. The people who didn't live on farms were about a fifteen-minute drive away from the firehouse. Well, they were fifteen minutes away going the speed limit. Sirens blaring and cars moving out of the way? It was more like nine.

The department was a combination career and volunteer house. There were ten guys working on salary: Tripp, the assistant chief, two captains, and six firefighters. As for volunteers, there were twenty-five of them scattered around Mirabelle.

Tripp hadn't worked in a combination house before he'd gotten this job, which had made him slightly worried. Sometimes there could be a little conflict between the career guys and the volunteers, but it wasn't a problem at this house. The community factor in Mirabelle was off the charts.

At any given time there could be as many as twenty people hanging out at the house…not even counting the guys on duty. Active volunteers, retired volunteers, and guys who just lived in Mirabelle. A lot would come over for a card game or a little food, or *a lot* of food, as it was never in short supply.

Whether it be a casserole from any of the church ladies, four dozen eggs and a bag of vegetables from a local farmer, or pounds and pounds of seafood from the wharf, there was always something to eat. It was a good thing, too, as a number of the older bachelors or widowers would stop in for a little conversation and a hot meal. The homeless population wasn't all that high, but there were a couple of Mirabelle residents who could use some help with a meal or two, and they knew exactly where to come.

Another problem they didn't have here was volunteers leaving their day jobs when more manpower was needed. With so many locally owned businesses there was never really an issue when there was an emergency.

Tripp took a lot of pride in the men who worked for him, and the house that his men worked out of. Mirabelle had become home for a multitude of reasons beyond his job, especially now that he had a group of really good friends, a dog, a house…

Are you ever going to settle down? The conversation from that morning's phone call with his mother echoed in his head. *Your father and I aren't getting any younger and we want grandchildren.*

His mother had called him to confirm the dates of his father's sixtieth birthday party, coming up in May. She'd wanted to make sure Tripp had gotten off for the date. Once she'd confirmed that, she'd asked if there was any possibility he'd be bringing a date.

She hadn't been pleased at all when he'd told her no.

Tripp loved his mother dearly. Alexis Black was the absolute best person he knew. The woman would walk into fire for those that she loved. She also wasn't one to let things go, and this grandbaby thing wasn't going anywhere, especially as Tripp was their only child.

The "settling down" conversation was one that Tripp had been having with his mother for the last ten years now. It had started right after his best friend Landon had gotten married. Over the last four years she'd upped the ante and mentioned it at least monthly, if not more. That had begun right after he and his girlfriend Autumn had broken up. Autumn just so happened to be his last serious relationship.

He'd often joked that it was the bachelor life for him, and really what was wrong with that? He hadn't found the woman that made him think about changing his life.

It wasn't that he'd written marriage off, because he hadn't. He'd be a liar if he said that he hadn't thought about a family of his own living in the house he'd just bought…or that he hadn't had the image of people gathered around that dining room table of his…a wife and kids.

The thing was, he had too many examples of good marriages around him. And he was by no means delusional that his family's or friends' marriages were perfect…but they were something special.

And he wanted something special.

Besides, he *was* settled down…it just wasn't with a family like his mother and father wanted...or like ninety percent of his friends had done.

And sometimes there was some merit in staying single, the prime example being the man who was currently in the driver's seat of the department's pick-up truck: Beaumont Giovanni Culpepper, the assistant fire chief.

Beau was a Mirabellian by birth, but he'd only just moved back the year before. He was forty-five and raising his eleven-year-old son Ethan on his own. He and his wife had divorced three years ago when she'd left him for a Baptist pastor.

A Baptist pastor who'd *also* been married.

If that wasn't an advertisement for singledom, Tripp didn't know what was, though maybe his current negative outlook had a little bit to do with the pounding headache he was sporting. He'd had another week of incredibly long days and very little sleep. The most recent calls hadn't been weather related or acts of God, either, so much as acts of stupidity.

Terrance Spurlock had had the half-brained idea that he was going to drink half a bottle of Jim Beam and climb onto the roof of the tallest of the six lighthouses in Mirabelle. It was only after he'd made it to the top that he remembered he was terrified of heights. It had taken five guys to get him off the roof, at three o'clock in the morning.

There'd been a couple of illegal beach fires, something that was only going to become more and more frequent as Spring Breaks were starting and people were vacationing in Mirabelle.

But a beach fire wasn't the reason he'd been pulled from bed at two o'clock in the morning the night before. Nope. That had been because of the Wigginses. Shelby had gotten sick and tired of her husband Herald and his constant infidelity. She'd set his belongings on fire on the front lawn...which had included his truck and a propane tank that had been sitting in the back. Yeah, more than Shelby's temper had exploded.

The two of them made another *incredibly* strong case for marriage.

The only thing Tripp had going for him was that when the day had been done he had a blessed three days off.

As the two head officers, Tripp and Beau worked on a rotating schedule: five days on, three days off. They always overlapped a day at the beginning and end. If there wasn't too much going on at the house on those days, they went around town to make sure businesses and such were up to fire code.

Those inspections were reason number fifty-two that Tripp's head was killing him.

There were some days where this particular task was a breeze. In and out of the establishments that were on their list with no problems. Today had not been that day. Out of the six businesses they'd inspected there'd been about fifteen violations, ranging from expired extinguishers, faulty alarm systems, and a broken emergency exit door. Which had meant disgruntled owners, paperwork, and the promise of another visit in thirty days.

His headache had only magnified as the day had gone on, a new jab of pain blossoming behind his temples as they'd left the last place. They had three more stops before they were done: LauraAnne's Liquors, the Gas-N-Go, and Farmer's Drugs.

"You want a coffee or something?" Beau asked.

Tripp looked at the clock on the radio. It was half past one, so he probably had about four more hours until he was done for the day. "Yeah, maybe that will help."

"Something is better than nothing. You've been a regular old ray of sunshine all day."

"Is that sarcasm I'm sensing from you, Romeo?"

The nickname—which Beau actually preferred to being called Beaumont—was because ever since he'd moved back, pretty much all of the single ladies in Mirabelle liked to hit on him. But the guy never acted on it. He hadn't dated since his divorce, and Tripp was pretty sure that wasn't going to change.

"Sure as hell is, Chief." Beau nodded as he made a left onto Whiskey River Lane.

"Remind me to write you up when we get back to the station for an inability at being funny," Tripp said as he looked down at his clipboard and finished with his notes on the inspection they'd just finished.

"I'll be sure to get right on that."

The best coffee in all of Mirabelle was hands down from Café Lula, but as the café was all the way down on the beach, they were going to have to go to the second best place.

When they pulled into the parking lot of the Stardust Diner, there were still a number of cars scattered around the parking lot. It didn't matter what time of day it was; someone was in the place and most likely enjoying a plate of pancakes and the crispiest bacon on the Gulf Coast.

But Tripp's favorite part was the pie—strawberry rhubarb, to be exact. Since he was there, he might as well get a piece to go with his coffee. The sugar *and* caffeine could do double team on his headache and foul mood.

As they headed inside, Beau's phone started to ring and he pulled it from his pocket and looked down. "I'll be right in. Get me a coffee, too."

"Sure thing." Tripp nodded before making his way to the building. The blast of cold from the air conditioner hit him in the face when he opened the door. Mabel Seamore was working the register and she was just finishing up with another customer when Tripp walked up.

"Hey sugar." She smiled. "What can I get you?"

"Two of your largest to-go cups filled with coffee doctored only that way you can, a slice of strawberry rhubarb pie, and a bag of Homer's Homemade Kettle chips."

Where Tripp had a sweet tooth, Beau was a fan of all things salty.

"I can get you the coffee and the chips, but we're all out of strawberry rhubarb."

Well, wasn't that just *great*.

"I'm afraid we just served the last slice." Mabel nodded behind him and Tripp turned to look at the booths lined up against the wall.

Beth was sitting on one side, her head bent over a book as she brought a fork full of *his* pie to her mouth. She was wearing bright red scrubs, her hair braided and hanging over her shoulder, showing off her slender neck.

Well, well, well, what do we have here?

"You want another flavor?" Mabel asked, forcing Tripp to pull his gaze from Beth.

"No thanks," he said as he pulled out a ten. Mabel went to make change but Tripp shook his head. "Keep it."

"Thanks, sugar. You wait five minutes and you can get some coffee from a fresh pot."

"Will do," he nodded.

Mabel smiled before she went off to help a customer who was sitting at the opposite end of the counter, and she wasn't the only one moving. It was an automatic reaction that Tripp turned around and walked across the diner to Beth.

He was like a moth to a flame.

"Just when I thought we could be friends."

Beth pulled her gaze from the book in her hands and looked up. "Tripp."

"You took my pie."

"What?" she asked on a confused laugh as she flipped the book onto the table to hold its place.

"My pie." He nodded to the plate as he slid into the seat across from her.

"Did you write your name on it?" She lifted the plate and looked underneath it. "No, no I don't see your name." Her eyes returned to him and a grin spread across her face as she lowered the plate back to the table.

And just like that the pain in Tripp's head disappeared, wiped away by Beth Boone's smile.

"It's a constant dibs on the last piece of *that* particular pie," he pointed at it. "It's always mine."

"I wasn't aware of this rule." She shook her head, scooping up another bite as she brought the fork to her mouth and wrapped her lips around it.

That little act had to be one of the sexiest things he'd ever seen in his life.

Now Tripp had always been a sucker for sweets...whether they were baked goods or beautiful women. When he'd opened his door last week to find this particular woman standing on the doorstep, he hadn't been sure which had been more tempting: her or the cookies.

Turned out, Beth *smelled* like a fucking cookie, too. The whole time she'd been over enjoying a beer with him, he'd had the strangest urge to lean down and press his nose to her neck. Or maybe it wasn't so strange at all.

It stood to reason that if the woman smelled like cookies she might taste like cookies…and that was all Tripp had been able to think about: what Beth Boone tasted like. And it was a thought that had plagued him since. And now? Well, now he was pretty sure she would taste like pie. His favorite pie.

Yeah, there was no hope for him. None.

It was a problem, to be sure. A *massive* one. He wasn't allowed to like her as anything other than a friend…or want her, either. She was off limits per his rules.

Rules…

Weren't they just talking about rules?

"You've been gone from Mirabelle too long, Beth. You're going to need to relearn all those rules." He was going to need to relearn a few rules himself…like which women were off limits.

"Apparently. There a book?"

"I'll put one together."

"How nice of you. Also, you do know that there are about a dozen other pies to choose from over there?" She pointed to the display case with her fork.

"I'm aware. But none of them are the pie I wanted. I needed a pick-me-up and you stole the last slice of it."

"You have *pick-me-up* pie?"

He sure did. And it turned out he was still getting that pick-me-up. It was just in the form of her as opposed to pie. Hell, she was almost like a dessert anyway. A *waaaay* better one.

"And that's strange to you?" he asked. "Don't you make *thank you* cookies?"

"Fair point," she said as she took another bite, and just like that he was distracted by her mouth again and the way it wrapped around the fork.

Well, she was just taunting him now…and flirting with him, too. That was new and he liked it. Liked it a lot.

Yeah, he had a thing for his neighbor…had had a thing for her since she'd shown up on his doorstep covered in mud and started screaming at him about Duke. He wasn't sure what it was about that moment that was sticking out to him now. Maybe those hot pink shorts and the outline of her breasts underneath her shirt.

But was that what it had taken for him to really notice her? No, it hadn't been.

Hell, he'd probably had a thing for her even before then…he just was too blind to see it.

He normally wasn't a man who needed to be hit over the head repeatedly…except, apparently, in the case of Beth Boone.

Fuck his stupid set of rules.

* * *

Oh Lord, Tripp Black looked good. How was it that this man was downright edible in his navy blue uniform pants and gray T-shirt? While he was sitting there looking like most women's fireman fantasy come to life, she was wearing scrubs that weren't exciting or lust-inducing in the slightest.

A little over a week ago he'd agitated her in every possible way. She wouldn't have cared what the hell she looked like when bumping into him randomly.

This was not the case today.

"Speaking of your *thank you* cookies," he leaned forward, resting his elbows on the table. "I'll have you know that there aren't even crumbs left."

"You ate all two dozen of them?" she asked, trying to recall if she'd even washed her hair that morning…or put on mascara?

She couldn't remember, especially not at the moment. His eyes were focused so intently on hers, holding her gaze as something that she swore was desire flashed through them. It was hot and…and it made her a little sweaty.

Granted, she'd been making a production of eating her pie—pie that he thought was *his* pie—but that had all been about messing with him. And she was pretty sure that he no longer cared about the pie in the slightest. She was also pretty sure she was about three-point-five seconds from spontaneously combusting.

"Beth, I think you underestimate my love of baked goods. Or what I'm willing to do for them."

And before she knew it, the fork was lifted out of her hand, and the plate was gone from in front of her. He leaned back in the seat, grinning as he put a forkful of pie into his mouth.

"You did *not* just steal that."

A few seconds passed as he chewed and swallowed. "Oh but I did. Sweets are my weakness. Couldn't stop myself," he said before he took another bite.

"I wouldn't think a man like you would have a lot of weaknesses."

"I don't." He shook his head. "It's a very short list." And with that he took the last bite of pie.

It was right there on the tip of her tongue to ask what that list consisted of when Mabel walked up to the booth, two cups of coffee and a bag of chips in hand. "You're good to go, Chief."

"Thanks, Mabel." He grinned up at her, drumming his fingers against the table.

"Looks like you got your pie anyway." Mabel grabbed the empty plate in front of Tripp.

"Beth shared with me."

"Well, aren't you sweet?" Mabel said to Beth.

Tripp turned to look at Beth, too. "Just the sweetest."

"Let me know if you need anything else, Chief," Mabel tapped the table with her free hand before she walked off.

"I shared with you?" Beth asked, her eyebrows climbing up her forehead. "Is that what we're calling your *stealing* now?"

"I thought we clarified that you stole first."

"I don't think we clarified anything."

"Huh. I guess we didn't." He shrugged. "I should go, though. I'm on the clock, and we can't all play hooky from work."

"Hey! I'm on my lunch break." She forced a frown onto her face.

Righteous indignation, that's the look she needed to be sporting right now—*not* insane attraction to the man in front of her.

Good luck.

"Well, you enjoy the rest of it, Beth," he said as he slid out of the seat across from her. He stood, grabbing the two coffees from the table before he winked at her.

Winked.

She couldn't pull her eyes from him as he walked away, watching as he said a quick word to Mabel at the register before he was out the door. As he made his way to the parking lot, her gaze moved down to that very fine ass of his. She didn't even try to stop herself from looking. Why would she? There was something to be said about the way he filled out every inch of those uniform pants…or *any* pair of pants, really.

Though he probably looked pretty damn good in no pants.

Probably? No, without a doubt he would look good in no pants.

Get it together, woman!

"I would've shared my pie with him, too, you know."

Mabel was back at the table and Beth looked up at her. "Oh, we're just friends." She shook her head. Denial was the best policy, after all.

"Keep telling yourself that, dear. I *almost* believed it."

Okay, maybe it wasn't the best policy. But continuing this conversation with Mabel wasn't an option, either. "Can I have the check?"

"Chief Black already paid for you."

He did what? "Tripp paid?"

The woman's knowing smile overtook her face. "Pie and everything. You want that sweet tea to go?"

"Sure," she said, unsure of how else to respond.

Beth turned to look through the window, her eyes landing on Tripp and Beau Culpepper. They were both walking to the fire department's pickup truck, their cups of coffee in hand. When Tripp got to the passenger door he paused for just a second and turned to look over his shoulder. He spotted her looking at him and his mouth turned up on one side.

And then? Well, and then he *fucking* winked at her again.

Yup, it was official. Beth Boone totally, one hundred and one percent, had a thing for Tripp Black.

Shiiiit.

Chapter Seven

Apology Pie

Attempting to not think about Tripp was a bit of a struggle for the rest of the afternoon...or if Beth was being totally honest with herself, a *massive* struggle. It didn't help in the slightest that the doctor's office was ridiculously slow, so there was pretty much nothing to distract her from picturing his smile...from hearing his deep voice...the way he'd looked at her as he'd told her sweets were his weakness...how he'd looked at her as if she *were* a sweet.

She'd read that correctly. Hadn't she?

And to add fuel to the flames—*her* flames—he smelled better than any other man. How was that even possible? Well, that was a question she was pretty sure she'd never really work out the answer to...in fact there were a whole list of questions.

Like, how was it that she'd found his pie stealing sexy? He'd purposely tried to antagonize her and a move like that shouldn't have been so damn attractive...yet it was. Apparently she was reverting back to kindergarten and liking the boy on the playground who pulled her hair.

Though if Beth were being honest with herself she did like her hair pulled a little; it just wasn't on the playground...

When four o'clock rolled around, and Beth was given the opportunity to go home early, she got out of the office like her ass was on fire. The second she was in the car the radio was turned up and the windows rolled down. What she'd needed more than anything were those few minutes with the music too loud to think and fresh air blowing in her face.

Maybe that would clear the glorious scent of Tripp out of her head...yeah, not possible. It was imprinted on her brain. *Permanently*.

When she pulled into the driveway she looked over toward Tripp's house. Holy crap, what in the world was she going to do about this whole situation? Well, as the driveway was empty and he was most likely still at work, she didn't need to worry about it at the moment. She'd have some time before she saw him again...time to figure this out.

Now Beth wasn't a "bury her head in the sand" type of girl. But this thing—that she wasn't sure if she was making into a *thing* all on her own—with Tripp was a whole different ball game. She hadn't worked any of it out yet...and she *really* needed to discuss it with someone.

As she got out of the SUV and headed for the house, she was beyond thankful that she was going to have an opportunity that very evening. A few of her friends were coming over and they'd be more than willing to talk. And as it was a Friday night—and no one had to go to work the following morning—there would be plenty of wine involved.

Yeah, that would be good. They could give her plenty of perspective on the situation, especially as every single one of them was married. They'd all gotten a man and kept the man.

Not that Beth wanted to get or keep Tripp.

No, no, no...that was a ridiculous thought...a thought that rolled around in her brain as she opened the front door and stepped inside the house...the very, *very* quiet house.

Well, that couldn't be right. Nora always had the TV on, or music blasting, or was chattering on the phone...or a combination of the three.

Beth dropped her purse on the center island in the kitchen and headed toward the empty living room. Out of the corner of her eye she saw something white move in the backyard and she turned to get a better look.

The sight that greeted her made her groan.

She'd found her niece and nephew, all right. Nora was laying in the hammock with a book in her hands and headphones stuck in her ears while Grant was laying out on the lawn...or more accurately, he was laying on Duke. The dog was stretched out, his big tail wagging back and forth in the air.

Grant was reading, too, a book balanced on his knees, and his lips moved as he presumably read aloud to Duke. The icing on the cake of the whole scene? In between page turns, Grant was dipping a spoon into a jar of peanut butter. One scoop for him...the other scoop for Duke, whose long pink tongue darted out to lick the spoon clean before it was dunked back into the container.

It was the exact same jar of peanut butter that Beth used on her bananas every morning.

She headed for the back door and the puzzle pieces started to come together. With each step that she took another one fell into place, until the whole picture was clearly laid out.

All of it…every single issue…every little hiccup…every little annoyance and aggravation…every single problem that had happened since Tripp had moved in, had been caused by her kids: Nora sneaking into his backyard to use his hot tub, the flat tires from Penny's toys, Grant with the peanut butter…and now this. The dog had been the only card she'd had…and yes, she and her neighbor were on perfectly okay terms now—they were apparently flirting with each other over pie—but…but she'd been *awful* to him before that…and he hadn't done anything wrong. Nor, would it appear, had the dog.

Now Beth wasn't above admitting when she was wrong…but this was *sooo* beyond that. This was a whole other level of wrong that she'd never experienced, and she was going to have to tell Tripp.

Well, so much for a truce.

She had to conjure up more than a little restraint as she reached for the door handle. Every part of her wanted to wrench it open and start screaming. Somehow she pulled herself together.

The second Beth stepped outside Nora sat up abruptly, causing the hammock to sway. "You're not supposed to be home for another hour."

"You're supposed to be watching your brother," Beth waved beyond the screened-in porch, glancing over at Grant and Duke.

Grant was sitting up now, his little face filled with horror as he looked at Beth. Duke stretched his large body, moving his head forward so he could give Grant's cheek a sloppy lick.

"I *am* watching him." Nora's indignant voice pulled Beth's gaze back to her niece, now out of the hammock and standing.

"This is watching him?" Beth asked, miraculously keeping her voice level. "Nora, he stole Tripp's dog."

"Tripp isn't even home. What's the harm in it?"

And there went the miracle of the level quality of Beth's voice. "What's the harm in it?! It's. Not. Our. Dog. That's the harm. What if something happened?"

"I'm right here! He's not even twenty feet away from me!"

"A lot of good that's doing! Is it really that difficult to take care of your brother? It's three hours, five days a week. You're seventeen, Nora. I don't think this is a lot to ask of you!"

"What the hell do you know?!" Nora shouted so loudly that Duke started barking.

"Excuse me?"

"You have no idea what I deal with everyday. No idea what you ask of me. I get that your part of the dead mothers club—"

Beth couldn't stop herself from flinching at those words. How could she not when Nora pretty much flung them at her?

"—but don't even act like you know what it's like to lose both of your parents. Don't even act like you know what it's like to have a younger brother and sister that you have no freaking clue how to help because you're going through the same shit. Grant had another bad day at school. Came home crying because some little asshole in his class was calling him an orphan—"

Beth flinched again at *orphan*.

"He wanted to play with the dog. Of course I said yes, and I don't care if you have a problem with it. Or if it causes issues with *the neighbor*. You can deal with it. You can also be the one to tell him no." Nora pointed out to the yard. "Because it isn't going to be me."

And with that Nora walked into the house, making sure to slam the door behind her.

Beth closed her eyes and rubbed at her temples. Well, that had just been absolutely perfect.

A soft sniffle filled the air behind her. She turned and opened her eyes. Grant was standing on the other side of the screened-in door, looking at her with tears streaming down his cheeks. Duke was at Grant's side, whining as he pressed his massive body up against the little boy.

"Am I in trouble?" Grant asked with a slight quaver to his voice.

Beth pushed open the screen door and crossed the few feet to her nephew. She knelt down in front of him, reaching up and running her fingers under his eyes.

"You aren't in trouble, Goose. But we need to talk about this. It's not okay to take Mr. Tripp's dog out of his yard," she said, looking over at Duke.

The dog moved forward, whining again as he gently butted his head against Beth's chest. Without thinking about it, she reached up and scratched his furry neck. His tongue lolled out and his warm peanut butter breath hit Beth in the face.

Lovely.

She looked back to her nephew, who was running his hand along Duke's back. "But I only ever do it when Mr. Tripp isn't home…or in the mornings when I'm pretty sure he's sleeping. I'm just *borrowing* Duke."

"Grant, we've talked about this before. You can't borrow someone else's things without their knowledge. It's not okay even if you do bring him back."

Something Grant had failed to do, as Duke had been left in their backyard on numerous occasions.

"So I…" He sniffled hard as more tears escaped. His eyes somehow looked even greener when he was crying. "So I can't play with him anymore?"

"Buddy, that isn't a decision for me to make. I'll talk to Mr. Tripp, but if he says no—" which he would be totally justified to do under normal circumstances…and even more justified to do now that all of the facts were out…Grant stealing his dog and all, "—then the answer is no. And you're going to have to listen to that."

Now his little lip was trembling. "B-b-but he's my best friend."

"Oh Grant, come here." Beth pulled the now sobbing boy into her arms as he lost it. He was breaking her heart. How in the world was she supposed to deal with this?

She looked over Grant's shoulder at Duke. The dog was now nudging his head under Grant's arm in an attempt to get closer. Apparently the attachment wasn't one-sided.

This was going to be *beyond* complicated.

* * *

Normally Tripp was home sometime between five and six, but that night he didn't pull into his driveway until just before seven. Because of that day's mountain of paperwork, he'd finished up at the department a little later than usual. He hated the paperwork part of the job.

Hated it.

At least he'd already had dinner, a massive bowl of shrimp étouffée over steaming rice. He'd eaten while finishing up, and his full stomach had done a pretty good job at making the task way more tolerable. But good food wasn't the main reason he'd been able to push through. Nope, that belonged to Beth.

Five minutes with her at that diner and he was good to go for the rest of the day. He couldn't stop himself from smiling every damn time he thought about her shocked expression when he'd taken that plate right out of her hands. He also couldn't stop himself from thinking about how her mouth had wrapped around that fork as she'd eaten the pie.

She was sexy as hell, even when she was taunting him… probably sexier *because* she was taunting him.

And look at that, he was smiling again.

As he walked up the path to the front door his gaze traveled next door. She'd been a complication ever since he'd moved into his house. And now? Well, she was a complication of an entirely different sort.

What sort? He wasn't sure yet, but he'd bet good money he was going to find out. It was just a matter of time before his "rules" were broken. Something he was oddly fine with.

Or maybe it wasn't that odd at all.

He turned back to the front door, fitting the key in the lock and flipping the bolt. The second he walked into his house Duke was there, fluffy tail wagging and paws clipping against the hardwood as he danced around. He barked a few times in greeting before he rubbed his massive body against Tripp's legs.

"Hey buddy," he said as he dropped the keys on the side table and bent down, giving the dog a good body scratch.

Duke sat back on his haunches, closing his eyes as his tongue lolled out of his mouth. When Tripp got to the dog's chest, Duke leaned to the side while his back paw started to beat out a rhythm against the floor.

It was a minute before Tripp stopped and Duke immediately cracked one eye open, giving him a *why you stop* look.

"Dinner?"

Both of Duke's eyes were now wide open and he took off down the hall.

"Yeah, that's what I thought." Tripp stood and followed the dog to the kitchen.

He had about thirty minutes to feed Duke and get changed before he needed to be out the door again. He was heading over to the Sleepy Sheep to watch a hockey game with some of the guys. He felt a little bad about leaving Duke on his own for another couple of hours, but it was lessened because Finn was going to drop off Frankie before they left.

Duke was sitting in front of his empty food bowl, his tail sweeping back and forth across the floor as he waited for his dinner. Tripp opened the pantry and flipped up the plastic top of the massive Tupperware container that sat on the floor. He filled the plastic cup to the top before he tipped it into the bowl.

Duke looked between the bowl and Tripp, waiting for permission. See, the dog *had* learned a few things.

Tripp nodded and Duke turned back to his bowl before lunging at it like he hadn't eaten in weeks. One thing his dog wasn't was underfed; that was for damn sure.

Leaving the dog with his dinner, Tripp headed to his bedroom. He had just enough time to get in a quick shower so he stripped down, throwing his clothes in the hamper. The warm steady spray of the water across his muscles made him groan. There hadn't been any calls that day, so he hadn't done anything too strenuous, but the last couple of weeks had pushed him.

He was probably going to spend a good amount of his time off in his hot tub. He'd be in it right now if he hadn't promised his friends he'd go out for a drink and watch the game.

Five minutes under the glorious heat was too short, but he forced himself to get out and dry off. He threw the towel into the overflowing hamper—making a mental note that he needed to do laundry at some point—before he headed into his room. Crossing over to the dresser, he pulled open the bottom drawer to find only one pair of clean jeans. He *really* needed to do laundry soon.

Duke trotted in, his nails clipping against the hardwood floor as he went over to his doggy bed in the corner and fell down with a muffled flump. He was asleep within a minute.

"Must be hard." Tripp shook his head as he pulled on his pants.

The doorbell echoed through the house, rousing Duke immediately. He was off the bed and running through the room within an instant. Tripp grabbed a clean shirt from his dwindling stack, pulled it over his head, and headed through the house.

He peaked through the peephole, thinking he'd find Finn on the other side, a few minutes earlier than expected. But nope, it was Beth…holding something in her hands. He grabbed Duke's collar before he opened the door and when Beth came into view he saw that she held a pie.

Oddly enough—or maybe not so oddly—the pie was the thing he was least interested in. He was way more intrigued by what she was wearing: a white T-shirt and what was quickly becoming his favorite pair of jeans. How could they not draw his attention when they molded to her body the way they did?

"Long time no see," he said when his eyes landed on hers.

She shifted, taking a deep breath before letting it out slowly. "Do you have a minute?"

She was nervous? Why? She hadn't been earlier at the diner...she'd been flirty. What had happened since then?

"For you? I have many minutes. Even more than that, considering what's in your hands."

"Is that so?"

"Well, I have a feeling this is going to be very interesting." He grinned.

"And why is that?"

"Because every time you show up on my doorstep *something* interesting happens. Come in." He stepped away from the threshold, holding the door wide and keeping Duke restrained by his side.

Beth walked past him, bringing with her that scent of baked goods that drove him out of his fucking mind. Today it was accompanied with something tart...

His dick twitched. He was going to need to take another shower, this one very, *very* cold.

Get it together, man.

He shut the front door before he let go of Duke. The dog trotted off after Beth, clearly more interested in her.

I get it, buddy. I get it.

Tripp followed, stepping into the kitchen as Beth set the pie on the counter. When her hands were free she moved her attention to Duke, who was sniffing around her.

"Hey, Duke." She bent forward toward the dog, her blond hair falling from her shoulders. Her hands were on the dog's head; she scratched his scalp before moving down to his neck and across his back.

Tripp pressed his hip against the counter as he watched them. "Well, that's new. You two make up?"

Beth looked up, still giving her hands-on attention to Duke. "You could say that."

"So what kind of pie did you make me?"

"Cherry."

Cherries. That was what she smelled like. Sweet, tart cherries... and sugar... and vanilla... and goodness.

"And what's the occasion?"

She gave Duke one last scratch before she straightened. "My nephew has been stealing your dog."

Tripp pushed off the counter. "I'm sorry, what was that?"

"You know all of those times Duke was in my backyard wreaking havoc?"

"They're a little hard to forget."

"Well, as it turns out, it was Grant letting Duke back there. Usually when you were asleep or not home."

"You're serious?"

"Yes. So really every single problem that we've had since you moved in has been the fault of my kids. And every time I yelled at you"—she gestured to Tripp—"or complained about Duke"—she gestured to the dog—"or called either of you names"—she shifted on her feet, her gaze not leaving his—"I was totally and completely out of line. And I'm sorry. *Really* sorry. I told Grant he wasn't allowed to take Duke anymore, and that he needs to apologize to you as well."

"So is that what that is?" he asked, gesturing to the pie. "Apology Pie?"

"Yes."

"And Apology Pie is cherry flavored?"

"Yes," she said simply. "It was between that and Humble Pie."

That had him laughing. "Which is?"

"Triple berry. I had raspberries and blueberries but no blackberries."

"I like cherry. How did you figure out it wasn't Duke's fault?" he asked, more than slightly curious at this new turn of events.

"I came home early today. Grant was in the backyard with Duke reading him a book…and feeding him peanut butter."

"So Grant *is* the peanut butter culprit?" Tripp couldn't stop the disgusted grimace from taking over his face. His dislike of the stuff was really that strong.

"He sure is." She frowned. "And he was feeding it to Duke straight from the jar that I use every day. Dipping the spoon in and letting him lick it clean before repeating the process."

"So you've been sharing peanut butter with my dog?" He laughed; he couldn't help it.

"You keep that up"—she pointed at his massive grin—"and I'm taking my Apology Pie back." She made a move to grab it, but Tripp stepped in front of her, blocking her path. They were only inches apart and she had to look up to see his face.

Something shifted in her expression. Her eyes dilated and a flush of color darkened her cheeks. Apparently she wasn't the only one affected by their proximity.

He moved just a little bit closer, his eyes holding hers. "You can't take back pie, Beth. That's a hard and fast rule."

"You and these rules…I think you're just making them up as you go." Her voice had taken on a husky tone.

"Nope, it's in the book, too." He moved his hands to her waist and the second he touched her she inhaled unsteadily. "So is this how it's going to work with this whole neighbor thing? You continually making me baked goods when something happens…or you wanting something?"

"Yes." The word came across her lips on a whisper.

He moved his hands, one skimming across her hip and around to her back to pull her closer. She was flush up against him now and it was perfection.

Per-fucking-fection.

His other hand reached up and cradled the side of her face, his thumb skimming her cheek. "So, what? You need a favor and you make me a cobbler?"

"No." She closed her eyes and leaned into his touch. "For favors you get fudge."

"On what occasion do I get cake?" He lowered his head, skimming his nose across her jaw and moving lower.

"Birthdays." And now she was touching him, too, her hands at his sides fisting in the fabric of his shirt.

"Well, in that case, mine is October nineteenth."

"I'll make sure to, uh, remember that." She moved her head to the side, providing him greater access to just where he wanted to be.

He placed an open-mouth kiss on her neck, the taste of her skin so much better than he could've ever imagined. Another thing he couldn't have come close to imagining? The sound of her needy little gasps filling his ears. He pulled back, moving his hand to the back of her head, his fingers spearing through her hair.

"How does this system work for other things?" he asked.

"What other things?" she asked breathlessly.

"What's the trade-off for a kiss?"

She shook her head slightly, glancing at his mouth for just a second before she looked back up. "You can't barter a kiss, Tripp."

"You're right. Kisses are meant to be stolen."

"That in your rule book, too?"

"Sure is." And with that his mouth covered hers.

Chapter Eight

Breaking All the Rules

Tripp knew within an instant that Beth Boone tasted better than anything he'd ever had in his mouth. There was no gentle coaxing necessary in the kiss. The second his lips were on hers, she opened for him, her tongue sliding against his.

And it wasn't just her taste, either; she felt better than anything he'd ever touched…or had been touched by. Her hands were under his shirt, her bare palms moving across his abs. She flexed her fingers, her nails just biting into his skin.

Okay, so she liked it a little rough. He could work with that.

He repaid the slight sting she'd left on his lower belly by nipping at her bottom lip. Her answering moan sent him over the edge and just like that he had her pushed up against the counter. He gently tugged on her hair, getting her to tilt her head and allowing him to deepen the kiss.

It was a whole new experience kissing Beth, the shock to his system setting off a chain reaction in his body. His blood ran hotter, his heart beat faster, his skin felt over-sensitized…stretched too tight and tingling.

The feel of her against him—her mouth, her hands, the scent and taste of her—burned him. She burned him. Kissing this woman was like something he'd never known.

"Holy shit." He pulled back, needing a full breath of air before his lungs exploded.

Beth's head was cradled in his palm and he took in the full picture as he looked down into her face. Her blue eyes were dazed, blond hair wild, lips slightly swollen, breath coming in and out in uneven gasps.

So damn beautiful it was insane.

"What are you doing to me?" he asked, shaking his head.

But he didn't give her a chance to answer before his mouth was on hers again—tongues tangling, breaths mingling, need consuming.

Yeah, *consuming* was the right word, which was why it probably took both of them entirely by surprise when *two* dogs barking echoed around them. Tripp pulled his mouth away from Beth's, keeping his hands firmly in place as he turned.

Duke and Frankie were already wrestling on the floor in front of Finn, who was standing in the living room. His eyebrows were raised in surprise at the scene before him. "I, uh, knocked…The door was open so I figured you were outside or something."

"I was just leaving." Beth pulled away from Tripp's hold, her face and neck flushed. Whether it was more from the kissing or being caught he wasn't entirely sure.

What he was sure about was that he really didn't like the fact that she wasn't under his hands anymore.

"You sure? I can just come back so you two can finish up." Finn pointed to the door as he bit his bottom lip, trying and failing to hide the smirk that was making his mouth twitch.

"That's not necessary." Beth moved farther across the kitchen, putting distance between her and Tripp. "I'll see you later. Enjoy the pie," she said before she turned and practically ran down the hallway.

But that wasn't how this was going to end.

"Give me a sec." Tripp made to follow Beth before he turned quickly and looked at Finn. "And don't eat my pie."

* * *

Beth practically sprinted from Tripp's house, her mind, heart, and pulse racing. Tripp Black had just kissed her…and she'd had absolutely no problem kissing him back. The instant his lips had touched hers she'd opened her mouth for him. Good gravy, if Finn hadn't walked in there was no telling what else she would've opened for him.

Oh, that was a lie; she knew exactly what else she would've opened for him. She'd have let that man carry her off to any hard surface and spread her out. Let him do whatever the hell he wanted.

He'd had his hands on her, those big masculine calloused hands that had been gentle and demanding at the same time. It had been so long since she'd been touched by a man…but no one had ever touched her like *that*.

And she'd touched him back. Her palms still burned with the feel of his skin, and she balled her hands in an attempt to hold on to the sensation.

She was almost to the side door that led to the garage when the sound of her name had her turning around. Tripp was rounding the side of his house at a jog, a look of fierce determination on his face.

Her stomach started to somersault immediately.

What are you doing to me? Tripp had asked that question right before he'd started the second round of kissing that had been damn near close to destroying her.

No, the real question was, what was *he* doing to *her?*

"What the hell was that?" he asked when he was only a few feet away. "You just walk away?"

"Tripp, I—"

But that was all she got out before he pushed her up against the brick wall. "I wasn't done kissing you."

His mouth came down hard on hers, and just like before, she didn't fight him one little bit. And why the hell would she?

He'd awakened a hunger in her that had been dormant for way too long, a hunger that in that moment was stronger than it had ever been. Maybe it was stronger because it was shared—the man seemed pretty hell bent on devouring her.

She had her hands in his hair this time; she hadn't reached that high before as she'd gotten distracted by touching his body. The strands were soft and damp between her fingers. He must've just showered; the scent of soap on his skin strong.

"God," he groaned as he trailed his lips down her neck. "If I'd known this was what kissing you was like, we could've saved ourselves a lot of arguments."

"Is that right?"

"You wouldn't have been able to yell at me if your mouth had been occupied with mine."

"But then you wouldn't have gotten cookies…or pie," she countered as his lips started to make the return journey up her throat and across her jaw.

"I'd rather have your mouth." And just like that he was kissing her again, his tongue stroking against hers and taking control.

When Tripp pulled back from her a minute—or five—later, Beth was slow to open her eyes, taking more than a second to focus on him.

"Consider everything forgiven." He brushed his lips against hers, the scruff of his beard just rasping against her cheek as he moved his mouth up to her ear. "And Beth?"

"Hmmm?" she hummed, unable to say any actual words.

"I'm still not done kissing you." With that he stepped back from her and walked away.

She stood there, unable to pull her gaze from him as he disappeared around the side of the house.

Holy fuck. Did that really just happen?

Yes, yes it had. Tripp had kissed the ever living daylights out of her. He'd thoroughly decimated her brain…which was probably why her back was still fused to the brick wall and she hadn't moved at all.

She'd go inside just as soon as she remembered how to walk again…whenever that was.

* * *

I'm still not done kissing you.

Those words played on repeat in Beth's head as she added the eggs one at a time to the cookie batter churning in the Kitchen Aid mixer. The whir of the motor was no match for the low rumble of Tripp's voice echoing around in her brain. That sentence was still making her a little bit weak in the knees...and more than a little damp between her thighs.

Good Lord, that kiss...*kisses*, actually, so many kisses that had blown her freaking mind. Each one better than the next. She'd never been kissed like that before, where her entire body was part of it, everything down to her very core.

It scared the shit out of her. This was the very thing she'd told herself not to go for. The very thing she knew she couldn't have. A fact that was so beyond clear.

Wasn't it?

It had to be...Tripp had made her lose her freaking mind...and every single one of her inhibitions. Well, at least *that* was clear. Very clear: as she'd plastered herself against the very solid length of him and kissed him back, her inhibitions had been long gone.

She wiped her hands on her apron before she grabbed the glass of wine from the kitchen counter. Glass to her lips she tipped her head back, finishing off the chilled chardonnay in seconds.

It had only been about thirty minutes since Tripp had left her pushed up against the side of the house and she'd already downed a glass of wine. And Beth's glasses weren't measured like they would be at a restaurant or bar. Not that *the glass is twenty-five percent full* nonsense. No, she filled that sucker up to the very top.

She was going to have to get a refill in a second, just as soon as she finished adding the vanilla to the batter.

Now, Beth having a little more to drink this evening was okay for a number of reasons. *One*: she had an empty house. The kids were spending the weekend with Papa Wallace. *Two*: she was more than capable of a little tipsy baking.

She'd made her mother's chocolate chip cookies so many times she could do so blindfolded and with one arm tied behind her back. They were going to turn out just fine. Good thing, too, as they were going to be sold the following day at the Mirabelle High School Baked Goods booth.

The town of Mirabelle never ran short on community gatherings. There was at least one festival, function, or celebration every month. The biggest and most successful were the Summer Seafood Festival, the Fall Festival, the Holiday Lights on the Harbor, and that weekend's event, the Spring Fling.

When Mel had asked Beth to help out and bake something, Beth hadn't even hesitated to say yes.

Speaking of Mel, she was going to be coming over soon with a couple of their other friends. Which was *perfect* as Beth needed to discuss what had happened... *pronto.*

As if thinking about them had made it so, Beth's cell phone rang on the counter behind her. Mel's number flashed on the screen. She turned the mixer off before swiping her finger across the screen to answer.

"Hey."

"Hey," Mel's voice filled the speaker. "On the way."

"Perfect. I've already polished off half the bottle of wine I had in the fridge."

Mel laughed. "There a reason you're getting liquored up before we get there?"

"Tripp kissed me." Even saying it out loud didn't make it feel true.

There was a beat of silence and then Mel said, "We'll be there in fifteen minutes."

Mel was actually standing on the front porch in less than ten, and she wasn't alone. Grace Anderson, Hannah Shepherd, and Harper James were standing there, too.

Grace and Harper were two of Beth's longstanding friends, going back about two decades just like Mel. Hannah, however, was a New York transplant who'd moved down two years ago. All three of them were married with children and were just as eager for a girls' night as Beth was.

There was only one person missing from that night's festivities, but their friend Paige was currently on a two-week trip in Italy with her husband, Brendan. Beth had no doubt the woman was having a grand old time.

"We brought reinforcements," Mel said as they all made their way inside.

"We saw the Bat Signal." Grace held up a bottle of wine in each hand.

"And by that she means the glowing light of an empty wineglass in the sky," Harper added.

Hannah held up a bottle of wine, too. "We knew we were needed."

"Oh, bless you." Beth held the door open wide for them all to pass through.

"We were told you had something good for us, but weren't told what," Grace said as they headed to the kitchen.

"I need to pour the wine first."

"Oh, it's *that* good?" Hannah asked.

"Well, get to pouring!" Harper demanded as she and Hannah took seats on the barstools at the kitchen island.

Mel sat on the other side of Hannah while Grace went over to inspect the cookie-making area. Beth had kept busy as she'd waited for her friends to get there, she'd finished mixing all of her dough and put the first batch in the oven. The kitchen was already filling up with the scent of baking cookies.

"I hope no one else is foolish enough to bring chocolate chip cookies to the bake sale tomorrow." Grace shook her pretty blond head as she peaked into the mixing bowl. "That's like trying to bring a knife to a gunfight."

As Grace was—in Beth's humble opinion—Mirabelle's best baker, she was going to take that compliment to the bank.

Grace and her grandmother Lula Mae were the owners of Café Lula, a quaint little place out on the beach that had some of the most glorious food Beth had ever put into her mouth. Lula Mae's fried chicken was unrivaled and what she could do with pastrami on rye should be illegal.

"Oh really? And what are you making?" Beth asked as she fished the corkscrew out of a drawer.

"I had to bring my A-game with you around now," Grace grinned. "I'm making double fudge cupcakes with cream cheese ganache frosting."

"And there goes my waistline and all my cash," Beth groaned. Grace's cream cheese ganache frosting was God's gift to any pastry. Beth was probably going to end up buying more of those damn cupcakes than anyone else.

"I can't help your waistline, but as for your cash?" Grace pulled a Tupperware container from the purse that hung from her shoulder. "I brought you the frosting leftovers," she said before she turned around to stick it in the fridge.

"And this is just another reason, on a long list of reasons, as to why I adore you." Beth pulled out four wineglasses before she grabbed the open bottle and started to pour.

"And that," Harper said, pointing to the now very full glasses, "is one of the reasons that we all adore you."

"You guys weren't planning on going anywhere for a while, right?" Beth grinned as she passed the glasses around. "You don't need to get back to relieve your babysitters or anything?" She looked between Hannah, Harper, and Grace.

"Are you kidding?" Hannah asked as she twirled a strand of her strawberry blond hair around her finger. "Mama Shepherd takes her grandmother duties *very* seriously. When she gets baby Nate for a night, she keeps him the *whole* night."

"Lula Mae is the exact same way with Rosie," Grace said about her own grandmother, who was Rosie's great-grandmother.

Grace and Beth had a number of things in common. They'd both learned how to bake at the hands of their mothers…and they'd both lost those mothers when they were young. Grace had been ten years old when her mother Claire had been taken from this life. The breast cancer had been aggressive, only giving her seven months from the time of diagnosis.

Neither Grace nor her older brother Brendan had ever known their respective fathers. After their mother's death, they'd been raised by their grandparents, Lula Mae and Oliver King. Grace understood a lot of what Beth was dealing with, and had always been there with good advice.

"Well, I'm not quite to the point of being without Sofie for a whole night." Harper shook her head. "But my parents were thrilled for an evening of babysitting. Liam and I will probably have to kick them out of the house when we get home tonight."

Grace laughed as she picked up her wineglass and held it in the air. "Well, no matter how it happened, here's to still getting a girls' night!"

"Cheers!" everyone said in unison as they clinked their glasses together and took a sip.

Beth had barely swallowed when Mel looked at her pointedly. "Spill."

"So to catch the three of you up on what Mel knows," Beth looked between Hannah, Harper, and Grace, "Tripp kissed me." That was the second time she'd said it out loud and she still didn't really believe it. "We got interrupted by your brother-in-law," she looked pointedly at Hannah, "I left…and Tripp followed and kissed me again."

"Finn walked in on the two of you making out?" Hannah's eyebrows rose high over her black, plastic-framed glasses. "Well, this just got way more interesting than I was expecting."

"Yeah it did." Grace nodded.

"Start from the beginning, Beth. And leave *nothing* out," Harper said before taking a hefty sip of wine.

Beth followed Harper's lead, taking her own fortifying drink before she launched into the story.

* * *

When it came to sports, Tripp's favorite to play was baseball. When it came to watching? It was hockey, hands down. Had been since he was six years old.

As Kingsland was less than an hour away from the home of the

Jacksonville Stampede, he'd gone to many games growing up. His dad had always gotten awesome seats and without fail, Tripp and his best friend Landon would scream themselves hoarse by the end of every single game.

It was a pretty exciting time to be a Stampede fan. They were the reigning Stanley Cup winners and were having another awesome season on the ice. Tonight they were playing the L.A. Kings, and it promised to be a good game as both teams were dominating that season.

Yet, Tripp was only half paying attention to the action on the screen in front of him. Why? Because he couldn't stop thinking about Beth.

Couldn't stop thinking about how her body had curved into his, about how she had felt perfect up against him. Couldn't stop thinking about how she'd put her hands on his skin. How she'd sighed in pleasure when he'd kissed her. How she'd moaned when he'd touched her. Couldn't stop thinking about how she tasted.

He was going to need to pour the ice-cold beer he was drinking into his lap in about a second.

"Yo! Tripp!" someone shouted as they jostled his shoulder.

He pulled his gaze from where he'd been blindly watching the game and looked across the bar at Nathanial Shepherd. Shep was Finn's older brother, and except for Finn sporting glasses and shorter hair, they looked ridiculously alike.

The Shepherd family owned the Sleepy Sheep, which was an institution in the small town. It had an Irish pub feel with its mahogany walls and floor, and the dollar bills that were signed and stapled to the ceiling. It had been built by Shep and Finn's grandfather right after World War II and was holding strong even after all these years. It had even been expanded to include a brewery next door.

The business was still family owned and operated, and most nights, some Shepherd or other was working behind the counter. Even Finn pulled a few evening shifts when he wasn't too busy with his day job.

"What the hell is going on with you?" Shep asked as he placed his hands on the bar and leaned forward.

"My brother just scored for the second time tonight, and while everyone in this bar is losing their shit, you're over here on the moon," Liam said from Tripp's right.

Not only was Liam a country musician who was married to the beautiful Harper James, he was also younger brother to Logan James. Logan just so happened to be one of the star players for the Jacksonville Stampede.

"So why is that?" Shep asked.

Finn was sitting to Tripp's left, and the second Shep asked the question he coughed into his hand. "Beth."

The other Shepherd brother wasn't working that night and was instead enjoying a beer while he watched the game…and apparently throwing Tripp under the bus. Well, that had taken no time at all.

Shep's gaze moved from Tripp to Finn in an instant. "What do you know?"

"Our friend here has finally gotten his head turned around by a woman."

Tripp looked at Finn, now wanting to throw his beer somewhere else. "Really, Finn?"

"What do you want from me?" He shrugged. "I walked in on

the two of you making out like there was no tomorrow. That's your own damn fault."

"You were kissing Beth?" This question came from Bennett Hart, who was sitting at the corner of the bar.

"Sure was," Finn answered. "She gave him pie, too."

"Is that a new euphemism for something?" Liam asked.

"Not one that I'm familiar with," Jax Anderson grinned.

Jax was a Deputy Sheriff for Atticus County whose beat was in Mirabelle. He and Tripp worked with each other every once in a while. When Tripp had first met the guy three years ago, he'd been pretty damn reserved and not quick to smile.

But that was before he'd married Grace.

Besides Tripp and Finn, all of the guys who were hanging out there were married. They were all perfect examples of *settling* not being a part of settled down. Each and every one of them had fallen hard for the woman in their life.

So it would stand to reason that if Tripp were going to ask for advice from anyone, it would be from his friends. But knowing his friends, it wasn't going to be necessary for him to ask. They'd be offering their advice up in no time at all. Just as soon as they started prying in three...two...one...

"So? Beth?" Shep grinned from across the counter. "This is an interesting turn of events."

"Because she definitely wasn't a member of the Tripp Black fan club," Finn said before he took a sip of his beer.

"Yeah." Bennett leaned forward and rested his elbows on the bar. "But that was before he went out on the lake and saved Grant."

"This is true." Jax nodded. "That *was* a significant catalyst for such a big change of opinion."

"But to go from thoroughly disliking someone," Finn said, looking at the guys, "to letting them stick their tongue down your throat? That's a pretty big leap."

"Also true," Liam agreed.

"And what about this pie?" Shep asked.

"Which we should all take into account," Bennett interjected, "is in addition to the cookies she'd already made him."

"Beth made him cookies, too?" Jax's reddish brown eyebrows rose up high.

"Which ones?" Shep asked, looking at Bennett.

"Chocolate chip."

"Damn." Finn groaned before he finished his beer. "Those bad boys are unrivaled."

"You guys going to talk to me while you talk about me?" Tripp asked.

"I don't hear you chiming in to help us decipher this new development." Shep shook his head as he grabbed Finn's empty glass and slid a full one into its place.

"We have precious little to go on here. Since we've known you, you've been almost virginal," Bennett said.

Finn choked into his beer.

"I'm glad this is so much fun for all of you." Tripp frowned. The thing was, he couldn't exactly contest what Bennett had just said.

Well, he couldn't argue with his friends about having very little to go on when it came to his love life. Since he'd moved to Mirabelle he hadn't been in a single relationship serious enough to bring a girl around to any of his friends. Sure he'd dated, but it hadn't gone any further than casual.

As for the virginal part? He could contest that. It might've been a few months since he'd had sex, but he wasn't anywhere near celibate. But come to think of it, he hadn't brought a woman home with him since he'd moved into the new house. Nor had he gone home with anyone.

Well, that was an interesting fact.

"Okay, all kidding aside." Shep placed his elbows on the bar and leaned over it. "Do you *want* to date Beth?"

"I don't know." He definitely wanted to keep kissing her. That was for damn sure.

"Well, you're going to need to figure it out." Bennett was looking pretty seriously at Tripp now. "You know anything with her isn't going to be simple or casual. Not when she has three kids involved."

"I'm fully aware of that." This thing with Beth, whatever it was or could be, was already so damn complicated. Was that something he even wanted to get involved with?

His mind flashed to the memory of her in his arms, her back pressed to the brick wall as he'd kissed her. He could still feel her hands in his hair.

He wanted *something*. That was for damn sure.

"And we also need to factor in Beth. Who's to say she even wants to date you?" Finn asked, raising his eyebrows at Tripp.

Well, that was a fair point. Who *was* to say that she wanted to date him?

"Hmm," Jax hummed. "I think that's something we can find out. We'll just have to ask our wives what they learned tonight."

"What are you talking about?" Tripp asked.

"Hannah, Mel, Harper, and Grace are all hanging out with Beth," Shep answered. "They're most likely drinking enough wine to float a raft."

"Probably a small ship," Liam agreed.

"Should be easy to get any information out of them at this point." Jax looked down at his phone. "Especially as Grace just texted me that she *has a tipsy.* She also sent this picture," he said, sliding his phone across the bar to Tripp.

But before Tripp could pick it up, Finn snatched it. "Let me see that." He studied it for a second before he turned to Tripp, grinning as he handed over the phone. "Well damn, look what's in the background."

His eyes immediately landed on Beth when he looked down at the screen. Her smile was genuine, reaching all the way up to her eyes, which seemed even bluer than he remembered.

Was that a trick of the camera? Or just something that happened when she was happy? The need to know the answer burned his brain.

He slowly took in the rest of the picture. Grace's arm was wrapped around Beth's shoulder and they were both holding glasses of wine. Then his eyes caught on the background, where trays of cookies cooled on the counter behind them.

Chocolate chip cookies.

Tripp forced himself to look up from the screen, trying hard to maintain some sort of poker face. He was pretty sure he was somewhat successful, which was good as there were five sets of eyes on him. But really, it wasn't one of the easiest things he'd ever done, especially since he was now thinking that Beth probably smelled like those damn cookies again.

"You think if we went over there we could snag some of her cookies?" Finn asked.

There was something about the way Finn said *her cookies* that had Tripp wanting to slug his friend in the face.

"No, I don't," Bennett shook his head. "She's making them for the high school bake sale at the Spring Fling. You want them, you're going to have to buy them."

"Well, I know where I'm going to be tomorrow." Finn waggled his eyebrows. "Buying all the cookies."

"Not if I get there first," Tripp said before he could stop himself.

Yup, he was fucked. He wasn't going to be able to maintain any semblance of a poker face when it came to Beth.

It wasn't possible, not anymore.

Chapter Nine

Control

Beth looked into her nearly empty wineglass, swirling the last few sips around and around. The strands of star-shaped lights that ran around the porch ceiling twinkled through the glass and seemed to float in the last of the liquid.

After the last batch of cookies had been pulled from the oven and left to cool, they'd all moved out to the back porch. Hannah and Mel were sitting in the hammock, their feet resting on the floor as they rocked slowly, careful not to spill their wine.

Harper was laid out on the love seat, her feet propped up on one armrest, her head on the other. Grace and Beth had stationed themselves in the matching chairs, and the table between them and Harper now held two empty bottles and a third whose contents were slowly dwindling.

The other thing that was dwindling was the tray of brownies that Grace had whipped up and then slathered with the cream cheese ganache frosting. They'd needed *something* to soak up all that alcohol.

"You know Beth, you aren't going to find the answer to my question in the remnants of that wine," Harper said.

The question? What Beth was going to do about her sexy neighbor.

Hannah laughed. "This isn't like tea leaf reading."

Beth looked up at her friends and grinned. "Ohhhh, that would be fun. Finding answers in an empty wineglass."

"An empty wineglass?" Grace asked. "I don't think any of us have had an empty glass all night."

"True," Mel nodded. "Now answer the question."

Beth sighed, shaking her head. "I have no idea what I'm going to do."

"But you like him. You *liiiike* him." Harper's emphasis on the word *like* was totally and one hundred percent true.

It was that thrilling—and more than slightly terrifying—flip-in-her-belly kind of like. Beth hadn't felt it in years. Those chasing days that happened right before *something* started.

Could a *something* start with Tripp?

"How did this even happen?" Beth asked, so beyond confused. It had just crept up on her out of nowhere. *He'd* just crept up on her out of nowhere with his sexy sexiness.

"Are you *seriously* asking how it happened?" Grace shook her head pityingly. "You looked at the man. *That's* how it happened. You were just too stubborn to realize it before."

"I am *not* stubborn."

"All right, Pinocchio," Mel said. "You can keep lying to yourself if you want to. Let us know how that turns out for you."

"Ugh," Beth groaned.

"Though I will say, you know what I really appreciate when it comes to this whole thing with Tripp?" Mel asked.

"What's that?" Beth turned to look over at her friend.

"His little line of not being done kissing you."

"I was a pretty big fan of that, too." Beth leaned her head back and looked at the ceiling, remembering exactly what it had been like to be kissed by Tripp. And if she was really honest with herself, she was pretty happy that he wasn't done. She sure as hell wasn't ready for that new development to be over.

Not even in the slightest.

But could she do it? Be in a relationship *and* be a mom? She had no freaking clue. She'd obviously never done it before. She was already trying to juggle so many things…one more ball could have everything tumbling down.

"Well, if you want my suggestion on what to do"—Harper's voice floated on the night air—"I think you should *do* him."

"What?" Beth's head came up so fast she probably gave herself whiplash.

"Oh, yeah. Do what Harper said," Hannah agreed before she brought her wineglass to her lips.

"You're serious?"

"Most definitely," Harper nodded. "Make a move on him."

"I can't do that!" Beth laughed, feeling a little hysterical. There was no way in hell.

"Why not?" Grace asked. "He's clearly interested."

"Why not?" Beth repeated the question. "Because it would complicate everything."

"Life is already complicated. Absolutely nothing is going to change that. You might as well get a few man-made orgasms out of it," Hannah said.

"Here. Here." Mel clinked her wineglass against Hannah's before both of them took a drink.

A man-made orgasm sounded more glorious than Beth could put into words. And the idea of a Tripp-made orgasm? Well, it left her a little breathless. She was pushing her thighs together at just the thought of his hands on her body again. He'd obliterated her brain when he'd kissed her earlier, so there was no telling what the man was capable of in other areas.

But it couldn't be just physical, at least not for her. There was always a layer of emotion involved. When it came to sex she'd never been able to separate the two. Could she handle something like that with Tripp?

What would happen when it ended? Not *if*, but *when*. Really? She was already putting an expiration date on it? That didn't bode well.

And with that thought taking over her brain, she drained the last of her wine. Then she leaned forward and grabbed the bottle on the table, pouring more into her glass. "Anyone else?"

"Yes please," Grace held out her glass.

Hannah shook her head. "Still working on mine."

"Me too," Mel said.

"You can top me off." Harper reached over and gently pushed at her glass, inching it closer to Beth on the coffee table. "Liam just texted me. There's twenty minutes left before the hockey game is over, so the guys won't be here for another thirty."

They'd all definitely had too much to drink that night and there was no way any of them could drive home. But it had always been the plan that they were going to drink too much, so their husbands had taken the responsibility for picking them up.

"All right," Beth said as she settled back into her seat. "Well, somebody else can be in the hot seat for the next thirty minutes.

Eenny, meeny, miny, moe." She pointed at Hannah. "It's your turn!"

They spent the next twenty minutes talking and laughing and doing a little more catching up. Beth hadn't realized just how much she'd needed a night like this. There'd been more times than she could count where she'd laughed so hard her stomach hurt.

With ten minutes until the guys got there, they headed inside and started cleaning up. Beth was loading the dishwasher with the wineglasses when she started laughing so hard she was crying.

How could she not when Mel and Harper were telling them about Bennett and Liam putting on a little concert with Hamilton and Dale's help? The boys had acquired a number of mentors in the last couple of years. Not only were they very close with Bennett; they'd also developed a relationship with Liam and Logan James.

Not too shabby for the two eighteen-year-olds to have the phone numbers of a country music star and a hockey legend in their phones. Nope, not too shabby at all.

"So anyway," Harper told them, drying the Pyrex dish that had earlier held the brownies. "They come out into the living room dressed as the members of One Direction. Tight pants, styled hair, everything."

"You're shitting me." Grace shook her head as she leaned against the counter.

"Not even a little bit. And the whole time they kept up with the accents. Didn't break character once. It was my favorite thing of *ever*." Mel grinned.

"Tell me you have it on film," Hannah begged, clasping her hands in front of herself and jumping up and down.

"You bet your sweet ass I do." Harper nodded, setting the dish on the counter.

"It is a sweet ass," Hannah said matter-of-factly. "You can ask my husband and he will tell you all about it."

"Of that I have no doubt," Beth said as the doorbell rang. She headed for the front door, opening it up to reveal Bennett, Jax, and Shep.

"You've come for your wives?" she asked, pulling the door open wider for them all to step inside.

"Yes ma'am," Bennett said, stopping in front of her for a hug.

"They're in the kitchen." She nodded before she was pulled into Jax's embrace.

"You look lovely as always, Beth," he said before he followed Bennett down the hallway.

Last, but certainly not least, Shep entered. He wrapped her up in his arms and lifted her from the ground. "Hello, beautiful!" He kissed her on the cheek before he set her back down and let go of her. "You and the other ladies get good and tipsy?"

"You betcha." She nodded as she led him into the kitchen.

"That's what I like to hear. Harper," Shep said as he walked into the kitchen, "Liam will be over in a second. He's next door with Finn checking out Tripp's new work on Koko."

"Koko?" Mel asked.

"His Yenko," Bennett said as he slipped his arm around Mel's waist and pulled her in close to his body.

"Was that even English?" Harper raised an eyebrow.

"It's a limited edition Chevelle." Grace was the first to answer.

Beth didn't have any clue what a Yenko was, but she at least knew that a Chevelle was a car.

It was true that both Beth and Grace had family members that were mechanics, but Grace knew a whole hell of a lot more than Beth did. She chalked it up to the fact that both Grace's brother and grandfather were the owners of King's Auto, the same shop where Beth's father worked.

"I love it when you talk car." Jax grinned at his wife. "It's sexy."

"If you'd like, I can tell you how a carburetor works when we get home," she smirked at him.

Hannah shook her head. "You two are strange."

"No argument there. You get all your cookies baked?" Jax asked, looking at Beth.

"Sure did. They're ready to go for tomorrow. Wouldn't have finished as quickly without all the help I got, either. Four extra sets of hands sure does make the process go faster."

"What was your job?" Shep asked Hannah.

"Bagging and tasting." Hannah grinned at him as he moved closer to her and leaned down to give her a kiss. She was a notoriously bad baker. Her cooking skills went about as far as a frying pan. She did make killer paninis and crepes, but that was pretty much it.

"Tasting?" Shep raised his eyebrows. "Don't tell Finn. He was wanting to get a few samples."

"Did you tell him he can buy them tomorrow just like everyone else?" Mel put her hands on her hips.

"Yes," Bennett nodded. "And I wouldn't be surprised if he and Tripp come to blows over them."

"What?" Beth asked, unable to stop the question from falling out of her mouth.

"Well, it appeared that Finn was a little jealous of the plate of cookies that Tripp already got." Shep grinned.

"And it also looked like Tripp had an issue with anyone else having some of your cookies, Beth," Jax said.

"Huh." Grace's blond eyebrows rose high. "I wonder why that is?"

"Probably because he got a taste of something he liked." Harper looked pointedly at Beth.

"Okay, I think I've had enough of this particular conversation." Beth clapped her hands together, bringing a finality to it...or so she hoped.

She had no doubt her cheeks were flaming now...and though she could blame some of that on the wine, it wasn't the main cause. It didn't help that everyone standing in the kitchen was looking at her. Seven sets of eyes were a lot to combat when a person was trying to look unaffected by the topic at hand...and considering the topic at hand just so happened to be Tripp? Yeah, looking unaffected wasn't going to happen.

Nope!

To make matters so much worse, when Beth walked outside five minutes later to see Harper off—all of the other girls had already left with their husbands—her attempt at unaffected went from poor to failing...or more accurately, it went to falling.

The tip of her flip-flop caught on the top step of the porch and just like that she was falling sideways right into the bushes—the very splintery, spiky, prod-a-person-in-all-of-the-places-no-one-wants-to-be-prodded bushes.

The absolute best part of it? It all happened right in front of Tripp. He was about ten feet away, standing on the walkway with Liam and Finn, illuminated by the floodlight on the corner of the garage, a light that clearly showed his smile when his eyes landed on her.

And that was how the ability to walk and think at the same time vanished from Beth's skill set.

Fuuuuuuuuuuuuuuuuuuuuuuuuuuuuuuuck.

* * *

Tripp looked up as the two women came out of the house. He'd been interested in what Liam was telling him, but the moment his eyes caught on Beth he had no idea what his friend was even talking about anymore.

All he saw was her…and the next second all he saw was her falling right off the front porch steps.

As his attention had been entirely on her, he was the first one that noticed what happened, and the first one to move toward her. He was halfway there before she even hit the bushes.

She landed on her side and the thick brush held her up, as opposed to swallowing her. As he pulled Beth from the bushes and to her feet, he was vaguely aware of the commotion around them. But he was intently focused on her and wasn't really paying attention to what they were saying—something about her general well-being after her fall, but clearly *he* was taking care of that.

Taking care of *her*.

Another reason he was more than a little preoccupied was that he was touching her. His hands cupped her elbows, his fingers stretched up the backs of her arms. Even after he'd gotten her steady on her feet, he wasn't able to let go.

"You hurt?"

"Just my pride," she said as her cheeks flamed red.

"That it?" He forced himself to let go of one of her arms and reached up to get the twigs out of her hair. The move caused the blond strands that had fallen across her forehead to pull to the side and he immediately noticed the cut right below her hairline. It was about an inch wide and starting to bleed.

"Shit, Beth, you're bleeding."

"I am?" She moved her hand up to touch her forehead but Tripp grabbed it and pulled it away.

"Your hands are covered in dirt." He looked down at the one he was now holding, taking in the scrapes across her palm. "Come on." He wrapped his fingers around her wrist and pulled her into the house. "Let me get you cleaned up."

"You know I'm capable of cleaning myself up, right? I'm a nurse," she said as he led her down the hallway.

"And I'm a firefighter and certified EMT...and I'm not drunk."

"I'm not drunk either!" She stopped walking, pulling her hand from his.

He turned around, taking in her narrowed eyes and the stubbornness transforming the set of her mouth.

"Then why did you just fall into the bushes?"

Her cheeks managed to flame redder, embarrassment winning out over the outrage from just seconds ago. "I tripped."

"Come on, Beth. Either we can do this the easy way and I can get you fixed up, or we can do this the hard way."

"And what's the hard way?" Her gaze somehow narrowed even more.

"I pick you up and carry you."

Her eyes went wide, with two emotions flickering in those blue depths: first agitation and then want. He wondered if they were separate, or if she was agitated *because* she wanted option number two.

She glared up as she walked around him. "I take back our truce."

Tripp couldn't stop himself from grinning as he followed. She rounded the corner of the hallway, heading through the kitchen to the sink.

He'd never been past the front door of the house, and he did a quick scan of the space as he walked through, more than impressed with what he saw. He had a decent kitchen, but hers was almost double in size.

His attention moved back to Beth, who was a few steps in front of him. She was already at the sink, pulling a paper towel from the holder, and being careful not to touch the part that she brought up and held to her forehead.

"Where is your first aid kit?" he asked her.

"Under the left sink in the bathroom." She pointed to the door at the back of the kitchen with her free hand.

"Stay here, I'll go grab it," he said as he headed off in that direction.

"Can you stop telling me what to do?" she called out as he walked away.

"Nope." He shook his head as he crossed over the threshold and reached for the light switch.

The second the room was illuminated he came up short. He was in the master bedroom...Beth's bedroom.

There was something about seeing her bed—about actually laying eyes on where she slept at night—that had him pausing for just a second. It felt...intimate, an intimacy that he wanted more of.

He wanted more of whatever this thing was with her. He'd wanted it ever since he'd tasted her.

He pulled his gaze from the bed and headed for the bathroom, turning on the light and taking a quick glance around as he went to the sink. Everything—from the tile floors, sunken tub, stand-up shower, sink, and cabinets—was white.

He grabbed the first aid kit from underneath the sink and headed back through the bedroom, doing his level best to avoid looking at her bed this time around. All he needed was to get distracted again...to think about being in that bed with her.

Not the time, buddy.

When he walked into the kitchen, Harper, Liam, and Finn were all standing around Beth.

"You guys can head home," Beth was saying as Tripp set the kit on the counter and went to wash his hands. "No use sticking around."

"You sure? I don't want to miss the second act." Harper was fighting a grin that played at the corner of her mouth as she looked between Tripp and Beth.

"There won't be a second act." Beth frowned, shaking her head at her friend.

"You sure about that?" Finn asked. "You got any popcorn we can pop?"

Beth's frown turned more severe. "Keep it up, Finn, and Tripp will be patching up more than me."

"Come on." Liam slipped his arm around his wife's waist and took a step toward the hallway. "Tripp can handle it."

Harper focused on Tripp. "You better take care of her. Otherwise you've got me to deal with."

"That a threat, Harper?" Tripp asked as he grabbed a paper towel and dried his hands.

"Nope." She smiled sweetly. "It's a promise."

"You've got nothing to worry about. I've cleaned more than a few cuts in my day."

"That's good to know, but it wasn't what I was talking about." Harper moved her gaze to Beth. "I'll see you tomorrow."

A fresh flush of red colored Beth's cheeks at Harper's words. "Yes. Tomorrow. Bye!"

Everyone filed out of the kitchen and down the hallway as Tripp unsnapped the latch on the first aid kit. It was fully stocked and neatly organized, and he immediately found everything that he needed to get her cleaned up.

"So," he said as he turned to her and moved closer. "You going to be a difficult patient or a good one?"

"I haven't decided yet."

"Of course you haven't. Let me see it."

She dropped her hand as he reached up and brushed the hair back from her forehead. His fingers grazed her skin and her next breath was sharp. He knew the reaction had nothing to do with him touching the cut and everything to do with him touching her.

"It's minor," he said as he got a closer look. "It's already stopped bleeding."

"I told you I could take care of it myself."

"You did." He nodded as he grabbed a washcloth from the kit.

"But you didn't believe me."

"Oh, Beth, I more than believed you." He turned the sink on, waiting for the water to warm a little. "I just ignored it," he hold her as he fought a grin.

"Are you laughing at me?" Her face got redder, though he was sure it had less to do with embarrassment now. "I'm glad my falling was so humorous for you."

"Actually, I didn't find you falling funny at all." He stuck the cloth under the water before wringing it out. "Though that string of expletives was rather interesting."

"What?" She looked up at him, horrified.

He pressed the cloth around the cut and started to clean it. "You have the mouth of a truck driver."

"I didn't realize I'd said anything out loud. And I would prefer to compare it to the mouth of a sailor."

"And why's that?"

"Because, in my experience, sailors are much sexier than truck drivers."

"That so?" He paused from his ministrations as he looked down into her face.

"Yes," she nodded. "It's the whole uniform thing."

"So you like a man in uniform? Well, that's convenient," he said before he went back to cleaning the wound.

"And why's that?"

"Because I wear a uniform."

"And?"

"And…" His eyes were on hers again. "You like me."

"Well, aren't you sure of yourself?"

He set the cloth on the counter as he took a step closer to her. Her eyes dilated and her breathing became shallow. "I'm sure of a number of things," he said as he leaned down, his lips hovering just above hers. "And I'm sure that you like me, mostly because of how you kissed me back."

"And how was that?"

"Like you had no control."

Before he could give in to the need to kiss her again—and before he made himself go from semi-hard to a full-on erection—he pulled away. The noise that escaped her throat was unmistakably a whimper.

Tripp went back to his task of getting Beth patched up, trying really damn hard not to be so smug about the effect he'd just had on her. But it would've taken a much humbler man than he was to succeed at that, and it didn't help that she caught the look on his face. Her eyes narrowed but surprisingly enough she didn't say anything.

But what did she expect of him? Hell, he wasn't a saint. The woman wanted him. And it wasn't like she was just *any* woman who wanted him, either.

This was Beth he was talking about here. Feisty blond neighbor extraordinaire with a talent for baking (that was beginning to become one of his favorite things) and a mouth that drove him wild (which, at the moment, *was* his favorite thing).

So really, it was only right that he was driving her wild right back.

Fair was fair.

* * *

So Tripp was going to taunt Beth…and look entirely too pleased with himself while he did it.

She took back her earlier assessment of him. He was a cocky, arrogant jerk. It was taking a lot for her to bite her tongue and not inform him of this fact. She forced herself to be quiet as he finished up with her forehead, putting some ointment on the cut before covering it with a bandage.

Another reason she was refraining from saying anything was because she was paying close attention to how he worked. The man had a very gentle touch and she had to stop herself from physically reacting every damn time his fingers brushed across her skin.

This was much easier said than done.

She somehow managed to gain some semblance of control by the time he'd moved on to her hands.

There were minor scrapes on them, and he found a few splinters in her left palm. After she washed her hands he went about pulling them out. She lasted another full minute before she spoke.

"It's mutual," she told him as he started working out the last splinter.

"What's mutual?" he asked, not looking up at her.

"You like me too."

"And what makes you think that?" Even though he was focused on her hands she still caught the grin that turned up his mouth.

"*Know.* Not think."

"All right. What makes you *know* that?"

"You paid my bill at the diner today."

"I ate some of the pie," he countered.

"You ate less than half the pie, but you paid the entire bill."

He pulled out the last splinter before he looked up at her. "Maybe I was just being generous."

"Nope, it was because you like me and wanted to impress me."

"Is that so?" he asked as he moved to the sink and started cleaning up.

"Yes," she nodded.

Tripp didn't say anything as he sterilized the tweezers and put them back in the case. After he threw everything away and washed his hands he leaned back against the counter and looked at Beth. "I think I'm going to need more proof than that."

She took a few steps closer, stopping when she was less than a foot away. "How about because when I fell you were the farthest from me, but the first to get there?"

"Well, I was looking at you when you fell."

"Which was because why, exactly?"

His answer was to reach forward, his hands landing on her hips, and pull her to him. Her breasts were now pressed up against his chest, her thighs aligned with his.

Okay, so she'd be lying to herself if she said that she wasn't a really big fan of this new touching phase in their neighbor-ness.

A really big fan.

"There's also the way you kiss me," she whispered as she gently braced her hands on his chest and leaned up, bringing her mouth to his ear.

"Which is how, exactly?"

What was she doing? This…this was so entirely out of character for her. Being this…forward, and consequences be damned. Yet she couldn't help herself when he was around. Some flirting switch had been flipped.

It was very true that she'd had a little more to drink that night than she usually did. It was also true that she was still just a little bit tipsy, but not tipsy enough to change the very real fact that she wanted him. And no amount of alcohol was going to change that fact. And judging by the man's very prominent erection pressing into her belly, he wanted her just as much.

"Tripp, you kiss me like *you* don't have control." Her teeth grazed his earlobe before she placed an open-mouthed kiss on his neck, a kiss that made him groan. The rumble vibrated through her.

But a moment later she was pulling back, stepping out of his embrace. She didn't even attempt to hide her self-satisfied expression at his now incredulous look.

So they were no longer battling over neighborly problems, but battling wills. That was fine, *perfectly* fine. He'd started this whole back and forth show of who was in more control anyway.

She could fight fire with fire. *Game on, Tripp. Game, freaking, on.*

Though she did wonder what the winner of this little game was going to get...or how they'd figure that out.

"Thank you for getting me cleaned up." She held her hands in the air, showing the fresh Band-Aids he'd placed across her palms before she indicated the bandage on her head. "I appreciate it."

His eyes narrowed, a twitch playing at the corner of his mouth. "You 'appreciate it'?"

"Yes. You'll have to let me know which dessert you'd like as a thank you for it. Patch-me-up Pineapple Upside-Down cake...or something."

A grin overtook his face and he shook his head. "Or something. You get this round, Beth," he said as he pushed off the counter, rounding the island at the center of the kitchen before he headed down the hall. "But the next round is mine," he called out right before the front door shut.

It was then that she realized she wasn't fighting fire with fire.

No, she was *playing* with fire.

Chapter Ten

A Dinosaur Called Flounder

It had been years since Beth had been to a Spring Fling, even longer since she'd participated in one. The thing had almost doubled in size since she was a kid. The fair—complete with a massive Ferris wheel, fun house, merry-go-round, and more booths of games than Beth had the patience to count—was a newer addition to the event.

The real draw was the animals. There was the petting zoo (complete with pony rides), the pig racing pen (where people were crowded around cheering on the hog they wanted to win...and placing bets), and the cow show (which was actually where people dressed up any animal that wasn't a cow into a cow).

Last, but certainly not least, were the vendors. About fifty booths and tents were set up around her, half local and the other half out of towners. There were those trying to sell their handmade goods and crafts, restaurants selling food, a pet adoption booth, and so on, and so on.

The bake sale, where Beth was currently stationed, was set up under a tent that sported the white and royal blue school colors. The school mascot, Paulie the Pirate, was printed on the overhanging border that ran around the whole tent. There were four massive tables set up on each side of the tent, two for the goods, one for the milk and coffee station, and the last was a sign-up station for the 10K color run the following month.

Mel had become the master of fundraisers, always having the next one in the works so that the community was in the know as to exactly what was going on.

Beth got to work with Mel, Dale, and Hamilton on her shift. The boys were on sign-up duty for the 10K…and flirting with every teenage girl who walked up to them. There were currently a group of five gathered around them, twirling their hair and giggling.

"You know every single one of those girls is going to sign up now, don't you?" Beth asked, looking over at Mel. "They don't stand a chance."

"Why do you think I put Dale and Hamilton at the sign-up in the first place?"

"Because you're an evil genius."

"And don't you forget it," Mel grinned before she moved off to check the status of the coffee makers.

Beth turned to look at the crowd of people moving around. It was after one in the afternoon so a lot of them were lining up around the food vendors trying to snag some lunch. As she'd eaten a late breakfast before coming here she wasn't all that hungry…though she could do with some more caffeine.

She hadn't exactly slept well the night before. It had taken her well over an hour to finally fall asleep. And once she had? Well, the rest of the night had been fitful.

Tripp was to blame.

Obviously.

She'd lain in bed, unable to get the events of the day out of her head. A lot had happened, starting with that damn piece of pie at the diner...and her realizing she had a thing for him.

But what was the thing? That was the question, wasn't it? And she had no clue what the answer was. Their flirting had morphed into something else in absolutely no time at all. In fact, the time from pie to kiss had only been about five hours. Five *freaking* hours. Oh dear Lord, that was fast.

Too fast.

Too *freaking* fast.

But whenever she started overthinking things—as she was prone to do—she remembered what his lips felt like on hers. Good Lord, kissing him had been...good.

Too good.

Too *freaking* good.

She was going to need to figure out what she wanted. Stat.

* * *

Tripp made his way through the mass of people that swarmed around him. He hadn't planned on going to the Mirabelle Spring Fling; but had every intention of spending the day working on Koko. He'd just gotten a new alternator he needed to install.

But his plans changed when he saw Beth loading up her SUV that morning.

She'd been wearing a bright blue Pirates T-shirt and jeans

shorts. The woman might be on the shorter side but that fact in no way detracted from her legs. She had fantastic legs.

Tripp found himself thanking the good Lord for the unseasonably warm weather, as it made it possible for her to show off those legs. He'd had a pretty intense fantasy of having those legs wrapped around his waist the night before.

One fantasy among many. All involving Beth.

When he'd left her house he'd walked in his own door and immediately headed for the coldest shower he'd even taken in his life.

It hadn't helped. Didn't even make a dent.

It had been a long time since he'd wanted a woman so much, and if he was being entirely honest with himself, he had *never* wanted a woman at the level he wanted Beth.

Which was why he was currently navigating the crowd in search of her. And when he finally found her he came up short at the sight. She was talking to some guy that Tripp had never seen before. She was beaming up at him, that smile getting bigger and bigger right up until she tipped her head back and laughed.

It was then that the schmuck reached forward, putting his hand on her arm before he pulled her into a hug. Tripp wasn't quite ready for the seething jealousy he felt at seeing Beth in another man's arms.

Yeah, that was... *unexpected.*

To top the whole thing off, when the idiot *finally* let go of her, he held up multiple bags of chocolate chip cookies. That had Tripp moving again.

Those were *his* fucking cookies.

Before Tripp could get to her, the asshole had moved off, but not before giving Beth a wistful look over his shoulder.

"Just keep moving it along there, buddy," Tripp grumbled under his breath.

He was still a good ten feet away from her when she turned to go back behind the table, but as she moved, her eyes came up and landed on him. Her smile was replaced with an expression of surprise, her eyes going wide as she came to a halt and her entire body snapped to attention, like she'd just been shocked.

But within a second that all changed.

She loosened her shoulders, her stance going nonchalant as her body relaxed. She gave him a friendly smile, a smile that clearly said *oh, you're here. No big deal.* Tripp continued to approach until he was standing right in front of her. Close enough to smell the vanilla on her skin…or was it in her hair? He had no idea. What he did know was that the scent was incredible.

She stared up into his face, still trying to look entirely unaffected by his sudden appearance.

She failed.

She might be trying to hide her reaction to him, but her blue eyes gave her away. They were bright with pleasure. Yeah, she couldn't hide that.

And she wasn't the only one who sucked at hiding how she really felt. He was about ten times worse.

"There a reason you're scowling at me right now?" Beth asked, taking a step closer to him.

Yes, because some other guy had just touched her. That was why he was scowling. But rather than answer her, he did something even he couldn't have predicted until the moment he decided to do it.

He kissed her.

Well, he didn't *just* kiss her. No, he needed to prove a point—the point being that no other man was allowed to have his hands on her arms…or anything else, for that matter.

Oh hell, who was he kidding? It had been an eventuality: he was going to do it the second he'd seen her. He'd known he was going to grab her and haul her up against his body. Known he was going to claim her at the first opportunity he got.

Which was what he did.

Not only did she fist her hands in his T-shirt to give herself leverage as she stretched up, but her lips opened immediately to his. There was no resistance, just like the day before. He swept his tongue inside her mouth, tasting her sweetness.

And God, was she sweet.

She was also kissing him back. Her hands tightened in the fabric of his T-shirt as she somehow pulled herself even closer to him. He had absolutely no complaints.

Not a one.

When he finally pulled his mouth back from Beth's—both of them good and truly breathless—he looked down into her beautiful face.

Mine.

That one word took hold in his mind and before he knew it, planted itself firmly and sprouted roots.

Well, that was definitely new. And not something he was going to analyze at the moment, not that he exactly had the brain capacity to analyze anything besides Beth being in his arms.

"How's your head?" He reached up and brushed her hair back and behind her ear so he could get a better look at her forehead.

"It's fine."

"Good." His fingers traced her hairline, moving down the side of her face to her jaw. "Who was that guy?"

"What guy?" Her eyes squinted in confusion.

"The guy who was just being overly friendly with you."

"You mean you? Do you normally just walk up to women in the middle of a crowd, grab them and kiss them?"

"Women in general? No. You? Apparently. Now answer my question: Who was the guy?"

"He means Jameson."

Tripp turned to see Mel a few feet away, standing behind the bake sale table. Her arms were folded across her chest and she was wearing the biggest damn smirk he'd ever seen in his life.

Before Tripp knew it, he was looking back at Beth, but not because he'd turned back. Nope. She'd grabbed his chin and forced his gaze back to hers.

"Did you seriously just kiss me because you're jealous?"

"I'm not jealous of that guy." *Anymore*, he amended in his head. He was the one who currently had Beth in his arms, and had tasted her mouth just moments ago.

"Oh, really now?" Her eyebrows rose high. "Well, to answer your question, Jameson is an old boyfriend. My first boyfriend, to be exact."

"Wasn't he your first kiss, too?" Mel asked.

It wasn't lost on him at all that Mel was trying to be an instigator. She was succeeding in her mission, too.

"Sure was." Beth nodded. "And as far as kisses go, it was—"

But exactly what it was, Tripp would never find out. His mouth covered hers, effectively stopping her from saying another word. As he kissed her, he was determined to make her forget about anything or *anyone* else. But it was Beth who was making him forget.

It had taken him absolutely no time at all to become completely and totally lost in her...and to completely and totally forget that they were in public...and currently surrounded by a hundred or so people. But who the fuck cared about that when she was running her hands up and down his chest...and grazing her teeth along his bottom lip?

What brought Tripp back to the moment was a piercing wolf whistle that echoed in his ears a moment later. He didn't need to look over to know who'd done it. Enough time playing baseball and going horseback riding with Finn had permanently engrained that noise in Tripp's brain.

And as much as he really, *really* wanted to keep kissing the beautiful woman in his arms, he needed to get a grip on himself.

When his mouth left hers—more than reluctantly—she looked up at him and grinned. "Not jealous, huh?"

"Jealous?" Finn asked, now at Tripp's side. "Of who?"

"Jameson Mitchell," Mel answered before anyone else could. "Why?"

"Because, he was flirting with Beth," Tripp told his friend.

"He was not." Beth shook her head. "Next time, you should get all the facts," she said as she pointed over Tripp's shoulder, a gesture that had him turning.

Jameson was a couple of booths down, holding hands with a beautiful and very pregnant redhead. There were two little girls—both sporting strawberry blond hair—at their sides, one pulling on her father's pant leg while she pointed to the very end of the row.

Tripp turned back to Beth to find her looking as smug as a person could look. "He's happily married. Has been for about ten years now. I went to their wedding, actually. Got them a bacon press in the shape of a pig and a griddle that makes their pancakes look like a cow."

He'd been wrong; her expression could get even more smug. A second later she stretched up and brought that smug mouth of hers to his ear, speaking low enough so only he could hear what she said next.

"Looks like I get this round, too, Tripp." She dragged her hands down his chest again, flexing her fingers when she got to his abs. Her nails just pressed through the material of his shirt and into his skin.

He'd lost, all right. He was also quickly learning that when it came to Beth, control was a thing of the past.

* * *

Tripp Black was determined to destroy every last brain cell, ounce of composure, and any semblance of decorum that Beth possessed.

He was doing a pretty damn good job of it, too.

One second she'd been looking up into his scowling face and the next he'd been kissing the breath out of her, something that appeared to be becoming a bit of a habit. But Tripp had gone and upped his game this afternoon.

He'd done all that kissing very publicly.

It wasn't that Beth had a problem with public displays of affection, not in the slightest. But gossip traveled fast around Mirabelle, and for him to have kissed her in front of so many witnesses said a lot…like he didn't care who saw all of that kissing.

Okay, just one more thing to add to the long list of things she was learning when it came to whatever this was with him. It made her stomach flutter.

And as she was learning full well with this man, flutters could be dangerous.

Another thing she was adding to the list of things she was learning about him was Tripp's reaction to her talking with Jameson. It was ridiculous for many, many reasons. The number one reason being that she and Jameson weren't anything more than friends, something that had been true for over a decade and a half now.

That didn't change the fact of the matter, though. Even if Tripp wanted to deny it, he'd been totally jealous. If she didn't know any better, she'd think he was trying to make a claim on her or something. But that would be crazy…wouldn't it? It was too soon for something like that.

Way too soon.

Way too *freaking* soon.

The conversation Beth had had with Mel the other day popped into her brain, the one about men going all caveman. The way Tripp was currently looking down at her definitely made her believe he wanted nothing more than to throw her over his shoulder and carry her off somewhere.

Well, she'd poked the bear with that last little move of hers, now hadn't she? And she'd only just been able to hold on to the last vestiges of her self-restraint as she'd leaned up against his body and run her hands down his perfectly muscled chest a few seconds ago.

She was definitely playing with fire.

It took a force of will to take a step away from him now, but she had to do it for sanity's sake. Because if she stood there looking up into those intensely warm brown eyes of his for one more moment—and with his hands more than possessively placed on her hips—her sanity was going to crumble. She was pretty damn close to letting him carry her off anywhere that he wanted…and she'd enjoy every single moment of it.

Nope. Nope. Nope. That was *not* going to happen. She needed to pull herself together, and it was only because someone was speaking again that she was able to do it. Finn was asking a question and it took everything in her to concentrate on his words.

"It's becoming a bit of a pattern with me walking up while the two of you are making out. This going to become the new norm?"

She really wanted to know the answer to that question, too. She had absolutely no idea what this was…and she really wasn't the type to stay in limbo over something like this. Answers; she needed answers.

But Tripp wasn't giving any. Instead he asked Finn a question of his own. "What are you doing over here?"

"I came for sweets." Finn clapped his hands together before he rubbed them excitedly. "Beth, you still have some of your cookies up for grabs?"

"I sure do." She started moving back to the table, beyond grateful for the distraction. But before she could get behind it, a high-pitched squeal of glee echoed through the air. The instinct to turn toward it was automatic; she'd know that sound anywhere.

Penny came barreling through the crowd, a green triceratops about half the size of her tucked underneath her arm. "Aunt B! Look what I got!" she said excitedly. Though what she actually said was, *wook what I got.*

Her hair was pulled up into pigtails that bounced up and down as she ran full tilt. Beth crouched down, opening her arms wide as Penny ran right into them. She stood with her giggling niece in her arms, looking into those delighted green eyes.

"What did you win?" Beth asked.

"A dinosaur! I named him Flounder."

"Like the fish?" Finn asked.

Beth looked over at him and couldn't help but laugh at his look of utter confusion. "Like the character from *The Little Mermaid*," she explained.

"Except my Flounder isn't a fish. He's a dinosaur," Penny said, holding the stuffed animal out for everyone to get a better look.

"We can see that," Tripp nodded. "How did you get him?"

"Papa! He knocked down all the bottles. He won Grant a bear!" She bounced in her aunt's arms as she pointed behind them.

All heads turned as Wallace and Grant made their way through the crowd. They were hand in hand, and Grant's other arm was wrapped around the neck of a fuzzy black bear. It was just slightly bigger than Penny's dinosaur, the head popping up above his elbow.

Grant was looking around, taking in the commotion that surrounded him with open fascination. It wasn't until he and his grandfather were twenty feet away that he saw Beth standing with Tripp and Finn. He stopped dead in his tracks.

The abrupt halt caught Wallace off guard. The man turned back to look at his grandson, saying something that had Grant shaking his head. Those big green eyes of his went wide as he looked back and forth between Beth and Tripp.

The look of fear that overtook Grant's face was not foreign to Beth. As usual, it made her heart hurt. She reached out for Tripp, the palm of her hand sliding up his forearm. What did it say that she found his warmth a comfort?

It said something that she wasn't going to analyze at the moment.

At her touch, Tripp turned to her, confusion in his eyes. "Why is Grant scared of me?"

"Because lately he's scared of everyone. But I think he's scared of you because of the whole thing with Duke."

"Right then. Well, I'll just have to take care of that, now won't I."

Before Beth could respond Tripp was moving toward Grant and her father.

"Pen, go show Dale and Hamilton Flounder." Beth kissed her niece on the head before setting her down on the ground.

Penny immediately ran off behind the tables and toward the boys, squealing excitedly. "Hammy! Dale! I got a dinosaur! His name is Flounder."

"Like the fish?" Hamilton asked.

Beth turned and followed Tripp, picking up her pace in order to catch up to his long stride.

When Tripp got to Wallace and Grant—the latter was now leaning against his grandfather's legs, looking about ten times more terrified than he had a moment before—he stuck out his hand.

"Hi, Wallace," he said as the two men shook hands.

"Tripp." Wallace nodded. His blue eyes—the exact same color as Beth's—twinkled as his mouth twitched into a smile, making his thick steely gray beard move.

Then Tripp focused entirely on Grant as he crouched down, getting on the little boy's level in one easy move. "Hey, Grant."

"Mr. Tripp," he whispered, shuffling his feet.

"I understand that you and I need to get a few things straightened out."

Grant nodded his head. "I-I was the one taking Duke from your yard. A-and bringing him over to our house. I'm sorry I took him. It-it was wrong."

Beth couldn't help but marvel at what a contradiction her nephew was, because even though he was clearly intimidated, he was still looking Tripp in the eyes.

Looking down at Tripp from her current position, Beth could see his scruffy jaw move as his mouth formed a grin. When he spoke, she could immediately tell that he was impressed with the boy. "You know, Grant, it takes a real man to look another man in the eye and admit he did something wrong."

"It does?" Grant asked imploringly. When Tripp nodded, Grant pushed off his grandfather's legs and stood up straight, squaring his shoulders. "I'm sorry I made you and Aunt B hate each other, too."

"We don't hate each other. Well, at least *I* don't hate your Aunt B," he said, turning to Beth and shooting her that grin of his.

Beth forced herself to look away from Tripp and focus on her nephew. "Goose, I don't hate Mr. Tripp, either."

She actually liked him a little too much. Liked his hands on her body…liked his deep voice whispering things in her ear…liked the feel of his lips on hers. Yeah, all of those things would be permanently ingrained in her brain for the rest of her life.

"You know, Grant," Tripp said, getting the little boy's attention again, "I think that Duke has become attached to you, too. When you were out on the lake, he was sitting at my back door very anxious to get outside, very anxious to get to *you*. He knew you were in trouble."

Well, that was news to Beth. She couldn't have been more wrong about that dog, either.

"He did?" Grant asked, letting go of Wallace's hand and taking a step closer to Tripp.

"Yeah, he did." Tripp nodded. "And he was very upset about it. He's bonded with you too, buddy, and I don't think he'd like it if he didn't get to see you anymore. So I'm going to make a deal with you. When I'm home and not busy with anything—and when you get permission from your aunt—you can come over and play with him."

"I-I can?" Grant asked, his eyes going wide.

"Yes you can. But like I said, you have to get permission first."

"I can do that! Can't I, Aunt B?" he asked, looking up at her with a huge smile on his face.

Beth was left momentarily speechless. She hadn't seen Grant's face light up that much since before Kevin and Colleen had died. A wave of gratitude crashed through her, and she was lucky it didn't knock her off her feet.

What was this man doing to her? Breaking down every last one of her defenses. *That* was what he was doing. For just a second her inability to speak was combined with an inability to breathe.

Was she ready for something like this? To be this vulnerable with a man again?

She forced herself to pull it together and nodded at Grant. "Yes, you can go over and play with Duke when all of those conditions are followed. And what do you say to Mr. Tripp?" she asked Grant.

"Thank you!" Grant was so excited now that he was bouncing on his feet.

"You're welcome," Tripp said as he stood back up.

"Hey Grant," Hamilton called out. "Come over here and show us what you got."

Grant glanced between Beth and Wallace, seeking permission. When they both nodded he shot off in that direction, the bottom of the bear bobbing up and down against the boy's back as he ran full tilt to Hamilton and Dale.

"Well, that was mighty nice of you." Wallace inclined his head in a small nod to Tripp.

"Yeah," Beth agreed, turning to look at the man who'd just made her nephew's day. She reached out and touched his arm…couldn't stop herself. "That was really kind of you to do that for him. I was going to ask yesterday, but I-I got a little distracted…"

…*by your mouth*, she finished in her head.

Tripp's warm brown eyes lit up, and she had absolutely no doubt that he knew exactly what she'd just been thinking. Nor did he leave her in any doubt that he was thinking the same thing when his gaze dipped to her lips for just a second.

"I see that the two of you have changed your tune about each other."

Beth turned to look at her father.

"Or, I at least hope you wouldn't be standing out here kissing some guy you didn't like." He nodded his head in the direction of Beth's hand, still on Tripp's arm.

She pulled her hand away as if she'd been burned, her eyes going wide in horror. "You saw that?"

Wallace reached up and ran a hand through his still very full head of hair, hair that was the exact same shade of dark gray as his beard. "I think very few people who are above four feet tall missed it." He moved his hand down from his head as he focused on Tripp and frowned... or at least tried to. His mouth twitched again as he fought a smile. "I've got my eye on you, Black. Understand?"

"Yes sir," Tripp nodded.

"Good," Wallace said before he moved off to the bake sale table.

Her father's words repeated in her mind as she watched him walk away: *Very few people above four feet tall missed it.* Meaning that Penny and Grant *hadn't* seen it. There was more than a small amount of relief coursing through her body at that information, and a whole hell of a lot of confusion.

She hadn't been over-exaggerating when she'd told her friends the night before that *anything* happening with Tripp (or anyone else, for that matter) would be complicated. And it was complicated for three very specific reasons: Nora, Grant, and Penny.

Beth had never been the type to fool around. She still wasn't. She had relationships, not flings. And now? Well, now a relationship with her also involved the kids.

Would Tripp even want a relationship like that? Would any guy? And what exactly did she want?

Hands were suddenly on her hips; Tripp's hands. They were such strong and firm hands. Steady. Sure. But why was it that when they were on her, she was unsure of everything?

He turned her to face him, and as she looked up into his eyes she decided she was sure of at least one thing: she wanted him.

But it wasn't that simple. It was *never* that simple.

She opened her mouth. To say what? She had no idea. But before she could get her brain to construct even a single sentence, Tripp spoke.

"You and I need to have a conversation."

"We do?"

"Yes." His fingers tightened on her waist as he pulled her closer, the pressure sending a thrill through her body. "Are the kids with Wallace tonight, too?"

"Yes." She nodded.

"And do you have plans? Because I'd like to make you dinner."

Tonight…tonight she was…what was she doing?

Well, since she was supposed to be having a quiet evening with an empty house, she hadn't had any plans that went further than a bubble bath and a bottle of wine. That had sounded absolutely glorious moments ago.

But with the way Tripp was looking at her, she had no doubt that an evening with him would be far more decadent…and dangerous…and would involve her ending up naked.

"I'm not doing anything. But…"

But…but what? Thoughts suddenly failed her as Tripp's hands started to move up and down her sides. He obliterated her thought process, time and time again. Hadn't she just come to the realization that she needed to be *way* more careful when it came to him, especially when she was around the kids?

What the hell was wrong with her?

She took a step back from Tripp's grasp, glancing over her shoulder to where Grant and Penny's attentions were being thoroughly occupied by Dale and Hamilton. She turned back to Tripp, shaking her head. "You don't play fair. I can't think straight when you put your hands on me."

He raised his eyebrows while a smirk turned up the corner of his mouth. "Yeah? Well, that goes both ways, Beth. You haven't exactly kept your hands to yourself, either."

"I know that. And I'm just wondering how much talking we're going to do if we're alone."

"What if I promise I'll keep my hands to myself?" He held his right hand up in a three-finger salute. "Scout's honor."

"You were a boy scout?"

"Eagle Scout," he told her as he dropped his hand to his side.

"Of course you were."

"Beth, the 'alone' part is because I'd like to talk to you somewhere where we aren't surrounded by a crowd of strangers...or interrupted by our nosey—but well meaning—friends. But," he said as that smirk of his transformed slowly into a full-on sexy smile, "if you don't think you can handle it, we can go out somewhere and get dinner."

Ohhhhhhh, no. He did *not* just challenge her. "Your place works just fine. You can cook for me."

"Perfect. It's a date. Six sound good to you?"

"Yes." She nodded.

"See you then. Now I'm going to buy some of your cookies." And with that he turned and headed off to the booth, where Finn was perusing the baked goods.

She couldn't take her eyes off his back, more than slightly overwhelmed by everything that had just happened. This man was a danger to her equilibrium, without a doubt. The path they were heading down was definitely, potentially, dangerous...but she couldn't help herself around him. Case in point: her entire body had warmed and her stomach was all fluttery.

How could it not be? She was going on a date with Tripp Black.

And there was that fear again. Maybe that had a little to do with how long it had been since she'd actually been on a date…almost a year and a half ago.

That one had been when Mick had taken her to dinner and a movie, about six months before their relationship ended.

Huh, maybe there'd been a few signs after all.

Beth headed back behind the table just as another one of Penny's high-pitched squeals rent the air. The little girl tore off again and ran straight to Nora, who was coming through the crowd.

"Nora! I gots a dinosaur!"

Nora scooped up her little sister and continued toward the tent, smiling as Penny went on and on about her new stuffed animal.

"What's his name?" Nora asked.

"Flounder."

"Like the fish?"

"Yes." Penny's little brow furrowed and she frowned. "Why does everyone keep asking me that?"

"Who else asked?"

"Mr. Finn and Hammy." Penny stuck out her free hand and pointed to the tent.

And just that quickly Nora's smile faltered, as well as her step. Her gaze came up and she looked in the direction that Penny indicated.

Hamilton was standing behind his post at the sign-up table, scowling as he looked at Nora. The expression on his face was very similar to the one Tripp had been wearing when he walked up to Beth not ten minutes ago. There was so much conflict in his eyes as he looked at Nora; sadness, mixed with a fair amount of anger.

Nora pulled her gaze from Hamilton and focused back on her sister, forcing a smile back in place as she started walking again. "Clearly they aren't as creative as you," she said as she moved past Hamilton, not even acknowledging him as she headed for Beth at the opposite end of the booth.

Such a quick exchange between the two teenagers, only a few seconds, but Beth had missed absolutely none of it. Not that she could say anything to Nora about it. Conversations of that caliber were strictly off limits.

"Penny," Wallace called out to his youngest granddaughter. "Come over here and pick something out."

"Yes, papa." She gave Nora a quick peck on the check before she was set on the ground and scurried off.

"Can I go out tonight?" Nora asked Beth by way of greeting.

Yup, that was how Nora started most conversations these days, straight to something that she wanted. No *hi, hello,* or even a *fuck you very much.*

Well, at least that last one wasn't spoken in words, though Beth did think that was the expression she got from her niece more often than not.

That wasn't the case today, but Beth wondered if Nora had been distracted by the proximity to Hamilton. It might have been brief but it was very evident to Beth that her niece was trying very hard to put on an air of nonchalance. She couldn't keep up with that *and* her usual contempt for her aunt.

"Who are you going with?" Beth asked, silently praying it wasn't any of Nora's new "friends."

"Monica and Gretchen."

Thank God. Monica and Gretchen had been friends with Nora since pre-school and though they hadn't been around as much as they used to, they hadn't been phased out like Hamilton.

"Where are you going?"

"Bubba's Burgers and then the movies."

Until two years ago the closest movie theater to Mirabelle had been in Tallahassee. People had had to drive over an hour to go see something on the big screen. So the novelty of the new local theater definitely hadn't worn off, and it was *the* place to be on the weekends for a lot of the high school kids.

"What's it rated?" Beth asked.

"PG-13."

"And Monica is driving?"

She was the only one out of the three girls who had a car. Gretchen had already been in two fender-benders and her parents had smartly revoked her license. But Monica was very responsible for a seventeen-year-old; she had to be. Her father was the county sheriff and he didn't tolerate any funny business of any kind.

As for Nora—well, Beth's niece was less than enthusiastic about getting behind the wheel of a car. Understandably so. Even though she had her driver's license she avoided driving as much as possible, though she was fine being driven by someone else.

"And what time will you be back at your grandfather's?"

"Well, that's the other half that I need to ask permission for," Nora said. "Monica and I wanted to stay the night at Gretchen's. We'd go back right after the movie ended, which is at ten."

"It's your grandfather's night with you guys. Did you ask him?"

"I did. And he said it was up to you. I also told him I'd make it up to him on a night of his choice, and we'd have dinner, just the two of us. My treat."

Beth's eyes moved over to her father, who was looking at the pair of them. He nodded his permission. "Well, that was nice of you," she said as she looked back to Nora.

"I'm capable of it sometimes."

Clearly; just not with Beth. "Okay. But I expect a phone call when you get to the McPhersons' house."

"All right. I'll call."

Beth could tell from Nora's tone that she was trying to hold back her exasperation. Because, at seventeen, she was apparently beyond checking in.

Nora's eyes left Beth's, moving to a spot over Beth's shoulder. Tension snapped her niece's shoulders and back into the most rigid posture imaginable. Beth didn't need to turn to know that it was Hamilton who'd caused such a reaction in Nora.

Didn't stop her from turning anyway. Immediately, it was clear to Beth why the scene was no match for Nora's attempted indifference. Both Hamilton and Dale were now very much occupied with another group of girls who'd wandered up.

One of the girls, a pretty blonde with legs longer than any teenager should posses, was laughing as Hamilton handed her a pen. She reached out and grabbed his arm instead, running her fingers over his forearm.

Beth turned back to find Nora already ten feet away. She sighed as she stared at her niece's retreating back, wishing for the millionth time that whatever was going on with Nora and Hamilton would get resolved.

Neither of them seemed happy about the current situation.

A gently nudge at Beth's side had her turning. Mel had two cups of freshly squeezed lemonade in her hands. She handed one to Beth.

"I do not miss being a teenager at all." Mel shook her head.

"You noticed all of that?"

"A blind man wouldn't have missed it."

"True." Beth nodded before she took a sip from her cup. The lemonade was the perfect combination of tart and sweet. "The angst and hormones floating in the air right now is enough to give me hives."

Mel raised her eyebrows. "You're a fine one to talk. I think half of those hormones in the air are leftover from you and Tripp."

At the mention of his name Beth scanned the nearby tables, looking for him. He'd said he was going to buy some baked goods. "They are not. He and I aren't that bad."

"He's gone," Mel said.

"Oh." Beth immediately stopped looking around, wishing she could ignore the flair of disappointment that he'd left. Not that it mattered…she was going to see him tonight.

Oh, good Lord. What the hell was wrong with her? Apparently she was no better than her seventeen-year-old niece.

Not wanting to make eye contact with Mel—who was more observant than was natural for any human being to be—Beth moved closer to the table of baked goods in front of her. There was a huge gap in the middle and as she went to shuffle some things to fill it, she realized the empty space was where her cookies had been.

She immediately turned to Mel, who was standing in the exact same position and sipping her lemonade—all calm, cool, and collected.

"What happened to my cookies?"

Mel took another drink, this one long and slow before she lowered her cup. "Tripp bought them all." Her mouth curved up in a grin.

"Excuse me?" Beth asked. That couldn't be right. There'd been about thirty bags left, and they were priced at five dollars a bag. "He did *not* drop one hundred and fifty dollars on cookies."

"You're right." Mel shook her head. "He didn't. He gave me two hundred dollars."

"*He what!*"

"Two hundred dollars. And that was after Finn bought five bags for himself."

"Why in the world would he do that?" She knew he liked sweets, but come on. Hadn't she just made him a pie the night before?

"Beth, it would appear that Tripp Black doesn't want anyone else eating your cookies." Mel took a step forward and lowered her voice. "And I believe that includes more than just your baked goods."

Chapter Eleven

Living a Little ... or Living a Lot

Music pumped through the speakers on the bathroom counter, the steady bass ricocheting against the tiles that surrounded the room. It was loud, but not loud enough to drown out the thoughts that were bouncing around inside Beth's skull.

What was going to happen tonight?

Her stomach flipped for the hundredth time and she reached for the glass of wine on the counter. She'd been nursing the merlot for over an hour, making it last all the way through the bath she'd indulged in.

Instead of cancelling her earlier agenda, she'd decided to just move things up. She'd hoped sinking below the foamy hot water would help to relax her. It had, until her overactive imagination had ventured off into thinking about Tripp...and the evening...and his mouth on hers...and then his mouth everywhere else.

Her plan had kind of spiraled after that. She'd left the tub more flushed than ever and had to take a cold shower to cool herself down.

It had worked for the most part, but she definitely wouldn't need to wear any blush tonight. She'd gone light with her makeup, anyway. Just a little mascara and eyeliner, and a touch of bronze eye shadow. There was no point even bothering with lipstick; she was under absolutely no illusions that lipstick had a prayer of staying on her mouth.

She wasn't kidding herself with Tripp's "hands off" promise. It wasn't that she didn't think he was a man of his word, because she did. It was just that it was becoming blatantly clear that there was something going on between the two of them that neither could suppress.

She glanced into the mirror as she downed the last of her wine, then set the now empty glass on the counter. "What am I getting myself into?" she asked herself as she started to pull out the big, turquoise, Velcro rollers that stuck out in a halo around her head.

Well, the answer to that question might be figured out very shortly. In twenty minutes, to be exact.

Beth fidgeted with the belt on her robe as she headed for the walk-in closet that was accessible from the bathroom. It was large enough that both Kevin and Colleen's clothing had fit inside.

Now, with only Beth's things filling the racks, it was probably about one-third full. Since her weekly outfits consisted mainly of scrubs, she had a little less in her wardrobe than some. And really, some of the things in there needed to be tossed, something that was made even more apparent as she ran her palm down a pale yellow dress with pilled material. She grabbed a gray cardigan that she hadn't worn in over a year, spotting a hole on the shoulder.

When was the last time she'd gone shopping for clothes? With a pang she realized it had been shortly before Colleen's death. Her sister had come up to Tallahassee with Nora and the three of them had spent the day shopping.

There'd been one department store, where all three of them had loaded up their carts until they were overflowing. When they'd gone into the dressing rooms it had been a revolving opening of doors as they'd tried on outfit after outfit, having their own little fashion show.

Beth had spotted a royal blue dress almost the second she'd walked into that store. It was sleeveless, with a high rounded collar and about five inches of matching blue lace that went to the top of the bustline. The back of the dress was the same as the front, with just a little lace at the top.

All she'd been able to think as she looked at it was, *it's sooo pretty.*

But the second she'd looked at the price tag she'd known she wasn't going to buy it. On sale it was seventy dollars, which was a little pricey for something she wouldn't wear all that often. Not only that, but there'd been no specific occasion that she needed it for. She would've been buying it just to buy it, which wasn't something she did. When it came to clothes she usually bought things more for purpose than to be pretty.

"Just try it on," Colleen had said, tossing it into the basket.

As Beth unloaded her loot in the dressing room, she'd hung the blue dress on the back of the door, separate from everything else. For the next twenty minutes, while she worked her way through the other clothes she'd grabbed, it just hung there taunting her. She was almost done with her stack of clothes when she finally gave in and tried it on.

When Beth walked out of her room, both Colleen and Nora had been standing outside waiting for the next round.

"Oh my gosh, Aunt B. You *have* to buy it," Nora said immediately.

"She's right," Colleen agreed. "That needs to be in your closet."

"It's too much for something I don't *need.*"

"Stop being so practical. Sometimes it's not about what you *need,* Beth. It's about what you *want.* Live a little."

Beth pulled herself from the memory of her sister, a smile tugging at her mouth as she moved to the back of the closet. The blue dress hung from the hanger, *still* unworn and with the price tags *still* attached. She reached out, rubbing the soft, stretchy fabric between her thumb and forefinger.

"Live a little," she whispered before she reached up and pulled it from the hanger.

* * *

The steady beep from the oven filled the kitchen for a full five seconds, signaling that it was preheated. Duke lifted his head from where it rested on his stretched out paws, and the moment the noise ended the dog barked in response. He looked back and forth between Tripp and the offending object that had created the noise, making sure his master was aware.

"I heard it, buddy," Tripp told the dog as he walked over to the oven. He pulled the door open, stepping back as a wave of 350-degree air escaped in a burst.

The lasagna, covered in foil, sat waiting on the counter. Tripp transferred it to the middle rack before closing the door and setting the timer for forty-five minutes. After that he'd have to take the foil off and cook it for an additional fifteen. As it was five minutes to six, dinner would be ready a little after seven.

"Perfect timing." He rubbed his hands together as he headed for the front door and walked outside.

It was a clear, cool evening. The sun hung low and was starting to paint the sky different colors. They looked like subtle strokes of a brush at the moment, touches of pinks and yellows. But in no time at all they would become deeper shades of purple and orange.

He had a feeling it wouldn't take much convincing to get Beth to join him on the deck for a drink to go along with their conversation. They had over an hour before they could eat anyway; might as well watch the sunset, too.

Tripp found himself grinning as he mounted the front steps to Beth's porch. How could he not? The evening laid out before him was going to consist of time spent with Beth. And though there was the whole hands-off condition, he could keep himself in check.

As he raised his hand to knock, he took a deep steadying breath. His fist rapped the door once before it opened with a suddenness that caught him off guard. But it was nothing, *nothing* compared to what happened when he saw what was on the other side of that door, or more accurately *who*.

Words failed him. His brain had left his body and he didn't know how to talk, let alone breathe anymore.

Beth stood on the threshold, her blond hair falling around her shoulders in soft, thick waves that begged for a man's hands. *His* hands. Her blue eyes popped, the color never more vibrant than at that moment, and he had no doubt it had everything to do with her dress.

And dear God, that dress. It just might be the most provocative thing he'd ever seen in his life. Don't get him wrong; she didn't look immodest. Not even in the slightest. It was more the subtlety of it. The lace at the top showed just a hint of her cleavage before transitioning to the solid blue material, material that flowed down her body, hitting at about mid thigh.

There was no outlining or accentuating of her lovely curves in this dress. For the most part it hung loose, giving just a little hint of the wonder that lay beneath.

And then there were her legs—magnificent things that they were—which ended in yellow wedges, her pink toenails peeking out.

At that moment Tripp knew he was good and truly screwed. Why in the hell had he promised a hands-off evening? It was going to be the sweetest torture, looking but not touching.

As his eyes wandered back up her body and to her face, he saw the confusion in her eyes and the frown on her mouth.

"Don't tell me you came over here to cancel."

At her words he somehow regained the ability to speak. "No." He shook his head as he swallowed, that one word coming out just a tad bit strained. "Not cancelling."

"Then what are you doing on my doorstep? Did you think I was going to get lost or be late? Because I still have"—she glanced at the small silver watch on her left wrist before she looked up at him again—"three minutes. And I was literally walking out the door when you knocked."

"Neither." He shook his head, hoping the motion would clear it a little. It didn't. "Just because you live next door doesn't mean I'm not picking you up for our date."

"Oh." Her mouth rounded on the word before transforming into a smile. It was like looking at the sun.

"You look...God, you look stunning, Beth."

"Thank you." The pleasure in her eyes at his words was unmistakable. "I, uh, let me just..." She held up her right hand where the keys to her house dangled from her fingers.

She tucked her small purse under her arm as she grabbed the handle and pulled the door shut, stepping down to the porch. The move put her about six inches away from him, and he couldn't bring himself to move back, so when she turned, she ran right into him.

Just that quickly he failed in his hands-off mission. They had been together for less than sixty seconds, too.

Instinctively he reached out to steady her, his hands on her bare shoulders. He didn't mean to do it, didn't mean to skim his palms down her arms, but he did it anyway. Another thing that he *really* shouldn't have done was take a deep breath.

Vanilla. All he smelled was vanilla. It filled his lungs and head.

Somehow—the *how* of which he had no idea—he let go of her and took a step back. It wasn't remotely what he wanted to do. Nope. What he wanted to do was pull her up against him...feel more of her...feel all of her. What he wanted to do was lean down and take her mouth, dip his tongue past her lips and taste her. And he wanted to do a whole hell of a lot more, all of which did not involve stepping away from her.

But he needed to get his shit together. Stat. Because if he didn't let go of her, he wasn't going to be able to stop touching her. This thing with Beth wasn't about a game of control to be won. No, it was about something else…about figuring out what was going on with the two of them…what could go on after this.

He'd come to that realization at the Spring Fling, when he'd kissed her and all he'd been able to think was *mine*.

That being said, if Tripp wasn't much mistaken—and he was pretty sure that he wasn't—Beth looked more than a little bit disappointed when his hands fell away from her body.

"You ready?" he asked, taking another step back.

She nodded, and they headed across the lawn to his house. He'd never wanted to reach over and hold a woman's hand more than in that moment. It took everything in him to resist. He was just going to have to be content with the close proximity.

Fat fucking chance.

When they walked in the front door, Duke was there to greet them. He headed straight for Beth, wagging his tale excitedly. Beth set her purse on the side table before she bent forward and scratched the dog's head. Duke's eyes closed dreamily and he sat on his back legs, more than thrilled with Beth's ministrations.

"It's like there was never a feud between our two houses," Tripp said.

She looked up at him, her hands continuing to move through Duke's fur. "A feud between our two houses?" She raised her eyebrows. "How very…Shakespearean of you."

"Well, that's as far as the Shakespeare is going to go. Because I'm sorry to tell you I won't be standing outside the window and spouting sonnets to you."

"Oh no? Well, that's thoroughly disappointing. Should I just see myself out?" She asked, pointing back to the door.

"I've got wine."

"Oh, well in that case." Beth patted Duke's head before she straightened, grabbing her purse and walking to Tripp.

"After you." He waved his hand in front of him, letting her lead the way, mostly so he could get a glimpse of this dress of hers from behind.

Big mistake. *Huge.*

The material flowed down her back, and as she walked it swayed in the most tantalizing way around her hips and thighs…and her butt. He was absolutely checking out every single part of her that he could lay his eyes on.

"Dinner won't be ready for another hour or so. I figured we could have a drink and a little conversation."

When she got to the bar, she turned to look at him over her shoulder. "An hour. I feel like you led me over here under false pretenses."

"False pretenses?" he asked as he walked past her and into the kitchen.

"You said dinner was at six."

"I said no such thing." He shook his head, rounding the counter so that he was in front of her. He didn't take his gaze from her face as he reached to the side and pulled two wineglasses from the cupboard, setting them on the counter in front of him. "I said come over *at* six. A dinner time was never established."

"And what are we eating for dinner?"

"Lasagna. Made from scratch."

"Sauce too?" she asked in challenge.

"What kind of an amateur do you take me for? The only thing I didn't make were the noodles. I know who I'm dealing with tonight, Ms. Break-and-Bake-Cookies Are A Sin."

"They are." She nodded. "The only thing more blasphemous is boxed cake."

"I'll remember that. How do you feel about red wine?" He held up the bottle for her to see. "It's a Cabernet. Or is that on your list of *no-no's*, too?"

She narrowed her eyes and shook her head, fighting a smile. "No, it is not on my list of *no-no's*. Cabernet is on my list of all things good."

"Perfect." He reached for the drawer next to him, pulling out a corkscrew and aerator.

"So, speaking of cookies. You have a pretty good stock of them now. It was a rather expensive investment, though."

Tripp fitted the sharp tip of the screw to the cork before he started to twist. "I would've paid more."

"Is that so?"

"Without even batting an eye."

"Why?" She shifted on her feet as she placed her elbows on the counter and leaned forward.

When the screw couldn't go down any more, he pulled the cork out with an easy tug before looking up at Beth. "Why do you think? Because I didn't want any other guy out there getting any ideas."

"What sort of ideas are those?"

He reached for the aerator, glancing down as he fit it into the top of the bottle. He poured each glass about a third of the way full before he stopped, setting the bottle on the counter and lifting his gaze to Beth.

"The kind of ideas I'm currently having in regards to you."

"Which are?"

Well, there was this new insane jealousy that he'd never had before. He didn't like other men touching her, let alone talking to her. Another revelation he'd had at the Spring Fling. Then there was the fact that he couldn't get her out of his head.

Good luck on ever achieving that last one.

He grabbed both glasses of wine as he rounded the counter and stopped in front of her. She reached for the glass he held out, her fingers brushing his as she took it. Such a simple thing, such a small light touch...but he felt it everywhere. Her warmth spread up his arm, setting him on fire. He took a deep breath to steady himself and immediately regretted it. Again, the scent of vanilla on her skin filled his lungs, clouding his brain.

"That's two questions you've asked. It's my turn to get some answers."

"Okay, I counted more of an answer and a half from you, but you can go." She shrugged. "What do you want to ask me?"

So, so many things.

"Do you want to sit outside?" He nodded to the back door. Maybe the fresh air would help him remember how to process coherent thoughts.

"Sure." She nodded as she turned and headed for the door. "Does that count as a question?" she asked as she looked over her shoulder at him, her blue eyes sparkling.

There was something mischievous going on with her tonight, and he couldn't wait to find out what was going on in that beautiful brain of hers.

"No," he shook his head. "It does not."

"Shame." She faced forward again as she made her way through the living room. "That was such an easy one to answer."

"Are you nervous or something?" he asked as he moved to her side, getting to the door before her to open it.

"About what you could possibly ask me?" Her eyes met his as she passed him and walked out onto the deck. "No."

Tripp waited for Duke to follow Beth out before shutting the door. "Why not?"

She pointed to the far end of the deck, where an all-weather wicker sofa and glass coffee table sat just beneath the extended roof. He nodded, following her as she headed for it. When she sat down, she crossed her legs, and the hem of her dress rose higher on her thigh, showing just a little more of her flawless skin.

He took a seat next to her, sinking into the cushion, leaving just enough space between them to avoid the temptation of accidentally brushing up against her.

Though really, there was no such thing as avoiding temptation when it came to Beth. He could be on the other side of the county…scratch that, he could be on the other side of the *country* and it still wouldn't be enough space.

Beth took a sip of wine before she settled back in her seat. "This is good." She held up her glass.

"Glad you like it." He nodded before taking a sip of wine himself.

"So to answer your question, I'm not nervous because I don't think you'd ask me anything that I really didn't want to answer. And if for some reason you did, you wouldn't push it if I told you *no*."

"So you trust me?"

"Yes, I do."

"And what led to that revelation?"

"Nope," she shook her head and held three fingers up in the air. "By my tally I just answered three questions. It's my turn now."

"Okay." He waved his hand in the air in a *please proceed* gesture.

"What are these *ideas* you have when it comes to me? These *ideas* you don't want anyone else to have?"

Tripp settled into his seat, stretching his legs out in front of him as he rested his wineglass-free arm on the back of the sofa, right behind Beth, close but not touching. But damn did he want to reach forward and wrap one of her blond curls around his finger.

He couldn't do that, though. He needed to focus on answering. Not that he had a problem with answering, either. He was pretty sure he'd tell Beth anything she wanted to know.

"Well, one idea is that your mouth tastes better than any baked good I've ever had, and I don't want anyone else to figure that out."

Heat flared in her eyes and she shifted, the tips of her hair brushing across his forearm and tickling his skin. "Is that so?"

"Yes, and it stands to reason that if your mouth tastes that good, then the rest of you will, too."

"You think so?" Her eyebrows rose as she lifted her glass to her mouth. If he kissed her now he'd be able to taste that wine on her lips.

"I do. And I don't want anyone else *testing* that theory out."

She lowered the glass, revealing a pleased smile. "And do you think you're going to get to test this theory out?"

"God, I hope so."

Beth reached over, grabbing the glass of wine from his hands before she uncrossed her legs and leaned forward. She set both glasses on the table before she pulled herself up from the sofa, turning to stand in front of him. "I hope so, too."

Those words distracted him beyond all reason. How could they not? She *wanted* him to taste her all over. He wasn't going to survive this night. That stupid promise of his was going to kill him, a fact that was proven just seconds later. Because what happened next almost had Tripp swallowing his tongue.

Beth reached for the hem of her dress with one hand, pulling the blue fabric up and exposing more of her thighs. And then? Well, and then she was leaning forward, her hand landing on his shoulder as she slid her knees to either side of his thighs and straddled him.

"Beth," he whispered her name as she settled herself on his lap. "What are you doing?" The last word came out on a groan as she pressed the very heat of her onto his rapidly growing erection.

"You wanted to know why I trust you?" she asked as her hands moved down to his chest, palms flat, fingers circling.

"I do." Heat and desire flooded through every part of him at her touch and he had to grab the sofa to prevent himself from moving his hands to her body.

"I trust you because you went out on that lake to get Grant without a second thought. I trust you because you told Grant he could come over here and play with Duke, and I know you did it solely for him and not because you were trying to impress me. I trust you because I have no doubt what an effort it's costing you right now not to touch me."

"I promised you." His words came out hoarse and strained, probably because he was having trouble breathing...and his throat had gone dry.

"Scout's honor," she repeated his pledge. "But the thing is, Tripp, I was never a girl scout." Both of her hands were on his shoulders again and she slid them to the back of his neck, her fingers spearing through his hair as she leaned down and covered his mouth with hers.

Resisting her wasn't an option. Stopping a bullet with his bare hands sounded like a more possible task than stopping a kiss from Beth. Her tongue pushed passed his lips and he welcomed her into his mouth.

He was right, she did taste like wine.

It took a force of will he had no idea he possessed to keep his hands fisted on the cushions next to him. He still hadn't made a move to touch her. He couldn't, because if he did, he was done for. He needed to hear her say it, and until the words left her mouth, he was going to hold to his promise.

As if she knew what he was waiting for, she moved one of her hands from the back of his head, sliding her palm down his arm and to his wrist.

"I want you to take back your promise, Tripp." She'd pulled back from his mouth just slightly to whisper the words, still hovering close enough for her breath to mingle with his. "I want your hands on me." Her lips brushed over his in the softest of kisses as she brought his hand up and placed it on her thigh. "I want you to touch me everywhere." She pushed his hand up under the skirt of her dress, and his fingertips brushed lace and satin. "I want you."

Chapter Twelve

Want

Beth's friends had advised her to make a move on Tripp. Now she'd done it, and what a move it was.

She currently had a very strong and powerful man between her legs. But the way he was looking at her—like a man barely holding it together—it led her to believe she had *all* the power in the moment.

Or she'd had the power right up until she said the words, "I want you."

Just that quickly Tripp was moving into action. His hand on her thigh moved around to her butt, pulling her against him with a firm tug. She gasped as she fell forward, her breasts pressed up to his hard chest. His free hand came up to the back of her head, his fingers delving into her hair as he slanted his mouth over hers.

The hunger in his kiss was more intense that anything Beth had ever experienced. It had no rival. Nothing came close.

There was no gentleness in the possessive way that he held her. Nothing sweet or simple in how his tongue delved into her mouth, demanding from her the same that he was giving. He made her entire body come to life. Made her desperate for more. Made her desperate for everything he offered.

His hand in her hair tightened, not too much to hurt, but just enough to make her scalp tingle with pleasure. He pulled her mouth from his, his lips sliding down to her throat.

The deep need that burned low in Beth's belly spread, the desperate throbbing between her legs now unbearable. She started to move against him, seeking the pressure that she craved. And oh, did she find it.

Tripp was gloriously hard, his cock straining the zipper of his jeans. Just moving over him was making her more than a bit delirious. She was pretty sure she was going to lose her damn mind when he was actually inside of her, which she was hoping would be happening here shortly.

"Tripp." His name escaped her mouth on a low throaty moan but any other words she'd been about to speak were cut off. He nipped at the sensitive skin just above her shoulder and her entire body shuddered.

She'd been slightly distracted by everything else—rightfully so—and hadn't noticed when his hand slipped from her hair to her back. It wasn't until he pulled the front of her dress down that she realized he'd undone the zipper. The material fell away from her body, the straps catching at her elbows.

"Look at you," he whispered reverently as he pulled the material from her arms and freed her. The strapless bra she wore was black lace over a nude base, giving the illusion of see-through material over bare skin.

"You said you wanted my hands on you." He reached up, pushing her hair behind her shoulders before he trailed his fingers down her throat and to her collarbone. It was the lightest of touches, just the very tips of his fingers across her skin.

She nodded, moving her hips again in a not even remotely subtle move. "Yes."

Tripp's nostrils flared as he took a deep breath. "I've imagined touching you like this more times than I can count," he said, tracing the swells of her breasts. "Imagined what it would be like to kiss every inch of your body. To learn the taste of you here." He touched the valley between her breasts.

"And here." He was at the front of her bra, rasping his thumb over the puckered nipple that was just visible through the fabric. "And here." His palm went flat as it slid to her belly. He ran his forefinger around her belly button before moving lower.

His hand delved beneath the fabric of her dress, his fingers at the very top of her panties. They matched her bra, more black lace and nude satin. He tugged at the lacy top just slightly before letting them fall back into place and moving down the front. It was then that he was touching her through the thin material, giving her just a bit of pressure where she wanted him the most.

Then he pulled her panties to the side. Beth grabbed onto his shoulders as he gently spread her, tracing his fingers over her folds. "I want to learn the taste of you here."

"I want you inside me."

"Which just so happens to be another want of mine," he said as he slid a finger inside of her.

The gasp that escaped her mouth was followed by a low moan. Neither could be helped, nor could they be stopped.

"You're so wet," he marveled as he pulled his finger out of her.

When he pushed back in he slipped two inside. "So perfect."

"Oh God." Her grip on his shoulders tightened, her nails digging into his skin through his shirt.

Tripp leaned forward and opened his mouth at the base of Beth's throat. His tongue rasped over her skin as he moved down to her breasts. "I need you naked," he groaned as he pulled at her bra with his teeth.

"Then what the hell are you waiting for?"

"That's a very good question," he said as he pulled his fingers out before pushing them back in. "I quite possibly could be waiting for us to be a little less exposed. Unless you're a bit of an exhibitionist."

It was at that moment that she remembered where they were, and she turned and looked around.

"No one can see us, Beth." He smiled against her skin, and she could hear the grin in his voice. "Not unless they come right up to the shoreline, or walk into my backyard." He pushed his thumb to her clit as he continued to move his fingers in and out of her.

The next moan out of Beth's mouth was in no way quiet, and it echoed through the evening air. She would've been embarrassed if she hadn't been going out of her mind with pleasure.

"Though, that doesn't eliminate the possibility of us being overheard." His mouth was on her throat again, trailing kisses along her jaw and to her lips. "And I don't think you'll be getting any quieter, so that could be a problem."

"Tripp." Beth grabbed his head in her hands, her fingers in his hair as she tugged. She pulled until he was just far enough away so that she could look down into his face, see the desire in his brown eyes. "Take me to bed," she demanded.

More of that barely controlled heat flared through his eyes. The glorious pressure that Tripp's fingers had been providing disappeared as he pulled his hand from between their bodies.

"Hold on," he told her as he wrapped his arms around her. He palmed her butt, getting a good grip of a cheek in each hand, before he leaned forward and stood.

Beth wound her legs around his waist, locking her ankles together and holding onto his shoulders. "Not letting go." She pressed her lips to his in a quick kiss before he adjusted her in his arms, holding her with one hand for a moment so he could let them inside the house.

He opened the door with ease, returning his hand to her ass as he stepped over the threshold, and kicked the door closed with his foot. His mouth captured hers as he made his way through the house, thrusting his tongue past her lips and making her squirm in his arms. She was vaguely aware that they were moving down a hallway, Tripp's boots echoing on the hardwood floor with each step he took.

He didn't lay her down on the bed when they made it to his room. Instead he moved his hands from her butt to her thighs, and then up to her waist as he let her slide down his body. Not until her feet were firmly on the floor did he pull back from the kiss, his lips hovering just above hers as they both let out unsteady breaths. When he shifted back a step, her dress fell to the floor, puddling around her feet.

And there she stood—in nothing but her strapless bra, matching panties, and wedge heels. There was just enough light from the setting sun streaming through the windows to illuminate the room. Tripp's eyes raked over her body in a way that almost, *almost,* made her knees quake.

"Do you have any idea how beautiful you are?" he asked as he reached out, placing his hands on her hips.

Her face flushed, the burn moving all the way down to her toes. She wasn't usually one to get tongue-tied…except, apparently, with Tripp. She couldn't find her own words to respond.

"I look at you and I forget everything except the color of your eyes. I touch you and I get lost in how your skin feels under mine." His hands trailed up her sides, making her shiver. "And then I kiss you," he whispered as he stepped closer to her, his hands slipping around to her back and pulling her up against him. "And I never want to stop." His mouth covered hers, taking possession in an instant.

His hands roamed over her body, up her spine, across her hips, down to her thighs, touching every part of her that he could. But why should he get to be the only one who did the touching? She needed her hands on his skin like she needed to breathe.

The buttons of his shirt proved to be simple enough to pull free. Good thing, too, because if they'd been the least bit difficult she would have ripped the front of his shirt open.

When each and every button was undone she pushed his shirt away and slid her hands down his sides. Palms flat, she ran them to his abs and then up to his chest. He groaned into her mouth as her exploration continued to his nipples, her fingers circling.

She needed more of him, needed to touch every part of him. Her hands skimmed down, down, down until she was at the front of his jeans. The top button was another that popped free with ease, and as she went for the zipper she couldn't stop herself from tracing the outline of his straining cock.

And just that quickly her hands were pulled away and pinned to her sides. The whimper that came out of her throat couldn't be stopped. Tripp pulled his mouth from hers, skimming his nose along her jaw.

"Beth?" He whispered her name and it came out all sexy and gravelly.

"I want to touch you."

He pulled back just enough to look at her, his chocolate brown eyes so full of desire and heat it threatened to set her toes on fire. "Believe me, there's nothing I want more than your hands on me...Well, that isn't true"—his mouth quirked to the side—"I want my hands on *you* more. But if you continue to touch me there I'm going to lose the last ounce of rational thought that I'm holding onto."

"And what happens when you lose it?"

He shifted his body and she inhaled unsteadily as the hard length of his cock brushed against her belly. Oh, how she wanted to feel him in her hands. Know the length of him. The weight of him.

"I throw you on this bed and fuck you hard and fast."

Yes please.

Beth's stomach flipped in anticipation. For the second time that night she asked, "What the hell are you waiting for?" She tugged to free her arms from his grasp, but he refused to let her go, his hold firm.

"I'm waiting for a number of things, Beth. First on the list? You still aren't naked." He let go of her hands and before she even had a second to react, he'd hooked his fingers in the sides of her panties and was pushing them down. They hadn't even hit the floor before he was reaching around her and had the hooks at the back of her bra undone.

"Well, look who has quick hands and nimble fingers," she said as her bra fell to the floor, too.

"You haven't seen anything yet."

Within the next second Beth went from being vertical to horizontal, the movement freeing her of her shoes and the clothes that had puddled around her ankles. She was flat on her back in the middle of the bed, Tripp firmly stationed between her thighs.

"And now we get to number two, which just so happens to be exploring your perfect breasts." His mouth covered one of her breasts, sucking her nipple deep into his warm, wet mouth. One of his hands closed over her other breast, squeezing not so lightly. The pressure was delicious and made all the more so when his thumb rasped over her puckered nipple.

It was a moment or two before he pulled his mouth away from her breast and kissed his way across to the other. A shiver ran through her body as cool air wrapped around her newly exposed nipple, damp from Tripp's mouth.

He looked up at her, the smile on his lips wicked. "Cold?"

"Not even a little bit." She shook her head, her hair rustling across the comforter. "Actually, I'm quite the opposite."

"Is that so?" he asked right before he rasped his tongue across her other nipple.

"*Yes!*"

"Maybe we should cool you off." He blew across the spot he'd just licked and her eyes were rolling to the back of her head.

"God, Tripp." She writhed against him, unable to stop herself as he pulled that nipple into his mouth a second later. "Not helping."

He let go of her breast as he started to kiss his way down her abdomen. "Then the next thing on my list *really* isn't going to help."

His weight left the mattress and Beth opened her eyes just as he grabbed her waist and pulled. "Tripp!" she gasped as he brought her right to the edge of the bed.

The sure, steady weight of his palms ran up the back of her calves and to her knees as he placed her legs over his shoulders. "And now we get to number three," he said as he spread her thighs apart.

Apparently the man was hell bent on taking his time, and he did just that as he kissed, nipped, and licked his way up the inside of her left leg. He started at her knee and stopped just before he got to where she was desperate for his mouth…and then he moved to her right knee, repeating the entire process.

She was panting by the time he finally buried his face between her thighs, and started kissing, nipping, and licking her there.

"Fuck," he groaned, the vibration of his voice shooting through her. "I was right. You taste incredible." He slipped two fingers inside of her as his tongue found her clit.

Beth cried out as her spine arched off the bed. Her hands went to the back of his head, her fingers in his hair, holding him to her. Though, with the way he was feasting on her, it wasn't as if he had any intention of leaving any time soon.

But just to make sure…

"Don't stop. Please don't stop." Yup, she was still panting.

He pulled his mouth away for just a second, his fingers continuing their delicious push and pull as he looked up her body and found her eyes. "I'm not stopping until you're coming across my tongue. Understand?"

She nodded but he apparently needed more than that.

"Say it, Beth," he demanded as he thrust his fingers into her harder.

"I-I understand." She tugged on his hair, not all that gently either, until he was exactly where she wanted him.

The pressure of his fingers inside of her disappeared, and a moment later both of his hands were at her waist. His grip moved higher, his palms and fingers spanning her ribcage on either side as he held on to her.

His tongue speared into the very core of her again, and again, and again before he moved his attention to her clit. It was a constant back and forth, bringing her to the edge before pulling away. Lapping at her folds and nibbling on the sensitive skin of her inner thighs before returning to the center of her and starting all over.

"Tripp, *please.*" How was it that he was the one on his knees but she was the one begging? Because his mouth was magic; that was why.

She leaned up just a little to look and it was the most erotic thing she'd ever seen in her life. Watching as his head moved between her thighs, watching as his mouth worked over her core. Lips sucking, teeth grazing. His beard rasped against her skin and his tongue licked and pressed against her clit.

The ability to hold herself up any longer was gone, and she collapsed back onto the bed, letting the sensations overtake her.

True to his word, he never actually stopped his attention between her legs. He'd just taken a few detours here and there to get her to the final destination. And ohhhh man, when he got her there…

Wave after wave of pleasure rolled through her body, spreading out to her limbs and the very tips of her fingers and toes. Her back arched off the bed; her hands fisted in his hair as she screamed his name and who only knew what else.

Tripp's grip on her sides tightened, his fingers pushing into her flesh as he held onto her. He brought her down from her orgasm with slow steady licks of his tongue and she trembled with the aftershocks that continued to pulse through her, her legs and arms shaking.

When she opened her eyes, it was to find Tripp looking up at her, that wicked grin of his still turning up his lips. He leaned forward, placing a kiss next to her belly button before he pulled her legs from his shoulders and stood before her.

"Damn." He shook his head as he reached up, wiping his mouth with the back of his hand. "The sounds you make when you're coming are the sexiest sounds I've ever heard." He took a few steps back and sat on the chair behind him. "I'm going to need to hear those again, but the next time I'm going to be buried inside of you when you make them." He leaned forward and started untying his boots.

Beth sat up, pulling her legs underneath her in a fluid move and kneeling on the bed. "Is that so?"

"It is." He nodded, not looking up as he pulled off one boot and then the other. His socks joined the pile a moment later.

"And you think you can?"

His head came up and he stood. "'That a challenge?"

Her eyes raked over his body, and for more than a moment she forgot his question. There weren't words to describe how unbelievably sexy he was. No words. And he was hers…or was for at least the night.

His dark brown hair was tousled from her hands, and her fingers itched to dive into it again. The sleeves of his gray denim shirt were rolled up to the elbow, showing off his tanned forearms, while the front of it hung open, exposing his chest.

His muscles rippled and flexed as he crossed the room to her, and when he stopped in front of her she reached out. Her hands glided up to his shoulders, pushing his shirt away from his body. He let it drop from his arms and it fell to the floor, leaving him entirely bare chested in front of her.

Now this wasn't the first time that Beth had seen Tripp with his shirt off, but that was before...before he'd ever touched her...before he'd ever kissed her...before she'd realized how much she wanted him.

And oh, how she wanted him.

She ran her palms over his shoulders and biceps, and then to his left side where she traced the tattoo inked across his ribs. Her fingers moved to his chest, touching the light dusting of brown hair that trailed down to his abs...and arrowed past the waistband of his jeans.

Speaking of his jeans, they were still unbuttoned and riding low on his hips, like they would fall down with the simplest tug. The zipper was still up but there was very little distance from the point where it joined to where the outline of his erection began. Apparently Tripp Black didn't wear boxers or briefs. Nope, the man went commando.

Beth licked her lips as her eyes came back up to meet his. "It is." She nodded as she grabbed the tab of his zipper and pulled down. "You think you can rise to the challenge?" She asked, slipping her hand into his jeans and wrapping her hand around his cock.

He was heavy in her hand, hard and hot. She stroked the length of him, enjoying the feel of every single velvety inch.

The deep masculine groan that rumbled out of his chest filled the room. "Beth, there is no think. Only know."

"Really?" She let go of him, moving both hands to his sides. Her prediction was correct; his jeans did fall from his hips with a simple tug, and slid down his legs. He stepped free from them, standing before her completely naked.

She wrapped her hand around his freed erection, the question of him being *up* for anything clearly answered. Her eyes didn't leave his as she moved her hand up and down, base to tip, swiping her thumb over the head. His nostrils flared with his next unsteady breath and she knew he was barely holding it together. He was so close to her, his chest hair tickling her nipples, his face inches from hers as she stretched up and closed the distance.

"Prove it," she whispered, pressing her mouth to his.

"Oh, but I'm going to."

He pulled her hand away before he stepped to the side, opening the top drawer of his nightstand and grabbing a condom. It was on the tip of her tongue to protest as he opened the package; she wanted to be the one to put it on him. But as he rolled it down his length, she was more than slightly distracted by the action. There was something about watching him touch himself that made her forget to speak.

But who needed to speak, really?

He took possession of her mouth, his tongue dipping past her lips. The next second Beth found herself flat on her back in the middle of the bed, his hips cradled between her thighs, spreading her wide.

One of his hands made its way between their bodies, his fingers running over her folds. And then it wasn't his fingers moving through her wetness, it was the tip of his erection. He pulled his mouth from hers as he notched himself to her entrance, pushing in just a little as he looked down into her eyes.

"Ready?"

But he didn't even give her a chance to answer. He didn't need to. They both moved at the same time, him thrusting into her as she arched her hips up to meet him.

It took her breath away…the sensation of him moving into her…the tight fullness at the very core of her…how she was wrapped around the length of him…they way he was looking at her.

God, the way he was looking at her. The amazement in his eyes, the sheer pleasure radiating out of him. Or was that radiating out of her? She didn't know where she ended and he began.

"You okay?" Tripp rested his forehead against hers, his breathing uneven as he waited for her to adjust around him. He was a tight fit to be sure, but he wasn't hurting her.

"Yes." Beth reached up, her fingers delving into his hair as she moved her mouth to his.

The kiss started off soft, just a brush of her lips against his. When she nipped at his bottom lip and pulled it into her mouth, he let out another groan. He took her action as a cue and started to move. His thrusts were measured at first; he was taking his time as he steadily moved inside of her. Each stroke seemed to go deeper as he built up the pleasure that stirred throughout her body.

"You feel so good," he said, pulling out of her before slowly sliding back in. "So damn good."

His hands were braced on either side of her, levering himself up from the bed so as not to put all of his weight directly on top of her. But she wanted that. She wanted him pushing her down into the mattress, wanted the pressure of his body. She would've told him, too, but his mouth was on hers, consuming her entirely. Besides, sometimes actions spoke louder than words.

Beth dropped her hands from his hair, looping her arms underneath his so she could touch his shoulders. Before she knew it, she was raking her nails down his back and to his ass. And oh, wonder of wonders, his ass was glorious. She gripped it in both of her palms, urging him on harder as she bent her knees. Her legs spread wider apart as she brought her feet to the backs of his thighs, changing the angle of their bodies. Tripp somehow slid into her even deeper than before and her back came off the bed in a high arch.

He wrenched his mouth from hers, a gruff "fuck" escaping his lips, while she started to chant, "oh God, oh God, oh God."

There was no more slow and steady. Tripp's thrusts became harder, more possessive, wild. He buried his face in her neck, his breath erratic across her skin. His weight shifted as he moved one of his hands between their bodies. He found her clit, circling and pressing as he continued to move his hips, thrusting and rocking into her.

It was then that she felt it, the pleasure reaching its crest. She was right there on the precipice, so close to going over. Tripp must've known it, too. His mouth was at her ear, his teeth nipping at her earlobe. "Come for me, Beth. Come for me now. *Now*!"

His words pushed her over the edge. She cried out his name,

her body spiraling out of control as wave after wave of her orgasm rolled through her. She pulsed around him as he slammed into her over and over again. Then his entire body tensed, all of his muscles going rigid. Her name escaped his lips on a long low growl as he came inside of her.

He rolled to the side, not leaving her body as he pulled her along with him. One of his hands slid to her lower back, his palm going flat just above her ass, and then he was kissing her again. Not the all-consuming kisses from moments before, but soft and gentle ones that still had the ability to curl her toes and prevent her from fully catching her breath.

But Beth was beginning to think that when it came to Tripp, she'd probably never be able to fully catch her breath.

* * *

The lasagna didn't burn.

By the time they'd finished their first round in bed, the lasagna had finished its first round in the oven. Tripp removed the aluminum foil and it went back in for another fifteen minutes, until the cheese was bubbling and golden brown.

While the main course finished its progression to perfection, Tripp and Beth finished getting dinner ready. He'd told her to sit down but she didn't listen. She never listened.

Instead she threw her hair up into a messy bun on the top of her head and went about figuring out where everything was in his kitchen. She pulled out plates and silverware to set the table and fetched their wineglasses from outside and refilled them.

There was something about her moving around his home—

barefoot and wearing the denim shirt he'd had on earlier—that fascinated him beyond words. Maybe it was because every time she stretched to get something out of one of his cupboards the back of the shirt rode up high on her thighs, giving him just a flash of lacy underwear.

Or maybe it was just her moving around his space with ease.

Or maybe it was just her.

They lingered over dinner, talking and eating, Tripp was constantly distracted by the fork disappearing between Beth's lips. He'd never been more fascinated by a mouth in his life. It was her smile and her laughter.

Even when their plates were clean they didn't move away from the table; instead Tripp pulled Beth's feet up into his lap. When he started massaging them she moaned, another favorite thing of his that she did with her mouth.

Their back and forth questions from earlier continued, usually one for one unless the conversation evolved…which it did a number of times.

They talked about music, favorite bands, the first live concerts they'd ever been to. Hers had been to see Britney Spears; her sister had gotten tickets to the show in Orlando and they'd gone down together. His first concert was the Rolling Stones, and he'd gone with his dad and his best friend Landon.

She told him more about her love for gardening, how she loved being outside with her hands in the dirt.

"Yellow roses were my mom's favorite flower," she told him, her words more than a tad wistful. "And they became mine and Colleen's, too. Every spring they'd bloom like crazy in the backyard."

"Those weren't the flowers that Duke destroyed, were they?"

At the sound of his name, Duke perked up from where he was lying a few feet away.

"No." Beth shook her head. "Duke didn't touch those."

"Well, that's something." Even though the truth of Grant borrowing the dog was all out in the open now, Tripp would still feel terrible if those had been a casualty.

"Speaking of Duke? Why did you pick that as his name? If I'm remembering correctly, you went to the University of Georgia, so it's not after Duke University, is it?"

"He's definitely not named after the school." Tripp shook his head as his thumb started in on the instep of her right foot. "He's named after *The* Duke, as in John Wayne."

"Ohhhh, so you're a classic Western fan."

"I feel like I lived in those movies I watched them so much. Until I was thirteen I was pretty damn sure I was going to be a cowboy."

"Why did you decide you wanted to be a fireman?"

His ministrations on her foot stopped, and as tempted as he was to break their gaze, he didn't. "The answer to that question isn't short or simple." Nor was it going to be easy for him to talk about. But she'd asked and for some reason he didn't want to keep his answer to himself.

"I've got time."

"That you do. Especially as we've already established you're staying the night." He'd made it pretty damn clear that he wanted her in his bed all night. She'd agreed with very little persuasion. "All right, well, I'm going to have to start from the beginning, when my parents met in college."

"Oh, we're going *way* back." Beth settled back into her chair; the foot that wasn't in his hands moved up his inner thigh.

"Yup. Forty years, to be exact." He raised his eyebrows at her as he stopped her foot's ascent. "You going to behave?"

"Probably not."

"Good." He put her misbehaving foot on his knee before returning his attention to the instep of the other. "My dad was a senior in college, my mom a junior. And my mom's best friend was my Aunt Caroline. They were sorority sisters, met their freshman year when they pledged at the same time. As for my dad, his best friend was my Uncle Westley. They'd played baseball in high school, and as things would go, they both ended up getting athletic scholarships to UGA."

His hands moved from her foot to her ankle, and then to her calf, his fingers increasing the pressure as he moved up.

"My mom and dad started dating first, and it was about a month before my aunt and uncle crossed paths. For my uncle, it was love at first sight. For my aunt? Not so much. It took him weeks to convince her. On his way to pick her up for their first date, he got a flat tire…in the rain. When he finally got there to pick her up, he was an hour late and covered in mud. My aunt was furious at this point and slammed the door in his face. But he wasn't giving up."

"Determination. I like it."

"As you should." He reached forward, grabbing the seat of her chair and pulling her close enough to drape her legs over his lap. "So he bangs on the door until she opens up again, and it was then that she notices the bags in his hands. He'd stopped by this hole-in-the-wall Chinese takeout restaurant and picked up about ten different cartons of food. He tells her she can either be pissed at him and go hungry, or she can let him in and share a Chinese food smorgasbord."

"She let him in, didn't she?"

"She sure did. They were married a year and a half later, right after Aunt Caroline graduated. As for my parents, they waited a few years until my dad finished law school. As it was bound to happen, my mom and my Aunt Caroline found out they were pregnant within a month of each other." Tripp circled his fingers around her knee before moving to her thigh.

"Of course they did."

"There was no other way for it. So my Aunt Caroline had Landon, and a month later I was born. As things were meant to be, Landon was my best friend."

"Obviously."

"They lived in Savannah, which was only an hour and a half away. We saw each other at least once a month, sometimes even more often than that, what with holidays and vacations. Summers were spent at each other's houses. Half the time at mine, half at his."

Tripp paused in his story for just a moment and he looked down. He started rubbing his fingers across the hem of the oversize shirt Beth wore.

He cleared his throat before he continued, still looking down as he traced the thread of the seam. "It happened during the summer when Landon and I were at my house. We were both twelve at the time. We'd been out riding our bikes all afternoon and my mom liked for us to check in every hour or so. As we rounded the corner to our house, I saw her sitting on the front porch, sobbing."

This was where the story took a turn. Beth must have sensed it, because she reached forward and covered his hand with hers, her thumb tracing over his knuckles.

Tripp looked up at her before he continued. "Uncle Westley was an accountant at a pretty big firm in the downtown area of Savannah. His office was on the fifth floor. The electrical fire started on the second."

Beth's eyes closed hard before she opened them again.

"Instead of just saving himself, he tried to get everyone else out of the building. He saved nine people's lives that day, but he lost his. It was a bad fire—seven people died, including two firefighters."

"Tripp." She whispered his name on a sigh, flipping his hand and pressing her palm to his. "He's the reason you became a firefighter. Your Uncle Westley. He ran into the fire when it wasn't his job."

"Yes." He nodded, twining his fingers with hers.

"What happened to Landon and Caroline?"

"They ended up moving to Kingsland a year later. Their house was just down the street from ours. Caroline still lives there. She didn't remarry; she couldn't."

"That's how it was with my dad after my mom died." She shifted in the chair, the back of her thighs moving against the top of his. "And what about Landon? Are the two of you still best friends?"

"We are. He lives in Macon now, with his wife Jasmine and their three kids. Wes is eight, Clarissa six, and Tiffany two."

"How did they meet?"

"Law school."

"Really?" A small smile turned up her soft lips. "So he carried on your dad's legacy, and in a way you carried on his dad's. How poetic."

"Poetic? I don't know that I've ever looked at it that way."

"Well, I do. What you chose to do with your life is an amazing tribute to your uncle." She pulled their joined hands up, placing a kiss to the back of his hand. "I'm sorry he's gone."

Such a small gesture, her lips brushing across his skin, but it was comforting beyond measure.

"He was a good man. One of the best men." His free hand was at her thigh, fingertips brushing just underneath the hem of the shirt.

"Thank you for telling me about him. For sharing that part of yourself with me."

"Thank you for listening." He looked into her soft blue eyes, knowing full well that sharing that particular part of himself was not something small…and he wasn't quite sure how he felt about it.

Chapter Thirteen

The Definition of Boyfriend

The hot spray of the shower pounded against Tripp's back and shoulders, doing absolutely nothing to ease the tension that tightened every muscle in his body. Typically, showers relaxed him. Not this one. No, this one required him to lock his knees and grit his teeth.

Not that he was complaining or anything. Not in the slightest. Why in the hell would he complain? Beth was currently on her knees in front of him, his cock in her mouth. This was a much better way to start the day than lingering over a strong cup of coffee first thing in the morning.

Much, *much,* better.

One of his hands was braced against the tile wall, the other cradled the back of her head. He didn't push her down the length of him; there was no need to guide her. He just liked to feel her moving over him. Her mouth descending before she'd come back up in a slow, wet pull. Every time she got to the tip she swirled her tongue before starting the process all over again.

"Beth…" Her name came out of his mouth on a long, low groan but he ceased to know how to speak when she reached up and started stroking his balls.

"Hmmm," she hummed around him, her lips the farthest she could go down his shaft.

The vibration shot through him like a live current, going to every nerve. His eyes rolled to the back of his head as pressure built at the base of his cock. And then he was letting go, giving into the warm, perfect suction of her mouth. Her tongue working him over until he didn't have anything left.

It took a second for his brain to reconnect to his body. When it did, he opened his eyes and looked down at the woman who still knelt before him. He reached for her, pulling her to her feet. Her skin was hot under his hands. Feverish. The heat in her blue eyes intense… needy.

"We aren't even close to being done," he told her as he reached behind him and shut the water off.

"Thank God."

He grinned as he moved both of his hands to her sides, skimming them down her hips and to her thighs. A second later he was pulling her up, her arms looping around his neck as her legs wrapped around his waist.

The glass shower door opened with a simple push and Tripp stepped out, carrying Beth through the bathroom and to his bedroom. They were both dripping wet, the water from her hair running in rivulets down her shoulders and back. But he had absolutely no intention of stopping to grab a towel.

The second he got her on the bed, his mouth landed on her neck, and then he was moving across her chest—pausing for more than a moment at each of her breasts—and down to her belly. Every place his lips touched, he licked the water droplets that beaded on her skin. She was panting by the time he pulled her legs over his shoulders, but that was nothing to the cry of pleasure she made when he buried his face between her thighs.

He'd never get over the taste of her, would never get over the sounds she made. They drove him out of his ever-loving mind.

It didn't take all that long before she was coming against his tongue, her fingers tightening in his wet hair as her hips moved, seeking everything he gave her. There was no stopping until she was good and truly finished, her core no longer clutching with her release, her hands loosening in his hair. It was then that he gently pulled her legs from his shoulders, kneeling up between her thighs and looking down at her body. Her skin glowed, her breasts rose and fell as her chest heaved for breath, her nipples erect.

Yeah, he was already hard again.

He reached for the nightstand, pulling out the first condom he touched. Beth's eyes were on him, watching as he opened it and rolled it down his length.

His cock bobbed against his abs as he moved closer to her, still kneeling between her thighs. Her feet were planted flat on the mattress, her legs bent. Skimming his hands up from her calves, he pushed out when he got to her knees. He spread her wide and she shifted restlessly on the bed.

"So perfect." He ran a finger across her glistening folds. *And all mine.*

The breaths that escaped Beth's mouth were still unsteady, and they became even more so as he played with her, dipping his fingers inside, touching her clit, making her wetter and needier.

"Tripp!" She moaned his name on a plea.

She wasn't the only one who was desperate. He replaced his fingers with the tip of his cock, grabbing her hips and pulling her to him at the same moment that he thrust forward.

"Yes!" Her scream filled the room as she closed her eyes, her back arching off the bed and her hands wildly clutching at the sheets.

The bed creaked as he moved in and out of her, her breasts bouncing with every thrust. He liked this position, liked looking down at her as he took her from this angle. The only problem? He didn't have access to her mouth.

He grabbed her hands as he came down on top of her, pinning them above their heads as he claimed her mouth. Their fingers twined, linking together. Beth's legs came up and wrapped around his waist, her ankles locking above his ass.

The harder he thrust into her the more her body responded. Her hands held onto his in a fierce grip, like she was never going to let go; her heels dug into his ass to spur him on; her mouth hungrily ate at his, demanding more. Neither of them let up, the push and pull of their bodies on that mind-bending, pleasure-filled pace.

He knew when she'd gone beyond the edge, knew when she was consumed by her orgasm. Her nails dug into the backs of his hands almost painfully as she ripped her mouth from his and screamed his name. He buried his face against her neck as she tightened around his cock, the delicious pulse of her core bringing forth his own release. A long, low groan rumbled out of his chest as he let go, getting lost in the pleasure…

…getting lost in her.

It took a minute for Tripp to surface, and when he did he pulled up and looked down into Beth's face. Her eyes were open and focused on him, filled with wonder and pleasure. Her wet hair was spread out across his pillow and that flush of passion stained her cheeks.

She wrecked him. He knew then, figured it out in that moment, that he'd never be the same after this woman.

She'd *already* changed him, and if that wasn't just a little bit terrifying he didn't know what was.

* * *

Beth spent the morning and a good part of the afternoon with Tripp, leaving his house a little before two. As she needed to get dressed in more than his T-shirt before picking up the kids, it was understandable, but he hadn't wanted her to leave. And since she'd stayed at his house until the last possible minute, it led him to believe she hadn't wanted to leave, either.

A small consolation.

When Beth headed out the door, it wasn't lost on Tripp that they hadn't *exactly* had that conversation he'd intended for them to have. Sure they'd quite accurately established that there was something going on between them…they just hadn't established what they were going to do about it.

It wasn't that he didn't want to figure that out, because he did. It was just that he'd seriously gotten distracted. It was hard not to when Beth hadn't really been wearing clothes almost the entire time she'd been at his house.

But they *would* have that conversation, just as soon as they were in the same room again…and fully clothed.

Tripp occupied himself once she'd left. Since he hadn't gotten as much work done on Koko as he'd planned on the day before—not that he was complaining about that change in his agenda in the slightest—he was spending a few hours under the hood. It was a nice day outside, and there was a cool breeze coming in through the garage door. He needed to enjoy this weather while it lasted; it would be like a sweatbox in there once summer rolled around.

Duke was lounging in the grass a few feet away, basking in the sunshine one minute and then rolling over into the shade of the house when he got too hot. After an hour or so he finally settled on staying in the shade, falling asleep on his back. The only movement coming from him was his steadily rising and falling chest and the occasional twitch of his paws as he dreamt.

The dog must've really been out for the count, because he didn't react at all when they were joined by someone else. Well, Grant didn't so much join them as hide in the bushes on the side of the house. Tripp spotted the little guy peeking around the corner. His sandy blond head was visible for just a moment before it disappeared again.

It was about three minutes before Tripp finally said, "You going to come over here or just keep hiding out, Grant?"

A small crash shook the bushes at the same time as Grant's yelp filled the air. Tripp pulled out from under the hood of the car, but before he could respond Duke was up and darting over to the commotion.

Grant had fallen backward, sprawled in the bushes much like his aunt had been the other night. Tripp forced himself to hide his smile at the similarity, mainly because he didn't want Grant to think he was laughing at what had just happened. He pulled the little boy up and onto his feet before crouching down on eye level. Grant ducked his head, hiding his face.

"You okay?" Tripp asked, holding Grant firmly by the shoulders and looking him over. It hadn't been nearly as much of a fall as Beth had taken the other day, and besides a smudge of dirt on his pants leg, the kid looked fine.

"Yes, sir," he mumbled.

"What happened to you looking me in the eyes?"

Grant tensed before he moved his head up, a bright red flush staining his cheeks.

Tripp let go of the boy's shoulders, resting his forearms on top of his bent legs. "There's no need to be embarrassed, Grant. Though I don't know why you were hiding from me."

Duke was circling them, sniffing all around Grant and brushing his big, furry body against the little boy's side.

"I didn't want to bother you. You looked busy."

The kid was obviously still frightened. Well, Tripp was going to need to put the kibosh on that. For one thing, he had every intention of spending as much time with Beth as possible, and was therefore going to be around Grant quite often. Second, he didn't like scaring anyone, let alone an eight-year-old boy.

"I'm working on my car, but that doesn't mean I'm too busy to talk to you, buddy. Or let you play with Duke, for that matter. I'm guessing that's why you came over here."

When Tripp said Duke's name and the word *play* in the same sentence, the dog sat back on his haunches, letting out a soft whine as he gently swatted at Grant's arm.

"Yes, sir." He nodded, reaching out and petting Duke's head.

"Enough with this *sir* and *mister* business. You can call me Tripp. Okay?"

"O-okay."

"You got permission from your aunt to come over here?"

"Yes, s—" Grant cut himself off. "She said it was fine. I just need to be home for dinner."

Tripp looked down at his watch. It was a quarter past five. "What time is dinner?"

"Six."

"That gives you forty-five minutes. You ever play fetch with Duke?"

At that the dog whined again, his tail wagging back and forth in excitement.

"No." Grant shook his head.

"There are some balls over there." He stood up straight, turning to point to a basket in the corner of the garage. "And a Frisbee. Be careful not to throw them in the street. Got it?"

"Yes, s—"

Tripp raised an eyebrow and Grant cut himself off again before he ran over to the basket, Duke at his side. The smile that turned up Tripp's mouth as he went back to the car couldn't be helped. As he leaned to get under the hood, he kept Grant and Duke in view out of the corner of his eye.

The kid grabbed three balls: one blue rubber, a tennis, and a baseball. He set them in the upturned Frisbee before walking back through the garage. The Frisbee was precariously balanced in his hands, and the balls rolled back and forth, bumping the rim before rolling in the opposite direction. Somehow the kid made it out of there without dropping one, the added obstacle of Duke dancing around him not hindering him at all.

Tripp pulled his eyes from the engine and looked over as Grant set the Frisbee and balls down on the grass. He was looking down at them as he chewed on his bottom lip like they were the hardest math problem he'd ever seen.

Duke grabbed the Frisbee between his teeth, knocking off the balls as he moved his head back up and nudged Grant's hand. When Grant took the Frisbee, Duke took a few steps back, eyes not leaving the bright blue disk. Grant turned it over in his hands a few times, still unsure about it, before flinging it out. The Frisbee wobbled in the air as it went down, hitting the ground on its side and rolling away a few feet.

Duke was off but there was too much momentum under his big body for the short distance that the Frisbee had traveled, and he bounded right on past it. He turned around, confused, and spotted it behind him. The dog took off at a run again, barely stopping as he grabbed it between his teeth and brought it back to Grant at a trot.

Tripp watched Grant throw the Frisbee three more times with very little success—and continually looking more and more frustrated—before he straightened from underneath the hood of the car and headed out of the garage and into the front yard.

* * *

Warm water gushed from the kitchen sink faucet and the lemon-scented soap foamed up as Beth rubbed her hands together.

She felt fairly accomplished for the day considering she'd only been doing things—besides Tripp—for the last three and a half hours. A load of laundry was in the washer while another was tumbling in the dryer, groceries had been purchased and put away, and dinner was in the oven and would be ready in about thirty minutes.

Her biggest accomplishment of the day? Not following Grant next door when he'd gone over ten minutes ago. That had been a battle for sure, the desire to see Tripp again almost driving her to distraction...

She liked him. *Really* liked him. And though there was still that lingering fear of getting hurt, she still wanted whatever this was with him. She just needed to figure out how to do it while keeping the kids her number one priority.

Beth shut the water off, grabbing the dishtowel by the sink as she turned and looked over at the dining room table. "Whatcha working on, Lucky Penny?"

Her youngest niece was currently stationed there, working on a picture in her farm animals coloring book. As Beth watched her, all she could think was that she wouldn't trade this precious time with Penny for anything. This time before she became a teenager and locked herself in her room for hours on end, which was exactly where Nora was at the moment...and where she'd been since they'd gotten home two hours ago. Beth's older niece was in an especially unpleasant mood today.

Instead, Beth focused on the soft strokes of the crayons moving against the page. She loved that sound beyond words. That and the constant chatter. Penny created stories with each picture that she colored, and she also wasn't bound to the color norms of the world. Her skies were very rarely blue, trees seldom green, the sun never yellow.

"Goats. The baby is named Thaddeus." Penny pointed to the

smallest animal that she'd colored a bright turquoise. "And the mama goat is Lucinda." Her finger moved to the medium-size goat.

Penny named *every* animal that she came across. Her stuffed animals, the chickens embroidered on some of the dish towels, the lizards on the sidewalk in the morning, the owls on the wallpaper border that ran around her room—and yes, she did know all twenty-six of their names. Albert, Beatrice, Cesar, etc.—all the way through Zeus.

"I like her purple coat."

"Li-lac," Penny enunciated. "She's lilac."

Lucinda the lilac goat, mother of Thaddeus the turquoise goat.

"Oh, I'm sorry. I like her lilac coat. So what about the daddy goat?" Beth asked, looking at the last, and biggest, of the animals on the page. He was a pinkish orange color. So was he salmon or coral? *That* was the question.

"I don't know yet. I thought Carlos, but that doesn't seem right."

So daddy goat was coral.

"What about Casper?" *Casper the friendly goat,* Beth thought to herself.

"No." Penny shook her head as she looked down at the picture.

"Cedric?"

"No, that's not his name."

"Chadwick?"

"Chadwick?" Penny giggled, repeating the name. "Nope, that isn't it, either."

Beth's eyes traveled to the herbs growing on the windowsill. "Coriander?"

"Cor-i-an-der." Penny said the name slowly, seeing how it rolled off her tongue. "Commander Coriander...Yes! That's his name. Thanks, Aunt B!"

Commander Coriander the coral daddy goat. Made total sense.

"Glad to be of service." Beth grinned as she turned back to the sink, hanging the towel on the hook by the window.

At that moment a bright blue Frisbee went whizzing by. A second later Duke came streaking across the lawn, his big white and brown body a blur of movement. Beth leaned closer to the window, just in time to see Duke snatch the disk from the air. The dog looked beyond proud of himself as he trotted back across the lawn with the piece of plastic clutched between his teeth. Beth couldn't see beyond the driveway from this window, but she knew the dog was bringing the Frisbee back to Grant.

"Hey, PenPen. Want to go outside with me?" Beth asked, pulling herself away from the window. "Your brother is playing fetch with Duke," she added before Penny's customary *why*.

Penny looked up, rubbing the end of her nose with the back of her hand. "Okay." She nodded, setting the crayon down on the table before scrambling down from the chair.

Beth set a timer on her phone for the dinner in the oven before she stuck it in the back pocket of her shorts. When she held out her hand, Penny's little fingers and palm slid into place and the two headed for the front door.

It was nice outside, a cool evening with the sun still shining a pleasant warmth.

A series of barks rent the air as they went down the front steps. Tripp, Grant, and Duke came into view along the walkway. Tripp—Grant at this side—was holding the Frisbee in one hand, while the other was up in the air, balled in a fist.

"Duke, no. Sit," Tripp commanded. When Duke listened and sat back on his haunches, Tripp indicated the ground with his hand. "Lie down."

Duke listened again, going flat on the ground but not taking his eyes off the Frisbee in Tripp's hand.

"That was good." Tripp handed the Frisbee to Grant. "But try snapping your wrist a little bit more and do it when your arm is *almost* fully extended."

"Okay." Grant nodded, moving a few steps away from Tripp, the Frisbee now in hand. He shuffled his feet, getting them into position. "Ninety degrees," he looked up for confirmation.

"Yup, and elbow up and out," Tripp nodded.

Beth and Penny stopped at the edge of the lawn just as Grant moved his arm, flinging the Frisbee in a pretty good throw. Duke tore off the second it was out of Grant's hand.

"Ohh!" Penny squealed, pulling her hand from Beth's as she started clapping. "Good! Good! Good Grant!"

Her nephew spun around to see them, his eyes lighting up with delight. "Aunt B! I'm learning how to throw a Frisbee."

"I see that, Goose." She grinned, her gaze moving to Tripp, who was looking right back. His eyes moved over her in that way of his that made her breath catch.

"Teach me tooooo!" Penny said, running toward Tripp. "Please, Mr. Tripp!" Except she pronounced it *Twipp*.

"It's just Tripp, Penny." Grant told his little sister before turning to Beth. "He told me to call him Tripp and not *mister* or *sir*."

"Is that so?" Beth asked, raising her eyebrows at the man in question.

"It is." Tripp nodded.

Penny started to tug on Tripp's pant leg and he pulled his gaze from Beth and looked down at the little girl.

"Yes?" He grinned.

"Teach me *please*, Tripp." *Peeeas.*

Duke was back in front of them, Frisbee in mouth. "Take turns?" He raised his eyebrows at Grant in question.

"Okay." Grant nodded, getting the Frisbee from Duke and moving to hand it to Tripp.

Tripp shook his head. "You can show her how to hold it. Where do you put your thumb?"

"On top," Grant moved in beside Penny. "And this finger goes here," he said as he put her index finger to the side. "And the rest curl around to the bottom."

Grant walked Penny through it all step by step, Tripp helping along the way when something was forgotten. He stood there for Penny's first few feeble attempts at throwing. It hit the ground hard in the beginning, like she'd been trying to lob it down into the earth.

The first time it was airborne for more than couple of seconds, it wobbled precariously before hitting a very confused Duke in the side. The dog grabbed the disc and brought it over, giving it to Grant before moving out of Penny's strike zone.

Smart dog.

But Penny was enjoying herself, laughing with delight every time she threw it, no matter where it went. As for Grant, every time he was up to throw, it was with more strength and confidence and the Frisbee traveled a farther distance. The excitement emanating from him was palpable.

Something so simple was making both of these kids happy. Beth's heart clutched at the sheer joy on their faces.

Tripp had done this.

As if he knew she was thinking about him he turned to look at her over his shoulder and winked.

This man and his winks. Ohhhh good Lord she was falling for him. *Hard.*

Her phone buzzed in her back pocket, the timer going off. Had she really been out here for twenty-five minutes now? It didn't feel like that much time had passed at all. She wasn't ready to walk away from this moment. Wasn't ready to walk away from Tripp.

"Keep throwing," Tripp told Grant and Penny before he crossed the space to Beth. "You about to leave me again?"

"Leave you again?" she asked, taking a step forward. The need to be closer to him was stronger than she had the ability to control.

"Yes." He nodded, reaching up and tracing her hairline down the side of her face to her ear. "You left me about four hours ago. I'm clearly still not over it."

"Are you really going to act like you've been pining away?"

"Not an act. I was forced to console myself with the last of the apology pie and some of the cookies I bought yesterday."

"You already finished the pie?" she asked, her eyes going wide.

"You ask that like it was a challenge."

"How in the world are you not four hundred pounds?"

"Vigorous activity. Generally running and lifting weights, though I did enjoy our workout last night and this morning." He gave her that wicked grin of his. "It's been a while since that was my cardio."

"Oh, really now?" She looked around to where Penny and Grant were standing. They were ten feet away and watching the

Frisbee soar through the air, not paying attention to Tripp or Beth at all. "How long?"

"Seven months. You?" He was fiddling with a strand of her hair now. Slowly wrapping it around his finger.

"Ten."

"Not since your ex?"

"Not since my ex." She shook her head.

"And what if I told you that for this particular brand of cardio, I don't want us to have other workout buddies?"

Beth grinned. "So you'd like to be *exclusive*?"

"Yes." He took a step closer to her.

"And outside of cardio?" She couldn't stop herself from asking. What? He'd opened the door for this conversation, so she was just going to walk right on through.

"Meaning what, exactly? Dating exclusively? Was that not implied? Beth, I think I've already proven that I don't do well with other guys and you."

"This is true, but it wasn't what I meant."

"And what do you mean?"

Beth looked over to Grant and Penny again. They were both still in their own little world throwing the Frisbee. Her gaze returned to Tripp, and those brown eyes of his focused intently on her face.

"I'm a package deal when it comes to dating."

"Four for the price of one." He nodded. "I know that, Beth. I knew it the first time I kissed you."

"And it doesn't scare you?" Because it sure as hell scared her. Scared her to be that vulnerable again with a man, to open herself up. Scared her to get the kids involved in any capacity.

"Now, I didn't say that." His voice drawled a little bit when he spoke, his smile quirking to the side.

"Tripp, I'm serious."

"So am I." His hand moved down, his fingers trailing across her check and to her chin. "I know what dating you entails and I'm not walking away."

He pushed her chin up at the same moment that he leaned in, capturing her mouth in one of those soul-searing kisses that she'd only ever experienced with him. He was now cupping the side of her face while his other hand had moved to the small of her back, holding her against him.

A little giggle burst out behind them, and Tripp pulled his mouth from Beth's. His hand at her face fell away as he turned, but the one on her back stayed steady. Both Penny and Grant were watching them, the former smiling hugely and the latter looking a little confused.

"Mr. Tripp, why're you kissing my Aunt B?" Penny asked, taking a step forward and doing a little pirouette as she moved.

"I told you, Penny." Grant looked at her, frowning. "It's just Tripp. No 'mister.'"

"Oh right," Penny nodded at her brother before turning back. "*Tripp*, why're you kissing my Aunt B?"

"Because I like kissing her," he said simply, his hand at her back flexing.

"Oh." She nodded like that answered everything. "Is he your boyfriend now?" she asked, looking at Beth.

And just that fast Beth's mind went blank. A clean canvas. A white piece of paper. Nothing. Nada. How was she supposed to answer that?

"That, uh, is a topic of conversation Tripp and I haven't exactly had."

"Oh." Penny nodded again. "You should come to dinner tonight, Tripp."

"Should I now?" Tripp asked, thankfully moving right on past that boyfriend comment. They'd just have to revisit that later.

"Yeah," Grant agreed, now nodding his head more vigorously than Penny. "Aunt B made Shepherd's Pie. It's my favorite."

"Pie, you say?" Tripp asked Beth, his eyebrows raising high as a huge grin took over his face.

"Also," Grant continued, "Sunday is movie night and tonight is my pick. So it's guaranteed to be *really* good…whatever it is."

"Pie for dinner *and* a movie? You holding out on me, Beth?"

She looked over at him, her stomach doing that whole swooping thing that made her head spin. "Would you like to come to dinner tonight, Tripp?" Shockingly enough, that sentence came out rather steady.

"I'd love to." Tripp's grin widened before he turned to the kids. "Hey Grant, can you put the balls and Frisbee away, and show Penny where they go?"

"Yes, s—" Grant cut himself off before he nodded and went off with Penny to collect the balls.

Tripp looked back to Beth. "I'll walk over with them."

"Okay." She took a step away from him before turning and heading toward her house.

"And Beth?"

She glanced over her shoulder, still walking away.

"I would've answered Penny's boyfriend question with a *yes.*"

Her step faltered as that swooping sensation rolled through her lower belly again.

How it was possible for Tripp's grin to get even wider, Beth would never know.

* * *

Apparently when it came to Tripp Black, Beth was going to be continually surprised by him. She wondered if that was his MO. Well, that along with kissing the breath out of her every chance he got.

But really, her surprise was warranted. It wasn't like she'd had a lot going on in the romance department of late. Nor had she had a lot going on in the luck department, either.

During the year that Beth had been guardian to the kids, she hadn't gone on a single date. Those first couple of months after losing Colleen and Kevin had been some of the worst of her life. She wouldn't have been interested in dating even if she hadn't just gotten the pieces of her already decimated heart trampled on by her ex, Mick the Prick.

There was also the fact that pickings were slim. There hadn't been anyone who'd come along that she would've wanted to date. The handful of guys who'd asked her out pretty much fit into one of two groups: guys who would run the second they found out she was now a single mother, and guys who tried to use the kids to get to her…and to get into her pants.

So, clearly they were all *real* winners.

But then Tripp had come along…and he'd gone and made the boyfriend comment.

Boyfriend…*boyfriend*? That had been an interesting turn of events, and one she was going to need a whole hell of a lot more clarification on.

Like, what did his definition of "boyfriend" mean? He'd said that he understood she was a package deal—*four for the price of one*, as he'd put it—but did he *really* understand all that it entailed?

Beth was a ball of nerves as she sat at the dining room table, picking at her Shepherd's pie with her fork. It took a bit for her to be able to take normal size bites. Tripp, on the other hand, was sitting across from her right as rain.

It had taken him absolutely no time at all to win over Grant and Penny; they'd been pretty much fascinated with him from the get go.

Now when it came to Penny, this wasn't all that shocking. She'd sometimes get a little shy when it came to a large group of adults, something that became even more evident when she wasn't used to the people or the environment. But usually she was pretty quick to warm up to a new person when it was on a smaller scale, especially when they gave her their undivided attention. And Tripp had the patience of a saint with her rapid-fire questions.

Penny: *What's your favorite color?*

Tripp: *Blue.*

Penny: *How old are you?*

Tripp: *Thirty-five.*

Penny: *Do you have any brothers or sisters?*

Tripp: *Nope. Only child.*

Penny: *What's your favorite movie?*

Tripp: True Grit *(the original) and* Ghostbusters *for a close second.*

Penny: *What's your favorite number?*

Tripp: *Five.*

Penny: *Why is it your favorite number?*

Tripp: *Because it was the number on my first baseball jersey.*

That was when Grant started asking Tripp all the questions. Her nephew had watched baseball games before, mainly with his Papa Wallace, but he'd never played. And just that fast, Tripp was offering to teach Grant how to play baseball.

As she sat there and watched Grant listen to Tripp in rapt fascination, the desire to nail down the definition of whatever this was with him hit her all the harder. She could already see how quickly Grant would get attached.

It would take no time at all.

In stark contrast to Penny and Grant was Nora...who couldn't seem less impressed if she tried. Beth was now very much used to her eldest niece's less than pleasant moods. Well, maybe *used to* wasn't exactly the correct way to phrase it, but Beth had learned to deal with it.

Nora had sat through the entire meal without saying a single word unless prompted. But that was pretty much Nora's MO, speaking only when spoken to. Oh, and adding in as many eye-rolls and sighs as possible.

"I'm sorry about Nora. She's exceptionally teenager-y today," Beth apologized after dinner. She stood across from Tripp, fiddling with a dish towel while he leaned back against the counter with his arms folded across his chest.

They were alone in the kitchen. The only light came from the bulb above the stove and the glow from the lamps in the living room. The table was cleared of all dishes, the food had been put away, and water sloshed around in the running dishwasher. The kids had all headed out when everything had been cleaned up: Grant and Penny to put their pajamas on and get ready for the movie, Nora to sequester herself in her room...again.

Tripp shrugged his massive shoulders at Beth's apology. "I know it's going to take a little bit longer with her. I'm under absolutely no delusions that she's going to warm up to me any time soon." He pushed off the counter and closed the distance between them, pulling the towel from her hands. He set it down behind her before he grabbed her hips and leaned in close. "But I'm not easily intimidated, Beth."

"No?" Her hands were on his chest, and his heat radiated through his T-shirt.

"No." He shook his head.

"Earlier, you said you would've said *yes* to Penny's boyfriend question."

"I would've." His brown eyes had gone dark and intense as he looked at her. "Didn't we establish that we're dating exclusively?"

"We did."

"Now correct me if I'm wrong, but isn't that the definition of a boyfriend?"

"I think it depends on the person defining it."

"Well, for me it *is* the definition. And I know we're going to need to take precautions. If I overstep my bounds, put me in my place. I'm a big boy. I can handle it. But Beth, I want to see what this is with you. I want to see where we can go with it." He leaned down and pressed his mouth to her neck. "Say yes."

"Yes." Beth melted against him, wanting his heat and strength. His hands slid underneath the hem of her shirt and his fingers traced the bare skin at her sides as he kissed his way up her throat and to her mouth.

He pulled back a minute or two later, looking down into her face. "God, I missed your lips this afternoon."

Beth's mouth quirked to the side. "It was what? Four hours?"

"Four of the longest hours of my life," he told her before he leaned down, slanting his mouth over hers.

Oh, look at that, he was kissing the breath out of her.

Again.

Chapter Fourteen

Afternoon Delights

Beth's hands and knees sank into the plush rug on Tripp's living room floor. The man who owned the rug was kneeling behind her, his hands firmly around her waist as he thrust forward into her body.

A gasp escaped her mouth as he stretched her, his hips stilling as he let her adjust around his length. One of his hands let go of her hip, moving to her lower back and slowly sliding up her spine.

The moment was more than a little surreal for Beth. If someone would've told her a week ago that she'd be rushing home on her lunch break so Tripp Black could take her from behind, she would've said they were crazy. Yet here she was, naked and currently wrapped around his glorious cock.

During Mirabelle's five o'clock traffic it typically took Beth eight minutes to get home from the hospital. When it wasn't rush hour, it took about five. Today? She'd made it in four.

Tripp had met her at the door and stripped both of them of

their clothing before they even made it down the hallway. She had no idea if the living room had been his intended final destination, or if that was just as far as he'd been able to go.

But to be honest, she really didn't care. What she did care about was how his palm was moving over her skin, how the backs of her thighs were pushed up against the tops of his, how he pulsed inside her.

"Beth?" His voice was rough, no doubt from the restraint of not moving. But he was waiting until she was ready.

And was she ever. "Fuck me."

His sharp inhale filled her ears, a reaction to her choice of words. "As you wish," he whispered, slowly pulling out of her before thrusting back in.

She knew this wasn't going to be a slow and easy lovemaking session, but she didn't want slow and easy. No, she wanted rough and grasping…desperate, something he emphasized a moment later. The palm of his hand came down on her ass, not hard enough to hurt, but a slight sting that made her moan.

"You like that?" he asked right before he did it again on the other cheek.

"Yes." She stretched her arms out in front of her, leaning down and pushing her ass further up into the air.

"Oh hell, Beth." Tripp groaned her name long and loud, his appreciation for the new angle clear. He was moving harder now, his thrusts inching them up the rug. She was going to have rug-burned knees at the end of this.

Totally worth it.

How the man was able to evoke pleasure throughout every nerve and fiber of her being was beyond her. But he did. Hitting every damn spot with each slide, filling her, stretching her. It felt better than anything she'd ever experienced.

And yes, Beth had had good sex. The kind where in the end, all parties were pretty damn satisfied. The kind that gave a person a noticeable pep in their step because they'd had a decent orgasm or two.

But this wasn't *good* sex.

This was...something else entirely. Sex with Tripp was so mind-numbingly good it went beyond satisfaction. It was the kind where you weren't walking with a pep in your step afterward because you couldn't walk at all.

Beth's hips undulated, doing her part to make Tripp just as mindless as he was making her. Both of his hands were on her hips again, his fingers tightening around her and pressing into her flesh.

The pleasure built, steadily mounting until she was falling over the edge. Her core started contracting around Tripp's cock, and she cried out as she came.

"That's it, baby," he ground out as he continued to move in and out of her. "Feel it. Feel me."

Wave after wave of orgasm washed through her, making her legs shake. If not for Tripp's hold on her body she would've collapsed. But he held her up, not letting go until the very end when he had his own release, his cock pulsing deep inside her.

"Fuck..." He groaned, his grip on her hips disappearing as he pulled from her body.

Beth's legs still weren't in any condition to keep her upright, and she found herself down on the rug. Tripp was flat on his back next to her, his unsteady breaths filling the air.

Somehow—she had no idea *how* because her arm felt boneless—she reached over and patted his chest. "Good job."

He chuckled, his mouth at her ear. "You too." He kissed a trail from her temple all the way to her mouth. "Don't go anywhere," he told her before he pulled away and got to his feet.

"Couldn't move even if I wanted to."

He laughed again, the sound echoing down the hallway as he made his way to his bedroom. A minute later water rushed through the pipes behind the wall, then there was the soft creak of a door opening, and bare feet moving across wood floors.

Tripp was back down on the rug beside Beth, grabbing a pillow on the sofa to lay his head on before pulling her into his arms. She rested her head on his chest as she snuggled into his side.

He slowly traced his fingers along her spine. "Think you can call in sick for the rest of the afternoon?"

This time it was Beth who was laughing. "Sorry pal, no can do."

Before she could blink she found herself on her back. Tripp was between her legs; her breasts were smashed against his chest and her hands pinned above her head.

"'Pal?'" He raised his eyebrows as he looked down at her.

"Would you prefer buddy? Amigo? Compadre? Chum?"

"No, I would not." His eyes narrowed and his mouth quirked to the side. "You know damn well what I prefer."

"I might need a refresher." She shifted her body beneath his, drawing her knees up and cradling his hips between her thighs. "And you have"—she glanced over at the clock on the wall before she looked back to him—"about another twenty minutes to remind me."

"What have I told you about challenging me, Beth?"

She grinned as she brought her mouth to his, nipping at his bottom lip as she rolled her hips. Tripp was already hard again, his erection pressing against her belly.

"That when rising to the challenge, there is no *think*, only *know*."

"Damn straight." And his mouth covered hers as he went about proving it.

* * *

To say that Beth had a very lovely Monday would be an understatement. She'd take two orgasms from Tripp and a grilled cheese sandwich—which he'd made for her while she'd gotten dressed again—over a big lunch any day.

Her time in the office hadn't been bad at all either; they were fairly busy, which meant a faster day. Before she knew it, it was five thirty and she was heading home. And the sight that greeted her when she pulled into her driveway was the cherry on top of everything.

Tripp and Grant were in the front yard playing catch.

Something in Beth's chest clutched, and for just a second it was hard to breathe. It took her more than a moment to get hold of herself. This man was...he was...well, he was unbelievable.

She reached over and grabbed her purse from the passenger seat, pulling it over her shoulder before getting out of the car.

Tripp was facing her, eyes covered by his sunglasses. She knew he saw her as his mouth quirked to the side. Grant, on the other hand, was not aware of her. Her nephew had his back to the driveway, and neither the sound of the car pulling in nor the snap of the door shutting made him turn around. The kid was beyond focused on Tripp as he wound his arm up and threw.

The ball curved too far to the left, causing Tripp to lunge to the side to catch it. His glove closed around the ball and he straightened, getting back into position. "Grant, you're too tense. Drop your shoulders." He circled his own shoulders before dropping them down. The movement made his gray T-shirt go taut across his chest.

"Oh, right." Grant mimicked the move Tripp had just made, rolling his shoulders and letting them fall.

"Better." Tripp grinned before he tossed the ball back.

Grant closed his glove a second too early and the ball hit the very tip before continuing through the air. It hit the ground and rolled, and Duke lunged for it. The dog had been attentively sitting at Grant's side waiting for stray balls like this one.

Grant turned, watching the dog run off and spotting Beth. "Hi, Aunt B!"

"Hey, Goose." She crossed over to him. "I see you're learning to throw a baseball today."

"I am." He nodded enthusiastically, holding his hand out for Duke, who'd just come ambling back, baseball clutched in his mouth. The dog gave the ball back to Grant, fluffy tail wagging. "Eww." Grant wrinkled his nose as he wiped the ball on his shorts. "Dog drool."

Beth had to bite at the corner of her lip to keep from laughing. She really didn't understand how *this* grossed him out, yet sharing a spoon with Duke while eating peanut butter had not. To each their own.

"Can I stay out here until dinner?" Grant asked, looking up at Beth.

"You finish your homework?"

Grant nodded enthusiastically.

"As long as it's okay with Tripp." Beth's eyes moved to the man in question as she raised her eyebrows.

He'd crossed the space to them, now standing only a few feet away. Even through the lenses of his sunglasses, she could feel his penetrating gaze on her. "It is." He nodded.

"I'm going to go get some water. Then can we start again?" Grant asked Tripp.

"Sounds good."

"Sweet!" Grant ran off to the shade of Tripp's garage, where two sweating water bottles sat on the concrete.

Beth pulled her gaze from her nephew and looked up at the man in front of her. "Thank you."

"For what?" He reached forward, putting his hand on her hip and sliding it around to her back. He pulled her closer, bringing her body flush against his.

"For doing this with Grant. Spending time with him. Teaching him."

"You don't need to thank me for any of that. I'm having a good time with him. He's a great kid."

"He is." Beth put her hands on his chest, moving them up to the collar of his shirt. She barely had to tug to get Tripp to lean down and press his mouth to hers. "You're pretty great, too," she said against his lips.

"Same goes for you."

Her hands slid out to his shoulders, his muscles flexing beneath her palms. "You going to join us for dinner tonight?"

"I'd love to. I seemed to have worked up a pretty good appetite today."

"Is that so?"

"Sure is." He leaned down and kissed her again, his tongue slipping inside her mouth and finding hers. He tightened his grip on her back, holding her firmly to him.

Grant's voice behind them had them pulling apart. "Are you two almost done?" he asked, sounding more than slightly exasperated.

Tripp's hands fell away from her body and they took a step back from each other. "Yeah, we're done, buddy," he told Grant before looking to Beth again. "What time do we need to be at the table?"

Beth glanced at her watch. It was five forty-nine. "Six thirty."

"I think we can handle that. Right, Grant?" Tripp reached over and ruffled the boy's hair.

"Yup." He nodded before turning his head up to Tripp, the unmistakable look of hero worship written across his face.

Beth's chest clutched again as she turned away and headed to the house. The happiness coursing through her almost felt too good to be true.

Almost.

* * *

It wasn't just Monday evening that Tripp joined them for dinner, but every single night that week. Another thing that continued were the evening catch sessions with him and Grant, they'd come in and wash up before sitting down at the table to eat. It quickly became one of her favorite things to see.

When Beth got home on Friday she found Nora sitting out on the porch. She was leaning back against one of the massive pillars with her legs stretched out and an open book in her lap. But she wasn't reading the book; no, she was watching Tripp and Grant.

That wasn't the only thing Nora participated in. After dinner she actually joined them in the living room to watch a movie. It was Penny's turn to pick, so of course it was Disney, but thankfully she chose *The Lion King* and not *Frozen*.

On Saturday and Sunday, Beth went over to Tripp's house at six in the morning. On both days he'd made her come twice before the sun even rose. She didn't feel even remotely bad about her crack-of-dawn adventures, either. She sometimes went for early morning runs, so it wouldn't have been that unusual if she happened to not be in her bed when the kids woke up. Besides, they always slept in on the weekends. She'd been back and had breakfast ready before any of them even opened their eyes.

Beth's lunch breaks on Monday and Tuesday had consisted of time spent with Tripp. As Monday and Tuesday had been his days off, she'd spent most of her hour naked and with him inside of her.

Just after three o'clock on Wednesday afternoon Beth's cellphone vibrated against the desk, letting her know she had a text. She finished updating a patient's file before she looked at it, seeing it was from Tripp.

Her stomach did that swooping thing it always did when it came to him, because good Lord this man affected her. And when she actually read his text? Well, her grin somehow got even bigger.

What are your thoughts on me picking up something for dinner for you, me, and the kids?

My thoughts are very, very positive, she typed out quickly and hit Send.

Beth pulled the corner of her bottom lip between her teeth, trying to contain her smile. But containing it was useless, had been useless since the first time he'd kissed her. Which had been twelve days ago.

Twelve freaking days. What was even happening?

"Well, look at you, Grinny McGrinnerson."

Vanessa was standing in the doorway. She had a piece of folded up paper in her hands that she was fiddling with absentmindedly.

"Does that current look on your face have anything to do with your new boyfriend?"

Beth turned in her chair to face Vanessa. "It just might."

"He's good to you." Not a question, but a statement.

And it was so damn true.

"He is." Beth took a deep breath, her stomach doing that weird flippy thing that was becoming the norm when she talked about Tripp.

Vanessa took a step forward, handing the piece of paper she'd been fiddling with to Beth. "Well, I was asked to give you this."

Beth looked down, unfolding the paper.

Which appeals the most?
*   1) Italian (I'm thinking pizza. Though a case could be made for calzones)*
*   2) Chinese Smorgasbord (I order ten things and it's a free-for-all)*

3) Burgers and fries (with enough ketchup to satisfy Penny and Grant)

4) Mexican (tacos or burritos, or we can live danger- ously and have both)

5.) _____ (You want something that I haven't suggested)

"He's out in the waiting room."

Vanessa had barely finished her sentence before Beth was out of her chair and down the hallway. When she pushed the door open she saw that Tripp was the only person in the room. Her man was wearing a black and white Mirabelle Firefighter T-shirt and his customary navy blue uniform pants. He grinned the second his eyes landed on her.

"Hey," he said as he crossed the space to her in four easy strides.

"Hey yourself."

His hands were at her hips and he was leaning down at the same moment that she grabbed onto his arms and stretched up. Their mouths met in the middle, and it was one of those long, lingering kisses.

"God, I needed that," he said against her mouth before pulling back to look down into her face.

"Bad day?"

"Just long. I needed a pick-me-up."

"They out of your pie at the diner again?"

"Don't know," he shrugged. "I came here first. You've ruined me for sweets, Beth. They just don't do it for me anymore. I want you." He reached up, cupping the side of her face and tracing her cheek with his thumb.

"That so?" She leaned into his touch.

"It is. And I think I was especially in need of a pick-me-up because I didn't see you this morning…or this afternoon."

"So you missed me." Beth lowered her voice, fully aware of Vanessa, who'd retaken her seat behind the receptionist desk…and slid the glass divider pane open an inch or two.

"That's a fact." He pressed his lips to hers again in another lingering kiss. They were only given a moment to get lost in it, though, because at the sound of someone clearing their throat, Tripp pulled back.

Beth looked past Tripp, seeing the assistant fire chief leaning against the doorjamb, a grin turning up the corners of his mouth.

Beau was another man of Mirabelle who had been blessed with good looks. Beth had always thought he looked like a guy who'd just walked off the cover of a romance novel. Probably one where the hero was a rogue or something…or maybe a pirate. He'd have to be something a little scandalous with his thick black hair that just brushed his shoulders and the salt-and-pepper beard that covered his very strong jaw.

The man had a body that rivaled a Greek god's: biceps that strained the fabric of his T-shirt, a wide and solid chest, and muscular thighs. And these were all observations that were easily made with him fully clothed. It was like knowing the sky was blue…well, except when it came to Penny, and then it was any color she wanted it to be.

But Beau had a lot more going for him than just looks. He was a supremely nice guy, something that hadn't changed even though he'd been screwed over—royally so—by his ex-wife. There was also the fact that he was a dad who loved his son more than life itself.

He was a great package, to be sure, though Beth was partial to the package that she currently had in hand. Well—Tripp *as a whole* being the package—not his package in particular. Though she was partial to that, too.

"Hi Beau," she smiled, hoping that her current train of thought wasn't written all over her face. "How are you doing?"

"Pretty good." He folded his arms across his massive chest. "You kiss him and make him all better?" He indicated Tripp with his chin.

"I think so." She patted Tripp's chest, but didn't turn away from Beau. "You having a long day, too?"

One of Tripp's hands slid around Beth's back, his fingers spreading wide at the base of her spine. It took some serious concentration to focus on Beau and not the way Tripp was touching her.

"Yup. We've had a day full of inspections. People aren't all that pleasant when you tell them they aren't up to code."

"Oh, I bet they aren't. So what are you going to do for a pick-me-up?"

But before he could answer, the door off to the side opened. Denise was escorting Annette Wharton, an elderly woman Beth had known since she was a little girl, out and over to the receptionist desk.

Beau's reaction to the new company was immediate as he pushed off the doorjamb. His back was ramrod straight now, all of his muscles tensed as his body went on full alert. And his eyes? Well, they were locked on Denise.

Vanessa pushed the sliding glass open the rest of the way and smiled at the patient. "You're good to go, Mrs. Wharton. There was a credit on your account." As Mrs. Wharton was a little hard of hearing in her old age, Vanessa enunciated the words loud and clear.

"No bill? Well, this day just got better," Mrs. Wharton pretty much shouted, which was the norm whenever she spoke. She adjusted her grip on her cane before she turned toward the exit. But she came up short when she spotted the people in the waiting room…and she wasn't the only one.

When Denise's gaze landed on Beau, her cheeks flushed bright pink. "Beau," she said, more than a little startled.

A very different expression was now playing over Beau's face, one that Beth had never seen on him before. The man's brown eyes went darker as they focused on the woman in front of him. It was the kind of look that a man reserved for a woman he was interested in.

"What was that, dear? You know Beaumont Giovanni?" Mrs. Wharton's booming voice filled the room as she looked between Denise and Beau quizzically.

Beau visibly winced at being called by his full first and middle name. Very few people ever called him Beaumont, let alone Beaumont Giovanni. It was mainly those people who'd known him when he was a child that did so, and as Mrs. Wharton had been friends with the late Cristiana Culpepper, she fit into that category. And so had Beth's mother Dory.

Personally, Beth thought that his name was pretty damn fitting. It went with her whole romance-novel-cover-model theory pretty damn well.

"I do know Beau." Denise nodded to Mrs. Wharton.

"Well, did you know he was single?" Again with the shouting. Really, a person who was so tiny shouldn't be that loud.

The pink flush on Denise's cheeks turned to a bright red and her eyes widened. "I...I did know that."

"And Beaumont, did you know that Denise is widowed? It's a damn shame, really. No woman who has legs like hers should be put out to pasture this early. I'm just saying."

Beau put his hand to his mouth and coughed into it. If Beth didn't know any better, she'd say there was some pink staining his cheeks, too. It was a little harder to tell because of his beard.

"Well, I just thought I'd point that out." Mrs. Wharton shrugged as she looked between Denise and Beau. It was then that she turned her attention to Tripp and Beth. "As for you two. I like this." She waved her hand at them. "Beth, he isn't too bad to look at. And Tripp—well son, you got yourself a beautiful girl, there."

"Yes ma'am," Tripp nodded.

"Don't screw it up. You aren't going to find yourself a better one than her." She pointed her finger at him and waggled it a bit for good measure. "Now I need to go. My ride is waiting for me," she said before starting her slow and steady walk out of the waiting room. As she passed Beau she added in another shout, "Seriously, she's got the legs of a thirty-year-old," before she continued on.

No one said a word, probably waiting for Mrs. Wharton to get a good distance down the hall. The shrill ring of Vanessa's telephone finally broke the silence. "Atticus County Hospital, Women's Health. This is Vanessa speaking. How can I help you?"

"That woman says whatever she's thinking." Denise shook her head, more than slightly mortified. "Does having an inner filter diminish with age?"

"Not when it comes to her." Beth shook her head. "She's always said exactly what she thinks."

"I can attest to that," Beau agreed, his eyes returning to Denise. He studied her for a second before he asked, "You guys have decent coffee around here?"

Denise merely nodded.

"Care to show me? I think I need a little caffeine."

Denise nodded again, lightly clearing her throat. She pointed to the hall behind Beau, in the same direction Mrs. Wharton had just ventured down. "It's, uh, that way."

"I'll follow your lead." He turned in the doorway, waving his hand out in front of him for her to pass by. "Carry on, you two. Nothing to see here," he told Beth and Tripp before he turned and followed Denise.

"Huh, that's interesting." Tripp's mouth was by Beth's ear, and he spoke softly so only she could hear him. Which was smart, because even though Vanessa was on the phone, she was no doubt still paying very close attention to what was happening in the waiting room.

"What? Beau wanting coffee?" Beth turned to face Tripp again, both of his hands now at the small of her back and pulling her in close to his body.

"He already has a fresh cup sitting in the truck."

"So apparently Mrs. Wharton is pretty damn observant, even in her old age."

"It would appear so. Looks like I'm not the only firefighter who has a thing for a nurse."

"Must be something in the water."

"Must be," he agreed. "So about dinner? What did you decide?"

"The Chinese smorgasbord."

"Good choice." He reached up, pushing back a strand of hair that had fallen across her forehead.

"Stick around, Tripp Black." She fisted her hand in the front of his shirt and tugged, pulling him closer. "I'm full of them."

"Oh, I plan on sticking around. Believe you me." And with that, he kissed her.

* * *

Beth was in an exceptionally good mood when she got off work that evening. She'd had a good day at work—part of that having to do with Tripp's afternoon visit—and she didn't need to worry about dinner that night, either. She could go home and just relax.

Or so she thought.

Little did she know that her good mood would have an expiration time attached to it—that time being when she walked in the door with Penny at six seventeen. Tripp wasn't there yet. He'd texted her that he'd gotten a little delayed at work, but would be at the house before seven.

"Hey, Goose. Whatcha reading?" Beth asked Grant when she walked into the living room. He was lying on the sofa, a book in his lap.

He held up the book for Beth to see the back. It was the book on baseball that Tripp had given him the other day.

"You finish all of your homework?"

"Yes. It's all done." He nodded.

"Good." She leaned over and pressed a kiss to his head before ruffling his hair with her hand. "Where's your sister?"

"I'm right here!" Penny giggled as she pulled her coloring book and crayons out of her backpack and stationed herself at the coffee table.

"Nora is in her room," he said as his eyes went back to the book in his hands.

Beth headed down the hallway, hearing the faint beat of music echo through Nora's closed door.

"Nora?" Beth knocked on the door.

There was no answer, but the music got louder. Oh, fantastic. Nora was in one of her moods. Well, that was just great. Beth knocked, then reached for the handle but it wouldn't turn.

Oh no, she did not *lock the door.*

"Nora, open this door now!" Beth knocked even harder, shouting over the music. "You have three seconds before I open it myself and you will not like what happens at the end of that. One…"

The music went off.

"Two…"

Footsteps echoed across the hardwood floor as Nora crossed the room.

"Three."

The lock was flipped and the door wrenched open. "What?" Nora demanded.

Beth's eyes widened and her mouth fell open in a horrified 'O' as she looked at her niece. Nora had dyed her hair bright blue.

"What did you do, Nora?" Beth asked when she was finally able to get hold of herself to speak without screaming. "What in God's name did you do?"

"It's *my* hair. I can do whatever I want with it."

"Oh really? Is that what you think?"

Nora didn't answer. She just stood there stubbornly glaring, her hands on her waist.

"Until you're either eighteen or not financially dependent on me, you actually can't do whatever you want. Fun time is over, sweetheart. You're grounded for two weeks."

"Two weeks?" Nora's hands fell from her waist.

"Or until you de-Smurf. Whichever is longer."

"I don't believe this!" Nora screamed as she slammed the door in Beth's face, locking it again.

* * *

Tripp heard the yelling as soon as he and Duke walked in the front door. Beth and Nora were going at it, their voices echoing down the hallway. With anyone else he would've turned right back around and headed out the door.

But not with Beth.

Whatever this incident was with Nora didn't scare him. He'd been around enough in the last week and a half to know the drill at least a little bit.

"If you think this is acceptable behavior you are beyond delusional, young lady!"

Or maybe it wasn't so much a drill as a full-on crisis. Tripp had absolutely no doubt that Beth was beyond furious, so much so that her voice was shaking. It reminded him of that morning with Duke.

"You can't do this!" Nora shrieked back. "You can't take away my phone! I bought that with my money!"

"Okay. Fine. Keep your phone, Nora. But you don't pay for the plan, so I will be suspending your service on it. *And* I'll be changing the WiFi password for the house. So you won't be able to use the Internet at all."

"What about my homework?"

"You will get it for an hour a day when I'm home. Nothing more. And if I so much as see you on Facebook you won't even get that anymore!"

The screaming continued as Tripp set the bags of dinner down in the kitchen before he headed into the living room. There he came across Penny and Grant.

Penny was sitting on the floor and hugging her pink elephant Evangeline, tears streaming down her face while she sniffled. Grant was huddled in the corner of the sofa, arms wrapped around his legs while he stared off glumly. Duke was immediately at the boy's side, pressing his nose into Grant's ribs.

"Come on. Let's go outside." Tripp bent down and scooped Penny and the elephant into his arms—the little girl burying her face in Tripp's neck—before heading to the back door.

Both Grant and Duke followed, and when Tripp closed the door behind them it shut out almost all of the yelling in the house. They went out onto the patio. Tripp sat down on the stone steps first and Grant took the space next to him.

"I don't like it when they argue," Grant said, running his hand through the fur on Duke's back. The dog had stationed himself at the boy's side.

"What happened?"

"Nora dyed her hair blue," Penny whispered into Tripp's neck as she nuzzled closer to him.

"Really? Blue?"

"Bright blue." Grant nodded. "At first Aunt B only grounded her for two weeks…but then Nora slammed the door in her face and it became three. They've been in there yelling for the last twenty minutes."

It was then that the door behind them opened, and Beth walked out to the patio. Her hands were shaking and there were bright patches of pink on her cheeks and neck.

But as she looked between Penny and Grant her anger deflated…and so did she. "I'm sorry, guys."

* * *

Tripp pulled the bottle of sauvignon blanc from the refrigerator and walked over to the kitchen island, where two wineglasses sat. He filled both up about halfway before tossing the now empty bottle into the recycling. Glasses in hand, he headed to the back porch where Beth was sitting on the sofa.

If anyone needed a drink at that moment, she did. It had not been the relaxing evening he'd planned. Not at all.

There'd been another confrontation over dinner when a blue-haired Nora marched into the kitchen, grabbed the carton of Lo Mein and some chopsticks, and attempted to head back to her bedroom.

Beth had stopped her and told her in no uncertain terms that she could either eat with them at the dinner table, or she wasn't eating at all.

Nora chose to eat, but she sat at the table without saying a word to anyone.

It was after nine now, and all three kids were in bed. Beth turned when he opened the door and stepped outside. She still had that deflated look about her, like she wouldn't be able to handle anything else for a while.

He handed her a glass before he sat down next to her, wrapping his arm around her shoulders and pulling her into his body. They took a few minutes to sip their wine, staring out into the darkness that stretched over the backyard.

"How are you still here?" she asked, turning to look up at him.

"What do you mean?" His gaze met hers and held.

"How are you not running out the front door?"

Run out the front door and go where? To his empty house? Yeah, the only way he would've left was if she'd asked him to. But she hadn't.

"I told you before, Beth. I'm not easily intimidated. Not even by a seventeen-year-old with blue hair."

"Oh God," she groaned as she turned her face and pressed it into his chest. "That blue hair."

"It could be worse." He moved his arm that was on the sofa behind her, bringing his hand to the back of her head, his fingers delving into her hair.

She looked at him again, frowning. "How? How could it be worse?"

"She could've dyed it orange."

A huff of air escaped her nose in a bitter laugh. "Orange would've been worse." She turned away from him before she said, "Tripp, I'm so bad at this. So bad at being a parent." Her voice caught on the last word.

Tripp leaned forward, setting his wineglass on the table before he moved his hand to her face, gently nudging her chin until she was looking at him again. Tears were brimming in her eyes, and when she blinked they fell, tracking down her cheeks.

These tears affected him a lot more than when she'd cried a couple of weeks ago. He hated them. He hated seeing her in pain like this.

"The only way you would be failing is if you gave up. Have you given up?" he asked as he ran his fingers beneath her eyes.

"On Nora? I would die before I gave up on her."

"Then you aren't failing."

She let out a long and low breath as she continued to look up into his eyes. "Thank you," she said after a moment. "Thank you for saying that. And thank you for staying."

"Where else would I be?" He leaned in and pressed his lips to hers.

Her mouth opened to his, and as he kissed her he knew beyond a shadow of a doubt that there wasn't any place he'd rather be, even with everything that had happened over the last few hours.

Nope. Nowhere else but in that moment with her.

Chapter Fifteen

Captain Commando

Before Beth even realized it, twelve days with Tripp turned into five weeks. He'd become a fixture in her—and the kids', for that matter—day-to-day life.

He ate dinner with them more evenings than not, even cooking for her and the kids on his days off. She'd come home on multiple nights to find him in her kitchen, Grant acting as his little culinary helper. The change in Grant had been amazing. He talked more, smiled more, laughed more.

Baseball had become Tripp's and Grant's *thing*, the catch sessions in the front yard continuing with regularity. Grant's progress had been remarkable, especially when it came to his strength, accuracy, and confidence. And something Beth really loved was that Tripp had even started calling Grant Goose. Adopting the moniker for her nephew had meant more than she could have ever imagined.

Then there was Penny. That child adored Tripp, following him around and asking him a million questions. She'd wrap her little fist in the fabric of his pants leg and tug, looking up at him before holding her hands out to be picked up. He always complied. He also never denied her a story at the end of the night. She'd crawl into his lap with a book in her hand, and politely ask him to read to her.

Nora was a different story. The blue hair incident had been a pretty significant setback. For a couple of weeks she'd been way more sour than usual. But as the blue faded from her hair—a process that had been sped along by a hair treatment Beth bought—her attitude seemed to improve slightly.

As for Nora's attitude toward Tripp…

In the beginning it appeared that her niece was just tolerating Tripp's presence. But as the days progressed her stone cold demeanor seemed to soften, showing that she might actually like having him around.

The biggest change had happened two weeks ago. Nora had asked Tripp for help with her chemistry homework. As Tripp was a science whiz it made perfect sense, but the fact that Nora had asked him? Yeah, Beth's jaw had almost hit the floor.

Tripp was beyond patient with Nora, too. He'd sit at the dining room table with her and go over the theories and formulas until she completely understood. And miracle of miracles, he'd even been able to make her laugh on occasion.

It didn't even upset Beth that for the most part Nora was nicer to Tripp than she was to Beth. Mainly this was due to the fact that *anything* good coming from Nora made Beth happy. She was able to get glimpses of the niece she knew, and she'd take that over nothing any day of the week.

Another part of Beth's optimism had to do with the effect Tripp was having on Beth herself. Many people had told her that she looked much happier and way less stressed. There'd been a marked change in her life and in the kids' lives, and Tripp had been the catalyst.

There were some nights and weekends where he wasn't around because he was working. When he was on call, he'd had to leave the dinner table a handful of times to respond to an emergency. Other times his truck was missing from the driveway when she got home, or sometimes it was already gone when she woke up in the morning.

The worry that accompanied those days was unavoidable for Beth. How could she not be concerned? Her boyfriend walked into danger for a living. She'd be lying if she said the risk involved in his profession didn't worry her. The relief that coursed through her when she saw his truck pulling into the driveway or when her phone would light up with his name on the screen proved that. But with what had happened in the last year there was anxiety involved in caring about anyone, really.

Other facets of their relationship were taking some time to figure out as well…like their sex life. It was pretty much a get-it-when-they-could situation, which meant they could only be together on her lunch breaks or early in the mornings on the weekends. As for sleepovers, those took place solely at Tripp's house, and those had been few and far between. Sleepovers only happened when the kids were with Papa Wallace.

They might have been over a month into the relationship, but Beth wasn't ready for him to stay the night when the kids were home. And that was something he completely understood: the kids were still getting used to him being around and she hadn't been ready to introduce that particular element to them…yet.

The "too soon" conversation was one that she was going to need to talk out with her friends, not just with regard to his spending the night, but to how quickly their relationship was moving. Luckily for Beth, she was getting together with them that Friday night for margaritas and mayhem.

Nora was no longer on house suspension. The blue was entirely gone from her hair and her three weeks of being grounded were up. Though she might still be the sullen teenager Beth was becoming accustomed to, her behavior—for the most part—was better. That, and the fact that she'd made the honor roll for the third time that year, made Beth a little more agreeable when Nora asked to go to the high school basketball game that night.

Since both Beth and Nora would be out, Wallace said he'd come over to watch Penny and Grant until Beth got home.

Friday was a supremely slow day at the doctor's office; there weren't even any appointments scheduled after the lunch hour. It was Beth's turn to go home early, and she jumped at the chance to spend a few extra hours with Tripp, who just so happened to have the day off.

She pulled out her phone as she headed out of the building and dialed Tripp's number. He picked up on the second ring.

"Hey, babe. What's going on?"

"I got off early today." She looked around the parking lot to make sure no one was within hearing distance. "And I was wondering what the odds were of us getting each other off."

"I'd say they were pretty damn high." She could hear the grin in his voice.

"You at home?"

"On the way now."

"I'll see you there." She hung up, picking up her pace to her car.

* * *

Tripp was just getting out of his truck when Beth pulled into her driveway. He leaned back against the door of the truck as she made her way across the lawn, letting his eyes linger over every inch of her. She was wearing dark purple scrubs today, blond hair thrown up in a high ponytail, sunglasses perched on her nose.

She walked right up to him, grabbing the front of his shirt and stretching up for his mouth. Her lips opened instantly, her tongue finding his. It was the kind of kiss that always let him know she was in the mood, and had the ability to make him hard in an instant.

Though her phone call had pretty much taken care of that.

"Hello, gorgeous." He smiled against her lips.

"You already know you're getting laid, right?"

"Doesn't mean I can't tell you the truth."

She raised her eyebrows at him.

"What? I'm becoming partial to these scrubs of yours. Maybe because I'm peeling you out of them more often than anything else."

"Well, then how about you get to peeling?"

"Come on." He grabbed her hand and led her to the house.

Once they were in his bedroom, they began to undress each other. He started with her hair first, pulling the tie out so all of that blond goodness fell down around her shoulders. She started with his belt buckle, her hands delving past the waistband and stroking his erection.

When all of their clothes littered the floor, Beth took charge, pushing him back onto the bed. She climbed on top of him, straddling his thighs as she slid the condom down his cock...and then she was sliding down his cock.

Now Tripp was an equal opportunity guy when it came to the bedroom. He liked a woman on top just as much as he liked being on top. But Beth? Damn, there were no words for her taking control. No words for watching her ride him, for watching her lose herself in the moment.

He held onto her hips, more for the opportunity to touch her than to guide her. She didn't need guidance. She knew exactly what she was doing and she was fucking magnificent at it, too.

They'd found their rhythm, him thrusting up as she moved down, her blond hair falling over her shoulders, her breasts bouncing with every movement. Then there were the sounds she made, those gasps and throaty moans. But his favorite thing? Well, his favorite was when she said his name.

"Tripp." She threw her head back as he brought one of his hands between their bodies and found her sweet spot, applying just the right amount of pressure.

"That's it, baby," he told her. "Take it. Take what you want." Lord knew he was taking exactly what he wanted.

"Oh God." She leaned forward, bracing her hands on his chest as she started to move on him harder...faster.

She cried out his name when she hit her peak, her body tightening around him in the most perfect spasms. He let go, giving in to the pleasure he'd been holding back from until she came first. Both of his hands were at her hips again, thrusting up hard and riding out his release.

Beth fell onto him, those perfect breasts of hers smashed against his chest, her face pressed into his neck. Her breaths were ragged, hitting his skin in uneven puffs. A thin sheen of sweat coated both of them, and when he opened his mouth on her shoulder he tasted the salt on her skin.

He brought his hand to her back, trailing his fingers up and down her spine and making her shiver against him.

"Cold?"

"No." She nuzzled her face into his throat. "I like your hands on me."

"That makes two of us." He rolled them, now hovering over her as he looked down into her face. "I'll be right back." He kissed her lips before he pulled from her body and got out of bed.

He cleaned up and when he stepped back into the room, Beth was sitting at the edge of the bed, pulling his T-shirt from the pile of clothes on the floor. She stood as she slipped it over her head, the blue fabric dropping down and covering her to mid-thigh.

"Now why do you insist upon covering up such an awesome view?"

She shook her head at him, but a grin fought at the edges of her exasperation. "I thought we already discussed that I'm not an exhibitionist. But you, Captain Commando, should feel free to walk around however you like." She gestured below his waist with one of her hands, eyes lingering for just a moment before she cleared her throat and looked up.

"Captain Commando?" He raised his eyebrows.

"Yup. Your aversion to underwear has been noted. Now I'm going to get some water," she said before she turned to the door. "I'm feeling rather parched. Probably from all of that screaming you make me do."

Tripp laughed as she walked away, reaching for his discarded jeans on the floor. He pulled them on before following her out into the kitchen. She already had a glass in her hand and was pressing it to the water dispenser on the fridge.

"Changed your mind, I see?" She asked before she took a long drink of water and then slowly lowered the glass from her mouth.

"I didn't want you to get distracted again." He moved closer to her, reaching up and catching a drop of water that clung to her lip with his thumb.

"I'm not inclined to believe you."

"You shouldn't." He grabbed the half full glass from her hands and finished off the water. "You eat lunch yet?"

"No, you?"

He shook his head. "Soup and sandwich sound good?"

"Perfect." She nodded, heading for his pantry for the bread. "Tripp?"

"Hmm?" He pulled a pot out of the cabinet before turning to her.

She was facing him now, a half empty jar of peanut butter in her hand. "I thought you hated this stuff. You have three jars of it in here."

"I do hate it. I bought it for Grant."

Besides her eyes going wide with shock, her entire body froze. "You did?"

"What?" He shrugged his shoulders. "Sometimes when he comes over after school, he wants a snack. I thought it would be a good idea to have something here that he likes. It isn't that big of a deal."

Beth had still been holding the jar of peanut butter up in the air like a statue, but her arm finally dropped as she shook her head. "I disagree." She turned back to the pantry and put the jar back on the shelf. When she grabbed the bread she shut the door and headed to the counter space next to him.

"You stocking up on stuff for Grant is super sweet."

"Oh yeah? Then what would you say to the fact that I stock up on stuff for you too?"

She'd been working on the twist tie at the top of the bag and she stopped as she turned to look at him. "What do you stock up for me?"

"Condoms." He smirked, waggling his eyebrows.

Her head fell back as a burst of laughter escaped her lips, and he swooped in close, lightly nipping her neck with his teeth. God, he loved that sound, could listen to her laugh all damn day.

Beth continued her sandwich making while Tripp pulled a Tupperware container of Lula Mae's homemade chicken noodle soup from the refrigerator. He'd just poured enough into the pot when Beth's cell phone started ringing. Britney Spears's "Toxic" filled the air.

"Be right back," she said as she wiped her hands on a towel.

Right after they'd gotten into the house, she'd deposited her purse on the table near the entrance. As she headed that way, the oversize T-shirt she wore swayed around her thighs. Thighs that had been straddling him not that long ago.

He grinned.

"Hey dad," Beth said as she came back into the room, phone held to her ear as she paused on the threshold of the kitchen. "Oh no. Do you need anything?" A beat of silence. "Are you sure? I'm not at work; I can get you something." Another beat of silence. "You don't need to apologize. It's fine. It isn't a big deal if I don't go. Just feel better, dad. And call me if you need anything. Okay?" After another moment she said, "I love you," then hung up the phone.

"What's wrong?"

"Dad isn't feeling well. He has a migraine and can't come over to watch the kids. I need to call Mel and tell her I can't make it tonight," she said as she started to press buttons on her phone.

"Why do you have to cancel?"

"Because." Beth looked up at him. "I already promised Nora she could go to the basketball game at the high school and I don't have a sitter for Penny and Grant. Besides, Grant doesn't do well with strangers."

"I can watch them."

"W-what?"

"I can watch Penny and Grant tonight. It isn't a problem."

Her mouth hung open for a second, words apparently failing her. "You're serious?" she asked after a moment, setting her phone on the counter.

"Yes, I'm serious. What, do you not trust me with them?"

"Tripp, I trust you more than most. I just didn't think that babysitting was how you'd want to spend your Friday night."

"I like spending time with the kids, Beth. We can order takeout and watch a movie. I have absolutely no doubt that it will be fun."

"All right." She was standing in front of him now, looking up into his face. "You never cease to amaze me, Tripp Black." She put a palm on his chest, stretching up and brushing her lips across his. "Thank you."

Chapter Sixteen

A Tea Party with a Possum, a Snake, a Turtle, a Toddler, and a Thirty-Five-Year-Old Man

At six thirty the chime of the front doorbell pealed through the house. As Beth was still in the process of getting dressed—and as he'd been kicked out of the room because he kept distracting her—it was Tripp who opened the door to find Mel and Bennett on the other side.

It was a given that when the girls got together for nights such as this, they drank. Tripp knew Beth had every intention of partaking in multiple margaritas, so obviously she—or any of the other ladies, for that matter—wasn't going to be driving. Bennett was acting as DD for his wife, and he'd drive Beth to the restaurant and back as well.

"Fancy seeing you here," Mel said as she stepped over the threshold, patting Tripp's chest with her palm before she headed down the hallway. "Where's your girlfriend?" she asked over her shoulder.

"Bedroom," he called out before turning to Bennett.

"I hear you're babysitting tonight. Looks like I'm not the only one having a sober evening," Bennett said as they headed for the living room.

"The only thing I will be drinking is imaginary tea." Tripp nodded to the low table in the corner, where Penny was setting up the tea party with all of the guests of honor.

The first was Mordecai the possum. Yup, Penny had a stuffed animal possum. Tripp had won it for her in the Papa Pan's Pizza claw machine last week. The thing was so ugly it was cute. A chair had been placed behind it so that its front paws rested on the table, and its whiskery little nose was pointed toward the butter dish.

The second guest was Elsa the lizard. This stuffed animal was so large that Penny was able to make it sit up right in the chair. How it was possible for the thing to look regal, Tripp would never know. Maybe it was because of the blue and silver scales, or the fact that the end of its tail trailed on the floor like a train.

The third guest was Steve the turtle. The little plastic figurine was about the size of Tripp's hand, and therefore too small to sit on a chair. Instead the turtle had been placed right there on the table, its head stretching out toward the toy blue berry muffin that sat on a tiny plate with pink roses.

"My goal tonight," Tripp told Bennett, "is to get Steve over there to come out of his shell."

Penny looked up at Tripp and giggled.

"Hey," Grant called out from where he was currently playing tug o' war with Duke in the kitchen. Tripp had brought the dog, along with a few toys, over with him. "Don't forget we're drinking Dr. Pepper, too!"

"My bad. Imaginary tea *and* Dr. Pepper," Tripp amended, holding his palms up in the air.

"Sounds like a real party," Bennett said.

"Oh, it will be, my friend. It *will* be." He gave Bennett a sideways smirk before his attention was entirely diverted to Beth, who'd just walked into the living room.

Her hair was curled around her shoulders and absolutely begging for his fingers to dive in. That pouty mouth of hers was painted a soft pink that he had every desire to kiss off. The turquoise sleeveless shirt she wore showed just a hint of cleavage and her jeans looked like they'd been painted on.

He crossed to her on instinct, a moth to a fucking flame. "Come here," he said as he put his hands on her waist, pulling her in close. "You look incredible." He pressed his lips to her mouth, deciding that kissing her lipstick off was a much safer bet then putting his hands in her hair.

She wouldn't be able to easily fix the latter.

When he'd made her good and truly breathless, he moved his mouth to her ear. "Feel free to text me any of your drunken inappropriate thoughts throughout the night."

She pulled away and looked into his eyes. "What makes you think I'll have such thoughts?"

"Because I know you, Beth Boone." He pressed another quick kiss to her lips before letting go.

"It's possible that you do," she said as she reached up and swiped her thumb across his lips, wiping away the lipstick. When she dropped her hand she looked over to Penny and Grant. "You guys going to be good for Tripp?" she asked.

"Mmm hmm." Grant barely looked over as he continued to play with Duke.

"Yessssss," Penny said as she ran over to Beth, arms held out wide.

Beth leaned down and scooped her niece up in an easy swoop, placing the child on her hip. Penny leaned forward, kissing Beth with a loud smack on the cheek. "Tripp said I could pick the movie tonight."

"Oh, did he?" Beth looked at Tripp. "I'm thinking you're in for a night with a Disney princess or two."

"And?" He shrugged. "Ariel is a pretty cool chick. I could hang with her."

"I'm totally all about Sleeping Beauty," Bennett said, looking at Mel with a massive grin. "Beautiful blonde who doesn't like to wake up."

Mel narrowed her eyes at her husband, her mouth in a frown. "You're hilarious."

"I know I am."

Beth set Penny back down, kissing her on the top of her little blond head before straightening. Beth's eyes were back on Tripp as she spoke, "I'll have my phone on in case you need to call me."

"I know you will. But I've got everything under control. Which means you should have fun tonight and not worry."

"Yeah." Mel linked her arm in Beth's and started to tug her toward the door. "No. Worrying."

"I'll do my best." Beth blew Tripp a kiss before she let herself be led away.

"I'll see you later. Have fun with the kiddos," Bennett said before he followed the two ladies out.

Penny stepped closer to Tripp, wrapping her arms around his leg and looking up at him. "Are you ready for the tea party?" she asked.

"All right, but dinner is going to be here in about twenty minutes, so when it gets here we're taking a break."

"Okay." Penny nodded and let go of Tripp's leg. She reached up for his hand, her tiny fingers engulfed by his massive ones. "Let's go!"

He complied, letting her lead him over to her expertly set table. And for the first time in Tripp's life, he had tea with a possum, a lizard, a turtle, and the cutest toddler on the face of the planet.

* * *

When Bennett dropped Mel and Beth off at Caliente's—Mirabelle's one and only Mexican restaurant—the place was fairly busy. They walked in and were led to a table in the corner of the back porch, where Grace, Paige, and Hannah were already sitting.

"I figured it was safer for us to stay a little bit away from other people," Hannah told Beth and Mel as they sat down. "Less likely to be overheard by strangers when our conversations veer to certain topics."

"Are you saying our conversations are inappropriate?" Grace held one hand to her chest, feigning offense.

"Oh, whatever do you mean?" Paige, a northerner born and raised, asked with a thoroughly exaggerated southern twang.

Paige had gotten back from her trip with her husband Brendan three weeks ago, and besides one hurried run-in at the Piggly Wiggly, they hadn't gotten the opportunity for an in-depth catch up.

But before Beth could even open her mouth Paige was speaking. "All right, woman, spill."

"Why do I have to go first?" Beth asked. "You just went on an Italian adventure."

"We can get to that later. I want to know how you snagged Tripp."

"You know he's babysitting the kids tonight," Mel smirked.

"Seriously?" Paige's palm came down and smacked the table. "Yeah, you are definitely starting."

"Should we wait until Harper gets here?" Hannah asked.

"Harper isn't coming." Mel shook her head.

"She isn't?" Paige broke a chip in half before dipping it into the bowl of salsa.

"No," Beth chimed in, fully aware of why Harper wasn't showing up. She'd been given permission to share from the source, too. "She had her post-baby check-up today and got the all clear from Dr. Walker."

"I don't think she and Liam will be leaving the house all weekend," Mel added.

"Sooo," Grace grinned as she waggled her eyebrows. "She is *coming*, just not here. She called me the second she left to tell me she wouldn't be joining us tonight. I'm pretty sure the only place she stopped on the way home was to stock up on the essentials."

"What, you mean condoms and wine?" Beth asked.

"Obviously," Paige nodded. "So, speaking of getting some, let's bring the topic back to Beth."

"You're a woman on a mission, aren't you?"

"You bet I am! Come on, Tripp has been friends with us for over three years now. Three!" Paige held three fingers up in the air to emphasize her point. "And not once has he brought a woman around. Then, all of a sudden, you come around and he's done for."

"All of a sudden?" Beth laughed. "Are you forgetting the part where I've known him for two of those three years?"

"That first year doesn't count," Mel chimed in. "For one, you had a boyfriend."

"*Jackass*," Grace coughed into her hand.

"Exactly." Mel nodded. "And two, you didn't live here."

"But I *have* lived here for the last year, and we've been neighbors for months. Most of that time was just massive amounts of resentment and contention."

At that moment their waiter came up with a tray holding five beautiful, lime-green margaritas, salt coating the glass rims.

"Okay, it's been a slow burn," Paige amended her statement when the waiter walked away. "But now everything is on fire, and I want to hear *all* about it. So start from the very first spark."

"You're not going to stop until I do, are you?"

"Nope." Paige shook her head, lifting her margarita glass to her mouth.

"We want to know what's got you so happy," Hannah grinned.

"You mean that smile she's been rocking?" Grace asked. "Regular sex will do that to a girl."

"Of that there is no doubt. And you better not leave anything out." Mel gave her stern teacher look, which always meant business.

"Fine." Beth grabbed her own margarita, taking a sip—actually, it was more like a gulp—to fortify herself before she began her tale. "So there I was…"

* * *

Beth was on her second margarita, feeling a mighty nice buzz, before she finally broached the particular topic she'd wanted to ask her friends about.

"I need advice," she said as she pushed her now empty plate of chicken enchiladas aside.

"On what, exactly?" Paige asked.

"How soon is too soon for Tripp to stay the night?"

"Wait." Hannah held up her hand. "I thought you said you *had* slept in the same bed as him."

"I have, just not at my house. It's always at his place and when the kids are with my dad."

"And you don't know when it's okay to have him stay the night when the kids *are* there?" Grace asked as she lifted her margarita glass to her lips.

"No, I don't."

"Babe, that's not something any of us have experience with." Mel shook her head. "We all started our relationships without that particular element."

"Yes, but you all had *things* to deal with." Beth sat up straighter in her chair. "Hell, Mel, you'd been shot not that long before you and Bennett started up. And Paige, it took you months to let Brendan into your bed."

"Actually, it was his bed that I let myself into, and he was only too eager to let me." Paige waved her hand in the air. "But please continue."

"Hannah, you and Shep had this heartbreaking past that made you question starting things up with him again. And Grace, well…Grace, your husband was blind to the fact that the two of you had been in love with each other for years. So all of you had *elements* to contend with, even if they aren't the same as mine."

"Okay, okay you made your point," Grace said as she finished off the last of her margarita.

The waiter came up to the table just as the empty glass was set back down. "Another round?"

"Please." Mel smiled at him before returning her attention to her friends.

"And it's not just about him staying the night, either," Beth told her friends. "It's our relationship as a whole. I…I worry that we're moving too fast. And the impact that could have on the kids."

"Speaking of the kids." Mel looked at Beth. "Are they still sleeping in bed with you? Because that would put the kibosh on Tripp staying the night real quick."

"Only during the really bad storms, which have been happening a little less frequently lately."

There was a beat of silence as everyone took a moment to think, and it was Hannah who spoke first this time.

"I think you should do what feels right when it comes to how your relationship progresses. That's my piece of advice for you. I fought what I felt for Shep for weeks when I came back down here. And it just made everything harder for both of us. I mean, when I really think about it, I actually fought what felt right for thirteen freaking years, which was being *with* him. It was only when I stopped fighting it that all of the good stuff started to happen."

"Like him moving in with you at the inn, getting married, and having a baby?" Paige asked.

"Exactly." Hannah grinned hugely.

"I agree with Hannah," Mel nodded. "I remember how great it was when I stopped fighting what I wanted with Bennett. When we both gave in to it."

"I, on the other hand"—Grace touched her chest—"never fought what I wanted with Jax. It was him who was fighting, and we all know where that got us."

"I'm not fighting anything." Beth paused for a second then

started to chew on her bottom lip. "I mean, I don't think I'm fighting anything."

"Maybe you are, maybe you aren't." Paige shrugged. "But there has to be some *instinct* that's leading you in a certain direction, and if the instinct isn't there yet, maybe it's not the time. I think it's just going to feel right when it *is* right, and there will come a moment when you stop overthinking and just do."

"Wasn't that how it was when you decided to start something with Tripp in the first place?" Hannah asked. "It just felt right?"

"I…" Beth trailed off. Well, yeah, straddling Tripp in his backyard while he'd touched and kissed her had felt pretty damn right. Everything after had felt even better.

"What do you want, Beth?" Grace asked.

"Because, really"—Mel raised her eyebrows—"that's the ultimate question."

Chapter Seventeen

Closer

After the third round of margaritas, they all had a fourth. Because the drinks had been spaced out over four hours, and because Beth had kept up with her water intake, she wasn't drunk. Though when Bennett dropped her off at eleven o'clock, she *was* feeling pretty damn good…and wasn't overthinking anything.

Beth unlocked and opened the front door before turning to wave to Bennett and Mel, who were sitting in his idling truck parked in the driveway. Then she stepped inside, locking the door behind her. The hall light had been left on and she dropped her purse on the table by the front door before making her way down the hallway.

The only sound coming from the living room was "A Whole New World" from the end credits of Aladdin. The only light came from the movie flickering on the TV and the soft glow from the lamp in the corner. When Beth stepped into the room, the scene before her had her heart catching in her throat.

Everyone in the room was asleep. Tripp was sprawled out on

the floor with Penny snuggled up on his chest, her little hand clutched in the fabric of his T-shirt. Grant was a few feet away, using a softly snoring Duke as his pillow. And last—but certainly not least—Nora was passed out on the sofa. She had changed into pajamas and her face was washed clean of makeup.

Beth stood there for more than a minute, committing the moment to memory. All three of her kids were peacefully asleep…along with the man that she loved. Because there was no doubt that Beth was in love with Tripp Black. He'd stolen her heart the very first time he'd kissed her; she just hadn't realized it until that very moment.

She reached up and wiped her fingers across her cheeks, unsure of when she'd started crying. Fresh tears fell with each blink, but unlike so many times over the last year, they weren't tears of loss or pain or frustration. No, they were tears of joy. It had been too long since she'd had those, and she savored them for everything that they were worth.

It was only when the credits stopped rolling and the room turned blue from the screen's light that Beth finally moved. She crossed to Tripp, kneeling down beside him and gently brushing her fingertips across his forehead. His eyes snapped open and his body tensed for just a second before he focused on her.

"Hey," he whispered, his voice groggy and rough.

"Hi." She brushed her fingers across his forehead again before she leaned down and pressed her lips to his. It was just a soft kiss, a simple brushing of mouths. When she pulled back her attention moved to Penny, still sound asleep on Tripp's chest. "They exhaust you?"

"I think it was a joint effort." He smiled at her sleepily.

"I should get them to bed." Beth ran her palm down Penny's back.

"Yeah." He nodded, sitting up.

Beth stood and Tripp handed Penny up. True to form, the child didn't wake, just stirred a little as she snuggled into Beth's arms. Beth held her niece close, kissing her soft blond hair as she made her way down the hallway to the second bedroom on the left.

By the time Penny was tucked into bed and her star night light turned on, Tripp had already moved the other two kids to their beds. Nora had rolled over onto her side, arms wrapped around one of her pillows. Beth grabbed the door and pulled it nearly closed, keeping it cracked by a few inches the way she had with Penny's.

When Beth crossed over to her nephew's room, Tripp was getting Grant settled. Duke was sitting at the foot of the bed, his big fluffy head resting on the end of the quilt that Tripp was currently adjusting around Grant's shoulders. Quilt adjusting finished, Tripp reached up and brushed back the hair that had fallen across Grant's forehead.

Such a simple gesture filled with so much affection. Just that quickly Beth's heart was in her throat again.

Tripp straightened and turned around, his eyes now on her. She didn't say anything, just held out her hand to him. He closed the distance, grabbing her hand and interlocking their fingers as she led him out into the hallway.

Tripp turned, about to call Duke, who was now lounging on the floor next to Grant's bed.

"Leave him for a minute." Beth tugged Tripp's hand. She turned to him, both of her hands landing on his chest as she looked up into his face. "The kids were good?"

"Of course they were. No issues. Well-behaved. We all had a good time."

"When did Nora get home?"

"Around nine thirty. She came home, got pajama'd and joined us for *Aladdin*...which we all apparently fell asleep to." Tripp reached for her face, tracing the line of her jaw. "Did you have a good time?"

"I did. It was nice to get out with the girls."

"I'm glad." He leaned down, his lips hovering above hers. "Just so you know, you taste like margaritas," he said before he opened his mouth over hers.

This kiss was not a simple brushing of mouths, but one that devoured. Beth's hands roamed across Tripp's chest while his migrated south to her ass, his fingers flexing and kneading as he held her to him.

Beth slid her palms up over his shoulders and to the back of his head. With her fingers tangling in his hair she pulled back and looked up at him, this man that she wanted...*needed*. And even though she wasn't prepared to tell him that she was in love with him, she could show him. Show him how much he meant to her.

"Stay." Never in her life had she felt more certain about one word, and she was definitely doing what felt right. "Stay all night, with me, in my bed. Please."

Tripp's hands moved up to her waist, his grip tightening as he leaned down close to her mouth, their lips barely a breath apart. "That's a request I'd never refuse." He kissed her again, his tongue finding hers.

She'd become well-versed in what happened when the two of them lost control in a kiss, and she had to stop it from happening right then.

"Bedroom," she gasped when she pulled back, breathless. "No wall sex tonight...Well, at least not these walls." She gestured to the space around them.

"That probably wouldn't be wise." His grip on her waist tightened and he turned her around. "Lead the way," he whispered in her ear.

Beth grabbed one of his hands and did just that, pulling him across the living room, through the kitchen, and into her bedroom. He closed the door behind them with a snap and then she was in his arms again.

The room was semi-illuminated by the moon glowing through the open blinds, so neither of them let go long enough to turn on a light. They didn't say a word as they undressed each other. The only sounds were of their unsteady breaths between kisses, and their clothes hitting the floor.

Once they were both fully naked, he pulled her against him, the hard length of his erection pressing into her belly. His mouth hovered over hers as his hands traveled down her bare back, fingers tracing her spine.

"I'll never get over how your skin feels under my hands. How you feel against me." One of his palms slid all the way down her back, and over the curve of her ass. Then he was touching her, his fingers running over her folds and finding her wet. "How it feels to be inside of you."

"Tripp!" She gasped as he slid one long finger inside of her, pumping his hand a few times before he pulled all the way out...and then slid in two fingers. Her body arched in his arms, her grip on his shoulders tightened.

"I'll never get over how you respond to how I touch you. How your body reacts to me. What it's like to kiss you. And Beth, I will *never* get over the taste of you." His mouth landed on hers, his tongue sliding between her lips. His fingers hadn't stopped moving in and out of her, applying pressure to every spot that made her squirm and rub up against his erection.

"I need to be inside of you, Beth." His mouth slid down her throat and he placed a hot open-mouthed kiss right above her collarbone. "I need you to be wrapped around me in every way."

"I need that, too." She said it to the ceiling, as her head was currently rolled back on her shoulders, giving Tripp greater access to her neck.

"Where are your condoms?"

His question had her head coming up, her eyes meeting his. "Tripp, I…I don't want anything between us." They'd been together long enough that he knew she was on birth control. "I know I'm safe."

"I have to get a physical every six months. I'm clean."

"I trust you." Her hand moved to his face, cupping his cheek in her palm. "I don't want any barriers, Tripp. I just want you. I just want *us.*"

"God, yes," he groaned before kissing her again, grabbing on to her thighs, and lifting her up in one easy move. He only had to take a few steps back until he could sit on the edge of the bed. She straddled him now, her knees sinking into the mattress on either side of his thighs.

One of her hands was at his shoulder, gripping it hard as she levered herself up. The other hand was between their bodies, wrapping around his cock and lining him up with her entrance. Her eyes moved back to his—eyes that were filled with a type of longing and heat that she'd *never* seen before—as she slowly lowered herself down, impaling herself fully.

They both inhaled at the same moment, stealing each other's air.

Tripp's hands were at her hips, holding her steady. "Give me…just a second." The words left his lips more than slightly strained. "You feel soo fucking good. *Too* fucking good."

Yeah, he wasn't the only one who needed a second to gather himself. Because really, Tripp bare, thick, and hard inside her was more than she'd ever experienced before.

And they hadn't even really begun.

His grip at her waist tightened and he lifted her up, the core of her dragging along the length of him, before he pushed her back down. She was just slightly higher than he was, only needing to lean down a few inches to get to his mouth.

"Slow," he breathed against her lips.

"Slow," she repeated.

They were both moving now. Tripp's feet were still on the floor, allowing him to get leverage. Both of her arms looped around his shoulders as she kissed him. One of his hands left her waist, moving to her breasts. He brushed his thumb across one nipple, then the other, and even more pleasure shot through her.

Her lips fell away from his on a moan, her back arching. Tripp's head bent, his lips at her breast where he rasped his tongue across one puckered peak, and then drew it into his mouth.

"Oh, oh, oh." Her hands were at the back of his head now, fingers in his hair as she held him to her.

The first orgasm was a slow build, a combination of how they moved together, how his mouth moved over her breasts, how he held her, touched her, tasted her. She had to hold herself back from screaming, but his name did escape her lips when she came.

Her body was still pulsing around him when she found herself on her back in the middle of the bed, Tripp thrusting in and pulling out of her still-clinging body. He looked down into her face, grabbing one of her hands and stretching it high above their heads, their fingers twining together. In their new position, she could just make out that possessiveness in his eyes as he lowered his head, kissing her in a slow lingering way that matched how his body moved over hers, moved in her. But when his mouth started to move harder, his kiss more demanding, so did his hips.

She was more than grateful that his mouth was still on hers when she came for the second time, because she wouldn't have been able to keep that one quiet. Not one little bit. And as Tripp groaned against her mouth with his own release, apparently he couldn't, either.

He collapsed on top of her—he had no other choice, really, as her legs were wrapped solidly around his waist—sweaty and shaking as he buried his face against her throat. She wasn't even remotely ready for him to move away from her. Wasn't ready for him to leave her body. She loved how he covered her, loved how his weight pushed her down into the mattress, loved how he filled her.

Loved *him*.

"What?" Tripp asked as he pulled up and looked into her eyes. "What did you just say?"

Her mouth fell open on a gasp. She hadn't even realized she'd been speaking out loud. Why did this always happen with him? Why couldn't she keep her thoughts inside her head?

"I—I didn't mean to. I—"

"Are you taking it back?" The corner of his mouth quirked up as he lowered his head, his lips just brushing over hers. "Because I'm in love with you, too, Beth Boone."

Beth gasped again, and he took advantage, his tongue dipping inside of her mouth. She brought her hands to the back of his head again, holding him to her. He rolled them both, him on his back, her sprawled across his chest.

She levered up on her arms, her hair swinging forward on either side of her face as she looked down.

"I've been waiting for you to figure it out." He looked at her as he reached up and pushed her hair back and behind her ears. "I didn't want to tell you before you realized you loved me back. Didn't want to freak you out."

"Me? Freak out?"

"Yes. You. I know you're worried about how fast this is moving."

"And you're not?" Her heart was still beating rapidly in her chest.

"No." He shook his head. "I've never wanted something more in my life. I love you, Beth. So damn much."

"When did you realize it?"

"It was one of those nights Wallace had the kids. And when I got home from work, I found you taking a nap in my bed. You were curled up around one of my pillows, and you looked so damn peaceful. All I could think was what I wouldn't give to know what you were dreaming about."

The memory of that afternoon came flooding back to her. She'd been exhausted because, courtesy of another thunderstorm, the three kids had joined her in bed the night before. She also knew exactly what she'd been dreaming about because when he'd kissed her to wake her up, she'd thought she'd still been dreaming.

"You. I was dreaming about you, Tripp." She leaned down and pressed her lips to his.

"Tell me again," he whispered against her mouth.

"I love you."

"Again."

"I love you."

"Again…"

* * *

Coming to consciousness was slow going for Beth the following morning. It took her more than a couple of seconds to realize she was naked, that the sheets were moving over her bare skin.

She never slept naked these days…unless she was in Tripp's bed. But no, she was definitely in her bed. She knew that without a doubt. Her mattress, her sheets, her scent of laundry detergent.

When she opened her eyes, it took a few bleary-eyed blinks to adjust to the sunlight that beamed through the window. She hadn't closed the blinds before she went to bed last night…

Last night…Tripp, in her bed. Her accidentally telling him she loved him…him saying it back.

Her eyes moved over to the empty space next to her. The sheets were rumpled and there was a definite impression in the other pillow.

He left?

The clank of a pan being set on the stove came from the kitchen. A moment later the low rumble of Tripp's voice hit her ears and the smell of coffee and bacon filled her nose.

Beth scrambled out of bed, making a quick trip to the bathroom before grabbing her robe from the back of the door and tying the sash securely around her waist. She opened the door and walked out to find everyone in the kitchen.

Tripp was at the stove in his jeans and T-shirt from yesterday, with a still pajama'd Nora at his side. A pan of bacon was crisping up in front of him while he held his hand a few inches above an empty pan on another burner, testing the heat.

"Put a little bit of that butter in the pan," he told Nora and pointed to the butter dish on the counter with his tongs. "Spread it around as it melts and then add the eggs." He indicated the bowel of whisked-up and seasoned eggs by the butter dish.

"Okay." She nodded as she cut off a dollop. "This good?"

"Yup. In the pan."

Both Penny and Grant were sitting on stools at the center island, flour spread all over the granite countertop, and just a little dusted across their noses and cheeks. Duke was at Penny's side, his head in her lap.

"Morning," Beth said as all eyes turned to her.

"Aunt B! We made pancakes!" Penny squealed. "But don't sneak Duke any of the chocolate chip ones because they aren't good for him."

Duke's head perked up at the sound of his name, but when Penny started to scratch the dog's ears, he rested his head back in her lap.

"Only the plain ones." Grant pointed to the center of the counter at a plate covered with a white towel.

"Is that so." She raised her eyebrows at Tripp, whose gaze was entirely focused on her.

"It is." He grinned at her.

"What do you have going on over there, Nora?"

"Super fluffy, and cheesy, scrambled eggs," Nora said, not taking her attention off the job in front of her, where she slowly ran the spatula across the bottom of the pan.

"Does anything else need to be done?" Beth asked as she glanced over at the dining room table, which had already been set.

"Nope." He shook his head. "Breakfast will be ready in about five. Coffee is brewed, though. You can make yourself a cup if you need a little caffeine."

"I always need a little caffeine," she said as she went over to the coffee maker, a smile turning up her mouth.

A girl could get used to mornings like this.

Chapter Eighteen

A Little Alone Time

Beth was pretty sure her niece was hell bent on making her lose her damn mind. Nora hadn't even been off of probation for a full week before she was grounded again. This time it was for piercing her belly button.

Apparently, the offending little diamond stud had been poking through the girl's abdomen for three months now. It was only by chance that Beth had found it. She'd gone into her niece's room to wake her up for school and Nora's shirt had ridden up while she slept.

One of Nora's less-than-reputable new friends had a cousin who was a tattoo artist and also did piercings. Beth was just beyond grateful it hadn't been something permanent.

The stud had been removed and Nora was grounded for another three weeks, though the first week would be broken up from weeks two and three. The week between was the kids' Spring Break and if thousands of dollars hadn't already been invested on it, Nora wouldn't have been leaving the house. Besides, there was no way Beth would ever deny Nora time spent with her grandparents.

Grand Cass and Grandpa D were Kevin's parents, otherwise known as Cassandra and Dennis Ross. They lived in West Palm Beach, which was about a seven-hour drive from Mirabelle. So they only got to see the kids during the holidays or when they made the trek up.

Cassandra and Dennis had asked Beth months ago if they could get the kids during Spring Break that year. They wanted to take them to half a dozen theme parks in Orlando. Beth had thought it was an excellent idea for the kids to get out of town, mostly because the anniversary of Kevin and Colleen's deaths was on a Saturday in the middle of April, which just so happened to be the first day of their break.

Yet another reason Nora was going to get a reprieve, even if she didn't exactly act grateful for it.

Everyone would of course be spending the anniversary of that day together. Cassandra and Dennis drove up on Friday so all of Saturday could be entirely devoted to celebrating Kevin and Colleen's memory.

It was still hard for Beth to come to grips with the fact that it had been a year since their deaths, a year without them. The loss was unbearable.

The day also marked what would've been Kevin and Colleen's twentieth wedding anniversary. For whatever reason, those were the images Beth's brain had decided to replay: Colleen walking down the aisle arm-in-arm with their father, her white dress simple yet stunning, a smile on her face as she only had eyes for Kevin, the two of them dancing their first dance as man and wife.

The day was going to be difficult, no doubt about it. But it was a pretty big comfort to know that Tripp was going to be right there by her side for it, from beginning to end.

He'd stayed the night with Beth, even with Cassandra and Dennis taking up residence in the den-turned-guest room. Beth hadn't been even remotely surprised that he'd proceeded to win both Cassandra and Dennis over in no time at all. And neither of them had made a comment about him staying, though Cassandra had given an approving nod. Beth thought it wasn't so much that she approved of Tripp staying as she approved of Tripp himself.

Besides, Beth wasn't going to hide how they were currently living, not from anyone. Hiding it would imply that she was embarrassed or ashamed, and she wasn't either of those things. Not even close.

And when Beth woke up on Saturday morning, she appreciated him being next to her. Appreciated it beyond words. She had no idea how long she'd stared up at the ceiling trying to fortify herself for the day. Nor did she know when she'd started crying.

"Hey, babe. Come here," Tripp whispered, his voice rough and gravelly in her ear, as he pulled her into his arms. She pressed her face to his chest as she let herself go over to the sadness. Full, body-racking sobs took over as he whispered, "I've got you, Beth. I've got you," over and over again.

She was so used to being the rock for the kids, and sometimes even for her father. So to not have to be the strongest person in the room was…freeing, in a way. She let herself be comforted by Tripp's strength, and at the same time, by his gentle touch. His kisses and caresses. His words.

He loved her.

It had been a week since they'd said those words to each other, and they'd told each other again and again every day since. So she let those words wash over her as he said them to her now, his lips at her temple, his hands moving up and down her back as he tried to sooth her.

He loved her.

He *loved* her.

* * *

Tripp knew the week without the kids would be a difficult one for Beth. Hell, she'd almost cried when Penny had asked if she could pack Herbert the hippopotamus. There'd also been the moment when Grant had gotten nervous about sleeping in a room without a nightlight, so Beth had packed a little plug-in one for him. But what had upset her the most was that Nora hadn't said good-bye when they left. Yeah, that one had hurt her a lot.

And it was more that just those incidents. It was the distance, too.

Since Colleen and Kevin's deaths, Beth hadn't been away from the kids for more than forty-eight hours, and even then they'd at least been in the same town as she was. The handful of times they'd left Mirabelle in the last year, she'd always been with them.

The thing was, Tripp found himself missing them, too. He missed Penny and her constant chatter, how'd she'd create a story from just about anything she saw. Whether it was a pasture of cows they drove by, or what Duke was dreaming about, or what the animals in her coloring book were doing when no one was looking.

He missed hanging out with Grant in the evenings, whether they were working on Koko or playing catch. He missed the easy conversation he had with the kid. How Grant had started to confide in him about things. He'd even started talking about the death of his parents. With anyone else it wasn't something he talked about unless prompted. But not with Tripp. He talked about it with Tripp.

And Grant wasn't the only one having some breakthroughs. Before the belly button-piercing incident, Nora had asked Tripp if he'd go driving with her. That one had been a pretty big moment, as she hadn't gotten behind the wheel of a car since her parents had died. Beth had told him that regardless of the grounding, Nora could drive with him whenever. That wasn't something she was going to stand in the way of. Not a development that big.

At the end of the day, Nora was a good kid, and she was actually pretty pleasant to be around when she wasn't being a royal pain in the ass. Tripp missed sitting down with her in the evenings and helping her with her math and science homework.

He also missed all of the kids helping him cook in the kitchen. It had become a thing now, where they all lined up waiting to be assigned a job.

It was a pretty big change for him, going from being alone a majority of the time to being in the midst of the day-to-day chaos that accompanied Beth and the kids. But he liked the domesticity, liked it way more than he would've ever imagined. He was more than a little surprised at how easy a transition it had been for him, but it was something he'd just slipped into, like the situation had been meant for him.

He missed the kids. They'd become part of his every day, something he'd gotten used to after just two months.

However, there was another side to the week: having Beth *en-*

tirely to himself. It was the first time since the start of their relationship that he'd gotten her, alone, for more than twenty-four hours. And he had every intention of taking advantage of every last minute of it.

He'd be a fool not to. Besides, he firmly believed distraction was the best policy, so him focusing her mind on other things was only helpful. And he did a pretty good job of it on Monday.

The second she walked through his door after work, he had her in his arms, pulling her against his body as the door slammed shut behind them. It took absolutely no time at all for the kiss to turn frantic, both of them trying to consume the other. He thrust his tongue past her lips and she welcomed him, just as eager.

He walked her backward until she was up against the wall, his fingers hooking in the sides of the waistband of her scrubs, pulling them along with her panties down her legs. She worked on the front of his pants—belt unbuckled, zipper unzipped. When his erection was freed, he lifted her up and her legs wrapped around his waist. Nails digging into his shoulders for purchase, she cried out as he plunged inside of her.

God, he loved that part. Loved how she reacted to him every damn time. His movements were wild, making her writhe against him. His mouth was at her neck, teeth nipping her skin.

"Tripp," she gasped. "Oh, Tripp!"

Her orgasm slammed into her, and she was screaming his name as she pulsed around his cock. He didn't stop moving, riding her as every once of pleasure ran through her body. And then he was letting go, coming inside of her.

He held her against the wall for a moment, letting the pleasure course through his body as well. Then he was pulling back to look into her face. Her beautiful, beautiful face.

"So, how was your day at work?" he asked.

She burst out laughing, her head falling back against the wall. He took advantage of her neck again, smiling against her skin as he kissed her.

* * *

Beth had never had more sex in her life. She was pretty sure that Tripp was hell bent on christening every room in his house…and hers. Well, except the kid's rooms—they did have some decency. Not a lot, but some.

On Tuesday morning he spread her out across his kitchen table, sitting in the chair in front of her and pulling her legs over his shoulders. After dinner that night there was a repeat at her kitchen table.

They went for a run together on Wednesday morning and afterward he pulled her into the shower with him. He had her pressed up against the wall before the water had even gotten warm.

That night, he worked late due to a couple of calls. The first had been a grease fire at Mrs. Sanderson's house. Then he'd been called to the beach because some drunken college students had jumped off the pier. Once in the water, two of them couldn't remember how to swim and had clung to the massive barnacle-ridden posts, screaming for help.

So Beth hung out with Duke, who followed her around the house. Since the kids were out of town, she figured she should take advantage and do a down and dirty clean of their rooms. And that down and dirty clean produced a lot of laundry.

When Tripp came home around nine he found her in the laundry room. Which led to the first time either of them had ever had sex on top of a running washing machine.

* * *

There'd only been a handful of nights Tripp and Beth had spent together when he'd had to respond to calls in the middle of the night. But as he always put his phone on vibrate under his pillow, she never woke up for those, and usually only realized he'd left when she woke up in the morning.

But when "Toxic" filled the silent room around two in the morning on Thursday, it woke both of them up. Beth scrambled for the phone on her nightstand, heart in her throat and fingers fumbling as she tried to get to it quickly.

A phone call in the middle of the night was never a good thing. She'd learned that from firsthand experience. And when she saw Nora's name on the screen she was pretty sure her heart would beat out of her chest.

She sat up, her legs coming over the side of the bed and her feet landing on the floor. She slid her finger across the screen before pulling it to her ear, hands shaking. "Nora? What's going on?" There was a frantic edge to her voice that she couldn't hide.

Tripp was immediately awake behind her, his hand going to her lower back.

A loud sniffle sounded through the speaker of the phone before

Nora said, "I had a dream you...you...you died and we had to move and go live with Gran and Grandpa. When I woke up and wasn't home...I—I just needed to hear your voice to make sure it wasn't real."

Beth's shoulders slumped in relief. It was a bad dream, just a bad dream. Something she could totally deal with. "Nora, honey, it's okay." She made a move to get up from the bed so that Tripp could go back to sleep, but his hand slid to her hip, fractionally tightening his grip.

"Stay here," he said softly into the darkness, his hand going to her back again. And while Beth soothed Nora, Tripp soothed her, his palm moving up and down her spine.

It took five minutes or so before Nora was ready to get off the phone, with her sleepy "I love you" filling Beth's ear.

"I love you, too, and I'll see you soon. Have fun."

"I will."

Phone back on the nightstand, Beth settled under the covers and against Tripp's body. "What was the dream?" he asked as his arms came around her, one of his hands sliding underneath the oversize T-shirt she wore to touch her bare back.

Beth pressed her face to his chest, felt his warm skin against her cheek. She hesitated for just a moment before she answered. "That I died."

He inhaled a sharp breath through his nose and his entire body tensed, his hands tightening their grip on her. It took him a second to relax again, his mouth going to her temple. "I would've woken up freaking out, too."

She pulled back from his chest and looked up at him. His face was shadowed in the dark, but she knew his eyes were on her. "But

I have quick ways to reassure myself that you're here. That you're okay."

"Yeah?" she asked before his lips landed on hers. It was a soft, sweet kiss, one that had her melting against him.

"Yeah."

He held her close as they both fell asleep again. And when she woke up in the morning, she was still wrapped in his arms.

* * *

As if things were meant to be, Tripp's days off that week just so happened to coincide with the weekend. So Beth would have him to herself for a solid forty-eight hours, and she wasn't going to share him.

But as it was bound to be whenever she was desperate to get home, the day dragged on. Her lunch break was rather interesting, though. She and Denise drove the ten minutes over to Café Lula to get a bite to eat together.

Grace had just delivered their food to them and turned around to go back to the register when Denise leaned over the table and said, "I need your advice."

"About what?" Beth asked as she took a sip of sweet tea.

"Sex."

Beth inhaled half of the liquid down her windpipe and started coughing. It took her a minute before she got hold of herself and was actually able to breathe right again. "I'm sorry. What?" She reached for a napkin and wiped at her watering eyes.

"This isn't funny." Denise frowned.

"I wasn't laughing. You just caught me off guard. That isn't exactly a topic of conversation the two of us have delved into before."

"I know. But I don't know who else to ask. Paige obviously isn't an option."

"I would imagine that your daughter would not be an option." Beth shook her head as she grabbed her bag of chips and opened them, dumping half of them onto her plate. "So…things with Beau are progressing, I'm assuming."

Beau had asked Denise out that day in the hospital when Mrs. Wharton had gone on and on about Denise having the legs of a thirty-year-old. Apparently Beau had noticed this as well. That had been well over a month ago, and the two had been seeing each other regularly since then.

"Yes…they are progressing." Denise nodded, color flushing her cheeks. "And I don't know what to do about the continuing progression. Trevor was the only man I was ever with."

"And things were good with him in that department?"

"Things were *very* good with him. But…what if *sex*"—her voice dropped when she said the word—"has changed?"

Beth grabbed one of her chips from the plate and nibbled it. "Well, from my experience, it's going to be different. But different isn't necessarily disappointing." None of the men she'd been with had been anywhere close to similar. "Are you worried about disappointing Beau? Or about being disappointed."

"I think, a little of both. And what if I'm thinking about Trevor the entire time?"

"I…" Beth trailed off, not sure how to answer that one at all. "You might…or you might not." She grabbed another chip. "Denise, would you feel like you were somehow betraying him if you *weren't* thinking about him?"

"No, it's not that." She shook her head. "Before he died, he told me he didn't want me to be alone for the rest of my life. He hoped I'd get to a point where I could let myself love like that again."

"Do you think you could with Beau?"

"I think there's the possibility for it. He's a very good man, and I enjoy my time with him. A lot."

"Do *you* want things to progress further?"

More color infused Denise's cheeks before she nodded. "I do."

"You know, I was told by some very wise women, one of them being your daughter, to do what felt right, to not overthink it and just *do*. Maybe that's what *you* need to do. Otherwise, you're never going to know. And Denise, in the end, I don't think either of you are going to be disappointed."

Beth sure as hell knew she hadn't been.

* * *

When Beth got home from work that day, she walked into the house to find Tripp sitting on the sofa, watching a baseball game on TV. But the second he saw her, he turned it off and stood.

"Pack a bag. We're going away for the weekend."

"Oh, are we?" She dropped her purse onto a side table.

"Yup." He nodded, moving across the living room to her. "Just you and me."

"Where's Duke?"

"Finn is watching him for me." Tripp's hands landed on her waist before they slid around to her back and he pulled her right up against his firm, solid body.

"So it really is just you and me."

"It is." He kissed her, one of his hands sliding down until he cupped her bottom. He squeezed lightly before he spun her around in the direction of her bedroom. "And no need to pack pajamas." He leaned in close to her ear. "Because you won't be needing them." He gave her a gentle nudge to get moving.

Beth headed to her bedroom, a grin on her face.

* * *

Tripp didn't tell Beth where they were going and she didn't ask. He really liked that she was perfectly okay with letting herself be surprised, that she didn't need to know the plan and trusted him. She just climbed into the passenger seat of his truck and settled in.

It was a two-hour drive to their destination, a small town that was just over the Georgia state line. She looked over at him as they passed the city sign, her eyes narrowing in speculation. But she didn't say a word about it; instead she just continued the story she'd been telling him.

But when they pulled up in front of a rather swanky bed and breakfast and he put his truck in Park, she turned to him and asked, "Seriously?"

The Adeline House was almost one hundred and thirty years old. It was a three-story white Victorian with a black roof and shutters and a red front door. The porch wrapped around the entirety of it, empty rocking chairs waiting for guests to sit.

"What do you say? Want to stay here for the weekend with me?"

"You bet I do." She unbuckled her seat belt and leaned across the armrest and kissed him. "Thank you."

"Beth, we haven't even gotten started."

He got out of the truck then rounded to her side and helped her slide out. Her hand firmly held in his, he led her to the front door. Jenson Peters, the man Tripp had talked to that afternoon to book the room, greeted them when they walked in the door. He had thick white hair and a pretty impressive mustache.

"Here are your keys to the Pembroke Cottage and the last thing I need is to know what time you'd like breakfast brought to your room in the morning."

"Nine will be good." It would be nice for both of them to sleep in a little bit...and probably a necessity, as Tripp had every intention of keeping her up most of the night.

"If you need anything, just ring the front desk." Jenson smiled at them both. "The extension is by the phone in the room."

They both thanked him before they headed outside.

"You got us a cottage?" Beth asked as they made their way down the steps.

"More privacy." He grinned as he leaned down and kissed the "O" her lips had just made. "Come on."

They went back to his truck, and he let go of her hand so he could grab both of their bags. Then they followed a stone-paved pathway that led to a little blue cottage with white shutters and a white door. Tripp set the bags down as he got the key from his pocket and opened the door.

He pulled the key from the door and put it back in his pocket before he grabbed the bags again. "After you."

Beth stepped inside and gasped. "Oh my gosh."

The walls were a light blue and white crown molding ran along the ceiling. The hardwood floors were a rich dark brown, almost the exact same color as the massive four-poster bed in the middle of the room. White hangings trailed down from the canopy and puddled on the floor.

Beth made a dash for the bed, flinging herself on it so that she was sprawled out in the middle of the lush white linens. Tripp dropped the bags on the floor before he joined her, stretching out next to her.

She rolled into him, grabbing his hand and leaning up so he could wrap his arm around her. "It's perfect," she whispered, settling into his side and throwing one of her legs over his.

"So your options are this: we can either stay here"—he turned his head and nipped at her ear—"and order food from somewhere that delivers."

"Or?"

"Or, you put on one of those fancy dresses you packed and I take you out."

"Hmm…" She turned to look at him. "Both very good options. I pick the second one."

She pressed a quick kiss to his mouth before she sat up and scooted off the bed. Her hips swayed as she walked over to her suitcase and unzipped it, pulling out her bag of toiletries and heading to the bathroom.

"Holy crap, Tripp!" she shouted and a second later peeked out from the doorway. "The bathtub is enormous. Make sure you add that to our agenda." She grinned wickedly before she disappeared again.

It was going to be a good weekend.

* * *

Twenty minutes later Beth was ready to go. She was wearing a light pink dress and strappy brown wedges that added about three inches to her height.

She was stunning, and he told her so. "Are you going to be okay if we walk?" he asked as she straightened the collar of his button-up shirt.

"What? These shoes are comfortable."

"I'll have to take your word for it." Comfortable, they did not look. Sexy as hell, yes. But not comfortable.

Dinner was at a small restaurant in the downtown area, about two blocks away from the Adeline House. They both catalogued the now-closed shops to visit the next day as they passed by hand-in-hand. Once settled at their table, Tripp ordered a bottle of wine and Beth told the waiter the four different appetizers they were going to split for their meal.

After sharing a dessert of chocolate hazelnut *crème brûlée*, they got back to the cottage around eleven. He barely had the door closed and locked before he had his hands on her. She worked at the buttons on his shirt while he took the time to explore her neck with his mouth. He was just about to get to work on the zipper at the side of her dress when she pulled back.

"Stop," she whispered, breathless.

He raised his eyebrows.

"Just for a minute. One minute." She turned and went to the bathroom, the door snapping shut behind her.

He started to count in his head as he sat down at the edge of the bed, kicking off his shoes before getting rid of his socks. Then he lay back, wearing only his jeans, as he stared up at the canopy. He had no doubt in his mind that whatever she was doing was going to be totally worth it when she opened the door. Didn't mean every damn second she wasn't under his hands wasn't painful.

He was at ninety-four seconds when the handle finally turned and he sat up. She was standing in the open doorway and as his eyes moved over her body, he forgot how to breathe.

She was wearing a slip made of light purple satin and white lace. The bottom hit high on her thighs, and there was a slit running up the left side. The satin covered her breasts, her nipples puckering through the fabric.

His mouth watered.

"God, Beth." He stood up and crossed the room to her. He reached for her hips, the silky material moving under his palms as he slid his hands up to her waist. "Do you have any idea how fucking sexy you are?"

And she was his. All *fucking* his.

He didn't give her a chance to answer before his mouth was on hers, his grip at her waist tightening as he pulled her up. Her legs wrapped around him and he walked back to the four-poster, laying her down on all of that white bedding. And then his lips were trailing down her neck to her breasts, pulling one of those satin covered nipples into his mouth.

Beth's moan filled the room as her back arched off the bed, hands going to the back of his head and fingers delving into his hair as she held him to her.

He took his time, exploring every inch of her that was covered in all of that satin and lace. Every delectable inch. The panties she wore were made of the same satin and lace as the slip, and when he flicked his tongue against the material covering her clit she cried out.

A stronger man than he was would've been able to hold out more, but he'd reached his limit. Fingers hooking in the material at her hips, he pulled her panties down her legs as he pulled himself up from the bed. He unbuckled his jeans and let them drop to the floor, then he slid over her body. Slipping a hand underneath her bottom, he lifted her just slightly as he thrust into her.

They moved together, both of them grasping and clinging to each other. Between the satin of her slip rubbing against his chest and her throaty moans, she was driving him out of his ever-loving mind.

His restraint at letting go hit the max, and he picked up the rhythm of his hips as he spent himself inside of her. Then she fell over the edge, his release triggering hers, her body pulsing around his and wringing out every last ounce of pleasure.

He collapsed on top of her, his lips pressed to the junction of her shoulder and her throat. "I love you," he said against her skin.

Loved her more than he'd ever loved anyone.

* * *

When Beth woke up the following morning she realized the night's activities had put her into a solid sleep. She hadn't stirred at all from when she and Tripp had finally gone to sleep around two, right up to when the alarm went off at eight forty-five. She was in the exact same spot, her body cushioned by the mattress beneath her and Tripp next to her. Well, Tripp wasn't exactly a cushion—more a wall of hard, hot, muscled male. And she'd take him any day of the week.

After breakfast was delivered to their room—goat cheese and

chive scrambled eggs, French toast made from thick slices of bread and smothered in blueberry syrup, and sausage from a local farm—they took the tub for a spin. Literally; the jets had the water swirling around them. Tripp pulled her onto his lap about halfway through, and she took him for a spin.

It was close to noon when they finally ventured out of the cottage and walked to the main part of downtown. The trees were in full bloom, the leaves rustling in the spring breeze. Cars drove slowly over the brick-paved road, cautious of the people milling around on either side of the street.

Tripp wanted to check out a sporting goods store, where he ended up buying a new baseball glove for Grant. After that they stopped into a bookstore, where they both lingered over the shelves—the children's section specifically. Both Beth and Tripp picked out a stack of storybooks for Penny, almost all of them involving an animal with a unique name. As for Nora, Beth was wandering around a little boutique shop when she found a simple silver necklace. It had three tiny hearts on it. One silver, one gold, and one bronze.

Around three they had a light lunch—their rather large breakfast had lasted them a while—at a little pizzeria. They got back to the cottage close to four o'clock, and after putting down their spoils, fell into bed. But besides a few kisses, there wasn't any funny business.

Being here felt beyond decadent, especially as she was snuggled up next to Tripp. They talked for a little while, but the hours they'd spent in the sun had made her sleepy. Besides, they were definitely going to have another night of *vigorous* activity. So she figured she might as well rest up.

* * *

For the second time that day, Beth woke up next to Tripp, although this time he was trailing kisses across her jaw. Because they had to leave in an hour, he let her get out of bed after only a couple more kisses.

After curling her hair and redoing her makeup, she pulled that night's dress from her bag. Zipper undone and back gapping open, she stepped out of the bathroom just as Tripp was pulling a gray polo over his head. She was more than capable of pulling up the zipper herself, but where was the fun in that?

Once his eyes cleared the material of his shirt and he saw her, he stilled. "You're wearing the blue dress tonight? The one you wore on our first date?"

"I figured I could wear it for longer than twenty minutes this time." She crossed the room to him and turned around, holding her hair up. "Can you get that for me?"

He moved in close to her, his breath washing across her skin as he kissed her neck. There was a slight tug at the base of her dress before she heard the snick of the zipper coming together.

Then his hands were at her hips, and he pulled her back against him, bringing his mouth to her ear. "You wearing it for longer might be a change, but it's still going to be in a pile on the floor by the end of tonight."

She turned, looking over her shoulder at him. "Really now?"

"Yup." He spun her around, his lips going to hers. She looped her arms around his neck, holding onto him as he kissed her...thoroughly. "You ready?" he asked after a minute. "Because we need to leave before I throw you on this bed."

"Lead the way."

He reached up and pulled her arms from his neck, letting go of one while he locked their fingers together with the other. She grabbed her purse before they were out the door.

There was still about an hour of sunlight left as they headed back into the heart of downtown. She was wearing her yellow wedges tonight, and they clipped against the ground with every step they took.

Dinner was at a steakhouse. Beth ordered a filet mignon and Tripp the prime rib. Their meals helped to soak up the bottle of red wine Tripp had ordered. The shared baked apple strudel covered in triple cream vanilla ice cream also put in a good effort, but in the end both she and Tripp were feeling pretty damn good when he led her out of the restaurant two hours later.

Night had settled in and the lamps along the streets had been lit. Music thumped softly in the distance, and as they got closer to it Beth recognized the song. Someone was covering Prince's "Raspberry Beret." They rounded a corner and found themselves in a spacious side yard filled with about thirty people or so, most of them dancing. Brick buildings with ivy-covered walls stood three stories tall on either side, and strings of lights had been hung all around, making the space glow.

"I realize we've still yet to dance together," he said as he turned to her. "And we need to rectify that."

Beth grinned as the song ended. "I like the way you think."

And with that Tripp led her out into the middle of the crowd as the band in the corner started to play the Pointer Sisters' "Slow Hand." He pulled her in close as his free hand went to her lower back, his fingers spreading wide at the base of her spine.

There was something different about being in Tripp's arms this way—how he spun her around, how his body moved with hers, how he whispered in her ear, how his lips lingered on her skin. Everything. God, it was *everything*.

It was close to midnight by the time they got back to the cottage, and a different type of dancing continued. It was a constant back and forth as they made love to each other, Tripp leading and then Beth. In the end, though, it was the two of them moving together.

Chapter Nineteen

Unexpected

Baby," a deep, rumbly voice whispered in Beth's ear. "Breakfast is here."

Beth's eyes were slow to open on Sunday morning, but with the scent of coffee in the air she somehow managed. Tripp was sitting at the edge of the bed, wearing a pair of jeans and nothing else. His fingers traced over her bare shoulder and down her arm.

"There she is." He grinned as she blinked up at him. "Hungry?"

"Mmm hmm."

He leaned down and pressed a kiss to her lips before he stood up. "Good. You should get it while it's hot."

Beth rolled onto her back and stretched, her arms going up while her feet stretched out. She was wearing the satin and lace slip, pajamas that Tripp *clearly* approved of, and the material slid over her skin as she moved.

"Are you talking about the food or y-y-ou?" She yawned. "Because it could go either way."

"Well, as I'm *always* hot for you, it's the food."

She grinned as she pulled her arms back up, flopping them down on the bed beside her. It was then that she noticed something blue and sparkly sitting on the ring finger of her right hand.

Beth sat up abruptly, her hand coming to her face as she looked down. The stone that sat at the center of the ring wasn't so much blue as turquoise. Tiny diamonds surrounded the circular stone, and there more diamonds inlaid into the top of the band.

It was beautiful. Absolutely beautiful.

Beth slowly lifted her head, her eyes not leaving the ring until the very last second. Tripp was standing at the little table and chairs where breakfast had been placed, watching her.

"Tripp…I…wh-when? Why?"

"Yesterday when we were at that boutique, and because I wanted to."

Beth hadn't even seen the ring the day before, probably because she'd been so focused on picking out something for Nora. But it was exactly something that she would've picked out for herself, if she spent money on herself these days…which she didn't. It had probably cost him upward of two hundred dollars. Maybe even three.

Words failed her, probably because the emotions that were rising up in her chest had gone to her throat and left her momentarily speechless. She pulled herself up from the bed and crossed the room, throwing her arms around him.

"Thank you." She buried her face against his bare chest, pressing her lips to the spot right over his heart. "It's perfect and I love it."

"You're welcome." He kissed the top of her head, his hands moving down her back. "You know, you aren't playing fair," he said against her hair. "Plastering your satin-clad body against me."

"Look who's talking." She looked up at him and held out her hand for him to clearly see the ring. "I mean, I'm not giving it back"—she grinned as she pulled her hand to her chest—"but it *is* too much."

"Consider it a birthday present."

"My birthday is in December. Four months ago." A fact that he remembered as the stone that sat in the middle of the ring was her birthstone.

"It's a late present, Beth. Consider it thirty years of late presents."

"Tripp, you didn't h—"

His mouth was on hers, covering it in a searing kiss. "I know I didn't have too." His lips brushed over her cheek and the shell of her ear. "But I wanted to. And Beth, if you don't put a robe on in the next ten seconds, I'm going to do something else I want to do, breakfast be damned."

She pulled away from him and took a step back. "Okay," she said before she turned around and headed for the bathroom. "And Tripp?" she called out, not turning around.

"Yes."

"I love you."

* * *

Because Cassandra and Dennis were going to spend the following week at a cabin in Georgia, it wasn't a problem at all for them to drop off the kids on their way up. Tripp and Beth got back to her house about two hours before their Cadillac Escalade was pulling into the driveway.

She and Tripp had swung by Finn's to pick up Duke, and though the dog had been pretty damn excited to see Tripp, he was beside himself when he saw Grant. The SUV had barely rolled to a stop before Grant flung the door open and was bolting out to Duke.

"Apparently I'm no longer the favorite," Tripp said as Grant tackled Duke in the middle of the yard. They wrestled for a little bit, with Duke doing everything in his power to lick Grant's face.

"Well, it's been a week since they saw each other…It was only forty-eight hours for you."

"Aw, look at you trying to make me feel better." He hooked his arm around her shoulders and pulled her in close to kiss her on the forehead.

At that moment Cassandra freed Penny from her car seat and the little girl made a mad dash from the vehicle. "Aunt B! Tripp!" She squealed as she came barreling toward them, a brand-new stuffed animal Tigger tucked under her arm.

Beth sat back on her heals, arms opened wide as Penny ran right into them. "PenPen!" Beth picked up her niece and pressed a kiss to her little rosy cheek.

"I missed you."

"I missed you too. So much. But did you have fun?"

"Yes! We rode the Teacups, and Dumbo, and ate Mickey Mouse ice cream, and there was a ride with Dinosaurs. But the dinosaurs were mean dinosaurs, not like Flounder, who is a good dinosaur. We went to Harry Potter World, too, and rode a train, and Grant rode a hippo…hippo…" She looked over at Grant. "Grant, what was it?"

"A hippogriff." He giggled as Duke continued to lick his face.

"Yeah, a hippogriff." She turned back to Beth and Tripp. "He rode that with Nora."

"Sounds like you guys had an adventure," Tripp said.

"We did." Penny turned to him, holding out her arms and indicating she wanted Tripp to hold her now.

He immediately complied with her demand, pulling her from Beth's arms. She stretched up and placed a kiss to his scruffy jaw before resting her head on his chest. "I missed you too, Tripp." *Twipp.*

And there was that now-familiar sensation of her heart clutching because of how he was with her kids. Out of the corner of her eye she saw Nora coming up the path, so she turned from the scene to focus her attention on her older niece.

Nora walked straight up to Beth and threw her arms around her aunt. Beth was more than a little shocked by the sheer force of the hug. It had been months since Nora had shown this much affection.

"Hey," she whispered as she pulled Nora close, leaning down and pressing a kiss to her niece's head.

"Hey," Nora repeated, not looking up as she hugged Beth harder.

"I'm glad you're home."

It was a couple of seconds before Nora responded in the softest of voices. "Me too."

* * *

The dinner table that night was a crowded one, with Cassandra, Dennis, and Wallace joining Tripp, Beth, and the kids. Tacos had been a relatively easy meal to get together and once everyone had eaten their fill and everything had been cleaned up, they'd all played a couple of rounds of dominos. Penny was the only one who couldn't play by herself, and she'd taken turns flitting between Beth's and Tripp's laps to help them play.

When nine o'clock rolled around and Penny was struggling to keep her eyes open as she leaned against Tripp's chest, Beth called an end to the evening. All three kids made the rounds saying good night to everyone, and Cassandra and Dennis asked if they could tuck them all in. Wallace was out the door not long after, and once Duke had done his business in the backyard, Tripp locked all the doors. As was the norm now, Duke made his way to Grant's room and curled up on the bed.

Tripp closed the bedroom door behind him just as Beth walked in from the bathroom. She was wearing one of his old Mirabelle Fire Department T-Shirts. It was faded gray and long enough so he could only just see her pajama shorts peeking out.

"You know," he started as he pulled off his shirt. "It's no wonder that Duke missed Grant more than me. The dog has become accustomed to sleeping in a soft, comfy bed."

"This is very true." Beth nodded as she went to her dresser, leaning her head to the side as she started pulling out her earrings.

He came up behind her, unclasping her necklace before he kissed her neck. "And we all know I won't be sharing my bed with anyone save you."

She turned to look at him and his hands went to either side of her body, bracing himself against the dresser and caging her in.

"This is *also* very true." She grinned up at him. Her hands went to his chest, palms sliding over his skin. "Thank you for this week-end. I had a perfect time."

"Perfect, huh?" He grabbed her right hand, brought it to his mouth, and kissed her palm. He gently bent her fingers down so he could see the ring that sat on her finger, the only piece of jewelry she hadn't taken off.

There was something about her wearing it that made him happy beyond all reason. Hell, being with her made him happy beyond all reason. He wanted this life with her. Wanted this life with the kids. Wanted it all.

He'd be putting another ring on her finger, except it would be on the opposite hand. And that fact didn't scare him at all.

Not one fucking bit.

* * *

Monday morning was business as usual when the alarm went off at six, though settling back into the daily routine was not so instantaneous. That took a couple of days. Sleep schedules were understandably off for everyone, including Tripp and Beth. The two of them couldn't make love into the wee hours of the nights and sleep in late the following mornings.

Now that wasn't to say he was no longer making love to Beth regularly, because he was; it was just at more reasonable hours. He couldn't help himself around her; the need for her was constant.

He wasn't complaining, though.

But after their days' long struggle of getting back into a somewhat regular routine, they were thrown out of whack again the following week. A few new volunteer firefighters at the house needed to be trained, not to mention that Tripp put his guys through the paces regularly to make sure they were up to scratch.

As the majority of the firemen were volunteers, they also had day jobs, so they weren't able to come to the station until after five in the afternoon. He decided to take advantage of those hours, as well as the entirety of Saturday and Sunday.

That Wednesday he didn't get home until close to nine. On Thursday it was after ten. Friday was going to be even later as it was officially the weekend. Before they got started on that night's drills, he headed outside with his cell, pulling up Beth's number.

"Hey," she answered on the third ring, the pleasure in her voice clear.

"Hey yourself. You home yet?" If she wasn't already, she was on the way there.

"Walked in the door fifteen minutes ago. And guess what? Nora is making dinner."

"Really now?"

"Yes, spaghetti and homemade meatballs. Tripp, she made the sauce from scratch, too. She also put together a rather elaborate garden salad. Cherry tomatoes, cucumbers in the shapes of stars, those crinkly carrots. It's pretty impressive."

"It sounds like it."

"So because she's cooking, I'm currently sitting on the back porch with a glass of wine and watching Grant swinging on the tire swing." The tire swing Tripp had put up a couple of weekends ago.

"Well, doesn't that sound like a lovely evening."

"It would be better if you were here."

"You know I'd be there if I could. I'd probably be massaging your feet as we speak."

"Hmmm," she hummed. "Or something else." Her voice had dropped low in his ear and he could just imagine her sitting on the back porch, legs curled up on the sofa with that glass of wine in her hand.

"God," he groaned, thinking about just what it was he'd like to be massaging. "What color scrubs are you wearing?"

She burst out laughing, the sound of it filling his chest. "They're blue," she attempted to say in a sultry voice once she got a grip on herself.

"Ohhh, really now?"

There was a muffled sound in the background, a door opening and Nora saying something.

"Yes, really. But I've got to go," Beth told him. "I'll see you later tonight."

"You will indeed. Enjoy your fancy dinner. I love you."

"I love you, too."

* * *

Mirabelle High School had another basketball game that Saturday night. It was the first day of Nora's freedom; her grounding after the belly button piercing incident was over.

So when she asked if she could go with Gretchen and Monica—and that the usual nine-thirty curfew be extended to ten o'clock—Beth complied. Nora had earned it with her exceptional behavior over the last two weeks, especially since she'd helped out with Penny and Grant that afternoon while Beth worked out in the backyard.

Though Duke's destruction from months ago had long been

cleaned up, Beth hadn't done any replanting. Spring was in full bloom, and there wasn't a better time. She had every intention of taking full advantage of the weekend.

It was close to five when Beth came in, wanting to take a shower before Nora left to go to dinner and the game. She had just finished scrubbing the dirt from underneath her nails when her cell phone started buzzing on the counter. Mel's name flashed across the screen.

After wiping her hands with a towel she picked it up and put it to her ear. "What's going on?"

"Bennett is going to the basketball game with Hamilton and Dale and I have no desire to go. Nor do I have any desire to sit around this empty house. Too much energy to sit still."

"Come over and have dinner with us tonight. I'm making fried chicken."

"I'm there. See you soon."

It had been a few weeks since the two of them had *really* talked and Beth was looking forward to catching up. So much so that she was beaming when she opened the door an hour later.

"I brought ice cream," Mel whispered, holding up a green shopping bag when she walked through the front door. "It has about five different kinds of chocolate."

"God bless you." Beth took the bag and stuck it in the freezer when they got to the kitchen.

"Okay, what's first?" Mel asked, looking at all of the ingredients Beth had pulled out and put on the counter.

"Mashed potatoes."

"Can I help, too?" Grant asked, coming into the kitchen. Duke trotted in after him. Pretty much the only time that the dog even spent at Tripp's now was during the day when no one was home and he needed access to a doggy door. Otherwise he was over at their house.

"You can help me peel potatoes," Mel said as she went to the drawer by the stove and pulled out two peelers.

"I want to help tooooooo!" Penny came charging into the kitchen, Paxton the platypus's head popping up from where she had a chokehold around his neck, his body flailing around behind her.

"All right, PenPen." Beth nodded. "But both of you go wash your hands first. And Penny, Paxton can't help us cook so put him in your room."

"Okay, it's time for his nap anyway," her niece said matter-of-factly before she charged out of the kitchen, Grant and Duke on her heels.

"You want some wine?" Beth asked as she headed for the refrigerator.

"Not tonight."

"What?" Beth turned around, surprised. The wine question had been a rhetorical one. "Who are you?"

"Beth, I'm four days late."

Beth's entire body froze as she looked at Mel, and then the words processed. Four. Days. Late. "Seriously?"

Oh, Lord, please let it be true. Please, please *let her friend be pregnant.*

"Yes, and you know I'm never late."

"Like clockwork, you are."

"I haven't told anyone. Not even Bennett. We've both been so disappointed in the past, and I don't want to get his hopes up yet.

But I had to tell someone, and you're that someone. Besides Bennett, you know more than anyone what a struggle this has been."

It wasn't that Mel begrudged any of her friends the ease with which they'd gotten pregnant. She loved all of them dearly and was beyond happy for each and every one of them. But that happiness didn't mean it was any easier for her. In fact, it just seemed to make it harder.

"Oh, honey." Beth crossed the space to Mel. "I'm glad I'm the person you told. Come here." She pulled her friend into a hug. They held each other for a good long moment, the joy and nervousness clear. When Beth let go and took a step back, she was full-on grinning. "So that *energy* you spoke of earlier, the *too much* you had to sit still. It was nervous energy."

"I haven't been able to think straight at all. It's been—"

But exactly what it had been, Beth would have to wait until later to find out. Penny and Grant both came back into the kitchen, hands washed and ready to start cooking.

* * *

It was a packed house at the Mirabelle Fire Department on Friday night. Between the full-time fighters and the volunteers, there were now thirty guys in the building and every single chair around the twenty-seat dining table was occupied.

With the day of training they'd had, all of the guys had sore muscles and raging appetites. Jorge Rodriguez's wife had made cornbread and two massive pots of Cuban black bean soup. Even with every man in that room eating their fill, there were still going to be leftovers.

Tripp leaned back in his seat, stretching his legs out as he listened to the great debate going on around him: Dean, Jess, or Logan. The guys had just started watching the sixth season of *Gilmore Girls*, and the firehouse was divided into three different teams.

"Logan is a douche bag," Freddie Griffin said, sounding more than a little disgusted. "Rory is way too good for him. Dean was the much better choice."

"Dean? *Dean*?! The guy who cheated on his wife." Jorge shook his head. "Not to mention he bailed on Rory when it got to be too hard for him. He's a pussy."

"What do you think, chief?" Dan Thompson asked, looking over at Tripp. "Who do you think is the best man for the job?"

Tripp shifted his feet, taking a deep breath and letting it out. "None of them."

"None of them?" Beau repeated, his mouth splitting into a grin. "Why? Because Rory reminds you of Nora?"

Okay, so this was a true statement. Tripp had made the connection a couple of weeks ago, and just that quickly he'd come to the realization that he wasn't a fan of *any* of Rory Gilmore's boyfriends.

Not. A. One.

"I'm not even going to deny it." It wasn't just Beth he cared about; he'd fallen for those kids, too.

Hook, line, and sinker.

Tripp pulled his feet back and stood, grabbing his bowl and heading to the kitchen. He went to the sink, turning the faucet on and letting the water heat up. Beau made his way into the kitchen, too, bowl in hand. When Tripp grabbed the dish, Beau moved to the side, pressing his hip into the counter.

"Sooooo, it looks like everyone in that family has you wrapped around their little fingers. That took"—Beau flipped his wrist as he glanced down at his watch—"no time at all."

"Look at you talk, Romeo." Tripp looked over at his second in command, eyebrows raised high. "If I'm not much mistaken, you're wrapped, too. How are things going with Denise?"

"Pretty damn good." Beau grinned.

"What about her and Ethan?" As Tripp was now well aware, it was a very different experience dating someone who had kids. They were an added element for sure, one that needed to be handled properly. Their lives were affected, too.

"Well, I think. He hasn't really had a consistent female figure in his life lately, so it took him a bit to open up to her. But he likes having her around now. Denise took him to the movies tonight."

"It took Nora a bit longer to get used to me than it did Penny and Grant. And I'm not under any delusions that it isn't a constant uphill battle," he said as he tested the hot water with his hand and grabbed the sponge.

"Oh, it's that for sure. Things are never easy with kids. Once you think you have a handle on it, all hell breaks loose."

It was at that moment that the alarm started to blare through the PA system, and the guys on call immediately went into action. They were already heading to the garage when Jeanette Kemper's voice came over the speaker saying there'd been a car accident at Alligator Lane.

There actually weren't very many alligators at Alligator Lane. It was the point where Whiskey River flowed into the Gulf of Mexico, and the salt level in the water was too high for them to stick around. With the backdrop of the Bartlett Forest, the four-mile stretch of beach was pretty damn secluded.

More often than not, it was high schoolers who took advantage of the privacy, either for a party or just going to park and make out…or other things. Tripp had heard more than a few stories from his friends at the sheriffs department about catching overly hormonally-charged kids going at it.

From the firehouse to Alligator Lane—with sirens blaring—it was less than a three-minute ride. By the time the fire truck and ambulance got to the location, red and blue lights were already flashing from two patrol vehicles parked along the side of the road.

The high beams from both trucks were on, pointing to a Jeep Wrangler that had crashed into a bank of trees. The engine was smashed and a massive low-hanging branch caged in the driver's side.

When Tripp got out of the truck he spotted one of the officers and immediately recognized Jax in his dark green uniform. Jax was making his way to Tripp at a jog.

"What's going on?" Tripp asked.

"Both the driver and the passenger are conscious. Eighteen-year-old driver has a laceration on his forehead, passenger has a possible broken wrist." By then Jax was only a few feet away, and the expression on his face was grave. "Tripp, the passenger is Nora."

A fear unlike any Tripp had ever known gripped him. He took off for the Jeep at a sprint, his heart hammering hard in his chest.

Chapter Twenty

Upside Down

So when did it happen?" Beth asked pretty much the second Penny and Grant had gone into the other room to watch a half hour of TV.

Just a half hour, though, so that Mel and Beth could talk, then they'd play whatever game the two kids picked out. To be honest, it was probably going to take them that long to agree on the same game.

"Well, I'm pretty sure it was the night we went to Caliente's. We got home and, uh, did our thing."

"Ahhh, after the margaritas. You know Harper's theory on tequila, it gets you knocked up." This was Harper's theory because it had actually happened that way for her and Liam. "So there's that. You take a test yet?"

"This morning. And it was positive."

"Mel." Beth put her hand over her heart, tears filling her eyes. Happy tears. Oh so happy tears.

"Don't." Mel shook her head at her friend. "Not yet. Not until

I go see Dr. McAndrews and he confirms it. I—I just want to be sure. I *need* to be sure."

"I know. I know. But there's hope. And I'm going to hold on to it."

"Me too."

The doorbell rang, and both of them looked toward the door. "You expecting anyone else tonight?"

"No." Beth shook her head. "I'll be right back." She went through the living room—stepping around Duke, who was rolling around the floor on his back—noticing the fifteen or so board games that were stacked on the coffee table in three piles.

"So this one goes in the 'no' pile," Grant said as he moved a box to the far left.

She grinned as she passed them, and it lingered on her lips as she wrapped her hand around the handle and turned. But the instant that door opened, her smile disappeared.

Jax stood on the other side of the door. He was wearing his deputy sheriff uniform and a grim frown.

Her mind immediately started to go through the list. Nora…her father…Tripp.

"Who is it?" The question came out of her mouth on a whisper.

"Everyone is alive," he started off and Beth's shoulders slumped, but the relief was short-lived. "Nora was in a car accident."

Nora…Nora…Nora…

In the second before Jax continued, a dozen images flashed through Beth's brain.

A sleeping newborn Nora in the basinet at the hospital the day she was born.

A giggling five-month-old Nora in Beth's arms as she bounced around the kitchen of Colleen and Kevin's first house.

A one-year-old Nora taking her first steps in a yellow onesie.

A four-year-old Nora grabbing Beth's hand and leading her into the newly painted purple bedroom that was still Nora's bedroom today.

A six-year-old, grinning, gap-toothed Nora sitting on top of a horse.

A nine-year-old Nora making a massive sandcastle with Kevin at the beach.

An eleven-year-old Nora decked out in hot pink knee pads as she roller bladed around the neighborhood with Hamilton.

A thirteen-year-old Nora snuggled up with Beth and Colleen on the sofa while they watched a movie.

A sixteen-year-old Nora wearing a black dress as she stood in front of her parents' graves. Penny was in her arms while Grant held her hand.

A seventeen-year-old Nora from this morning, sitting at the table in the kitchen drinking orange juice and eating a piece of toast slathered in blackberry jam.

And the last image was a car smashed into a tree. It was the picture she'd seen from Colleen and Kevin's accident.

No, this wasn't happening. Not again. Please, Lord, not again. She stopped breathing, her chest constricting tight and preventing her from speaking.

"Beth, she's fully conscious and it looks like she broke her wrist."

She was surprised she could still hear Jax's words, as her ears were ringing. She looked down at her side, where the warm steady weight of Duke rested against her leg. *When had he come over?* Her hand dropped down to the dog's head as Jax continued talking.

"Tripp was in the fire truck that was called to the scene to get her out. He went with her in the ambulance."

Tripp was with Nora. She wasn't alone...wasn't alone...not alone...

"I came here to take you to the hospital."

"Beth, I'll stay here with the kids." Mel was speaking now, her voice steady next to Beth. *When had she come over?*

The words going on around her were only slightly processing, like hearing sound through water.

Nora...Nora...Nora...

"Beth." Jax reached out and touched her shoulders. "What do you need?"

"Shoes." She shook her head lightly, trying to clear it. She needed to focus. "And my purse."

"Mel?" Jax asked.

"I'm on it." And Mel was gone, heading down the hallway.

"Beth, I know you're terrified right now." Jax's grip on her shoulders tightened. "But it's going to be okay."

"You don't know that." Her voice cracked on the words.

"Gut instinct tells me it is."

"How often has your gut been wrong?"

"Never. Not when it comes to stuff like this. Nora was fully conscious, talking, and aware of everything that was going on. She didn't hit her head and she was wearing her seat belt. Tripp made the exact same call I did, as well as the other firefighters on scene and both of the EMTs. She's on her way to the hospital, or is already there. And a doctor is going to check her out from top to bottom. So let's get in my truck, and you can hear it from whoever that doctor is. Okay?"

She nodded, only just slightly consoled by Jax's words.

"And Beth, it would also be good for you to start taking regular breaths again. You passing out on me isn't an option. Understood?"

"Understood."

"Aunt B?"

"What's going on?"

Penny and Grant's voices had her spinning around, both of them standing at the end of the hallway.

"Hi, Jax." Both Penny and Grant greeted him at the same time, though Penny had spoken rather exuberantly as she bounced around, while Grant waved shyly.

"Hey, kiddos."

Beth pulled some semblance of composure together as she headed down the hallway—Duke still at her side—to the kids and knelt down in front of them. "Jax needs to take me somewhere right now, but Mel is going to stay with you. So you better be good for her. All right?"

"Is everything okay?" Grant asked, reaching out for Duke.

"Yes," Beth said, hearing Jax's words repeating in her head on a loop. "If I get home late, I'll see you in the morning."

"'kay." Penny nodded before she threw her arms around Beth's neck.

Once Penny let go, Grant hugged Beth, too, the look of disappointment on his face clear.

She kissed both of them on the cheek before she whispered, "Mel brought ice cream."

"You brought ice cream?" Penny all but shouted as Mel appeared at the end of the hallway.

"I sure did." She nodded as she handed Beth her purse, and a pair of socks and sneakers.

"Thank you." Beth leaned in and pressed a kiss to Mel's cheek before turning to Jax.

"Come on," he said as he led her to his truck. "Let's get you to your niece."

* * *

There was an empty spot for emergency vehicles right by the entrance to the emergency room. Pretty much the second the locks were popped on the doors of Jax's truck, Beth had hers open and was climbing out. The automatic doors for the hospital slid open when she walked up, and the blast of cold from the air conditioner hit her in the face, cooling her clammy skin.

Beth's eyes landed on Tripp the moment she walked into the waiting room. He was leaning back against the wall, his arms folded across his chest and his mouth in a flat line. When he spotted her, he pushed off the wall, his long strides eating up the distance.

"Nora's with Dr. Eamon. He's checking her out to make sure her only injury is her wrist…" Tripp started giving Beth the rundown before she even opened her mouth, reaching out and grabbing her shoulders. Her hands went to his waist, her fingers fisting in the material of his shirt like that was where they belonged.

His palms moved up and down her arms as he talked, repeating a few of the things that Jax had already told her. It didn't hurt to hear for a second time that Nora had been conscious, hadn't hit her head, and that she had been wearing her seat belt. But even with all of those affirmations, all Beth could envision was Tripp pulling Nora from the smashed-in Jeep.

"Oh God." She slammed her eyes shut, the image too much to handle.

"Beth, babe, come here." He pulled her into him, his arms coming around her.

She let him hold her. Let his strength and confidence and reassurance wrap around her. His hands were now at her back, moving up and down her spine in slow, steady strokes. He pressed his warm lips against her temple and whispered. "I've got you, Beth. I've got you."

She could only let herself be soothed by him for a moment, just a moment. One, she needed to get to Nora. And two, the longer he held her the closer she was to falling apart. She desperately needed to keep herself together, needed to not lose it.

Later. She could lose it later.

"I need to see her," she whispered, looking up at him. Maybe when she actually laid eyes on her niece, she would stop freaking the fuck out…and maybe not feel like her heart was going to beat out of her chest.

Or maybe this feeling wouldn't ever go away.

"I'll be right here." He leaned down and kissed her forehead. "I'm not going anywhere." His hands fell away from her body as he took a step back.

"Thank you." Beth nodded, squeezing his hand before she let go and headed for the double doors that led to the examination area.

A nurse named Gail Sumner was sitting behind the desk next to the entrance. She stood up from her seat as Beth drew near, compassion on her face. "Nora is at the back left corner."

"Thank you," Beth managed to say before she pushed the doors open with shaking hands.

There were thirty beds in the ER, and about ten of them held patients tonight. The one with Nora in it had blue curtains drawn up around it. Dr. Eamon was just coming out from behind the curtains as Beth walked up.

"Oh good; you're here. We just got Nora in there, and I want to do a complete check-up to make sure it's just her wrist that's hurt. Do you want to help her into the gown, or do you want me to get another nurse?"

Beth shook her head. "I'll help her into it."

"Okay, I'll be right back." He reached out, grabbing Beth's shoulder as he looked her in the eyes. "We're going to take care of her."

"I know."

"Good." He nodded before he let go and headed off to another patient.

Beth took a deep breath before she pulled the curtain back, but there was really nothing she could've done to fortify herself for the sight of her niece in that bed.

There was a bright red mark across the left side of Nora's jaw and some scrapes on her forehead. Her face was blotchy from crying. All of those tears had tracked black mascara down her cheeks from her green eyes; green eyes that always got greener when she cried.

"I'm sorry." Those two words escaped Nora's mouth on a breathless whisper, right before her shoulders bent forward and she started to sob.

Beth moved, crossing the distance to the side of the bed and pulling Nora into her arms. Nora turned her head into Beth's chest, her entire body shaking as tears soaked through the fabric of Beth's shirt.

She brought her hand up to the back of her niece's head, running her fingers through Nora's hair. "I've got you, Nora. I've got you." Beth found herself repeating what Tripp had said to her just moments before.

"I was so scared," Nora said through her body-wracking sobs. "He was driving so fast and he wouldn't listen to me."

Beth's hand stilled and she pulled back so she could look down into Nora's face. "Who?"

Until that moment she hadn't spared a single thought for whoever else had been in that Jeep. Absolutely all of her focus had been on getting to her niece.

Nora's eyes widened and she took an unsteady breath before she spoke. "I...uh...I was with Brick Mason."

There were very few people in Mirabelle who didn't know who the Masons were. The entire family had their life played out on billboards.

The one and only car dealership in Atticus County had been a Mason-owned and operated business for three generations. It had been started by Mortar Mason, then given to Welder Mason, and now it was run by Stone Mason.

Yup, those were the names of the Mason men. No fucking joke.

Stone's wife Kittredge, or Kitty, was also part of the business. Twenty-five years ago, Kitty had been hired to be a model for the dealership. For years there'd been billboards of her sporting the tiniest hot pink bikini imaginable.

This was during the time the TV show *Baywatch* was popular, and Kitty had pretty much had a Pamela Anderson-esque body—still did, thanks to the wonders of plastic surgery. At forty-three she was also still the face of the dealership, but now those billboards featured her in a Grace Kelly-style advertisement, covered in diamonds while driving a Porsche.

There'd also been a few years there where Stone, Kitty, and Brick had been on those billboards. A family values type of advertising. Because Brick had been playing football from the moment he could walk, he was usually pictured sporting a jersey and had a ball in his hands.

Brick was a legend in Mirabelle. He'd taken the high school football team all the way to the state semi-finals two years in a row, and they'd won state last fall. He was a senior this year and had gotten a full ride scholarship to the University of Miami. Most people thought of him as a small-town hero.

Beth was not one of them. She'd always gotten a smarmy feeling whenever she'd seen him. And there'd been more than a few rumors about some of his misdeeds getting covered up.

"Nora, why were you with Brick?"

"We were dating."

"*Were,* as in the past."

Nora nodded. "I ended it tonight."

"How long have you been seeing him?"

She hesitated for just a moment before she answered. "Since the Spring Fling."

There was an unpleasant sinking sensation in Beth's belly. Nora had been seeing this guy for as long as Beth had been with Tripp…She chose not to focus on that fact at the moment.

"So you ended it tonight? Is that why he was driving the way he was?"

"Part of it." Shame flickered in Nora's eyes and she looked away.

"And what was the other part?" Beth asked, dreading the other half of the answer.

"He…he wanted to go further than I was ready for." She shifted uncomfortably on the bed. "And I told him no." She whispered that last part, still not looking at Beth.

A different kind of fear was now taking over Beth's emotions, the kind of fear that was accompanied by anger…then rage. Mama bear kind of rage.

Beth reached for Nora's chin, gently pressing up until they were looking eye to eye. "Did he stop?"

"Yes, but he was pissed. He got back on the road and started driving like an idiot. I begged him to stop, to let me out, but he wouldn't listen. He just kept driving faster and faster. There was a bend in the road, but he didn't turn enough and then we were heading into the trees."

"He's here too?"

"Yes. He had a pretty deep cut on his forehead but I don't think he was hurt too badly. He was wearing his seat belt, too."

Wasn't hurt too badly, huh? Beth had no problem changing that. It took everything in her not to turn around, pull back the curtains, and go find Brick *Fuck Face* Mason. The desire was strong, but the need to stay with Nora was stronger.

"We'll talk about this more later." Mainly because Beth couldn't handle hearing anything else at the moment. "You need to get into the hospital gown so Dr. Eamon can get you looked at."

"Okay." Nora nodded, knowing her reprieve on this front was temporary. However, her reprieve on the pain front was nonexistent.

It took a couple minutes of maneuvering to get Nora's shirt off and not upset the delicate state of her left wrist. But as it was a T-shirt featuring one of Nora's favorite bands, Beth complied and didn't just cut it off.

The second it was over Nora's head, Beth got a glimpse of Nora's chest. A massive red mark from the seat belt was imprinted on Nora's pale skin, her white bra making it stand out all the more. Beth inhaled sharply through her nose. It was going to be an ugly bruise before long, an ugly bruise that was going to be pretty damn painful, too.

Every scrape, bump, and bruise on Nora hurt Beth as if they'd been inflicted to her own body.

A minute or two after Nora was all gowned up and settling back on the bed, Wallace pushed back the curtains, his face full of panic and fear. Beth had called him when Jax had driven her over, and he'd gotten right in his truck.

"What's going on? What happened? What do we know?" he asked as he held Nora's uninjured hand.

"I'm going to be okay, Papa," Nora said as Dr. Eamon pushed through the curtains next.

Beth stood by Nora's side as the head-to-toe exam was administered. She was listening to everything that Dr. Eamon said, but in the back of her mind, she kept going over what Nora had just told her about Brick.

The little shit.

Nora's final diagnoses? A broken wrist and bruises.

In the scheme of things, Beth knew it could've been way worse. She'd experienced way worse in her line of work. Hell, as an obstetrics nurse she'd been around screaming, emotional mothers giving birth to children. But that broken bone in Nora's body was more than she could really handle. There was a distinct possibility that had to do with the circumstances that created that broken bone and how the accident was so similar to how Colleen and Kevin had died.

A temporary cast was put on Nora's arm; there was too much swelling for a permanent one at the moment. So Beth and Nora would be returning to the hospital later in the week.

It was close to ten o'clock when Beth, Nora, and Wallace exited to the waiting room, a waiting room that now held many people who were there for Nora. Tripp and Jax had been joined by Grace, Paige, Harper, Hannah, Finn, Bennett, Dale, and Hamilton.

Nora came to an abrupt halt next to Beth, no doubt also shocked by the amount of people who'd shown up.

Beth looked around at the crowd, and when her gaze landed on Hamilton she saw a range of emotions run across the boy's face. Fear turned to relief before transforming into anger and frustration.

I feel your pain, buddy.

"I need to get some fresh air." Hamilton shook his head before he turned around and headed outside. He was clenching and unclenching his fists with each step that he took, tension radiating from every single one of his muscles. Dale lifted one of his shoulders in a half-shrug to Nora before following Hamilton out.

Nora watched them both walk away, that look of misery on her face intensifying. She reached up and ran her fingers under her eyes, brushing away the fresh tears that had fallen with her fingertips.

Tripp was the first to step forward, pulling Nora into a gentle hug and saying something only she could hear. When he let go he moved to the side and grabbed Beth's hand. They both stepped back so that everyone else who'd been waiting could get a hug of their own.

Tripp turned to Beth, pulling her close. "How are you doing?"

"I'm not going to lie to you, Tripp. I've been better."

"Brick left with Stone and Kitty about forty minutes before you and Nora walked out. He got his forehead stitched up but that was the only thing I could spot. He looked fine otherwise."

Of course he did, the stupid little shit.

"Beth, why was she with him? I thought she was going to the basketball game with Monica and Gretchen tonight."

"I thought so too. I don't know the entire story yet. And what I do know…" She shook her head as she trailed off, looking to Nora, who was now getting a hug from Bennett. She looked back to Tripp and sighed. "I can't handle anything else tonight, Tripp."

"I know." He reached up to cup the side of her face in his palm.

Beth closed her eyes as she leaned into his touch. More than a small part of her craved for his arms around her body. But she knew if he held her again she'd lose it for real this time, something she couldn't do in the middle of this waiting room.

That wasn't the only thing she had to contend with. There was that new nagging voice at the back of her mind, the one that kept repeating she'd been too distracted by her relationship with Tripp to pay attention to her niece. Nora had been dating this whole time and she hadn't even noticed.

But she wasn't ready to delve into that at the moment, either.

She pulled away from him, opening her eyes and shaking her head as she stepped back.

Confusion flickered in his eyes. "Beth?"

"I need to get Nora home. It's been a long night."

"Okay," he said slowly, his eyes searching her face. "Finn took me to pick up my truck at the station, so I can drive you. But I need to go back to do the accident report."

She just nodded before she turned and went back to Nora.

They were able to leave a few minutes later. All of Beth's friends told her that if she needed anything, all she had to do was call. By the time she headed outside with Tripp, Nora, and Wallace her head was pounding.

Tripp's hand rested at the small of her back. It was an odd thing to both crave his touch and want to run away from it. It was just that she couldn't handle being comforted right now. Instead of soothing her, his touch was about to make her break down into a sobbing mess. There was also the fact that she could never truly think properly when he had his hands on her—and if there was ever a time she needed to think properly, it was now.

When they got to the truck Wallace pulled Nora into another hug, probably his twentieth of the night. "I love you, granddaughter."

"I love you, too, papa."

When he pulled back, that stern look Beth had grown up with transformed his face. "You and I are going to have a conversation tomorrow."

"I know." Nora nodded.

Wallace helped Nora into the backseat on the passenger side, and as Beth was rounding to the driver's side, Tripp seemed to figure out pretty quickly that she would be sitting in the back as well. He helped her up, but when his hands left her body a slight sense of relief ran through her.

It instantly made her feel guilty.

Once she and Nora were settled in with their seat belts on, Nora leaned over and rested her head in Beth's lap. Beth's hand went to her niece's hair, gently running her fingers through it.

Tripp started his truck and backed out of the parking spot a moment later. The five-minute car ride home was a silent one; none of them uttering a single word. Beth stared out the side window into the darkness, unable to stop the evening's events from replaying in her brain.

She felt like she was going to throw up.

When they got to the house, Tripp helped Nora out of the truck while Beth unlocked the front door.

Mel was coming down the hallway as everyone made their way inside. She stopped when she saw Nora, letting out a sigh of relief. As Beth and Mel had been texting for most of the night—Beth had been sending updates on Nora while checking on Penny and Grant—Mel knew exactly what had happened. But seeing was believing, and Beth knew that full well.

"Oh, thank God you're okay." Mel pulled Nora into a hug and kissed the girl on the temple before letting go. "I'll leave you guys to it. Penny and Grant went to bed about an hour ago. Duke is with Grant."

But just as Mel said the dog's name, the clicks of Duke's nails sounded on the hardwood floor.

"Or he *was* with Grant," Mel corrected as Duke went right up to Nora and butted his furry head against her thigh. "Good night. Call me if you need me tomorrow." She grabbed Beth's hand and squeezed gently, patted Tripp on the shoulder, and then was out the door.

Beth, Tripp, and Nora stood in the silent hallway for just a moment before Nora turned and looked up at Tripp. "I…I'm glad it was you." Her voice trailed off at the end and she looked so damn lost.

"Come here, kiddo." Tripp pulled her into a hug, pressing a kiss to the top of her head.

As Beth watched them, her throat constricted and she took an unsteady breath, fighting back her tears.

"Get some rest." Tripp pulled back, Nora's shoulders gripped in his hands.

Nora just nodded before turning to Beth, a question in her eyes.

"I'll be there in a second."

"Okay," Nora said before she headed for her bedroom.

Beth watched her niece walk away, beyond relieved at having her home again. When Nora disappeared around the corner, she turned to Tripp.

"You know, that's twice now that you've saved one of my kids." She shook her head and blinked. The tears that had threatened just moments ago now fell freely.

"Beth." Tripp had her in his arms not even a second later and she found herself falling off the edge of that precipice she'd been precariously balanced on all night.

She couldn't summon the strength to pull away, and she didn't want to. Instead she pressed her face to his chest and good and truly lost it. The emotions her body had gone through over the last couple of hours had exhausted her beyond all reason and she wouldn't have been able to hold anything back even if she tried. Body-wracking sobs had taken over, but Tripp didn't let go of her; he just held on tight.

"She's going to be okay, Beth," he whispered against her ear.

"It could've been so much worse."

He pulled away only far enough to look down into her face. "Babe, this world is full of could'ves, would'ves, and should'ves. They're all hypotheticals, but Nora making it through what happened today? That's a reality." He ran his fingers along her hairline. "This wasn't your fault."

She dropped her gaze at his words, unable to look at him because she didn't believe him. Didn't believe what he'd just said in the slightest.

"Beth." He whispered her name as he touched her chin, gently nudging it up until her eyes were on him again. "This wasn't your fault," he repeated. "Tell me you know that."

"I can't tell you that, Tripp. If I did I'd be lying."

He didn't say anything as his eyes searched hers. What he found there she didn't know, but he must've realized he wasn't going to convince her. Instead he leaned down to brush his lips across hers.

"I love you," he said against her mouth.

"I love you, too."

"I don't know how late I'm going to be tonight. Do you want me to text you before I come back?"

"Actually, Nora asked if she could sleep with me tonight. And I told her yes."

"All right. It's probably for the best. I'm going to have to get up early in the morning anyway, and you need a full night's sleep. I'll see you tomorrow then. And you'll call me if you need anything?"

"I'll call you."

He kissed her again, his lips softly working over hers before he pulled away. Duke had been sitting at the entrance to the hallway, and when Tripp took a step back the dog approached and gently brushed against Beth's legs before following his owner. She watched the two of them head out into the night.

She flipped the deadbolt before she turned around and leaned against the door, taking a few unsteady breaths.

Everything just felt wrong. *Everything.* And she had no clue how to fix it.

It was an effort to force the feeling down before she pushed off the door a second later and headed down the hallway. She peeked into Penny's room and then Grant's, seeing them both sound asleep in their beds, before continuing on.

Soft light filtered out into the hallway from the open door of Nora's room. When Beth got to the doorway she found Nora sitting on the edge of her bed, staring off into space. When she lightly knocked, Nora looked over, swiping at her tears with her uninjured hand.

Beth entered and sat down next to Nora, who leaned over and rested her head on Beth's shoulder.

"We can talk about all of this tomorrow," Beth said as she leaned her head against Nora's. "After some sleep and a strong cup of coffee." Or five.

"Okay." Nora nodded slowly, her hair brushing against Beth's cheek with the movement. "I'm sorry," she whispered after a moment.

"I know." Beth lifted her head, turning so she could place a kiss to her niece's hair. "I know."

Chapter Twenty-One

Burning House

Sleep proved an elusive bitch for Beth that night. She probably had a dozen nightmares—full of would'ves, could'ves, and should'ves. No matter how hard she tried, those what ifs wouldn't stop. The last dream—which woke her up just after five in the morning—had been the worst: Nora dressed in a blue dress, eyes closed, skin pale and cold as she lay in a casket.

Heart slamming hard in her chest, Beth rolled over in bed and pulled a warm and very much alive Nora into her arms. Nora snuggled in closer, her soft breaths moving across the skin of Beth's neck. Beth lay there for an hour, counting every single one of those breaths.

It was around six when she finally got out of bed, heading for the kitchen and turning on the coffee maker. Ten minutes later she was sitting on the sofa on the back porch, a steaming cup of coffee in hand.

Her brain started to run through the last couple of months with Nora, going over what she knew, everything that she'd learned so far, and trying to puzzle it all together. But she didn't have all of the pieces yet, and she wouldn't until she talked to her niece.

But whether she had all of the pieces or not, there was a part of the puzzle that was pretty damn clear. This was partly her fault...her fault because of Tripp. There was no way around it; she'd been so wrapped up in him that she'd missed this whole thing with Nora. Because really, this was a massive freaking thing to miss.

She shouldn't have been this blind to it. Should've realized something was going on. Anything.

But no. The only things she'd noticed were what were right there in front of her face. Like bad attitudes and blue hair. Hell, she'd missed that stupid piercing for months. And that had happened *before* Tripp had even come into the picture.

So many things had happened before Tripp, so many things that she hadn't seen. Like Grant "borrowing" Duke. And Grant going out on that lake during a thunderstorm. She still cringed when she thought about that.

The only reason she hadn't missed anything with Penny yet was because Penny was too young to start hiding things. And that was probably going to change in no time at all. Beth cringed again at that thought.

She'd been so focused on going through all of her failings that she didn't even realize that an hour had passed, but it had. The sun was starting to light up the sky—not to mention her cup of coffee was empty. She'd been about to get up to get another cup when she heard Duke running around next door, and not a moment later Tripp was outside.

Everything in her stilled as she just sat and listened. She closed her eyes, letting his voice fill her ears. She wondered what time he'd gotten home last night, how much sleep he'd gotten, how late he'd be today…

It would be so easy to find out. All she had to do was open her mouth and ask. She only needed to say his name and she knew he'd come over, sit down next to her on the couch and let her curl up into his side.

She said nothing.

He stayed outside for about twenty minutes playing fetch with Duke before heading back in. A half an hour later she heard his truck engine turn over before he drove away.

Regret filled her chest and it only intensified as the sound of his truck disappeared. She hadn't even realized when she'd started crying, but her cheeks were definitely wet with tears.

* * *

It was close to nine and Beth was working on her third cup of coffee when Nora finally ambled outside. Her light brown hair was tousled around her head, her eyes sleepy.

"How are you feeling?"

"I hurt all over," Nora said as she gingerly sat down next to Beth. "I took some of the pain meds they gave me last night."

The prescription Nora had been given was definitely going to do more for her than over-the-counter stuff, but Beth had no doubt she'd still be feeling the aftereffects of the accident for a few days.

"Can I have some?" Nora nodded to Beth's cup.

Beth handed it over and Nora let out a satisfied sigh after her first sip. They sat in silence until Nora finished the entire cup, leaning over to the coffee table and setting it down on the glass surface.

"Okay, I'm ready," she said as she pulled her legs up onto the sofa and crossed them, grimacing for a moment before her face relaxed.

"Oh, are you?" Beth's eyebrows rose.

"Yup. It's time for me to face the music."

"You're going to tell me everything? Honestly?"

"Yes." Nora nodded. "I don't want to lie to you anymore."

"Good. I don't want you to lie to me anymore, either."

"So I told you it all started at the Spring Fling. I'd never really talked to Brick before then, but he saw me and came up to me. After talking for a little bit he asked me out. He, uh, was there when I went to the movies with Gretchen and Monica that night."

"Now I know I specifically asked who you were going with."

"Yes." Nora looked more than a little chagrined. "But you never asked if anyone was going to be meeting us *at* the movies."

"You still lied to me."

"I know."

"What else?"

"Well, he's been at all of the basketball games, the party at Greg Inglewood's a few weeks ago, and…and he's been driving me home from school."

"Have the two of you been inside the house by yourselves?" Beth asked, glad she was no longer holding anything breakable in her hands.

Nora pulled her bottom lip between her teeth and started chewing. It was a moment before she let go. "Yes. We'd make out on the sofa before Grant got home."

"Nora!" Beth closed her eyes and sighed, trying hard to keep calm. The more she learned the more appealing her dream of locking Nora up in a tower became. Too bad that wasn't an option. She took a deep breath before looking at her niece again.

"I know he shouldn't have been in the house. I know the rules. But I wanted to be with him and he never pushed me beyond my comfort zone before. Whenever things…" she trailed off for a moment as her cheeks turned red, "escalated, I would tell him to stop, and he would. Without hesitation. But last night"—she shook her head, confusion in her eyes—"it was like a switch flipped. I told him no and he freaked out. He called me…" She paused, her cheeks flushing with embarrassment again. "He called me a cocktease."

Beth bit her tongue, stopping herself from saying what *she* thought about the stupid little shit. "But he stopped?" She'd already asked that question the night before, but she needed to hear it again.

Nora squirmed uncomfortably. "After a minute he did. I had to…I had to say it more than once."

Beth's hands were balled into fists, her nails painfully digging into her palms.

"He's not who I thought he was." Nora shook her head.

"Who did you think he was, Nora? Because if you thought he was something great, why would you hide him? Why would you not tell me about him? Why would you keep him a secret? Why would you sneak around?"

"I don't know." Nora raised her shoulder in a small shrug and then winced at the movement. "I really don't. I just…did it."

"You know you're grounded, right?" Beth asked.

"That I actually do know." Nora nodded.

"No phone, no going out, no friends coming over. Two months, Nora."

"I understand." She nodded again. "Last night really scared me." Her gaze dropped as she started fiddling with the hem of her sleep shorts. "It brought everything from a year ago back. All I could think about were Mom and Dad, and how…and how it had happened to them. How they died. How *I* could've…" Her voice had gotten smaller and smaller as she talked, before finally trailing off. She didn't need to finish the sentence for Beth to understand.

"That's all I could think about, too." Beth reached out and grabbed Nora's hand, the gesture causing Nora to look up.

"I'm sorry for lying to you, Aunt B. I really, really am."

"I believe you. But no more lying, Nora."

"I promise. No more."

"I want you to know something. Sneaking around and lying aside, what happened last night wasn't your fault. You're not in trouble because of that accident, or because of what Brick did. You're supposed to be able to trust the person you date. Supposed to believe that they will respect your boundaries, sexual or otherwise. That's the healthy way to approach dating. What he did…his reaction to you saying 'no'…" Beth shook her head, taking a moment to breathe past the constriction in her throat. "This wasn't your fault. Do you understand that?"

Nora blinked, tears falling from her eyes, before she slowly nodded. "I understand," she said thickly.

"Come here." Beth let go of Nora's hand, shifting on the sofa and pulling her niece in close. They sat there for a few minutes, just holding each other, before Beth kissed Nora on the top of the head and whispered, "I love you."

"I love you, too."

The next breath that Beth pushed out from her lungs released a little bit of her tension and worry…but it wasn't enough to take all of it away.

* * *

Tripp had been a firefighter for thirteen years, six of which had been in the Air Force, and two spent in a war. Yet, nothing, *nothing* had ever terrified him more than learning that it was Nora in that smashed-in Jeep.

And when he'd seen her, hurt and scared? It had taken everything in him to remain calm and not lose it. There was also the fact that he'd wanted to beat the crap out of the asshole behind the wheel.

Once he'd really looked at how the Jeep had crashed, he knew that Brick was to blame. Knew it wasn't an accident, just sheer stupidity. Carelessness. And if there was anything that anyone should not be with Nora, it was careless.

He'd never get the images out of his head. They were burned into his brain, right next to the ones of Beth. Her walking panic-stricken into the ER waiting room, her sobbing in his arms, her not believing it wasn't her fault.

After finishing up the report that night, he'd lingered at his desk, going over the evening again to make sure he hadn't missed anything. Duke had come to the firehouse, too, and he hadn't left Tripp's side for a second, resting his big shaggy head on Tripp's thigh.

They'd gotten home well after midnight. The house had been

lonely and quiet. Since the kids had gotten back from their Spring break two weeks ago, he hadn't really spent too much time there. Just stopped over to change his clothes, really.

He slept like shit without Beth beside him.

There hadn't been a prayer of him getting anything close to adequate rest. Four straight weeks of sharing a bed with Beth had permanently changed him. Not just because of the sleeping arrangements, but because of everything. There was no going back and he damn well knew it.

When his alarm went off at seven, he was beyond exhausted. He knew he was going to need cups and cups of coffee to get through the day ahead. After hanging out with Duke outside for a bit, and after finishing that first cup of coffee, he'd gone back in to get dressed. He'd wanted to go next door and check on everyone before heading out, but he didn't want to wake up Beth or the kids. Just because he'd slept like shit didn't mean she had. They all needed some rest. He'd just have to call her at a more reasonable hour.

He brought Duke with him to the station, not wanting to leave the guy by himself all day. Beth and the kids had enough to contend with without adding Duke to the mix. And he knew that Wallace was going to be coming over for a conversation of his own. It would be a crowded house…

Though there was something in the back of his mind that kept telling him he should be a part of that crowd.

He'd been around for a couple of months now, been a part of their lives, but there was a huge difference between what happened on a normal day and what had happened the night before. He was fully aware of that fact.

There was no doubt in his mind that he needed to make it perfectly clear to Beth that he was in this for the long haul. It was a conversation he was going to need to have once all of this calmed down.

* * *

Tripp talked to Beth just a little bit that day, a handful of text messages and a very short phone call during lunch. She told him she was feeling better than the night before and that Nora was doing okay; in pain, but okay. She also told him to stop worrying and to focus on the training.

That had been easier said than done.

Everything was finished up at the firehouse around five, and as he and Duke headed out to his truck, he pulled out his phone to call Beth. He needed to stop by the store and get dog food—there was only enough left for Duke's dinner and breakfast—and he wanted to know if she needed anything while he was there.

She didn't answer, and his call went over to voicemail. He left a quick message and hung up, putting his phone in his pocket before letting Duke into the back, and then climbing into the driver's seat.

When he pulled into the parking lot of the Piggly Wiggly—Mirabelle's one and only grocery store—Beth's SUV was already parked in a spot. He found an empty space a row over. It was a cool night, and he rolled down all four of the windows just enough for Duke to stick his snout out and catch the breeze.

He found her in the juice aisle, stretching up in an attempt to grab a bottle that was pushed back on the top shelf. The back of her shirt had pulled up, exposing a strip of skin. In four strides he was right behind her.

"Need a little help?" he asked as he reached over her shoulder for the bottle.

"Oh!" She gasped, startled as she spun around and fell into his chest. He caught her, his free hand going to her waist to steady her. "Tripp," she breathed his name as she regained her footing.

He looked down into her face, immediately noticing her tired blue eyes and the dark circles beneath them. Every part of her looked weary.

"I thought you were going to call me to tell me if you needed anything," He let go of her before leaning to the side and putting the bottle of juice in her shopping cart.

"Dad came over so I figured I'd give him some time with Nora. Besides, I needed to get food and figure out dinner."

"I would've taken care of dinner."

"Tripp, you were busy today. You had stuff to do. I can handle it."

"I know that, Beth, but I want to—"

But he was cut off as a hatred-filled voice pretty much started screaming behind him. "I can't believe you have the gall to show your face in public!"

As his eyes were on Beth, he noticed how her expression changed from surprise and then almost immediately to anger. He turned around and came face to face with Kitty Mason.

The woman was wearing a designer suit, a cloud of perfume, and an expression that had probably made many people cower.

Tripp wasn't even remotely intimidated.

"And you"—Kitty reached up and poked Tripp's chest with her finger—"are just as bad."

"Mrs. Mason, I suggest you take a step back," he said calmly, fully aware of the people in the aisle around them that were turning to stare.

"Or what?" She raised her voice, poking him in the chest again. "You don't scare me."

"I'm not trying to scare you." He held his hands up, palms out. "But you need to take a step back."

"I will not!" She shouted before her focus moved to Beth. "You need to get that niece of yours under control! She put my son at risk last night! That accident was *her* fault. He's a good child, a role model to be looked up to, and I will not have him getting distracted because your niece likes to spread her legs like you do!"

An anger unlike anything Tripp had ever known started coursing through his veins. But before he could say anything Beth was the one now screaming.

"Are you kidding me? Your *model* son tried to force himself on my niece, and when she said no, he took it out on her by driving like a freaking lunatic and getting in a car accident. *Your* son put *my* niece in danger when he drove recklessly. She broke her wrist because of *him*!"

And just that fast Tripp was angrier than he'd been a moment before. "What?" He asked, turning to look at Beth. She glanced at him for only a second, a palpable pain in her expression over what she'd just revealed.

"You're a liar," Kitty hissed out.

Beth pulled her eyes from Tripp and looked back at Kitty. "I'm not. But you're lucky I'm not suing you for medical expenses or pressing charges for attempted sexual assault. If I see him anywhere close to her, I'm going to call the sheriff's department faster than you can blink." She grabbed her purse from the half-filled shopping cart, leaving it in the aisle before walking away.

Kitty stared after Beth's retreating form, daggers in her eyes. Tripp slid in front of the woman, blocking her view. Her eyes widened in surprise at his menacing expression.

"Kitty, understand this. If your son *ever* comes near Nora or Beth—or Penny or Grant, for that matter—he's going to have to deal with much more than the sheriff's department. Same goes for you."

She bristled at his words. "Is that a threat?"

"No." He shook his head. "It's a promise." And with that he turned around and followed Beth out of the store.

Once he got to the parking lot, he had to jog to catch up to her. She made a beeline for her SUV and as she rounded it, she put her hand on the side of the vehicle for balance.

"Beth?"

"Just give me a second."

The emotion in her voice was at that level where he knew how hard she was trying to not break down in the middle of the Piggly Wiggly parking lot. It was a minute or two before she got a handle on herself and was able to speak.

"I can't believe I just said that." She slowly turned to look at him, her hands shaking. "Oh God. Why did I say all of that?"

"Beth." He reached out for her but she shook her head, taking a step back.

"Don't touch me."

Those three words were a blow to the center of his chest and for just a second he couldn't breathe, let alone speak.

"It's just that every time you touch me, or comfort me, I feel like

I'm going to lose it. Like I can't hold anything together, and I can't deal with that right now. I'm *sorry*." Her voice broke as she said that last word. "I know you don't understand it. I just can't deal with this. Not right now."

"This?"

"*Us*."

What the fuck does that mean? It took everything in him not to ask that question out loud. But somehow—he wasn't sure as to the *how*—he stood there not saying a word. There was something unsettling in her expression, the same damn thing he'd seen in her eyes last night when he'd told her it wasn't her fault…and she hadn't believed him.

"I don't know how to do this, Tripp. I was failing at being a mom before you, and now I'm failing even more. Nora started sneaking around with that stupid jerk when we started seeing each other."

"So it's my fault?"

"No; you don't get it. It's *my* fault. *I* missed what was going on. This whole thing is entirely on me, and I brought you into it."

"And what? Now you want to take me *out* of it."

"It isn't about what I want. It's about what's best for the kids." Tears were streaming down her cheeks, and he desperately wanted to reach forward and comfort her. The pain in her eyes was breaking him in half and there was nothing he could do. Nothing.

Every time you touch me, or comfort me, I feel like I'm going to lose it. Well, he felt like he was going to lose it because he *couldn't* touch her.

"And you think ending this might be part of the answer? Are

you really going to tell me you think I've had a negative impact on the kids' lives?"

"No, I don't think that at all."

"Then why are you making this into an either/or thing? It doesn't have to be either the kids, or me. You *can* have both and you don't have to do it alone. Beth, I want to do this *with* you. From here on out. I want this life with you, with the kids."

"Tripp, it's been two months."

"And?"

"And two months isn't enough time to figure that out."

"It was for me. You've been it for me since the day you were banging on my front door covered in mud. I love you, Beth."

"Sometimes love isn't enough." Her words were barely a whisper, but he heard her loud and clear.

She might as well have slapped him.

How was it that less than twelve hours ago he'd been thinking there was no going back with her? No going back with the kids? No going back with any of it? But that wasn't the case. This whole conversation was the very last thing he'd expected.

He'd never been this blindsided before. It hurt like hell.

"Did you really just tell me that my love for you isn't enough?"

"Tripp, that wasn't what I meant." She reached up and wiped at her eyes, but fresh tears just filled them again a second later.

"Then what did you mean?"

"Love doesn't fix everything, and I need time to figure this all out."

"Time? I thought we'd already figured this out. Figured *us* out. Obviously I was wrong." His instincts screamed at him as he took a step back. He shouldn't be putting *more* space between them. They were miles and miles apart already. "You're right, Beth. Love isn't always enough."

And as he stood there he had no idea what else to say or do. What *would* be enough? What would be enough for her to realize he wasn't going anywhere? Not knowing the answer to fix it was beyond painful.

What was he supposed to do? He was standing in the middle of a burning house, watching the walls catch fire around him. And he had no idea how to stop it.

Chapter Twenty-Two

Sound of Your Heart

Beth hadn't thought it was possible to feel worse than she did on Sunday morning. Well, when she woke up on Monday she found out just how possible it was.

She'd gotten even less sleep Sunday night. Not all that surprising; every time she closed her eyes all she could see was that hurt look on Tripp's face, and how every single one of his features had hardened.

And apparently she was a masochist because for the second day in a row, she started out by listening to him playing fetch with Duke next door, not saying a damn word.

Once the kids were off to school, she'd gotten dressed and headed out the door to work, unable to keep her eyes from drifting over to Tripp's truck parked in his driveway.

"Nora doing okay?" Denise asked when Beth walked into the office.

Denise had called the day before—another one of her many

friends who'd asked if she needed anything. But the only person Beth had actually accepted help from was her dad.

"Yes." Beth nodded. "Her wrist is still pretty swollen, but the pain meds are helping."

"Well, that's good."

"I heard you had an eventful weekend," Vanessa said a moment later as she came in, cup of coffee in hand. "Everyone's talking about how upset Tripp got."

"After the accident?" Denise asked. "Well, of course he was upset. He was the one who got Nora out. Beau said he's never seen Tripp almost lose his control in an emergency before."

"No, not that." Vanessa shook her head. "They're talking about what happened at the Piggly Wiggly with Kitty Mason."

"What happened with Kitty?" Denise looked to Beth.

"I don't want to talk about it, actually. I really, really don't want to talk about any of this." And with that Beth turned around and headed down the hallway.

* * *

Tripp had never really been one to sit around and wallow in his own misery. And damn, was he fucking miserable.

He was more of a *distraction is the best policy* kind of a guy. The problem was there wasn't a distraction big enough to take his mind off of everything that had happened in the last two days. After their conversation—or whatever the hell it had been—in the Piggly Wiggly parking lot, he didn't have a clue where he and Beth stood.

It was killing him.

He'd been dating since he was thirteen years old, and there'd been a number of women he'd cared about in those years, but none like Beth. Not even close. Being with her had shown him the difference between loving someone and being *in* love with someone.

The second night without her next to him was even worse than the first. And that second morning it had taken him absolutely no time at all to realize he couldn't stay in the house. He was already itching to get out, and maybe, possibly, needed to have a conversation with someone other than his dog.

So he called Bennett and asked if his friend needed any help on the current construction project going on. Bennett and Mel lived in a small two-bedroom/one-bath house that Mel had inherited from her grandmother. It was now in the process of being turned into a three-bedroom/two-bath house, the add-on being a master bedroom with a pretty elaborate bathroom.

Mel and Bennett's dog, Teddy, was a chocolate lab who was always up for some canine companionship, so Tripp brought Duke with him. He was pretty sure his dog didn't want to be cooped up in the house, either, lonely place that it was.

"How is Nora doing?" Bennett asked when Tripp got there.

More than a sharp pang radiated through his chest, because he didn't really know the answer to that question. "Better than Saturday, but she's pretty sore from the accident." He repeated what Beth had told him the day before.

"You all right?" Bennett asked, really looking Tripp over.

"Long weekend. I'm fine. So what do you want me to do?" Preferably it would be a job demolishing something. That would be a great way to spend his day.

So when Bennett handed him a sledgehammer, he was over-joyed.

Well, as much as he was capable of being overjoyed...which wasn't a whole hell of a lot.

* * *

The traffic at the doctor's office was pretty steady throughout the morning, so there weren't any opportunities for Beth to get pulled into a conversation with Denise or Vanessa. But patients were a different story.

Most of the questions she got were out of concern, but there were a number of people that just wanted good gossip.

You know I never liked that Kittredge Mason. She thinks just because she put her clothes back on that she's better than everyone else.

I can't believe it was Brick behind the wheel. He's such a good kid. Are you sure Nora wasn't distracting him while he was driving?

You should keep a better eye on her. You know how kids like to run around and get in trouble. At least her hair isn't that god-awful blue anymore.

I'm sure you weren't a saint at that age, either, but some of those girls that she's been hanging out with like to play it fast and loose.

It didn't take very long before Beth was counting down the time, desperate for her lunch break. But she didn't even make it to one o'clock. Just after eleven, Vanessa met her coming out of an exam room.

Her instinct told her to flee, but the look on Vanessa's face didn't appear to be a prying one. "Nora's on extension four." Vanessa frowned. "She sounds upset."

Vanessa didn't need to follow up that last part of the message; of course something was wrong. Nora had only called Beth at work twice in the last year, once on her dad's birthday and once on her mom's birthday. On both of those days she's cried so hard she'd given herself a migraine.

Beth was down the hallway and at the phone in less than twenty seconds. "Hey Nora, what's going on?"

A sniffle sounded through the speaker and rang in Beth's ear, and her stomach fell the rest of the way to her feet. *Oh God, what was it now?*

"Nora?"

"Can you come down here?" Her niece's voice was raw and scratchy. She'd been crying for a while.

"What happened?"

"Bethelda Grimshaw."

That was all Nora needed to say. Bethelda *Fucking* Grimshaw.

"I'm on my way."

* * *

For Beth to say that she hated someone took a lot, but Bethelda Grimshaw had always fit into that category. She was an *evil* woman who took great joy in hurting other people. The reason behind this? No one really knew. It had started years ago when Bethelda had worked for the town newspaper. When her local interest pieces had gone from just a tad gossipy to downright defamatory, she'd been fired. Now she liked to spread her vitriol on her personal website.

Bethelda was one of those anomalies in Mirabelle—no one

would admit to reading her pieces, but everyone knew what she was writing about. In the last couple of years this rotten-to-the-core, poor excuse for a human being had gone after Brendan and Paige, Jax and Grace, Bennett and Mel, Shep and Hannah, Liam and Harper, and countless others.

Absolutely no one was off limits. This was clearly true as Nora, along with Beth and Tripp, were in the most recent article. And the woman had gone *way* too far this time.

THE GRIM TRUTH
WHORES OF BABYLON

It's a sad state of affairs when a child loses a parent, especially when it's at a young, delicate age. It's even sadder when a child loses both parents in one fell swoop. To be motherless and fatherless is absolutely horrible. And when you multiply that by three children? Well, it's just tragic.

That being said, there's no excuse for reckless (or indecent) behavior. Grief or no, there are ways to conduct oneself, something that Short Stack should really learn. But who's going to teach her?

Well, it certainly isn't going to be her current guardian, Sloppy Seconds (a name given for both her lax parenting skills and her track record with men). And do you want to know why? Because both of these ladies (a word I use loosely . . . loose being the operative word) have issues when it comes to good morals and decency.

Let's start with Sloppy. She's now embarking on a relationship (or something) with her neighbor Smokey the Bear. I mean really, what kind of a woman flaunts her sex life around the three kids she's supposed to be taking care of? It's rather tasteless, if you ask me. I've been witness to the two groping each other around town on multiple occasions, whether they're feeling each other up at family events such as the Spring Fling or playing tonsil hockey and copping a feel in diner parking lots.

There isn't any wonder that Short Stack (who was sporting horrendous blue hair for a while there) has been sneaking around town doing pretty much the same thing. And what else should be expected when you are being raised by a woman like Sloppy Seconds?

Short Stack has taken a leaf out of her aunt's book and decided that whoring around is a family business. Her current target? Well, he's none other than the star quarterback for our high school. We can call him Boulder Brains, as he clearly has no sense unless it's on a football field.

The young couple apparently decided to drive out to what I've been told is our town's favorite hook-up spot. And when they were driving back—no doubt after mauling each other in the back seat—they put not only their lives, but the lives of everyone on the road at risk. Reckless driving is no joking matter and it's troubling behavior for sure. They were in a car accident, for heaven sakes. That Jeep of Boulder's was wrapped around a tree. We're just lucky more people weren't involved.

I certainly hope that our law enforcement officials checked to make sure that no one was driving under the influence of something stronger than teenage hormones.

But I've found our "officials" somewhat lacking of late. I'm sure anything unlawful was covered up as family friend Deputy

Ginger was Johnny-on-the-spot . . . not to mention Smokey the Bear was there, too. But that's a different conversation for a different day.

Let's just say Smokey thinks he's above such limitations of what's legal too. He has absolutely no qualms about threatening people (Boulder's mother Bleached Blond Bimbo, or BBB, to be exact) in our local grocery store. Because clearly he prescribes by the philosophy that violence is the answer. And don't even get me started on Sloppy screaming like a lunatic.

Anyways, I predict that Short Stack will be part of the teenage pregnancy statistic before we know it. You mark my words.

Rage, all-consuming rage, coursed through Beth's body. She was torn between wanting to scream and punch a wall, or to just start crying herself.

The situation went well beyond that stupid article, which had been handed to Beth by Mel as soon as she got to the school. After reading it, she'd found out from a near hysterical Nora that Brick *Fuck Face* Mason had made a bet with his friends. All of them had been competing to "bag a virgin" by the end of the school year. Even though he hadn't actually done it, the piece of shit said he'd slept with Nora.

After that, Beth had gone to sit down with an administrator to discuss the situation. It was the decision of Vice Principle Vance Shields—a mouse of a man with wispy hair and a pointed face—that Nora should spend the rest of the week at home. It was not a suspension; he was just giving her time to be away from everything until it died down, or until Principal Mitch Bolinder got back.

Shields was currently in charge while Bolinder was out of the state dealing with a death in his family. Beth liked Mitch Bolinder…She was not a fan of Vance Shields. When Beth asked Shields what was going to happen to Brick, he'd told her nothing was going to happen.

"So Nora has to leave school, but Brick gets to stay? Even after what he did?"

"We have no actual proof of this *bet*, Ms. Boone." His hands had moved slightly, as if he'd wanted to raise them and make air quotes. "It's just a rumor. We can't punish him for a rumor."

"What about what happened this weekend?"

"You mean the car accident that didn't happen on school property or school time? There's nothing I can do about that."

"Nothing you *can* do or nothing you're *willing* to do? A month out from graduation I'm sure a suspension would affect his college prospects, scholarships, recognition for this school. All you're concerned about is Brick's reputation; you could care less about Nora's."

"I don't like what you're insinuating, Ms. Boone. You want me to potentially ruin this young man's future because of something that might or might not have happened. He and your niece have been dating for a while now. And she went with him willingly on Saturday night. She isn't exactly innocent, either. She's been sneaking around. Dyeing her hair. Spending time with the less-than-reputable crowd around school."

In other words, he didn't believe Nora.

"You don't like what I'm insinuating? You're taking the lies from Bethelda Grimshaw and using them against Nora." Beth stood up, grabbing her purse from the chair next to her. "What does it say about our society that if you're good at sports, you can pretty much do whatever the hell you want, consequences be damned? He crashed that car, Mr. Shields, wrapped it around a tree because Nora *wouldn't* sleep with him. Two years from now, when he rapes a girl during a frat party, that's going to be partially on you. You and his parents and everyone else who've let him get away with stuff like this."

And with that Beth turned around and left.

It was Mel's lunch hour, but instead of eating she'd been by Nora's side, sitting in the row of chairs outside the office. Nora's head was bent and she was looking at her lap, shoulders slumped. There was a tissue in her uninjured hand that she'd periodically pull up to wipe at her eyes.

Mel looked up at Beth in question. When Beth gave a small shake of the head, anger transformed Mel's expression, an anger that filled the air around them.

Beth crossed the space and knelt down in front of her niece. "Honey," she whispered as she reached for Nora's chin and gently lifted it. Her niece's eyes were streaming with tears, her cheeks red and blotchy. "I know how much this hurts, how upset you are, and I'm so sorry. This isn't your fault. Okay? This is in no way your fault."

"What's going to happen?"

"Well, I'm going to take you home right now. And you're not going to come to school for the rest of the week, and hopefully things will calm down."

"I have to stay home? But I didn't do anything. Not at school, at least. I never did anything wrong here!"

"I know, sweetie. This whole situation is crap."

Mel's eyes narrowed as she looked to the closed office door behind Beth. "Coward," she muttered under her breath. "They're all a bunch of freaking cowards."

"Come on." Beth stood. "Let's go get your stuff." She held out her hand, and when Nora grabbed it, gently pulled her niece to her feet. "And let's get out of here."

* * *

Besides the radio softly playing in the background, the inside of the SUV was quiet as Beth drove through downtown Mirabelle. It wasn't until the car rolled past their neighborhood that Nora spoke.

"Where are we going?"

Beth glanced over for just a second, the stark pain on her niece's face clear, before she turned back to the road. "A place your mom and I used to go. I need to stop and pick something up, though."

It wasn't like Beth was going back to work. There wasn't a snowball's chance in hell that she would've been able to do her job even close to effectively. Her mind was completely and totally preoccupied with everything else that was going on in her life, searching for the answers to all of the questions rolling around her thoroughly exhausted brain.

In that particular state, what better place was there to go than hers and Colleen's spot? She and her sister had always gone a handful of times throughout the year. Some visits were random, but the two consistent ones were on their mother's birthday and the anniversary of her death. Over the last year those had been the only two days Beth had been able to go. Both times had been beyond painful.

But the desire to take Nora there was so damn strong, and she wasn't going to fight it.

The Gas-N-Go was right before the turnoff to the beach. Beth left the engine running as she went inside, and Nora locked the doors while she waited. When Beth came out two minutes later, her loot was in a small brown paper bag.

Nora raised her eyebrows at the bag, but Beth just shook her head. "It's a surprise."

As it was early May the beach was good and truly occupied. Though most of the tourists were laid out on towels down on the sand, there were a good number of people strolling along the pier.

Beth parked the SUV and grabbed the brown bag. She looked over at Nora before nodding toward the door. "Come on."

They both got out and headed to the pier. It was a pretty day, and though the sun was shining high in the sky, it was pleasant with the humidity low and the sea breeze constant.

There were a dozen benches running along both sides of the pier, so more often than not, people used those to sit on and enjoy the view. Not Beth and Colleen, though.

Their *spot* was right next to the second to last pillar on the right side, optimal for sunsets. The railing that bordered the edges had two levels: one rail came up higher than Beth's waist, and the other was about knee level. But when they sat right there on the wooden planks with their legs hanging over the edge, that knee-level barrier became the perfect armrest.

Beth settled into her spot and Nora followed suit, sitting where Colleen had always sat. They both stared out at the view for a minute or two, and the emerald green waters were just as beautiful as ever. Beth reached for the paper bag and opened it up, pulling out one of the items.

The crisp release of carbonation filled the air as she twisted the cap off of a bottle of Dr. Pepper. Beth took a sip before passing the bottle over to Nora. "It was your grandmother's favorite, and your mother and I always split a bottle when we came here. That, along with a bag of plain potato chips." And with that she pulled out the other item in the bag, opening the bright yellow packaging and setting it down on the dock between them.

Nora nodded before she took a sip from the bottle. They passed the bottle back and forth for another couple of minutes while nibbling on chips and staring out at the Gulf of Mexico, then Nora finally spoke again. "Everyone thinks I'm a whore. But I didn't..." she trailed off, shaking her head. "I *never* slept with him."

"I know and I believe you. And a plethora of other people will, too. Not everyone in this town thinks Brick Mason is a Golden God."

"I wish I'd never let him touch me. All I want to do is sit in a shower and scrub at my skin."

"Oh, honey." Setting the bottle down on the pier, Beth reached over and grabbed Nora's uninjured hand, linking their fingers together. "Just because he's slime does not mean that it's on you. You are not a whore. Even if you had slept with him, you still wouldn't be one. Do you understand that?"

Nora gave an almost imperceptible nod before she looked back to the water. Beth let go of Nora's hand and they went back to passing the bottle of Dr. Pepper back and forth and working through the bag of chips. Again, it was a minute or two before Nora said anything.

"How old were you?" Nora turned to Beth. "The first time… you…when you lost your virginity?"

"I was seventeen." It wasn't lost on Beth that she'd been the same age Nora was now, which was more than slightly intimidating. But they'd made a promise of no lying to each other.

"Who was he?"

"Davis Benson," Beth said, just a bit wistfully. "He had the curliest light brown hair and dimples. I was a total sucker for him. His family moved down here at the end of my junior year, and I spent every moment with him that summer. We were officially dating by the time the new school year started up."

"And how long after did it happen?"

"A couple of months. It was in the fall. I went over to his house when his parents were out of town."

"Did Mom know?"

"Yes." Beth nodded. "Your mom was the only person I told."

"And what did she say?"

"She told me to be smart, with both my heart and my body. Just because Davis was my first did not mean I was his. And, as it turned out, I *wasn't* his."

"Do you regret it? Davis being your first?"

"Not even a little bit."

"Did you love him?"

Beth tilted her head to the side in thought. "At the time, I thought I did, but I didn't really know what love was then. To be totally honest, though, I don't have any regrets in that department."

"What about Mick?"

"I don't regret being with him. I did love him, very much, and in the time we were together I learned a lot about myself. And when it ended, well…" Beth wasn't exactly sure how to finish that statement. Nora didn't know why it had *really* ended with Mick.

"I know he didn't want to be a father to kids who weren't his."

Beth's mouth dropped open. Apparently Nora did know. "How?"

"I overheard you telling Mel. It was a couple of months after you two broke up, but…" She gave a small shrug. "It sucked hearing that we weren't wanted. You know? He'd been a part of our lives for years, acted like he cared about us. 'Acted' being the operative word."

"Honey, don't ever think that you, or your brother or your sister, are unwanted. And I don't think Mick was acting. I think he did genuinely care about you."

Nora frowned.

"And I'm not just saying that to make you or me feel better. It just wasn't the life he wanted, and he walked."

Sometimes love isn't enough. She knew as soon as she'd said it yesterday that Tripp didn't understand it, but she sure as hell did. Because it wasn't always enough to make people stay. And what was going to happen when he realized *he* didn't want to stay?

She thought she'd gotten over this fear in the last few weeks, but clearly that wasn't the case.

"Well, Tripp is different." Nora said before taking a sip of Dr. Pepper and swallowing. "And he'd never walk."

What the hell? Was Nora *in* Beth's brain at the moment?

"What makes you say that?"

"First of all, he knew exactly what he was getting into when he started dating you. He knew that we came along with you."

A package deal. God, that conversation with him felt like it had happened years ago, not months.

"And he tries with all of us," Nora continued. "It's different with him around. Better. And it isn't like he just does stuff with us because he has to, but because he *wants* to. And now I know how much he loves me, and Grant and Penny, for that matter." Tears started to well in Nora's eyes and her bottom lip trembled. "I mean, I felt it before, but there's a difference between feeling and knowing. And I *know.*"

"*How* do you know?" The question crossed Beth's lips on a whisper, probably because she'd been holding her breath.

"When we got to the hospital, they wouldn't let him go back with me because he wasn't family. And the nurse said, 'It would be different if she was your daughter.' And he said, 'She might as well be.'" Nora blinked and the tears fell from her eyes.

Oh God. How *stupid* was Beth? Why in the name of everything good and holy had she pushed him away? This man who loved her? This man who loved her kids? This man who'd said he'd wanted it all with her?

She was an idiot.

Beth reached up and started wiping at her cheeks; tears had long been streaming from her own eyes. "He said that?"

"He did. But I knew he was here to stay a while ago."

"Why's that?"

"Because of the way he looks at you. It's how Dad looked at Mom, like there was no one else in the world. I want someone to look at me like that one day."

"Oh honey, come here." Beth pulled the almost empty bottle from Nora's hand and set it down on the pier. And then she was wrapping her arms around Nora and holding her niece to her chest. "Someone will."

Beth had to stop herself from saying what she'd initially thought, which was that someone *already* looked at Nora that way.

They sat there for a little bit, Beth rubbing her hand up and down Nora's back, thinking about the last couple of things her niece had said.

"So it's *better* with Tripp around? Huh?" Beth dropped her arms as Nora straightened and sat up.

"I didn't mean that in a way that it was miserable with just you. But, it's like it was…incomplete or something, without him and Duke. Little things."

"Such as?"

"I don't wake up during a thunderstorm terrified out of my mind anymore. And neither do Penny or Grant."

Beth had to let that sink in…how had *she* not noticed this? Yes, she'd known there'd been storms that rolled through in the last couple of weeks, but as they hadn't woken her up, she'd just figured they hadn't been loud enough…

Another startling fact hit her: it wasn't the kids crawling into bed during a storm that had always woken her up; it was the storms themselves. She'd been scared of them, too. And now, with Tripp sleeping next to her in bed, she slept through them.

"It isn't like I hadn't witnessed how a man is *supposed* to treat a woman. I mean it wasn't like Dad wasn't an awesome example. Because he was. He's just been gone, you know? Also, *hello*, there are enough of your friends with husbands that make that point perfectly clear. But being around someone who is *constantly* like that is a different thing altogether. And seeing Tripp day in and day out, it made me really know that being with Brick was wrong. The instant I realized he didn't respect me or what I wanted, I... I just knew. You know?"

"Yeah, I know."

Nora took a deep breath before she let it out on a sigh. "You asked me yesterday *why* I didn't tell you about Brick in the first place. And I think maybe it was because I knew, deep down. I knew he was a jerk and that you wouldn't approve."

"But he showed you attention, and you wanted it. Even if it wasn't good attention."

"Yes."

"I still feel like I was blind for not realizing."

"Why?" Nora's eyebrows furrowed. "I got away with plenty of stuff with Mom and Dad." As soon as the words were out of her mouth, her eyes widened in shock and she covered her mouth with her good hand.

"I'm sorry; what did you just say? You're going to need to elaborate. No lies, remember."

Nora dropped her hand. "Only if you promise I can't get in trouble for past offenses."

"It's a deal."

* * *

Just after two o'clock that afternoon Hamilton's big blue truck rolled up into the driveway of Bennett and Mel's house. The front doors opened a moment after the truck engine was cut off, and both Hamilton and Dale got out and headed up to the house.

Tripp immediately noticed the swollen lower lip Hamilton was sporting, and so did Bennett.

"What happened to your face?" Bennett asked by way of a greeting.

Hamilton paused for a second, debating how to answer. "Brick Mason," he finally said.

Bennett's eyes widened in surprise. "You got into a fight with Brick Mason?"

"You know," Dale started, a huge grin turning up the corners of his mouth. "I've always wanted to say, 'you should see the other guy.' And really, you *should* see the other guy. Brick's got a black eye and a broken nose."

A pretty big part of Tripp was beyond proud of Hamilton at the moment. He wished he could've been the one to do it.

"Your sister see your face?" Bennett asked.

"Not yet."

"Anyone else see your face? Or the fight, for that matter?"

"No one saw the fight." Hamilton shook his head. "And I'm not worried about Brick saying anything, either. He's the big bad football player and he won't want it getting around that the band nerd kicked his ass."

That made sense. Even though Hamilton had filled out in the last couple of years, he was still on the leaner side compared to Brick. Though Hamilton had a couple of inches in height on him, Brick probably had about twenty more pounds of muscle.

Tripp set down the crowbar he'd been using to pry up baseboards and crossed the yard. "And *why* did you kick his ass?"

Hamilton took a deep breath, looking between Bennett and Tripp. "He had a bet running that he'd sleep with Nora by the end of the school year."

"What?" Tripp pretty much growled the word, and this was the part where he started to see red.

"Saturday he figured out that wasn't going to happen. But today he was telling everyone it did. And what with the newest Bethelda Grimshaw article out, which is all about Nora along with Beth and you"—he gestured to Tripp—"everyone believes him."

"Are you shitting me?" There was a sharp edge to Bennett's question.

"No, I'm not. And that asshole didn't get in any trouble. They sent Nora home for the week, though. Beth picked her up during the lunch hour."

Bennett cut a glance to Tripp, his question clear. *Why the hell didn't she call you?*

Tripp didn't answer. Instead he asked, "Bolinder suspended Nora?"

"It wasn't Bolinder; he's out for the week," Dale explained. "It was Shields. And she isn't suspended; she just can't come to school while *everything cools down*. At least that was what Mel told us. Whatever the hell that means."

All of the information Tripp had gotten in the last few minutes was ricocheting around in his head. And as loud as it was all was jumbled together, there was something inside of him screaming louder than everything else. He was *not* going to sit back and watch everything burn down around him. He was not going to let this relationship with Beth end without a fight.

No fucking way.

"I've got to go," Tripp said as he pulled his keys from his pocket and whistled. Duke got up from where he and Teddy were lying in the shade of the trees, and immediately bounded over to the truck.

Chapter Twenty-Three

All I Want

The steady knocking echoed around the house, only getting louder as Beth headed toward the front door. It had taken Beth a little while to hear it as she'd been buried in her closet with Nora. They'd also turned the music up on the speakers attached to Beth's phone and were both singing a little throwback Madonna pretty loudly.

How else was she supposed to pick out the outfit to wear when she went and told her boyfriend just how wrong she'd been about everything?

But Beth knew even before she opened the door that Tripp was going to be on the other side. So changing would not be happening.

"Hot pink scrubs it is," she said to herself as her hand closed around the knob and she pulled.

Yeah, Tripp was pissed. She figured that out immediately. His brown eyes had darkened, his mouth was in a firm grim line, and his hair looked like he'd run his hands through it a dozen times. He wasn't alone, either. Duke was standing at his side, tongue lolling out as he happily panted.

For whatever reason the whole thing reminded her of that morning all those months ago, the morning where everything had really started. And that was when his words from the day before echoed in her head...

You've been it for me since the day you started banging on my front door covered in mud.

And he'd been it for her since that moment, too.

She didn't say anything as she stepped forward and pretty much threw herself into his arms. He caught her, holding her close as her mouth landed on his and she thoroughly kissed him.

She savored the feel of him—her body pressed to his, her hands in his hair, his hands at her lower back. His fingers were spread wide, like he had to touch as much of her as possible. His beard lightly scraped against her skin as he kissed her back, his tongue moving against hers.

It took everything in Beth to break the kiss, but she had to tell him, had to tell him how wrong she'd been.

Hands still firmly locked in his hair, she pulled away, her lips hovering just over his. "I'm sorry. I was wrong. So, so, so wrong. I told you I needed to do what was best for the kids, and you being a part of their lives *is* what's best for them. It's what's best for me, too. I want this life with you, Tripp. I want all of it."

A soft laugh escaped his mouth. "You're unbelievable, you know that? I came over here to tell you that I'm not going anywhere, that I'll never stop fighting for you, for us, for the kids, and then you beat me to the punch."

"Oh." She bit her lip to stop herself from grinning and took a step back, pulling from his arms. "Do you want me to go inside?" She pointed to the door behind her. "I can walk back out and we can do this again?"

"Come here." He reached for her, his palms sliding across her hips as he pulled her against his body again. "We don't need a do-over; I'll just spend the rest of my life proving it to you."

"I like that plan."

"Good, because it's what's going to happen. Every day, Beth. Every *damn* day."

Her hands went to the back of his neck, pulling slightly as she stretched up. "I love you."

"I love you, too. More than I've ever loved anyone. I never had a chance in stopping it."

"Didn't we establish this a while ago?" she asked. "Neither of us has ever had any control when it comes to the other."

He grinned against her mouth. "No control at all."

And with that, he kissed her, neither of them letting go for a long time.

Epilogue

To Love and to Be Loved

One year later…with Nora

Nora leaned forward and looked into the mirror over her dresser. She pressed the lipstick down, coloring her mouth a soft pink. After rubbing her lips together she straightened and looked at the whole picture.

The sweetheart top of her dress was black, the corseted bodice helping with cleavage control. She'd had to wear a strapless bra as the top of the dress was made of sheer chiffon, showing off her shoulders and back. The skirt of the dress was a soft pink, layers of black and white tulle making her look a bit like a ballerina.

She loved it.

Aunt Beth had taken her prom dress shopping in Tallahassee a few weeks ago, and after a fairly extensive search through five different stores, they'd found the perfect one.

Nora reached up and pressed a bobby pin deeper into her hair, hiding it among the curls that had been pinned in a slightly messy up-do. She twisted one of the curls that hung in her face around her finger before letting it bounce back up.

"I don't think it's possible for you to look any more beautiful than you already do, honey."

Nora looked over to see her Aunt Beth leaning against the doorframe and beaming, though she was usually beaming these days. Ever since the morning sickness had stopped a month ago, her aunt had been rocking the pregnancy glow like it was nobody's business.

Aunt Beth and Tripp had wasted absolutely no time at all in the procreating department. They'd gotten married in December and a month later had found out a baby would be joining the family. Just last week they'd found out the baby was a girl.

Nora's family.

Aunt Beth had been like a second mother to her throughout her entire life, and in the last year Tripp had become a second father to her. He was a man who she knew would do absolutely anything for her.

"I think you're missing one thing, though," Beth said as she walked into the room. She held her hand in the air, a delicate silver chain dangling from her fingers, the pearl pendant slowly swinging in the air.

"That's the necklace you wore to your wedding." Nora reached up and touched the pearl.

"It was your grandmother's. She gave it to your mother on her wedding day. And your mother gave it to me when I went to my senior prom. And I want to give it to you now."

Two years. Nora's mother and father had been gone for two years, and the pain of it still caused her to lose her breath when she thought about either of them. The only reason she'd been able to get through the last two years was because of the woman standing in front of her.

Tears welled in her eyes and she had to take a deep breath and look at the ceiling to hold them back.

"Turn around," Beth whispered, the emotion in her voice clear as day.

Nora did as she was told, and Beth looped the necklace around her neck. When she spun back around, her aunt was giving her a watery smile. "I'm so proud of you, you know that? So beyond proud of you."

"Thank you. For more than just the necklace." Reaching up, Nora touched the pearl. "For everything. I love you, Aunt B."

"Oh, honey. Come here." Beth pulled Nora into a hug. "I love you so much."

When they pulled back Nora had to reach up and run her fingers underneath her eyes. Thank God her mascara was waterproof.

There was a light tap on the door and Nora straightened to see Mel in the doorway. She was holding a sleeping baby in her arms. Juliet was four months old with a head full of curling blond hair like her mother's, and piercing gray blue eyes like her father's.

"You about ready? I think Tripp is about to give my brother *the talk*, which, you know, is awkward, considering you and Hamilton have been dating for almost a year now."

Nora grinned; she couldn't help it. It was her automatic response whenever it came to her boyfriend.

She would never forget the afternoon he'd come knocking on the front door, and very politely asked Aunt Beth if he could have a conversation with Nora.

"I know she's grounded for two months, but I'd like to talk to her," he'd said. "Because I need her to completely and totally understand exactly how I feel about her, and I don't know that I can wait that long."

"Is that so?"

"Yes ma'am." He'd nodded, looking down to the end of the hallway where Nora stood, her mouth hanging open in shock.

"The rules don't exactly apply to you, Hamilton. Never have." Beth had waved him into the house. "Good luck. I'm rooting for you."

Hamilton had walked straight for Nora, grabbing her hand and leading her out into the backyard. Once he'd pulled her to the side of the house and out of view of any and all windows, he'd pushed her back up against the bricks and kissed her.

Like, *really* kissed her.

What she'd felt for him over the years had always been a little bit scary, mainly because she wasn't sure if he felt the same way. After her parents had died, what she felt for him had terrified her. So she'd pushed him away.

But with that one kiss she'd known, known just how much she could lose.

And she hadn't turned back since.

Hamilton—and Dale, for that matter—had decided to go to Florida State University. It hadn't been exactly *easy* the last year not seeing him every day, but he'd visited often and they'd made it work. And next year, they'd be together every day again.

Nora hadn't made her college choice based solely on Hamilton. Though, she'd be lying if she said he wasn't a factor. There were other things involved in her decision; the full ride scholarship hadn't hurt at all. There was also the fact that Aunt Beth and Mel had gone there, so she'd grown up with a fondness for the school.

But the main reason had been that whenever she went to the campus, it felt like a home away from home.

It also didn't hurt that it was only an hour away from her actual home, and she'd be able to visit whenever she wanted. She didn't want to miss out on the next family adventure. Not even a little bit.

Besides, she had a tradition to up hold as second mom. Her mother had been Beth's, Beth had been hers, and she was going to be one to her cousin.

"We'll be right there," Beth said, bringing Nora back to the moment. Mel nodded before she turned and left the room, heading back down the hallway. "You ready?"

"Yes." Nora nodded before she reached out and grabbed Beth's hand. "You know, if it can't be Mom here with me, I'm glad it's you." Nora said before she bent down, putting her mouth close to Beth's baby bump. "You hear that? You're going to have an awesome mom. One of the best ever. And your dad's pretty freaking awesome, too."

Then there was another soft knock on the door, and this time when Nora looked up it was Tripp standing there. He was looking at her with a grin turning up his mouth. "I've had good practice on how to be awesome from getting trained by you. Now get over here so I can get a good look at you."

"Get your shoes, sweetie." Beth nodded to the pink satin pumps in the corner. "He needs the full picture."

Nora slipped her shoes on before crossing over to Tripp, doing a little spin in front of him.

"Hmmm." His grin turned down a bit. "I think I need to go have another talk with Hamilton."

He made to move but Nora grabbed his arm, stretching up and

pressing a kiss to his scruffy jaw. "Thank you, Tripp. Thank you for being here."

"There's nowhere else I'd rather be." He pulled her into a gentle hug, his lips at her temple. "You look beautiful, Nora. Go out there and knock him dead."

When they let go of each other, Beth reached her hand out for Tripp. "We'll see you out there," she said before the two of them left the room.

Nora looked in the mirror one final time before she grabbed her black silk clutch and headed down the hallway.

When she stepped into the living room her eyes immediately landed on Hamilton. He was standing there in his black tux, as handsome as ever and looking right back at her like she was the only person in the world.

About the Author

Shannon Richard grew up in the Florida Panhandle as the baby sister of two overly protective but loving brothers. She was raised by a more than somewhat eccentric mother, a self-proclaimed vocabularist who showed her how to get lost in a book, and a father who passed on his love for coffee and really loud music. She graduated from Florida State University with a BA in English Literature and still lives in Tallahassee where she battles everyday life with writing, reading, and a rant every once in a while. Okay, so the rants might happen on a regular basis. She's still waiting for her Southern, scruffy, Mr. Darcy, and in the meantime writes love stories to indulge her overactive imagination. Oh, and she's a pretty big fan of the whimsy.

Learn more at:
http://shannonrichard.net/
Twitter: @shan_richard
Facebook: http://facebook.com/ShannonNRichard

Don't miss the next installment of
Shannon Richard's Country Road series!

Untold

Available Fall 2017

CPSIA information can be obtained
at www.ICGtesting.com
Printed in the USA
LVOW11s0842041116
511421LV00001B/11/P